Gu

"Caris Roane . . . with a sexy, cool, edgy, romantic fantasy that gleams like the dark wings and lethal allure of her Guardians of Ascension vampires. Prepare to be enthralled!"

—*New York Times* bestselling author Lara Adrian

"The latest Guardians of Ascension romantic urban fantasy is a great thriller . . . another fantastic entry in one of the strongest sagas on the market today."

—*Midwest Book Reviews*

"Roane's worldbuilding is complex and intriguing, and in addition to her compelling protagonists, she serves up a slew of secondary characters begging to be explored further. The Guardians of Ascension is a series with epic potential!" —*Romantic Times* (4½ stars)

"A super urban romantic fantasy in which the audience will believe in the vampires and the Ascension . . . fast-paced . . . thrilling." —Alternative Worlds

"A great story with a really different take on vampires. This is one book that is sure to be a hit with readers who love paranormals. Fans of J.R. Ward's Black Dagger Brotherhood series are sure to love this one too."

—Red Roses for Authors Blog

"*Ascension* is like . . . ve and colorful dream. . . . dable, terrifying, beauti . . . round and envelop you i . . .

—Barnes an . . . e Blog

"Incredibly creative, *Ascension* takes readers to another level as you learn about two earths, vampires, ancient warriors, and a new twist on love. I felt like I was on a roller-coaster ride, climbing until I hit the very top, only to come crashing down at lightning speed. Once you pick this book up, clear off your calendar because you won't be able to put it down. Best book I have read all year."

—SingleTitles.com

"Tightly plotted and smoking hot . . . a fantastic read."

—Fresh Fiction

"Nail-biting romance . . . hot sex . . . I can't wait to see what's going to happen next." —Bitten by Romance

Also by Caris Roane

ASCENSION

BURNING SKIES

WINGS OF FIRE

BORN OF ASHES

OBSIDIAN FLAME

GATES OF RAPTURE

BORN IN CHAINS

UNCHAINED

CARIS ROANE

St. Martin's Paperbacks

This is a work of fiction. All of the characters, organizations, and events portrayed in this novel are either products of the author's imagination or are used fictitiously.

UNCHAINED

Copyright © 2014 by Caris Roane.

All rights reserved.

For information address St. Martin's Press, 175 Fifth Avenue, New York, NY 10010.

ISBN: 978-1-250-03531-8

Printed in the United States of America

St. Martin's Paperbacks edition / December 2014

St. Martin's Paperbacks are published by St. Martin's Press, 175 Fifth Avenue, New York, NY 10010.

10 9 8 7 6 5 4 3 2 1

*To my sister, Nancy, and her
tremendous support over the years*

ACKNOWLEDGMENTS

Many thanks to Rose Hilliard and the team at St. Martin's Press for bringing the Men in Chains series to the shelves, for the outstanding covers, and for the fine editing. All blessings.

CHAPTER 1

Shayna Prentiss left the bar near the University of Washington, wondering if someone had slipped her a roofie. She felt light-headed and from the corner of an eye, she was sure she saw a man, dressed in black, floating in the air. When she turned to look, though, nothing was there.

Had to be drugs.

But she'd been so careful, never letting guys buy her drinks and, once she had a drink in hand, keeping it there. In her undergrad days she'd been through the gauntlet of insanity that accompanied the college journey and had made it a point to learn vicariously from stories that traveled like wildfire around the dorms. More than one student had ended up in the hospital.

But tonight, something must have gotten past her. Had she been distracted? Had she turned her back to talk to someone? Yet she couldn't think of a single moment when she'd let her guard down.

Or maybe it was just stress. Her replacement passport hadn't come through yet and she was leaving for Malaysia in two weeks to start her fieldwork. She'd booked the flight months ago to get a solid cheap rate. But she'd gotten so caught up in putting together as many chapters of her dissertation as she could before she left that she'd somehow managed to lose her passport.

She wasn't the most organized person, but she loved anthropology with a passion and intended to earn her PhD before she was thirty.

The dizziness returned, forcing her to stop to plant a hand against a light standard. And now she had a headache as though someone was tapping on her mind, wanting in.

She took deep breaths.

On a Friday night students headed everywhere, even at ten at night. She'd met up with friends for a drink, happy to unwind for a couple of hours, but now she was ready to get back to work. She tended to pore over her books until the early-morning hours and loved it. From the time she'd started college, she'd scheduled afternoon and evening classes whenever possible. She did her best thinking after the sun went down, preferably with books and papers scattered all around her. Antique statuary helped, as well as the oh-so-stereotypical midnight pizza. She had a fine collection of geodes she looked at or turned over and over in her hands when she was puzzling out some aspect of theory.

The air smelled of rain and the clouds overhead had

gathered to form a thick, familiar mass. A distant rumbling of thunder explained things loud and clear.

Great, now it was going to pour—and as usual, no umbrella.

A couple of guys stopped in front of her. "Shayna, how's it going?" They were in one of the classes she was required to teach as part of her doctoral program. They were young and had that hungry, Friday-night, hoping-to-get-laid look. And unfortunately, she never looked older than eighteen no matter how much makeup she wore.

With thoughts of her latest paper on her mind, she wasn't interested in encouraging any kind of male attention. "I'm fine. You boys move along and flirt with girls your own age."

They both grinned. She didn't always get the same respect as other teachers because of her youngish features. She'd be carded forever, but there was nothing she could do about that.

Waving them off, she hurried up the street, half walking, half running as thunder once more sounded from the north. She was cold now, grateful she'd worn her jeans and not the short skirt she'd actually considered.

As she rounded the corner, however, she swore that flying man appeared again, floating in the air, tracking her. So long as she didn't look directly at him, she could see him, and this time she took a hard look. He was handsome in a scary way, with short, roughed-up hair and dressed in black leather. He was big, too, like he kept a gym in his garage and spent most of the day there working out.

As hallucinations went, he was amazing.

She forced her gaze away from him and kept moving. Maybe she'd ingested some kind of psychedelic.

But the pressure on her mind increased then broke through. Words followed that set her heart racing. *Are you Shayna Prentiss?*

She stopped in her tracks and shifted slightly and now she could see the flying man clearly. But it also seemed like wavy lines floated in front of him. "I don't know what the hell you are, but would just leave me alone?"

His voice penetrated her head once more. *So you can see me?*

She shook her head in disbelief. The man she'd somehow fabricated from her apparently way-too-vivid imagination now communicated with her telepathically. Before answering his question, she analyzed the situation as best she could. Drugs seemed like the most sensible explanation, but other than some dizziness, she didn't feel drugged out.

She responded mind-to-mind. *Are you talking inside my head?*

I am. Shit, you've got power and you're human, right?

Yes, I'm human. Okay, an *alien* might make a statement like, *You're human, right?* although the words seemed earth-colloquial in nature. She'd never been much of an extraterrestrial believer. Intellectually, she knew that unexplained phenomena existed, but she also thought that science could eventually offer a rational explanation.

And you can see me. The flying man wasn't asking this time.

Should she even respond? The more prudent course would be to get back to her apartment, take two Advil, and go to bed. Hide under her comforter.

Yet the whole situation set her curiosity on high flame, and his question had a simple, scientific basis. *I can sort of see you. I mean sometimes I can, better from the side. You have wavy lines in front of you right now.*

This really couldn't be happening. She added, *I have to go home now. Maybe you should find someone else to talk to. I'm real busy these days.* Understatement.

Once again, she put her feet in motion and kept her head down. Had to be stress. She'd probably just been pushing too hard, as usual.

The flying man ignored her suggestion. *The truth is, Shayna, that I've come to talk to you, so it's great that you've got so much latent power for a human. That you can communicate easily mind-to-mind is a big plus.*

There it was again, *for a human*. What the hell did her hallucination mean by that? She wasn't into science fiction. When she needed to chill, she watched documentaries.

She shook her head and forced her gaze to the sidewalk. "Keep one foot in front of the other, Shayna," she whispered. "You'll be okay. This too shall pass. You're just stressed out. Losing your passport clearly was too much for you. At least you booked your flight. Just hang in there and you'll be fine."

The man's deep, resonant voice once more penetrated her mind. *You're not hallucinating. I'm real and I need your help.*

She must be going crazy because now the hallucination was asking for her help.

The first raindrops struck her shoulders and she started to run. Her apartment wasn't far, just a couple more blocks.

Maybe if she focused on the reality around her, on her life, on the fieldwork she'd planned for her yearlong stay in Malaysia, her mind would clear.

She had a meeting with her adviser in the morning, something she was not looking forward to. She often argued with Greg Michelson, and it didn't help that she'd broken her sacred rule and had not only slept with him but actually engaged in a very intense six-month affair with the bastard. Turned out, the man with such lofty ideals was a complete narcissist, especially in bed. He'd given her self-esteem a serious blow with all his attempts to remake her in his image as well as how often he called her selfish when she insisted that her needs be treated with as much respect as his demands.

I need you to come with me.

Even her hallucination appeared to be just another man wanting something from her, needing her to set aside her own goals in favor of his.

"Like hell I'm going to do that," she shouted. She took off on a sprint.

She tried to draw her keys from her purse, but her hands shook. If she could just get inside, she'd be okay. Bed, Advil, a shot of Ketel One if necessary.

I'm not going to hurt you. Dammit, would you please just stop and listen to me. I need your help.

She wished he didn't seem so real, and another part of her wished the drug would kick in and she'd pass out because right now she was scared out of her mind.

She turned the corner and groaned. The street was poorly lit and there wasn't a single person around. Even though she was only a few yards away from the front door of the complex, the man swept ahead of her, flying, his long black leather coat flapping as he moved.

He reached the door to the apartment building first, dipping beneath the overhang. He floated to land on the sidewalk, but this time he spoke aloud. "Are you Shayna Prentiss? I really need to know. It's important."

She squeezed her eyes shut and gave her head a shake, willing him away. "This is all in my head. It will pass." She repeated the words several times.

But when she opened her eyes, he was still there, and closer now. The rain had started to come down, lightning flashed, thunder boomed closer still.

"Please confirm your identity." He scanned her hair, her eyes, her face as though looking for something specific. "White-blond hair, unusual light-blue eyes, tall, pretty. Has to be you."

"Fine, I'm Shayna Prentiss, but who are you?"

"Marius Briggs." The hallucination had a specific name? "You're not seeing things, Shayna. I'm real."

She trembled now. "I don't understand any of this. What do you want with me and how were you doing all those tricks in the air?" When she started to back away, he moved in and took hold of her arms, his grip like steel.

"I need you to know that I don't usually do this kind of thing, but I'm desperate. My world is in trouble and we need you."

"Your world needs me? Are you an alien?"

"Not exactly. We live here, right alongside you. We just have the ability to disguise ourselves, to keep hidden from your kind."

"My kind." Oh, God.

Every horror movie she'd ever seen flipped through her head, except that this man didn't look like a monster.

But that's when things went haywire all over again because suddenly she saw *just him,* the faint cleft in his chin, the sharp angle of his cheekbones, and his unusual hazel eyes, flecked with gold. He was incredibly handsome.

But there was something more, almost as though she could sense what he was feeling, the level of his determination and, as his gaze skated over her features, his sudden male interest in her.

You're beautiful slid through her mind.

She didn't react; instead she held herself open to him, wanting to understand him. She no longer thought she was in the grip of a mind-bending drug, and she never drank more than would give her a nice buzz.

No, the man was real.

Oddly, her fears began to dissipate as her curiosity rose. She felt like she did when she was deep into some aspect of her studies, like she'd come home, as though she belonged here talking with this otherworldly man.

She resonated with him.

The term wasn't exactly scientific in nature, but that's what came to her as she stood in front of—what was his name? Marius Briggs. The questions came, the ones that rolled through her mind as familiar to her as breathing. "What hidden world? And you're not human? Yet you look human. Are our species related?"

He seemed exasperated as he shoved a hand through his loose, slightly messy dark hair. He grimaced. "I don't have time for this." He glanced around, worried.

Michelson, her former lover, had often been exasperated with her. If Mr. Briggs hoped to get her help, he'd better lose the attitude and start talking.

Despite his hold on her, she wiggled just enough to fold her arms over her chest and lift her chin. "I'm going to need some answers if you expect me to cooperate."

"I'd better just show you."

He pulled back his lips slightly and the next moment, she watched a set of what appeared to be extremely sharp fangs descend.

More horror movies popped through her mind. Really? Fangs? Flight? The black leather coat and all this supreme sexiness?

She wrinkled her nose. "You're a vampire?"

"We've lived in a secret cavern-based culture, right alongside yours, all this time, with our own customs and beliefs, our own problems. But we have disguising abilities, something that apparently you're good at seeing through but have kept us as separate species from the beginning of life on earth."

A number of thoughts and questions rattled through her brain, some of a scientific nature stemming from her curiosity about other cultures. But he'd already told her enough that she sensed she was in some kind of danger. "Does your kind prey on ours?"

"The worst of my kind does, yes, and they need to be stopped, which is why I've come to you for help."

"And I'll need to go with you, right?"

He breathed a sigh of relief. "Exactly."

"Well, I'm sorry, Mr. Otherworld Vampire, but I'm going to Malaysia to do critical fieldwork. I'm leaving in two weeks and I have a boatload of work to get done before I go. I have my own life, my own goals, and sorry but you're out of luck."

She'd spoken with confidence, but he still had hold of her arms and his face was taking on a tight, stubborn look. "You're still not understanding either the depth of my world's need or why it has to be you."

"Oh, come on, I can't be that special."

"That's where you're wrong. You have specific, latent

abilities that dovetail with my world. The fact that you can communicate telepathically with me no problem at all is a profound indication that what I'm telling you is true. And we need you, desperately."

"Well, I don't know what to tell you. I'm still kind of in shock."

"As you should be."

He looked so damn sincere. If she'd met him anywhere else, like at a party, she would have trusted him.

The flying man got a strange look on his face, his gaze still pinned to hers. "I saw pictures of you, but I didn't think you'd be this beautiful. My God." His voice had dropped into the lower registers.

She knew that man-sound. For all his fine words about looking for someone to help him save his world, maybe he was just cruising the university bars looking to get laid. Maybe this was just his line. No doubt male vampires, sharing DNA with humans as he suggested, had a lot in common with males of her species.

Except that his kind could fly.

Yeah. Except for that. And they had fangs for a purpose well documented in human fiction.

Her dizziness returned, only different this time. As she stared at him, he seemed to fade as well as the grip on her arm. She thought maybe she was fainting, but instead the space around her began to spin, increasing the sense that she could topple over.

She remained upright, but new images arrived. She saw Marius standing in the doorway of what had to be a bathroom. He wore a robe of some kind, silk maybe, and dark blue with a pattern on it.

She moved, only it wasn't her, but some future version of herself in the vision. She couldn't see it clearly, because strange dark waves covered parts of it. But from what she could make out, she was in a bathroom unknown to her and she was completely naked. What was he saying? Something like he thought she could use the robe. She watched as he hung it up on the back of the door.

Shayna did not understand what she was looking at, except that she was now drying off with her towel and didn't seem in the least distressed. Which meant that she was incredibly comfortable with Marius although he seemed to be uneasy.

She felt herself speak within this weird vision, a very strange sensation: *Thank you. I love the paisley in your robe. Is that silk you're wearing?*

For reasons she couldn't explain, she felt that this was some kind of vision of the future. She knew then that she'd slept with Marius and that she'd loved it.

Oh, dear God, what the hell was happening to her?

When she closed her eyes, the present returned, and she found that Marius still had hold of her arms but was essentially holding her upright.

"Shayna," he called sharply. "What's going on?"

"I don't know, but you and I . . . we were together. In a bathroom somewhere. You were dressed, but I'd been showering."

"Shit, have you just had a vision of the future?"

"I think so. Or maybe one possible future. My head aches from trying to make sense of everything. This really can't be happening."

Marius Briggs saw her confusion. He hated doing this to her, confronting her about issues in his world and trying to persuade her to come with him.

And now she'd just had a vision of the future. He could

hardly wrap his head around that, or around the fact that she'd seen them together, as a couple.

More than anything else, she'd just confirmed his belief that she could help his world. She had more power than he'd seen in a long time, and she was human, another confirmation that she was the right choice.

But how could he make her understand how much she was needed? The fact that she could see him also reflected the nature of her latent power and that Rumy had been right to send him here to Seattle.

He just had a couple of problems. First, he shouldn't have left Italy when he did, because he was still recovering from the effects of blood-starvation and the long flight had weakened him.

Second, what he was about to do went against every single one of his principles. He believed in the rights of the individual over everything else. But in this situation, if Shayna didn't actually agree to come with him, he might have to abduct her.

Even thinking about it made him sick in his gut, but he was out of options. He had an entire world to save, maybe even human earth as well, and Shayna Prentiss was the only woman on the planet who could help him right now.

She just looked so damn young to be the last, best hope for his world.

But Daniel was driving relentlessly through the vampire world, going after the final extinction weapon full-bore. The weapon, through the use of a pre-set decibel, had the ability to kill any vampire within its proximity with just a flip of the switch. If Daniel got hold of the weapon before Marius did, his entire culture was doomed to either slavery or annihilation. Daniel, the psychopath that he was, would take great pleasure in either venture.

Torture was Daniel's specialty, but mass murder would no doubt have tremendous appeal to his sick mind.

Shayna, according to Rumy's best information, had a unique, human ability to form a tracking pair with Marius. If she would agree to work with him, together they could secure the location of the weapon before Daniel. The trouble was, Daniel was offering a fortune to anyone who could find the weapon.

And the hunt was on.

Essentially, Marius was running out of time. He'd taken precautions to make his way secretly to Seattle, to find Shayna, and to bring her back to Italy with him. But Daniel was a powerful Ancestral and might have sent his men to watch his movements. He could be under attack at any moment.

Then there was Shayna herself. He didn't want to intrude in her life in this way, but he had no other recourse. She was *the one*. The telepathy, that she could see through his disguise, as well as her unexpected vision had confirmed it.

Knowing he had to do everything he could to persuade her, he released his disguise fully, something he hadn't wanted to do in case he'd been followed. But he wouldn't just snatch Shayna without trying to talk to her, to persuade her so that he didn't have to resort to abduction.

He glanced around, but so far so good. He'd know if any of his kind had shown up.

"The wavy lines are gone." Her light-blue eyes went wide. "Why is that?"

"I just dropped my disguise, which makes me vulnerable, but I want you to be able to trust me. Your vision has confirmed that you're the right woman, the one I've been looking for. Please come with me. Let me show you my world and talk to you in depth about what's going on."

"And you really are a vampire?"

He nodded.

She put two fingers to her temple and rubbed in a circle, squeezing her eyes shut. "I feel so dizzy."

"It's probably the telepathy. I had to punch pretty hard against your mind to break through, another indication of your level of natural power. I can explain everything later. I don't want you to be scared, but I need to take you away right now."

"You don't want me to be scared? You're gripping my arms, you're the size of a tank, and now you're talking about needing to cart me off somewhere."

"Shayna, we've got a bad guy running lose and he's trying to take over our world. The thing is, if he succeeds, he'll be after yours next and there will be nothing you can do to stop him."

She searched his eyes for a long moment, frowning. "Even if all this is true, what can that possibly have to do with me? I'm an anthropology grad student here at U-Dub. I'm not exactly superhero material. More like an egghead-type who happens to be curious about other cultures."

"Then maybe look at it this way: You'll be able to see an entirely different civilization firsthand. Doesn't that intrigue you a little?"

He saw her eyes flare and knew with just a little more back-and-forth he could persuade her. This could almost work. If only she'd stop looking so pale and shocked out.

She pressed her hands to her face. "I'll wake up soon. I just know it. This isn't a hallucination, this is just a really vivid dream. Those crab cakes I had at dinner tasted funny."

Marius didn't know what else he could say and his instincts told him it was only a matter of minutes before he was discovered here.

And she'd had a vision in which they'd been together. She'd seen the future.

As he looked at Shayna, as he factored in her vision, suddenly time slowed to a crawl. Though he had seen pictures of her on her blog, a few candid photos from a recent trip to Honduras, he hadn't seen her close up, not like this, just inches away.

Her complexion was like milk, her hair white-blond, and her eyes a light, unearthly blue. She was so beautiful that he swore his heart stopped beating for a few seconds. When it began again, it was a dull thud against his rib cage.

He hadn't expected this, to be so drawn to the woman who could save his world.

Her hair was straight, and she wore it past her shoulders. She had a lovely nose with a beautiful curve near the bridge. Her brows were arched slightly.

His gaze drifted to her neck, then down to the notch at the base of her throat. He watched her heart beating and his fangs began to thrum in his mouth. His hunger rose as well, followed sharply by a desire so profound that without thinking he drew her against him. If somewhere in the back of his mind he knew his conduct was completely inappropriate and not at all useful, he couldn't seem to help himself.

"What . . . what are you doing?" Her voice was a whisper.

She stilled in his arms as he sniffed her hair and

nuzzled along her cheekbone, then toward her ear, smelling what was the softest, most intoxicating scent, a delicate floral. He flicked his tongue over her skin.

You taste like heaven, Shayna. My God, I hadn't expected this.

What would her blood be like filling his mouth, easing his deepest vampire need?

He slid his lips down the side of her cheek, kissing and tasting as he went.

Then he found her lips and began kissing her, willing her to respond, loving the feel of her mouth beneath his. He had to get inside her, so he traced his tongue along the seam of her lips.

Part of his rational mind knew he was spinning out of control to be kissing the woman he'd have to kidnap if she didn't agree to come with him. But nothing else seemed more important than making a physical connection with her.

He heard a warbling sound coming from her throat as he began to thrust his tongue in and out. Her scent now filled his nostrils, no longer the light floral but heavier now and sultry as though the flower had just bloomed. She liked what he was doing; she wanted him.

A thrill ran through him, stronger and more powerful than anything he'd ever known. But why?

Shayna was utterly and completely shocked that she was allowing this bizarre kiss. And not just allowing, but enjoying.

First the vampire had said he needed her help; then he got this funny look on his face, pulled her against his muscular chest, then started sniffing her hair.

After that, she'd moved into some kind of strange enthralled state in which all she could do was let the kiss happen. But what stunned her was how she felt, like she could float, or sing, or fly. She didn't want the kiss to end.

Finally, she drew back, the dizziness having returned but for a different reason this time. She placed a hand on his chest and in a soft voice asked, "What was that?"

He shook his head slowly, which told her he was as confused as she felt. "I don't know. I didn't mean to do that. I don't think I'm helping my cause very much right now."

He closed his eyes and took a couple of deep breaths, maybe trying to regain control of himself.

Shayna took a step back. She needed to do the same thing, to find her rational mind. Besides, she still wasn't sure the man even existed, although he was becoming more real by the second.

But there was one thing she knew for sure, she had her own life, her own plans, and she wasn't willing to toss them aside for the sake of problems in a world not even her own. "I'm sorry, Marius, but I can't go with you. I wish you well, even if I'm still questioning your existence."

He released her right arm, but only enough to rub the side of his head and squint. He looked like he was in pain.

"Are you okay?"

"No. I'm sensing something or someone nearby."

Movement beyond his shoulder brought her gaze shifting to a new apparition, a much more complex one. This time several men, a dozen by her count, dressed similarly in black leather and big like Marius, arrived about thirty feet away, landing on the sidewalk and in the street, as though they'd been in flight as well.

To a man, they had the look of military, just as Marius did. Had he brought reinforcements in order to persuade her to get on board with his plans?

"So let's say I wasn't slipped some kind of hallucinogenic, or a roofie, or anything else—do you know who those men are? I'm guessing by the way they arrived that they're from your world. So did you bring them to intimidate me, because it's kind of working."

Marius turned and, at that moment, everything changed. For one thing, Marius started cursing up a shitstorm, then, "Daniel sent his troops. We are so fucked."

He said other words, but when he turned to her he looked really upset, even guilty as hell. "I'm sorry, Shayna, but we just ran out of time."

She didn't know what he meant by that until he grabbed her, pinned her to his chest, then launched straight up into the air.

For at least two seconds, she didn't know what had happened. But as Seattle disappeared below her, she realized he'd abducted her and that she now flew toward a heavy bank of dark clouds that streaked lightning like crazy.

She'd get killed by the storm.

Fear shot through her skull, her heart pounding hard.

She started to struggle, but he held her clamped in his arms. He shifted his flight, angling so that she now had a different, more distant view of Seattle. She screamed long and loud.

No one can hear you. I've created a disguise. Let's just hope like hell it holds. His voice again, once more inside her head.

He started flying faster and faster.

But what she didn't understand was that despite the

thunder clouds, the lightning, the rain, she passed through all that mass as though surrounded by a gentle breeze. How was this even possible?

But the next moment, pain pierced her head like nothing she'd ever known before. She writhed and screamed all over again.

Sorry. Altered flight hurts humans, but it can't be helped. I had to make this happen fast.

Though she had no idea how she was communicating telepathically, the words formed in her head and she responded. *Oh, God, I hurt. You bastard, you're killing me.*

Somewhere in the middle of things, the world turned black.

CHAPTER 2

Marius thanked God when Shayna passed out. He knew the pain he'd caused, but it couldn't be helped. He didn't have higher levels of power like some vampires, which was the only thing that could have prevented the pain, and he needed to lose the small army that Daniel sent after him by flying at top speed. If they caught up to him, he'd die and so would the woman in his arms.

Then where would his world be?

He had one advantage: He was faster than the men chasing him. His father's DNA had given him that. All he had to do was get out far enough in front, then shift course, and they'd never find him.

What he wanted more than anything was to get back

to Rumy's place, to The Erotic Passage, because he and Shayna would be safe there. However, he'd bet every cent he had on the likelihood that Daniel had men waiting to intercept. He'd never get within a thousand yards of Lake Como, maybe not even Italy, without being attacked.

As he flew, he glanced down at the Great Plains stretching out beneath him. Shifting slightly to check his back trail, he saw Daniel's men in the form of a few specks scattered in a long row, essentially on course for Italy and Rumy's club. They'd lose visual in a few more seconds. But he knew one way to help things along, a trick he'd learned from his surrogate father, Gabriel, a vampire of tremendous power.

Slowly, he built a secondary disguise around himself. Daniel would have been able to see through the disguise, but not his lackeys.

When the shield was complete, he decided to test it out and dropped three hundred feet, straight down, then hovered in the air. He held Shayna tightly against him, keeping her safe.

Slowly, he levitated backward until he semi-reclined in the air. In this position, he could watch the men in flight above him, but still remain levitating in altered flight. Yeah, he had some chops.

Daniel's men drew closer and closer, but remained in the same horizontal line as well as altitude, eyes forward.

Not one vampire hesitated in the air. No one looked around or down or anything. Besides the fact that they couldn't see him, they weren't even looking for him.

He took a breath, then another, and finally heaved a sigh when the warriors disappeared from sight. He could feel their flight pattern as if he'd built it inside his head.

He was right. They were all were headed east in the direction of Lake Como.

And that meant Daniel had called them back, no doubt to join a second contingent already waiting to intercept Marius near Rumy's famous sex-club complex.

Marius remained in position pondering his next move. Now that he knew for sure he couldn't return to Rumy's, he had to find shelter elsewhere. He needed to hide out, regroup, explain things to Shayna, and hopefully get her on board.

Like both his brothers, Adrien and Lucian, he had several secret homes scattered around the world, places he could escape to when needed. He had a place in the States, but decided against remaining in North America. Daniel may have left some of his forces behind to search the continent for him.

Keeping his disguising shield tight, he shifted course to the south and formed a mental image of his home in the Andes. He had a residence in the hill caves near General Carrera Lake on the Chilean side.

Once he fixed his mind on the bedroom of that dwelling, he took off, flying on autopilot toward South America, unconcerned about weather, planes, birds in flight, mountains, anything. Traveling in altered flight would allow him to pass easily through anything solid, and his internal vampire guidance system kept him on course.

Fifteen minutes later, after traveling thousands of miles, he closed in on the lake. If he'd been at Ancestral power, like both Daniel and Gabriel, he could have made the trip in a tenth of that time. More than once over the past year of imprisonment and torture at Daniel's hand, Marius had considered engaging his latent Ancestral power. Yet he hesitated, for the simple reason that he didn't want to follow in his father's footsteps. He'd long since made the decision to avoid rising to Ancestral status if he could possibly help it.

He began to slow, and eased through the hills, descending through solid matter as though it were no more significant than heavy fog. His cavern was sealed off from the outside, which made it ideal in terms of remaining secure from human trespassers.

But it had one other advantage. Three hundred years ago, he'd hired an Ancestral to create an intricate layered disguise over the small private home so that very few vampires would ever know of its existence. With luck, Daniel didn't know about it, either.

He touched down in the bedroom, dropping out of altered flight, and carefully settled Shayna on his bed. She looked absurdly pale against the dark-gray silk comforter. She was probably cold as well, being human. His own vampire genetics kept him warmed up no matter how low the temperature fell.

He took a down comforter from an adjacent armoire and covered her up. The fact that she released a sigh and visibly relaxed told him that he'd called it right.

Removing his coat and hanging it on a peg next to the armoire, he crossed to the fireplace. He stacked up a bunch of kindling, then created a tepee of smaller logs. Within a few minutes, the fire took hold and started warming up the room.

He'd left almost everything about the cave in a semifinished state. The original architect had hired craftsmen to square up the walls and to create a rough-hewn ceiling that flowed in a circle, with a portion indented to a peak. But nothing was smooth or polished.

He'd always liked the effect.

With the fire heating the room, he returned to the bed. Two stone shelves, also carved from rock, created shallow bedside tables. He lit a branch of candles, the only lighting in his home. His own vampire vision kept the space in a glow, but he didn't want Shayna coming to consciousness in a pitch-black room.

He sat down on the bed next to her, frowning. She represented something to him, something he had a hard time placing. Maybe it was her innocence, even though a year and a half ago, she'd made a fairly typical mistake of falling for one of her professors.

Once she'd won Rumy's online game that identified her as a human with tremendous if latent tracking abilities, he'd had her investigated. Marius knew quite a bit about her, including the fact that she had no immediate family left. Though she'd been on her own for a long time and very independent, her life as an American college student would in no way have prepared for the things she was likely to see and do if she stuck with him.

He slid a finger under the blood-chain at his neck. The metal had been infused with his blood when it was forged, and he had a matching chain in his pants pocket ready to bind Shayna to him. Once bound, their powers would combine, they'd form a tracking pair, and they could then go on the hunt for the extinction weapon.

He rose up slightly and drew the second chain out of his pocket, holding it in his hand as he settled down beside her once more.

The prudent course would be to slide the chain over her head right now and be done with it. She'd be enraged, but he could force her with any number of threats to get her to help him find the last weapon. And for a long moment, he debated doing just that.

She moaned softly, though still unconscious. She'd be coming around quickly now, and she'd be in pain.

But there was something he could do to help. At least he was pretty sure it would work.

Using the second bonding chain, he spread it out in a double line, laying it over Shayna's throat. She arched slightly, then relaxed. He could feel some of his power leaving his body and he knew the proximity of the chain next to Shayna's skin now allowed her to siphon his power and start healing. Altered flight was hard on humans, causing severe headaches and nausea.

Watching her draw a deep breath, he again considered slipping the chain over her head. If he did, she'd really be able to take on his power. The latent abilities that she'd previously exhibited would grow stronger, and her healing would progress quickly.

He was damn tempted.

He touched the chain at her neck and touched his own and felt a corresponding power surge within his own body. Her body arched again, stronger this time.

He'd gain from the bond as well, maybe even enough enhanced power and ability to battle his father if it came to that.

But he hated the thought of violating her freedom. It was bad enough that he'd basically abducted her from Seattle. But to go this far, to actually make it impossible for her to take the chain off without risk of dying—shit, he didn't think he could go through with it.

But he was tempted.

The sooner they started hunting the weapon, the better.

He leaned forward, planting an elbow on his knee, then dropped his head into his hand.

He couldn't do it.

When Rumy had first given him information on the winner of his little online game that proved Shayna's ability, Marius had thought he could rip Shayna out of her life and force the bond. Once her power came online, she'd be able to find the last of several dangerous, mass-destruction weapons and keep them out of the hands of Marius's maniacal father. In that way, Shayna would help save not just his world but the human world as well, since Daniel had designs on both.

Despite his belief that two worlds hung in the balance, though, he couldn't force her to do anything against her will.

He just couldn't.

Shayna must be given the chance to choose.

As he debated, his stomach cramped and without thinking, he began to rock as he attempted to force the pain away. Daniel had kept him blood-starved during his last incarceration, which had left him with a problem he'd have to deal with sooner or later. He would be cycling through a bout of blood-madness at some point, a condition caused by being deprived of blood, but hopefully not before he had everything settled with Shayna and maybe even the extinction weapon already in hand.

For now, he worked to control the pain in his gut and the disorienting swirls in his head. After a few minutes, he brought his symptoms under control and the debilitating pain eased back. Based on past experience from other episodes of blood-madness, he'd be good for several hours, possibly even a couple of days.

As Shayna came to consciousness, she felt that Marius was close by, even though she couldn't open her eyes. She could sense his presence in a way that was as much a mystery as his sudden arrival in Seattle.

She pressed a hand to the top of her head and moaned. She was in so much pain that she was pretty sure knives whirled inside her head.

She'd been abducted just outside her apartment building—that much she could recall. She also knew that she needed to pull it together to figure out just what kind of hell she'd gotten mixed up in. But right now, the pain was the only problem she could focus on. She didn't even know how she was surviving it.

She put both hands over her eyes, aware that she lay prone on some kind of bed. At least a comforter was keeping her warm. The space was cold and dark except for the glow from a fireplace opposite and what might have been a few candles on a stand to her right.

Barely opening her eyes, she saw that Marius sat on the side of the bed near her.

"Shayna, how you doin'?" He spoke quietly and sounded so compassionate for a vampire.

"I . . . hurt." She wanted to say something more, to explain about the knives, but she couldn't.

"I need you to focus on the chain at your neck. Can you do that? It will help you to heal more quickly. You'll be able to siphon my power, and the pain will start to subside."

"What . . . are you talking . . . about." Her stomach boiled.

She felt Marius's warm touch as he picked up her hand and moved it very slowly and gently to her throat. She felt the solid links beneath her fingertips just as he'd said. And the moment she made contact, a stream of power flowed through her hand and up her arm.

She gasped, because the same energy touched her mind and sent healing waves through her embattled brain. "Oh, God, that feels so good."

"Keep siphoning. This will all be over in a few minutes. You'll see."

She didn't know how it was working, but her mind knew a good thing and blocked out everything except the warm waves. She sucked in the sensation, and with each second that passed the pain lessened.

Marius was right. It didn't take long.

When she finally opened her eyes, his brow was furrowed heavily. Maybe it was the chain, but as soon as she looked into his eyes she could feel that he suffered in a way that hurt her own heart.

"What is it?" she asked. "I'm sensing this heaviness, a kind of weight that lives inside you, hurting you."

He stared at her, not answering for a moment. "I'm desperate about the fate of my world."

She felt certain there was more to the story, but she hardly knew him. It would be improper to probe further.

Shayna rubbed the chain at her neck. The pain in her head was now a dull throb that she knew would soon disappear so long as she kept her fingers on the chain and kept siphoning.

As she held Marius's gaze, she thought how strange it was to be here with him in a world completely hidden from human earth.

Above all, she was knocked out of stride by the way she responded to him. Again, he felt like home to her, which made no sense.

And his eyes.

Her thoughts funneled down to the small gold flecks set in an exquisite hazel. In her world, he would have been a supermodel, maybe even a movie star—he was that gorgeous.

She recalled the unexpected kiss outside her apartment building. The moment had been surreal and she was still shocked by how much she'd responded to him.

Her fingertip moved over the links as she looked at him. With each slide, desire started to build, a swell of more unexpected sensation inside her body that arrived so swiftly, she had to catch her breath.

She really didn't understand why she was responding to him like this, at the speed of light. Or why she resonated with him like she did.

Was this love at first sight? Or maybe it was more like the kind of animal attraction that generally led to a hot-and-heavy one-night stand. Whatever it was, her cheeks flamed at the thought that she could easily tumble into bed with him, even though that was something she never did. As a rule, she had to get to know a man first, feel that she could trust him, before she had sex with him.

Maybe it was a vampire thing, an enthrallment power. But even as she had this thought, she knew it wasn't true. For reasons she couldn't explain, she felt confident Marius would never do that to her.

Suddenly a wave of a scent rolled toward her, reminding her of grassy fields, very male, very worked up. Marius held her gaze, his chin lowered, gold-flecked hazel eyes dilated. Apparently, a response similar to the one that had just swamped her held him captive as well, and it was rampantly sexual.

At the same time, the scientific part of her brain lit up, adding a different kind of chemical into the mix. She felt rabidly *curious* about what was happening. Maybe for that reason, she didn't try to stop it or to remove her hand from the chain. Whatever this was, this knowing that flowed back and forth between them, she wanted to understand what was happening. The dangers that she'd already experienced told her that she needed information and she needed it now. Her life might just depend on how well she gained a raw set of parameters to define his world.

"Again, Marius, what's happening between us? Can you explain it to me? We just met, but suddenly my hormones are in overdrive." Her gaze fell to his lips. He had full lips that had felt so warm and moist on hers. And his tongue. He'd taken possession of her mouth without apology.

He'd make love to her that way as well. A kiss said an awful lot about a man.

She resisted the temptation to touch him. He'd removed his long leather coat to reveal a short-sleeved black T-shirt outlining a whole lot of muscle beneath. Her gaze drifted across his massive shoulders and, for a moment, she almost couldn't breathe.

She drew in a deep breath, settling back against the pillows. She continued to press her fingers against the chain to keep it in position across her throat. At least her head no longer hurt, but she sure wished her body would settle down. She wanted Marius way too much for just having met him.

Marius wasn't sure how to explain what was going on between them. He wasn't sure he understood the intensity of it himself. He knew that blood-chains always enhanced an experience, but the basic building blocks had to be there in the first place. When it came to having sex with Shayna, those blocks were piled sky-high.

"I'm not sure what to tell you."

He watched her gaze shift from his face to his shoulders, to the chain at his neck, then back to his eyes. She narrowed her gaze. "So do the chains cause the desire? Or is some other factor at work? And what are these chains, anyway, that they helped me heal?"

She had an interesting mind, seeking to know. She asked a lot of questions and was amazingly composed for having arrived in his home with so much pain that he'd had a hard time bearing her suffering. The chain around his neck and his proximity to her kept him informed moment by moment just how much the swift, dangerous flight had hurt her.

He explained about the chains, adding, "If you decide to put these on, you'll be bonded to me, sharing my power as you are now, only more of it. Blood-chains are known to enhance sexual desire, but only if there's an attraction in the first place. Apparently, there is. Also, for reasons I can't explain, you have a certain level of latent power, as I mentioned in Seattle, that I'm drawn to. Together we can form what's called a tracking pair, which might account for the strong attraction we have to each other."

"You're talking as though you're assuming I'll do this chain-bonding thing with you, but Marius, I can't possibly stay in your world. I have a very long list of things to do in order to get ready to . . . fly to . . . Malaysia." She glanced around as though just now becoming aware of her surroundings. "Okay, we're not in Seattle anymore, are we? But what is this place? Because it looks like a cave."

"It is a cave, much more rustic, you might say, than most modern dwellings." He shifted his gaze to the arched doorway, also chiseled in rough strikes, then to the wall opposite that housed a tall antique armoire. "I own several."

"I'm recalling that you mentioned a 'cavern-based' world. Is this your home?"

"One of them."

"How many do you have?"

He turned to her, chuckling. "Are you cataloging in order to collate and analyze later?"

She looked sheepish, but her eyes crinkled as she smiled. "I suppose I am. You'll have to forgive me. I collect data like some people collect bugs or stamps."

"I'm getting that, but I don't mind answering your questions. Given what I've put you through so far, it's the least I can do. I have six cave homes and was working on a seventh before the imprisonment."

She clamped her lips shut, but he could feel a whole host of questions bubbling in the air between them. He applauded that she politely refrained from asking.

He gave her permission anyway.

She stared at him. "Imprisonment? Where and why?"

He released a deep breath and decided that for her to make a decision she ought to know about his father and the scourge he was in his world. He told her about Daniel putting him and his brothers in the Himalayan cave, how he'd had them tortured.

"But what were you imprisoned for?"

"Daniel called it treason. Essentially, he recently took over our government, with plans to rule our world—and the only way to do that was to get rid of me and my brothers, because we fought him. We always have."

She stared at him, and he could feel how hard she was working to digest all that he'd said. "Let me understand.

Earlier you mentioned we would form a tracking pair. So if we did that, what would we be tracking?"

Marius explained about the extinction weapon, that the last one was hidden somewhere in his world. "With this weapon, he could take over our world. And if he succeeds, trust me, he'll go after human earth."

She clutched the chain in her fist, her light-blue eyes wide. "You're serious."

"With every fucking bone in my body. We're in trouble, Shayna, and that's why I'm asking for your help."

She sighed heavily. "So, who is this Daniel person?"

Marius felt a familiar queasiness anytime he had to own to his connection to Daniel. "He's my father."

"What?" Her brows rose.

"Yeah. Four hundred years of having to live with the fact that my brothers and I were sired by a monster. It sucks."

"What do you mean 'four hundred.'" She figured it out and her brows rose. "You're long-lived."

He nodded.

She looked away from him, but her gaze settled on his forearm. "You mentioned having brothers."

"Four of them, all half brothers. Two are aligned with Daniel, the other two are my best friends: Lucian and Adrien. We've been through a lot together."

She cocked her head. "So how is it you turned out so well? You and your brothers?"

"When we escaped Daniel's control, we had a lot of great teachers and counselors who got us through."

She glanced down at the chain in her hand.

"What is it?" Marius asked.

"I'm just so surprised by what I'm experiencing here.

I can sense who you are." She lifted the chain. "Which is why I know what you're saying is true. But it's just so strange to be in this situation, let alone to feel and know these things about someone I've just met."

"When I came to you in Seattle, Shayna, I didn't want to rip you out of your life. I need you to know that. Only the arrival of Daniel's security force would have caused me to take you into the air and bring you here."

She now had the chain wrapped around her fingers, her thumb rubbing over the links. After a moment, she lifted her gaze to her surroundings. "You know, you have very little lighting in here but I swear this room has started to look like it's lit in a glow. How's that possible?"

"You're starting to experience what our vision is like. We are, as your human lore suggests, extremely sensitive to sunlight, and yes, it can kill us. Humans moved out of cave living very early on, but our kind had to remain hidden deep in the earth. It's the perfect environment for us."

She nodded her gaze flitting around his rustic bedroom. "You must be very content here, Marius."

He was surprised by the statement. "Do you actually like this room?"

"I do. I think the stonework is fantastic. Rugged. Simple. Very clean. The craftsman clearly had a steady hand. There isn't one cut that jars the eye and I'm seeing some unique patterns." Her gaze drifted upward to the chiseled-out ceiling. "I like this design, how the indentation reaches to a point in the center of the ceiling. It's very aesthetically pleasing."

Marius tilted his head back. "I've never tired of looking at it."

"And it's just symmetrical enough that I doubt you've ever felt the need to improve it."

He'd had the same thought about this space. "No, never." Funny to think that he'd kidnapped this woman, only to find out she appreciated this room for almost the same reasons he did.

He rose from the bed, crossed to the fireplace, and added a couple more logs. He liked Shayna a lot. She had a calmness about her he hadn't expected. She was of course shocked out by where she was; he could sense it in her underlying tension.

He shifted his gaze back to her and saw that she'd scooted up to a sitting position. She thrust a couple of pillows behind her, but kept the comforter tucked around her legs and waist. She still siphoned his power, maybe fearing that if she didn't her head would start to hurt again.

He drew a chair close and sat down, but leaned forward to clasp his hands between his knees.

"So you want me to find this weapon before Daniel does."

"In a nutshell."

CHAPTER 3

Shayna stared at Marius, holding on to the blood-chain as though it was a life preserver—and maybe it was. Besides, she liked the feel of his power as she streamed it. She also loved being able to see so easily in the dark, and of course she really liked being out of pain.

Her brain whirred, working to process so much new information, and she let her thoughts fly in whatever direction they chose.

Her first musings went to the obvious, her overwhelming attraction to Marius, which made her current predicament even that much more complicated. The last thing she wanted to do was to make a decision about this strange chain-bonding, weapon-finding plan of Marius's simply because the breadth of his chest made her weak in the knees.

It didn't help that she hadn't been with a man since her breakup a year ago with Michelson. She'd wasted six months on him. But even after what seemed like a decent twelve-month interval, she still wasn't quite over him. He'd done something to her during their brief relationship, step by step tearing at her self-esteem so that in the end she'd allowed him to do things to her she hadn't confessed to a living soul.

So it came as a complete shock that when she finally felt the powerful stirrings of interest in another man, it was with a vampire.

She closed her eyes and leaned back against the pillows once more. She needed to stop thinking about her interest in Marius and instead focus on making sense of all that he'd just told her. A decision needed to be made.

Opening her eyes, she met his gaze once more. "The thing is, Marius, though I can appreciate that you've essentially asked for my help in resolving an issue in your world, I don't see how I can agree to help. What you're asking goes against everything I believe in. I've discovered a new secret world, but the last thing I should do is launch into an intervention. At the very least, I should make a study of what's actually happening. Perhaps in time I might come around to helping you, but it wouldn't be right to dive in with only your version of events."

Her adrenaline kicked in. "Of course, I would love to study your world, to perhaps visit a number of your caverns, to speak with a cross section of your people, which would help me to begin understanding your culture. But assisting you without sufficient knowledge is out of the question."

He remained leaning back against the chair. His jaw shifted slightly. "You do realize I could force you to help me."

"Yes. I suppose you could." She frowned, wondering if he would do just that. Her thumb rubbed the links back and forth, which increased her sense of him. He was incredibly determined, and that frightened her. "But you wouldn't, would you?"

"No, but I think maybe we need to take a trip."

"A trip?"

He nodded. "To another part of my world, something I think you need to see. You said you needed more information and I'll happily supply it."

His eyes suddenly took on a haunted look. Maybe she needed to make things clear. "I want you to take me home, Marius. I have no intention of forging this strange tracking-pair thing with you. I'm not an adventurous type, for one thing, but I think I've already explained my reasons. I will not intervene, not without a systematic review over a period of months, even years. My conscience won't allow it."

"It's not that simple. If Daniel gets the weapon . . ." His gaze slid away from hers and she knew he'd started thinking hard. He rose to pace to the fireplace and back.

Finally, he returned to stand in front of her. "Shayna, you don't know how much my thinking is aligned with yours on this subject, philosophically I mean, but I'm desperate here. For that reason, I want to show you something, and it won't be pleasant, but you need to see what I've lived with for such a long time. You said you can sense my guilt, and you're right. I live with tremendous guilt all the time because I haven't been able to help erad-

icate the worst criminal to impact our world in my lifetime.

"But even until a few days ago, even I didn't understand the level of horror he's inflicted on women of *your*
world. Not just women of my world but *yours*. I want you
to see for yourself what he's done. Then, if you still want
me to take you home, I will. Would you at least agree to
do that, to see what Daniel has done to your people?" He
drew a deep breath. "Again, it may be one of the hardest
things you'll ever have to see."

Shayna saw the philosophical loophole, since he'd spoken about women in *her* world. But she wasn't happy
about the position he'd just put her in at all. If humans
were involved, maybe she had responsibility after all.

She had a couple of questions she needed answered
before she agreed to go. "Are we talking human slavery?"

"Of the worst, most brutal kind, but it will mean going deep into Daniel's Dark Cave system, which will be
dangerous."

Shayna frowned. She couldn't believe how clearly she
could sense him, almost reading his mind. "He tortured
you there recently, didn't he? I say that because some of
your guilt comes from there, doesn't it?"

He nodded slowly.

Her throat began to ache. Why was this on her? She
was a university student, not a soldier. She didn't have
the kinds of abilities Marius possessed. Yet he'd brought
her here and asked for her help, assuring her she had
something of tremendous value in the situation.

But what did she owe him really?

Tears burned her eyes. She hated being put in this
position—as some kind of savior in his world. She'd

never asked for this, and she definitely didn't want any part of it.

And yet as Marius stared at her, a fire in his eyes, and as she felt the chain still wrapped around her fist, she could sense his desperation. She knew then that she couldn't refuse to take the trip with him. She had to at least agree to do that much, if only to assuage her conscience once she gave him her final answer.

Afterward, she could simply tell him to take her home and be done with the whole horrible thing.

Despite what was going on in his world, she didn't want to travel this path. She wanted to go back to her life, her careful plans to spend a year in the field then return to the University of Washington and work steadily on her dissertation. She had a doctorate to earn and she truly hoped one day to make a serious contribution to the field of cultural anthropology.

She didn't look at him as she said, "I'll go with you, but only because I can sense this is what you need from me in order to let this whole thing go." Finally, she lifted her gaze to him.

"Thank you," he said. "And I promise you that I do know how much I'm asking of you and that none of this is fair to you."

"How can you possibly understand what I'm feeling? You don't know what it is to be human and whipped into the air suddenly by a species that's only supposed to exist in folklore."

He smiled ruefully, then put his hand on the chain he wore. "In the same way you can feel my guilt, I can sense how you want more than anything to just go home right now."

Of course the street ran both ways. "Right."

He moved the chair back to its original position, angling it by the armoire. "We should go now. I suggest you put the blood-chain in your pocket while we fly. You can keep siphoning my power by touching it, but you need to be prepared that the flight will hurt despite the chains. Only vampires of special power, called Ancestrals, can fly humans around our globe pain-free. But you'll able to stream the healing power, and that will help."

She'd just gotten rid of the pain and could hardly stand the thought of launching into flight once more. But she'd never been one for holding back once a decision was made; she'd always had a tendency to jump in with both feet.

She pushed the comforter back and slid off the bed. With the chain secured in her pocket, and her hand tucked inside so that she could grip it at the same time, she nodded to him. "I'm ready."

Marius found himself admiring the woman in front of her. She had principles she tried to live by, and she'd just agreed to do something that would physically hurt her. She could have thrown a fit, gotten hysterical, but she didn't.

He held out his arm to her, and when she didn't move toward him, he remembered that all she knew about flying was what had happened in Seattle when he'd grabbed her and launched into the air. She didn't know the drill. "Step onto my right foot with both of yours and put your arm around my neck."

She didn't hesitate, another thing he liked about her: Once she made the decision, she was committed. But would this trip to Daniel's heinous Dark Cave system be enough to persuade her to join him?

He clamped his arm around her waist, pulling her tight against his side. "Do you feel secure?"

"Very."

"Good. You were unconscious for most of the trip here, but you probably won't be for this one because you're siphoning my power. You have hold of the chain?"

"In my tight, frightened fist, yes."

"Just wanted to be sure. I can feel my power streaming in your direction, but I needed to know what it was like on your end. As for the journey itself, we'll be able to communicate telepathically the entire distance." He switched just to be sure. *You okay with that?*

She turned into him so that she could look him in the eyes, a half smile on her lips. Because he held her pinned against him, his ever-present desire for her swelled. She was exquisite, and something about the blue of her eyes— or maybe it was the shape of her nose or possibly her smile—hit the center of his brain like a drug.

You're beautiful.

She frowned slightly. *Thank you. I . . . I wasn't expecting you to say that.*

Right. What the hell was he doing talking to her like that? He pulled himself together. *You ready?*

Yes.

Good. Let me switch to altered flight so you can feel the difference this time. I'd apologize again for just shooting us both up into the air in Seattle, but you already know why I had to do it.

I do. Go ahead.

He watched her for a second. Her gaze flitted around his room as though studying the space, categorizing maybe.

With the experience of four hundred years, he levitated

into the air then switched to altered flight. *What do you feel?*

Her eyes flitted once more. *A soft vibration, and the air appears to have gentle waves through it.*

You might want to close your eyes for this next part. We'll be flying through solid rock.

Really?

You're surprised?

Well, sure. She glanced toward the doorway. *Are you saying this cave doesn't have an outlet? That you didn't enter through, like, a front door?*

He chuckled. *No, nothing like that.*

So this isn't just flying.

We call it "altered" flight because it allows us to fly through anything solid.

Wow. Okay, but I'm not closing my eyes. I want to see this, to experience it.

When he took off, he headed straight up so that she wouldn't see a solid mass of rock coming straight at her.

It's like fog or something. And there's the sky. It's still dark. Where are we exactly?

South America.

That would explain it. So which direction are we traveling? I'm feeling like we're going east.

We are.

He felt her excitement so he kept the pace slow for now. Slower would mean less pain, and she could look around at the passing landscape below. Eventually, he'd have to move faster, because at this speed they were visible to other vampires either in the air or on the ground.

My head doesn't hurt. Is it the chains?

I'm not sure. Are you feeling any discomfort?

No, not really, but I'm holding the chains tight in

my fist and I do feel your power like a steady pulse through me.

That might change once we go faster.

Okay. I'll be ready.

Her arm tightened around his neck as she leaned forward and looked down. He wished he could show her more of the earth right now—what it would be like, for instance, to pass over one of the bigger human cities like Rio de Janeiro.

When his instincts suddenly told him that vampires were nearby, he started to speed up. He never ignored it when his senses warned him of the proximity of his kind. For all he knew they could be friendly, but he couldn't take the chance. *Gotta do this, Shayna. We've got vampires around here and I don't know if they're part of Daniel's crew or not.*

Go for it, but my head is starting to hurt.

I know. Just hold on to the chain in your pocket and focus on streaming my healing power. Can you do that?

She turned into him and nestled her head beneath his chin and damn him for liking it so much. What was it about Shayna, whom he barely knew, that got to him?

Had to be the blood-chains. But even if it was, the chains could only enhance what was already there. Which meant that on a very basic level, he was into her. And the feeling seemed to be mutual.

Just what he needed, the situation to become complicated with his desire for her. How much easier this would be if he didn't like who she was as a human female.

This hurts so bad.

But you haven't passed out. That's a good sign, Shayna. Hold tight. This won't take longer than ten minutes.

I know and streaming your power really does help. She rubbed her head beneath his chin, and even in the middle of altered flight, as he crossed over the African continent, he was hot for her. She was in pain, and he wanted to kiss her and do other things. Mostly, he wanted his fangs buried in a quick strike and her blood flowing so that he could taste what smelled so sweetly floral right now.

What are you thinking about? Even her voice in his head sounded wonderful.

You really don't want to know.

He felt her chuckle. *The chains have clued me in, and it helps if I think of you in that way as well. My head doesn't hurt so much. So I'm going with it. I'm really attracted to you, Marius. And the way you look in your T-shirt. I'm glad you didn't put your coat back on. Is this bothering you? Should I stop talking like this?*

Is it really helping? He should discourage her. He was liking the flirtation way too much.

Yes, it's helping, more than I can say. Once more, she rubbed her head against his neck and beneath his chin.

She stuck close and kept nuzzling him. But he felt her breathing hitch and he knew it wasn't good. *It's getting worse?*

Yes.

He hated the idea that something they might end up having to do often would be a source of pain for her. He sought around in his mind and finally said, *Listen, I don't know if this will work, but get a good grip on the chain in your hand then lift it to touch the chain at my neck. Can you do that?*

Yes and right now I'd try anything.

He felt her movements as she worked her hand out of

the pocket of her jeans, gliding her fist up his chest to make sure she didn't drop the chain.

She shifted just enough to bring her hand against his neck. The moment the chains connected, he felt a sudden jolt of power erupt between them and Shayna cried out.

Are you okay? Had he just hurt her?

It's so much better. I can't believe it. The connection has created a surge and the pain is leaving.

Good. I was hoping for that.

He breathed a little easier. The chains were functioning in a surprising way even though she hadn't yet put hers on. That she could siphon his power without actually wearing the chain and forging the bond meant something, though he wasn't sure what. The only thing he could deduce was that, for whatever reason, they were extremely compatible in terms of his power and her ability to siphon.

A few minutes later he swung north then began his descent into the Dark Cave system, miles away from the nearest improved cave. He knew Daniel's setup well, since a good year prior he'd snuck inside and spied on it, believing one day he'd return to tear the operation apart. He hadn't exactly planned on bringing a human female here, but she needed to see what was happening to tens of thousands of innocent human women every day.

He landed her at the far northern end of the system, a place he knew Daniel ignored. During several scouting missions, he'd never once seen a security team in the vicinity.

Shayna glanced around then smiled. "Hey, this is just a cave."

"Yep. Stalagmites and stalactites. Completely unimproved."

She stepped off his foot and took a moment to re-arrange the chain, wrapping it around her wrist several times, then lacing it afterward through her fingers. Clearly, she didn't want to lose it, and he didn't blame her.

She turned in a circle. "I'm still so stunned how well I can see in the dark."

"You've definitely tapped into my power. And you really do feel okay?"

Shifting to face him, she nodded. "The moment my chain connected with yours, the resulting wave of power quickly wiped out the headache. It was amazing. So yeah, I'm fine."

He stared at her and what he'd felt on the sidewalk in Seattle, as well as in flight, returned. He was so drawn to her. He moved close and took her arm gently in hand. "I'm glad you're okay."

His heart pounded as he stared into her light-blue eyes. He wanted to kiss her again, but he wouldn't do that to her.

He watched her lips part as a sliver of concern appeared in her eyes. "Of all that I've experienced so far," she said, shaking her head slowly, "what has surprised me the most is this." She waved her hand between them. "I know you want to kiss me and I want you to as well, which makes no sense. I don't really know you, and yet it's as though I've always known you." She lifted her hand that held the chain. "And these don't lie."

"No, they don't. They can only amplify what's already there."

"I know this won't make sense, but what comes through is that I can trust you. It would be foolish to act on it, though, wouldn't it? I mean, even another kiss might be asking for trouble." Her gaze fell to his lips. He sensed her desire, as well as her astonishment, that she was even thinking about kissing him.

"Completely foolish," he murmured. The air crackled between them, and he drew a little closer, not surprised when she took a small step as well so that only inches separated them.

Maybe because he thought it possible he'd never get the chance again, he closed the distance, pulled her into his arms, and settled his lips over hers.

Shayna's voice moved softly through his head, *Marius . . . yes.*

She surrounded his neck with both arms, pressing up against him.

He couldn't believe he was doing this, that he was kissing her for the second time. When her lips parted, he slid his tongue inside and couldn't repress the groan that followed.

Shayna could hardly breathe as Marius kissed her. She clung to him as though kissing him had become air to her starved lungs. She didn't understand her drive toward him at all, except for the obvious—she was painfully attracted to him.

He smelled so good, like summery grasses. Each drag of air had made her want him more, a sensation she'd tried to repress.

When he'd taken a step toward her just now, her feet had moved almost on their own. Now she was in his arms, her body pulsing with desire, the chain vibrating around her hand, saying, "Yes, yes, yes."

She knew the chain had done this, at least in part. She only wished that she'd met him at a Seattle bar and not under these difficult and bizarre circumstances.

When he began to pull back to end the moment, she withdrew as well, though her breathing had become erratic. He held her gaze and for a long moment, just looked at her. She couldn't imagine his thoughts, but she sensed he felt bemused, like he didn't know what to do with her.

She stood very still, waiting. He turned away from her and she felt his thoughts slide and his emotions grow dark. She'd felt this from him before, a powerful wash of guilt that led to feelings of unworthiness. Something tormented Marius, something so horrible that he couldn't even feel right about kissing her.

In this moment she felt her age. She was far too young to be dealing well with a four-hundred-year-old vampire who seemed to be filled with remorse.

Instead of saying anything, she drew inward as well, tapping into what life experience she had, the things she'd studied, the classes she'd taken in psychology. But nothing came to mind, no special synthesized wisdom that she could use to get Marius from where he was to a place where he might be willing to take her back in his arms.

Time to shift gears. "Is the Dark Cave system far from here?"

He made a half turn so that he met her gaze over his shoulder. He gestured with a toss of his hand. "We're already here. This is just a distant cave from Daniel's primary improved caverns." He glanced at the floor of the cave, then back to her. "I shouldn't have kissed you. I'm sorry for that."

"You don't have to apologize. You gave me what I wanted, that's all. And I loved it."

He stared at her for a long moment, his expression now grim. "The blood-chains are already creating a connection between us, can you feel it?"

She nodded. "I can. It's such a strange experience."

"It is that. And it's raw and magnificent and hard as hell to withstand."

"I would agree. It's amazing."

He narrowed his eyes. "You're not afraid of me, are you?"

"No, should I be?"

"I don't know. I would never want to hurt you, Shayna, but I'm afraid you'll get hurt."

She figured something out and moved close to him, putting her hand on his arm. "Until right this moment it didn't occur to me that what we're experiencing would be new ground for you as well. But it is, isn't it?"

"I've never worn a blood-chain before."

"And you're worried about me."

He released a heavy sigh. "Yes, I am. I don't want you to get hurt."

"Okay." She nodded briskly several times. She analyzed the situation and decided it would be best to forget about this moment and move on.

She'd told Marius she would do this, to look at what she understood to be Daniel's sex-slavery operation, involving human women, but she'd already made the decision that she needed to return to Seattle. This was not for her on any level. She was in no way trained to be part of what seemed to be a war within Marius's world or to deal with him personally. "Then how about we shift our attention back to making a trip through Daniel's operation."

He turned toward her and held out his arm once more. "Good idea."

But suddenly Shayna didn't want to see what it was that Daniel did to women from her world. She'd read enough articles about human trafficking to know that if it came close to any of what she'd learned, the images would probably never leave her mind.

It was one thing to be tucked up in Marius's bed with a fire burning in his fireplace and hearing about how vampires in his world steal human women and make sex slaves out of them. But it was another to travel halfway around the world and see it in person.

She crossed her arms over her stomach. "Actually, maybe you should just take me home right now. I don't plan on staying despite how horrible this reality is."

Marius lowered his chin. "It's the only thing I'm asking, then I'll take you home. But I need you to see how bad this is and why, against every principle, I would have brought you here in the first place. I'm asking you to have courage, most likely more than you've ever had in your life, and to see beyond your own life and plans."

She felt sick to her stomach. Why had it suddenly become her job to solve either problem, the war in his world or the issue of trafficking? "Marius, please don't make me do this. I just want to go home and resume my life."

Only then, when she lost heart, did he come to her, planting his hands on her arms. "You can do this, Shayna, and I need someone from your people to see what's being done to innocent humans. We've lived a secret life apart from your human world, but maybe that needs to change in order to protect women just like you."

Taking the ball out of the vampire court and lobbing it into her very human one calmed her down. She knew in her gut she had to do this thing. Maybe he was right. Maybe if she saw what was happening, she could report back to the US authorities and get the kind of help that was really needed to resolve the issue. She could still help, just not in the intense, chain-bound role she was currently assigned.

"Okay. Fine. I'm ready, but I'm really hoping that we'll do this fast. Get in, get out."

He nodded, then drew close, offering his booted foot once more.

As she stepped on top of his foot, he slid his arm around her waist and pulled her close. Despite the tension in the air, her proximity to Marius got to her all over again; honestly it was all she could do not to bury her nose in his neck and just take a whiff. Did all vampires smell this good?

Ready?

That he could breach her mind so easily once more sent another layer of sensation flowing through her.

I'm ready.

Still, she flinched as Marius shifted to altered flight and immediately spun them in a circle and headed not up but down. She had that nauseous, roller-coaster feeling *You're traveling fast.*

Have to. The speed keeps us invisible, but this will be a short trip.

She put her chained-up hand against his neck anyway. This time she felt a quick surge of power that seemed to set a block in place, preventing the pain. It was wonderful.

The next moment he slowed but didn't leave altered flight. They hung suspended at the end of a long hallway.

A large, muscled vampire walked away from them, down what appeared to be a central aisle. Minimal lighting was strung along the ceiling in twenty-foot increments of bare, sixty-watt bulbs.

Can he see us? she asked.

No. I have us cloaked in a heavy disguise. Only Daniel would be able to see through this, or maybe Quill and Lev, my half brothers who serve him.

Shayna was hardly listening. She could hear moaning as well as a sound she hadn't been able to place until she realized it was a cacophony of women weeping. *What is this place?*

An initial holding cell. The women are incarcerated here first, for a few hours. Most of them are raped at this point, a few kept pure for other harsher experiences down the line.

He started moving down the two rows of cells in which there were anywhere from one to three women on a cot, most of them huddled together, faces grimy, bodies bloodstained, eyes swollen from crying.

Screams erupted twenty yards away.

The guard stopped at what was an open cell door and smiled.

As Marius drew near, Shayna heard the guards laughing first, then some heavy grunting and more screams. She caught a glimpse inside and her stomach turned. Several of the guards were taking turns raping the two women in the cell.

I'm sorry you have to see this.

Shayna hadn't wanted to come here in the first place, but Marius was right. These women were human captives, and every nationality appeared to be represented. If she turned away without even observing, she was part of the problem. To not acknowledge their suffering and torture was to dishonor each and every one of them. *Isn't there something we can do?*

I'm afraid not. If we stopped and disrupted this crime, we'd be hunted down by the thousands of guards in this system. I'd probably be killed and you'd be put in one of these cells.

Shayna shuddered at this bald description and said nothing more.

The hallway ended, turned at a right angle—and Shayna gasped, for another hall extended farther than she could see. There were more guards and as Marius moved past the end of yet another long, double row of cells, and another, and another, the same scenario repeated: more weeping and screams from the women, laughter and grunting from the men.

Her own tears started to flow and she couldn't make them stop. *Marius, how many rows are there of just these initial holding cells?*

Can you see the horizon? He kept moving.

Shayna turned to look but it went on and on. *Oh, God.*

Marius's voice sounded distressed inside her head. *Shayna, thousands are brought here every week. Thousands die. Try if you can to process that number.*

I don't know how much more I can take.

Marius suddenly shifted course and flew straight up. For reasons she couldn't explain, she knew he held her in the middle of solid rock. *Shayna, this is the tip of the iceberg. Don't you understand? I showed you this part to help get you used to what the rest of this operation will look like.*

Oh, God.

But I will give you a choice. If you don't think you can see the rest, I'll take you away right now. She heard the compassion in his voice and knew he'd be as good as his word.

She grew very still, processing. What she'd seen so far made her want to throw up. Yet somehow, she couldn't speak the words ordering him to get her the hell out of here.

Do I want to leave? Yes. But, God help me, I'll stay. She swallowed really hard, brushing away her tears. Though she hated speaking the words that followed, she had to say them. *Show me everything you intended to earlier. Don't hold anything back because you're right; I need to see this for so many reasons. I live in my clean, simple, protected university world, but this is reality. I have to do this.*

It was at this moment, feeling Shayna tremble and knowing through the blood-chains that she was suffering, that Marius knew his relationship with this woman would never be simple. What he had just put her through, no woman should ever have to watch, the violation of her own gender.

And now she'd agreed to see the rest.

She showed tremendous courage when she should have been out of her mind, hysterical, even enraged that he would dare to disrupt her life and her worldview in this way. She should have demanded that he take her home.

Instead she'd faced up to the situation and chosen the harder path.

He barely knew her, but what he sensed through the chains, what he'd examined online about her life, and now her decision to see the rest of Daniel's operation spoke of her character and her abilities. He approved of her and his damn heart swelled.

I promise you that I'll make this quick for your sake.

He shut his emotions down, knowing that he was about to put Shayna through an unimaginable hell. In his own mind, he set up the course he'd take, traveling at the fringes of Daniel's immense operation in order to avoid detection. At the same time, he'd layer the level of atrocity and sexual violations she'd have to witness, beginning with the mildest first. There were a couple of venues, involving animals, he'd avoid altogether.

But she'd be witness to the rest.

Let's go.

She didn't say anything but her arm tightened around his neck. In turn, he held her more firmly at her waist. All the while, she continued to stream his power.

He flew deeper still and showed her a vast holding pen in an enormous cavern. The whole place was kept filthy in order to continue demoralizing the women, all of whom were naked and chained at the neck, and at the wrists and ankles. Hundreds milled around feeding troughs, or open latrines. Fights broke out. Groups of guards armed with Tasers raped or beat the women at will.

Daniel makes them live like animals to break them. He starves them and gives the guards license to do whatever they want. The women are sorted here as well. Those who show spirit, who aren't broken, are usually sent to auctions and go to the highest bidders. Those vampires who buy at auction tend to be the worst sadists, the ones who want women who will hold on to their humanity as long as they can while being brutalized in calculated stages.

The women who become dominant, who will hurt other women to survive, are put in sex shows and orgies. Some work in the cavern system for as long as two years. But Shayna, very few live beyond the two-year point. This is a death sentence. Sometimes it happens quickly. At least two percent won't leave this holding area.

She was very quiet, and he sensed she was shut down in order to handle what he was showing her.

Next, he took her to the adjoining bathing rooms where guards oversaw the cleanup of women ready to be moved through the system. Even here, the women were slapped or beaten, forced to become docile or risk being hurt again.

He flew up this time at a shallow angle to an open sex club with a ring of private booths and a large pit in which male vampires brutalized more women. A few slaves served drinks, but sex acts were rampant everywhere, as was the use of drugs. Vampires liked opiates.

It's the screaming. Shayna's voice sounded small and wounded within his head.

Unfortunately, the screams are part of the thrill.

She was trembling now and couldn't seem to stop. But she didn't say anything more. He pressed on, even though there was worse to come.

He took her through several private suites, slowing his pace only long enough for her to see and to understand. The individual woman, or sometimes several women, were being bitten, cut, and hung in chains, or laid out on tables, bound, and held spread-eagled, sometimes on their backs, sometimes on their stomachs. More than one died as he moved her from room to room. The floors were mostly made of cement with drains, the easiest ways to keep a slavery situation free of debris once a session was over.

Shayna's body stiffened next to his. He knew what was coming. Again, couldn't be helped.

Marius, I'm gonna throw up.

As before, he drifted into solid rock. *Just let it go.*

She heaved repeatedly. *Does it get worse than this?*

No, not worse, just more. I'll breeze you through the rest only to give you a feel for the volume of this setup.

Okay, because I really can't take much more.

I know. We're almost done.

She wept now and as she slid her arm around his neck, she kept wiping at her face. *I can't stop crying.*

I know. It's okay. He realized tears of his own had started leaking from his eyes. He'd lived with this a long time, but experiencing everything fresh through Shayna's eyes just plain hurt. The blood-chain let him experience all that she felt.

For the next several minutes he moved swiftly, passing through club after club, each with a slightly different theme, but always with women, and a few male humans, being raped and often tortured.

Finally, he wanted her to see where Daniel had held him captive, trying one last time to strip away Marius's determination to hold on to his view of what their world should be.

Shayna, this last place I'll be taking you is where Daniel recently tortured me. I need you to see, to understand what he did, so that you can also understand where I'm coming from.

Okay. Again, her voice had shrunk down.

But when he arrived, passing through a long stretch of solid rock, he was horrified to discover that a number of the bodies hadn't been removed. These were the corpses of the women that Daniel had killed in front of Marius in an attempt to force his hand.

I don't understand. What is this?

Shayna, I'm sorry. I thought this space would have been cleared by now. Let's get out of here.

No. Wait. You brought me here for a reason, so let's

finish this. Why were so many women killed here and what did it have to do with you?

Marius stayed in altered flight. He'd intended to set down, but not now. He felt the horror return, and for a moment was back in chains forced to watch each death.

Marius, tell me. I need to know.

He gestured in a forward motion. *I was strung up against that far wall. Daniel used a whip on me and a dagger at times for deep puncture wounds. He used the pain to try to force me to join him. Each time I refused, he tortured and killed another woman.*

Oh, God. She took more deep breaths. *Is this why you feel so guilty?*

One of many reasons, I'm afraid.

Marius, something is wrong. I'm feeling something strange. I think you need to get us out of here now.

He didn't know what she meant by that. But the next moment he heard a voice behind him. *Hello, son. Have you returned to me at last?*

As soon as Marius heard his father's voice, he reacted on instinct, refusing to turn to face him. Instead he gripped Shayna harder still and a split second later shot straight up through the cavern system, into the air, hurling them both in the direction of The Erotic Passage.

He opened a telepathic channel to Rumy. *Daniel found us. We're coming to you.*

Aw, shit. I can't let you in by either the front or the back door because Daniel left some of his men here in case you came back. Looks like he's determined to take you down this time.

Then I need fighting support. He glanced back and saw that Daniel was keeping pace and had a large detail with him. *I'm thinking we go with one of our earlier plans*

*involving your security team. Daniel has about twenty
men with him.*

How far out are you?

Two minutes.

*Jesus H. Christ. What? Are you like flying at super-
Ancestral level?*

*Hell if I know. I'm just damn determined to save
Shayna.*

All right. All right. Let me think.

Marius knew there was no place in the vampire world
he'd be safe with Shayna, not right now, not with Daniel
so close.

Marius had a safe house in New Zealand that Daniel
didn't know about, but if he'd headed there with Shayna,
Daniel could have followed them, just as he was doing
now.

His only hope was in facing off with Daniel and his
force, making use of Rumy's security personnel. Rumy
could summon at least a hundred men, but it might take
a few minutes.

The only problem was speed. Rumy would have to or-
chestrate and pull his team together while Daniel was
right on Marius's ass.

Timing would be critical.

However, Marius was confident he could hold them off
long enough for Rumy's men to arrive.

As he flew the last stretch to Italy, Marius now ques-
tioned his wisdom in taking Shayna to the Dark Cave system in the first place. Except that in his desperation, he
was hoping against hope that if she actually saw the atrocities committed against her people, then she might be
willing to engage with him and help him find the extinction weapon.

It had been a last-ditch effort that might just prove fatal to Shayna. Then he'd have one more death on his hands.

But what else was fucking new?

Rumy came back on the telepathic line. *Okay, we're moving to plan B. I'll contact you as soon as I have a location locked in, about thirty seconds.*

Got it. Plan B involved Rumy setting up a battlefield deep inside the Como system, well away from the various clubs and restaurants associated with The Erotic Passage.

Because Marius was flying at top speed, he could feel that pain piercing Shayna's head once more; even the power she streamed from the blood-chains wasn't helping.

Marius, can you slow down? You haven't gone this fast before.

I can't, because Daniel's after us. Just hold on. I'll be putting us down in less than a minute.

Hurry. Oh, God, the pain. It's worse than before. She started to scream.

Shayna, I'm so sorry.

He felt nothing but relief when she passed out.

CHAPTER 4

When Rumy came back on the line, he said, *I've got it set it up and my men are on the way.* He then sent Marius a visual.

Marius homed in on the image until he locked onto the exact cavern. *Got it.*

I'm sending my toughest two dozen. But they'll come in waves because they were on maneuvers in the north. Just keep Daniel talking. That bastard loves the sound of his own voice.

Thank you, Rumy.

Just stay alive. We need you, Marius. He felt Rumy shut the communication down.

Marius was only seconds out now. Once at Lake Como,

he headed into the hills and dipped through solid rock. He could feel the cavern's pull on him as he held the image fixed in his mind.

When he reached the location, he shifted from altered flight to regular levitation then sought out a stretch of even ground close to the cavern wall. At the same time, he started building the layered shield that Gabriel had taught him to construct. With any luck, Daniel wouldn't find him right away.

With great care, he laid Shayna next to the rock wall, then rose up, turning to face into the massive cavern space. The area was completely unimproved. The ground was boulder-strewn, with scattered pools of old water, as well as a number of stalactites and stalagmites, the dripstone making it hard to do battle. Rumy had chosen the place well.

He hated that this was the best he could do, but he didn't have an auxiliary fighting force like Rumy did. Building an army in his world was illegal.

Just as Daniel and his men started to arrive, he pulled two long battle chains from deep, narrow pockets in his leathers, then started them spinning. He still held his disguise, but Daniel took one long look around the cavern and began spacing his men out.

Then he turned to Marius because he could see right through his layered shield. Daniel waved an arm and Marius's disguise faltered and fell away. Shit. Just when he thought he knew the breadth of Daniel's power.

"Don't be a fool, son. I don't want to kill Shayna or you, but I'm so sick of you boys rebelling. It's been four hundred years and you'd think by now life would have shaped you up and brought you to serve at my feet."

"Then you shouldn't have hurt us like you did. We

would have had no reason to rebel otherwise." Stating the goddamn obvious.

Daniel looked as he always did, like an elegant dictator. He wore an expensive, tailored suit of dark-blue silk and a goatee trimmed close, with his short, dark hair slicked back. He had unforgettable eyes, teal, and flecked with gold. Marius shared the gold flecks but his eyes were a less impressive hazel, a distinction Marius preferred.

Daniel represented everything evil in their world and Marius hated him with a passion. Like all the Briggs boys, Daniel had tortured Marius, slicing the length of his spine and flaying him open again and again in order to preserve the scar for posterity. Only repeated cuts could leave a scar on a vampire. Daniel called it a character-building exercise. That's how he justified his pleasure in brutalizing his children. How often had he heard Daniel say that the beatings, cuttings, and slicings-up would make men of his sissy-boys.

Daniel hovered forty feet away, levitating behind his line of fighters. He wouldn't dirty his hands unless he had to.

"You were always my biggest disappointment, Marius. You were the little boy that cried all the time, looking for Adrien and Lucian to protect you. I know how much you used them—and don't pretend you didn't. You and I both know the truth. Of course it pleased me to see you writhe in your guilt when one or the other of your brothers would take your pain for you."

Daniel always got to the heart of things.

"Fuck you, Daniel." Hatred boiled in Marius, stronger than ever, especially recalling how his father hadn't even bothered to dispose of all the dead bodies in his most recent torture room. He'd left them there to rot as though even in death they had no value.

Daniel waved his arm and three of his fighters shifted in Marius's direction.

Marius lowered his chin. His nostrils flared. He'd battled a long time and the adrenaline flowed like fire through his body. With his battle chains spinning, Marius levitated, rising five feet into the air.

The men attacked, one in the front, and one from each side.

Marius flipped his wrist, and the spinning chain in his right hand flipped to wrap itself around that vampire's neck. He did the same with the left. From his periphery, he could see he'd brought both down and each now struggled to remove the chains.

The center assailant, as big as Marius, barreled down on him. But Marius pulled a dagger from his leathers, shifted to altered flight, whipped behind the attacker, and drove the blade deep into his kidneys.

The big body arched, then fell.

Three down.

Marius flew back to stand in front of Shayna. This time, Daniel sent five toward Marius, each maneuvering in levitated flight through the various dripstones, but no one moved against him.

Daniel shouted. "Ten thousand dollars to the one who cuts the woman's throat."

Marius contacted Rumy. *Need your men here. Now.*

They're on the way. Ten seconds out.

Marius backed up a little more. His reputation as a fighter, and the fact that he'd just killed the first three attackers, made the men wary as they approached him.

Marius counted backward, bloodied blade in one hand. His other outstretched for balance.

Three, two, one . . .

The next moment the cavalry arrived. Twenty of Rumy's best men shot into the cavern, shifting from altered flight. Three flew from behind Marius, the rest from various entrance points all over the battlefield.

Chaos erupted.

Marius moved to position himself just inches away from Shayna, body hunched as he shifted his blade from hand to hand, waiting for one of Daniel's men to break free and attack.

Rumy's security hands fought like maniacs, all of them set against Daniel and his kind. Not a life in their world had gone untouched by Daniel's tactic of systematically taking over smaller enterprises, forcing the courts to side with him in critical civil disputes. Nor had Daniel limited his sex slavery to just humans. Many innocent female vampires had been ripped from their homes and put to work.

To his left, one of Daniel's men struck down one of Rumy's and flew slowly in Marius's direction. He was a big motherfucker, taller than Marius, and one of Daniel's finest.

He rounded a stalagmite, whipped a long chain held in his right hand, and caught Marius's left wrist, trapping him as the chain held tight.

Marius flipped his blade with precision and caught the bastard in the throat. He went down, which pulled Marius with him.

The chain around Marius's wrist had him trapped since it was locked to a manacle on the attacker, now bleeding profusely from his throat. Marius knew he was trying to self-heal, but a wound like that was almost impossible to repair fast enough. Blood drained quickly.

Daniel skirted the battle, heading in Marius's direction. If he didn't figure this out fast, Daniel would kill him—every other guard in the place was battling hard.

He mentally called out to Rumy. *Need a few more men.*

Sending another dozen, but it'll be three minutes.

Thanks. It wouldn't be soon enough, but what else could he say.

When Daniel reached him, Marius was on his knees trying to work the chain off his wrist. "You're in a bit of a fix, Marius. Looks like your luck finally ran out. Or more to the point, Shayna's did."

He saw a blade flash.

"Don't hurt the woman. Take your vengeance out on me, but leave her alone."

"Attached already, I see. Well, this should be fun." He turned and moved slowly in Shayna's direction.

Typical of Daniel to take his time when he was about to make a kill.

Shayna hurt in so many places, she could hardly move. She felt as though the two hemispheres of her brain had gone to war and planned to be fighting for a long time. Marius had flown so swiftly out of the Dark Cave system that no amount of his siphoned power had helped. And now, yeah, she was in pain.

Her hearing was screwed up as well. Everything was muffled, maybe because she hurt so badly.

With Marius's blood-chain still wrapped around her wrist, and vibrating softly, she could also feel that whatever was happening to Marius, the vampire was in a rage. And something else: She felt a kind of fear that went deep and had ugly layers, something Marius had known his whole life.

Which meant Daniel had to be nearby.

She wished she could help, but she was so disoriented.

She had no idea where he'd taken her. She lay on some kind of rocky surface and could smell that this cave had a lot of damp. She tried to shift position, but the rocks made it hard to move without more pain.

Some kind of whirring sound reached her ears, but it was like listening through thick cotton balls. At the same time, she felt really sick to her stomach again, no doubt as a result of the flight. Of course it didn't help that images of the Dark Cave system still poured through her mind, especially the last location where Daniel had killed all those women in an attempt to subvert his son.

She breathed through another heavy wave of nausea.

Her hearing began to clear up and she realized that some kind of battle was taking place. She lifted up just enough to shift her head the other direction and then she wished she hadn't. Some kind of brawl was going on with thirty or forty huge men. Blood was everywhere as well as knives and chains used as weapons. A vampire nearby had died not ten feet from her, a chain around his neck, his tongue hanging out of his mouth, eyes bulging, the tips of his fangs showing.

That's when she started dry-heaving. She'd already been sick earlier and there was nothing left, but she heaved anyway.

Suddenly Marius's voice was in her head. *Shayna, look out. Daniel's behind you and I'm caught. If you can move, try to get away, hide behind one of the bigger dripstones.*

Fear now started moving like lightning through Shayna, and she forced herself to rise to a sitting position.

Her head was killing her.

Then she saw the one that had to be Daniel, standing in front of her maybe ten feet away. He stood like an untouchable god in the middle of the battle, wearing a dark-blue suit and looking pristine against all the blood and gore.

He smiled, a terrible smile full of a desire to cause pain, probably to cause her pain.

He was extremely handsome with unusual teal eyes, his dark hair plastered against his head, his goatee tight to his face.

Daniel.

The evil in this world.

The monster who had hurt his own sons, who enslaved tens of thousands of women, who wanted to rule his world.

Crossing her arms over her stomach, she could do little more than watch as he started moving toward her.

She clutched the blood-chain in her hand harder and siphoned as much of Marius's power as she could. She grew dizzy with pain and something more, something that made the smile on Daniel's face grow dim. Even Daniel grew dim, as though fading away, but not quite.

She felt herself moving backward, though not moving. She felt suspended in time and space. But where had she gone? What was she doing?

She knew three important things: First, that whatever she'd just done had bought her some time; second, that Daniel could no longer see her; and third, that this thing was damn temporary. She searched the blood-chains for knowledge and found that she had exactly thirty seconds; then she'd leave this bizarre safe space.

Marius, can you see me?

Marius, struggling with something on his arm, shifted in what should have been her direction, but his eyes went wide. *No, where are you?*

I'm not sure, but in twenty seconds, I'll return, then Daniel will have me. You've got to help, got to figure this out.

Daniel advanced on her position. "Where are you, Shayna, and what kind of power do you possess that you can disappear yet I'm able to feel you nearby?"

Nine, eight, seven . . .

Shayna felt the momentary power surge begin to fade. *Marius, he's right there. He's standing in front of me and I'm about to become visible.*

Daniel searched her previous location. "Where are you, pretty Shayna? Ah, I can see you now. How clever."

He reached for her and she felt his hands graze her arms; then he arched and grimaced, shouting his pain.

Marius had freed himself and stuck him with a blade.

Daniel suddenly just disappeared.

Shayna glanced upward, sensing where he was. She caught a glimpse of him, blood trailing as he shifted to altered flight and headed through the rock of the cavern ceiling.

Shayna saw Marius's bloody dagger as he turned away from her. The battle still raged all around the cavern.

Then suddenly, a new host of fighters entered the space, which changed everything abruptly.

One of Daniel's crew shouted an order and just like that, the rest of Daniel's force shifted to altered flight and retreated, disappearing through dripstone and rock alike.

Silence reigned for about ten long seconds. Then Marius gave a cry of triumph, a guttural masculine shout that vibrated all the way through to Shayna's heart. She'd never heard a better sound in her life. Tears flowed down her cheeks.

She'd survived something horrible, despite the severe headache that still hurt her.

She was safe. She released a deep sigh and the odd thought went through her that apparently she would live to see another day.

Through the haze of her pain, however, something sparked within Shayna's mind as she realized all over again that she was looking at a brand-new, never-before-discovered civilization. Yet the men celebrated as warriors had through the millennia, with shouts of triumph.

Marius turned toward her, his face blazing with passion and a sense of victory. But almost as quickly the expression died away and concern filled his hazel eyes. "Shayna. Shit, I'm so fucking sorry you had to see all this. And you're hurting. Let me get you out of here."

She nodded. She tried to gain her feet, but the pain in her head was too much. Marius leaned down and gathered her up in his arms once more as though she were as light as air.

She slid her arm around his neck. Despite the fact that he'd been warring, he smelled amazing, that wild grassy scent of his. He called out a few orders, mostly involving the disposal of the enemy fighters. There was some discussion about the one called Rumy, then suddenly she was airborne once more, moving through solid rock as though it were little more than a bank of fog.

However, he must have taken off too fast, because once again her brain felt skewered with swirling knives. She tried to access his power, but it was too much. She screamed, then blacked out. Again.

Marius settled Shayna on his bed, this time in his secret New Zealand home, a place even more secure than the one in Chile.

She looked horribly pale against the black linen, her blond hair fanning out. He still couldn't believe that she'd made herself disappear like that, a trick very few vampires could do. And it wasn't a layered disguise. She'd actually made herself invisible, even to Daniel, but how?

He trembled as he looked down at her. The battle adrenaline was easing back but had left him with the shakes. Not a good thing since it wasn't a normal reaction of his after a battle, which meant his other problem had started to surface. He wasn't in trouble yet, but he soon would be. He'd already been through one round of blood-starvation recovery, which involved a violent madness. And now it looked like the second one was on him.

And he needed to be tied up in order to keep Shayna safe.

A few years back, in anticipation of his world going from bad to totally wrecked, he'd searched for the best hiding places he could find. Though he'd used other Ancestrals to create the layered shields, for this one, his most secure location, he'd had Gabriel create the heavy layer of disguise around the entire system.

No one could find him here, not even Daniel.

For the moment, they were safe.

He worked to get his boots and socks off. For what he had to go through, his wrists and ankles would have to be bound. If he thrashed and the boots connected with Shayna, he could kill her.

The process of blood-starvation recovery was never simple and was similar to an addict's withdrawal process except in reverse. Instead of the body reacting to the absence of drugs, a vampire had a difficult time adding blood back into his diet once deprived.

His system was now in the process of beginning the second violent episode that would include sweating, shaking, and dementia. He probably wouldn't even be aware of most of what he would go through.

But Shayna would.

When he'd escaped from Daniel just a few days ago, he'd gone through his first round, then Rumy had sent him to bring Shayna into their world. He had hoped by now to be back in one of Rumy's apartments where several of his staff could tend to Marius, strap him down, and even donate blood during the process.

He had one option and contacted Rumy telepathically. *Hey, Rumy. Your security team did a great job as usual.*

They did. I've been listening to their reports. Seems a couple of them saw Shayna disappear right in front of Daniel. What's up with that?

He paced the bedroom, an arm pressed against his stomach. *She's got so much latent ability, I'm constantly astonished. Daniel would have killed her if he could have caught her.*

Instead, you stuck him.

At that, Marius smiled. *Yeah, I did. But listen, I've got a problem.*

I can hear it in your voice; you're close to a second round, aren't you?

Yes, and I'd really hoped I'd be back at The Erotic Passage.

You know we would have taken care of you.

I know. Except for his brothers and Gabriel, he had no better friend than Rumy.

So where are you?

I'm holed up in the one place no one knows about. He stopped to stare down at Shayna. *I'm going to need help, but I'm reluctant to bring anyone here. This has been my primary hiding place all these years.*

Rumy was silent for a moment, then said, *You want me ready as backup in case Shayna can't or won't donate?*

Yes. Even to his own ears he sounded relieved. He didn't want to do anything to jeopardize the secrecy of his home, so his current plan involved Shayna opening a vein. But if she wasn't up for that, yeah, he needed an option.

I'll have someone on call in case things don't work out over there, okay?

Thanks. He was grateful to be understood so quickly.

Just give me a shout if you need me.

Will do.

He cut the communication and moved to sit down on the side of the bed as he'd done before in Chile. He gently pushed her hair away from her face. She'd be in pain for a while and there was nothing he could do about that except to encourage her to keep siphoning more of his power once she woke up. He glanced down at her right hand, clamped in a fist, the chain laced through her fingers. No matter what, she wouldn't let it go.

Smart. Very smart.

Just as she began to stir on the bed, his stomach

cramped. He leaned over, holding his breath, a hand to his forehead. Shit, this was bad.

Shayna moaned. He glanced at her and watched her eyes flutter open. "Where are we? Are we safe?"

When she met his gaze, she stared at him for a long moment. "You stabbed your father."

"I did, but he still got away."

"I know. Oh, my head hurts, but there's something else. Marius, are you in some kind of pain? Because that's what I'm getting and you're kind of bent over. Were you wounded in the battle?"

He shook his head. "No. It's nothing like that. I'll tell you in a minute. I just want you to be free from your pain. Why don't you try putting the chains together like you did on the flight from Chile."

She struggled to sit up, then leaned close and pressed her chain against his. The power surge caused her to moan softly. "Oh, that is just so incredible, the way the healing power flows."

After a moment she looked around, though keeping the chains touching. "I thought maybe we would have returned to the other cave. But this one . . . is amazing. My God."

Marius glanced around as well. He'd been too caught up in both Shayna's suffering and his own to recall just how much money he'd put into this home. He'd had all the work done in secret, which meant putting the craftsmen through enthrallment each time he brought them in and when he took them home.

He'd spent over five million dollars getting the cave livable and sealed from damp, all the bats relocated to other parts of the system, water rerouted from underground rivers to create the critical indoor plumbing as well as the aesthetic waterfalls in several of the rooms, not to mention dealing with all the solar-electrical issues.

Shayna's gaze had become fixed on the angled waterfall some thirty feet away, which flowed from a space just beyond the tall ceiling line. This particular feature had lighting at the bottom that caused a glitter effect from the flecks of gold pyrite in the natural gray stone.

He breathed through another cramp.

"Is the fireplace functional like the one in Chile?"

He glanced back at Shayna, whose gaze had settled on the massive arched stone fireplace to the right, set at an angle in the direction of the bed. "It is."

"Where does the smoke go?"

"It's vented to the outside through an intricate piping system."

"You must be a world of engineers."

"We have many talented people and universities."

In the space between, a shelf held a three-tiered silver candelabra. The stone was etched behind in an intricate pattern of lines.

"There's that pattern again."

"Oh, that's right. I had the craftsman use that design in the Andes house." When another cramp took hold of him, he knew he had to start addressing his issue and get things sorted. "So, how are you feeling?"

She pulled her hand away from his neck, disconnecting the chains. "The pain's all gone." She even smiled.

"Good. I'm glad to hear it and I'm really sorry you had to go through that again, twice."

She nodded, frowning this time, her gaze fixed on him. "Wait a minute. You're in some kind of pain yourself. What's going on? Marius, this is serious, isn't it?"

"Yes, it is, and it's getting worse. I might need your help, but if you can't do it, I'll contact Rumy. He can bring someone in." Even his breathing had changed; this was coming on fast.

"What do you mean, if I can't do it? What exactly do you need me to do?"

"I'll need to be bound so I can't move, or hurt you, and later you'd need to donate."

She swallowed hard. "As in donating blood?" She touched her throat absently.

"Yes." He told her about blood-starvation and the resulting madness that comes from the reintroduction of blood into a vampire's depleted system.

Shayna stared at Marius, her eyes wide. "And this is what's wrong with you now?"

He nodded. He leaned over and wrapped both arms around his stomach.

Images of a frying pan and a fire came to mind. She'd just left two different kinds of horror, first with the atrocities at the Dark Cave system and then the recent battle. But given how pale Marius had just turned, she was about to enter a third.

"Tell me, Shayna, whether you can do this. Otherwise Rumy will send someone in."

"To feed you?"

He nodded. "And tend to me. Blood-madness recovery isn't very pretty."

Shayna grew very still. The oddest sensation went through her, a kind of possessive vibration that made her clamp her hand around Marius's wrist. And before she'd actually formed the words in her head to analyze their merit, she stated in a voice she barely recognized, "The hell anyone else is feeding you. I'll do it. You saved my life. My blood is yours."

He shifted slightly to meet her gaze. "Thank you." But his jaw looked stiff, and sweat had beaded up on his forehead. Because of the chains, she could feel how quickly his condition had turned for the worse.

He was breathing hard now, trying to hold himself together. She swung her legs over the side of the bed and quickly removed the chain from around her wrist and fingers. She wouldn't be able to do anything very fast if she wore the chain, but she tucked it into the pocket of her jeans to keep it close. Even with a layer of fabric separating her from the metal links, she still siphoned his power.

"How do I tie you up? What do I use? Where do I do this?"

"We'll have to do it here. Look under the bed. The chains are secured into the stone floor. Oh, God, Shayna, hurry. I'll hurt you if I'm not tied down within the next minute."

"I understand." Shayna had already seen enough of Marius's world, and of him, to believe him.

"Shit, this is coming on fast."

"I know. I can feel it, too."

She dove beneath the wood frame to see what the chain setup looked like. She found four sets of coils, with leather bands for the wrists and ankles.

Without being told what to do, she rose up, stripped the bedding off the bed except the bottom sheet, then pushed Marius to lie on his back. He'd started to shake all over.

She grabbed the strap and tied up his left wrist, then his left ankle.

"Good. Dammit, hurry, Shayna!"

She flew around the foot of the bed and grabbed the wrist strap from under the bed. She had to work to keep him steady enough to tighten the strap.

By the time she was working on his right ankle, he'd started thrashing and the sounds of the jangling chains scared her more than anything else. As a result, she lost control of his powerful leg twice. Capturing it a third time, she almost had the strap in place when he kicked out and threw her backward several feet.

She plowed into a chair and now she'd have a lovely bruise on her shoulder and back.

She stood up, knowing by his wild movements that she'd be in trouble if she didn't get the leg secured.

Marius's back started arching as though he was in terrible pain, his face twisted in agony. He started shouting incomprehensible things at the ceiling. His leg swung from side to side.

He'd kill her if she got too close. For just a handful of seconds he grew quiet, then the whole thing started again.

All she could do was stand back and watch him thrash though she still held the strap in her hand.

He arched and cried out repeatedly as though in great pain. But after a few minutes, she watched then timed those moments when everything slowed down and he looked as though he'd passed out.

She started practicing buckling the strap around the base of the chair leg. She did this over and over until she could do it at lightning speed.

When she felt ready, she siphoned Marius's power and focused on the leg. The moment his limb settled down, she moved in, wrapped the leather around his ankle, and buckled.

She stood up, lifted both arms, and shouted in triumph because now he really was contained. She would have shouted again, but that's when the horror really began.

Marius, now unable to move his legs, began straining with all his might against each of the bindings. He screamed and sometimes cried out, "Stop hurting me! Why are you hurting me?"

Shayna started moving backward until she hit the wall near the fireplace. Tears streamed from Marius's eyes and suddenly she couldn't take it anymore.

She sank to the floor and wept.

It was all too damn much.

She hadn't asked for this, to be taken into some freakish world where vampires existed and bad men tried to kill her, where sadists enslaved, raped, tortured, and killed thousands of human females, and where her abductor lay strapped down on his bed shouting and cursing because he had to go through some kind of withdrawal that she didn't understand.

She hugged her knees to her chest and covered her ears with her hands.

She sobbed. She was frightened and alone and didn't know what to do.

She stayed like that for a long time, tears flowing down her cheeks, using her shirt to wipe her nose, feeling damn sorry for herself.

After probably a good half hour of meltdown, her tears finally dried up.

She had a strange view from the floor and could only see one arm flail and one leg. She watched his muscles tense up in what must have been painful cramps. He still wore leather pants, which must have been unbearably hot because he was sweating.

Thank God he'd gotten his boots off. They sat askew near a side table next to the bed.

She rose to her feet and saw that he rolled his head back and forth as he moaned. The flushed, deep-red color of his skin alarmed her. Maybe she didn't understand what he was going through or why this was suddenly her fate, but she already knew that Marius was a good man, who worked hard on behalf of his world.

And right now, he needed her help.

A door on the other side of the bed led her into a bathroom. She had to make do with a large plastic container beneath the sink, something she would have used to soak her feet. She put it beneath the faucet and filled it with a couple of inches of water.

Hunting through the drawers, she found a stack of washcloths and a pair of scissors. The latter she'd use to cut his clothes off. This would be tricky, of course, because he moved so much, but she knew she had to cool him down.

Taking everything back to the room, she set the basin on the nightstand. She dipped a washcloth in the cold water, wrung it out a little, then—keeping her arms well away from his hands—she moved in close, trying to reach his forehead. But she couldn't extend her arm without Marius hitting her or even grabbing hold of her. The chains had too much give. If he caught her, she knew she wouldn't escape him.

She dropped the wet washcloth back in the basin.

She remembered seeing a sort of clamp near each set of chains. She lay on her stomach and examined the one near his ankle. She almost cried out with relief when she realized it was a ratchet setup that could tighten down each chain. If she could just make the noise of all that rattling stop, she'd be ahead of the game.

Using the levered handle, she tightened up the first one, and it worked. The sounds of the jangling chains had just about driven her crazy. Even though she knew it would distress him to limit his range of motion further, she decided to end that part of the nightmare right now and went to his other ankle, then both wrists, tightening each chain.

All the rattling stopped. She could breathe.

But now Marius pulled with all his might on each chain. She waited, just in case the whole thing flew apart. She held her breath, because if even one chain snapped, she'd be dead and she knew it.

However, the chains held and Marius finally laid back on the bed. Though his eyes were open, his mind was gone at least for the present. "Why, Father, why?"

Picking up the washcloth, she wrung it again, then laid it over his forehead.

He grew very still and a soft sigh left his lips.

She took a moment to wash his arms, each in turn, with the cold water. He had dried blood on him from the recent battle, which of course turned the water pink as she continued to cleanse the washcloth in the water. But she kept going and he made soft moaning sounds that told her she was giving him some relief. He even settled down, at least for now.

Next, she took the scissors and while he lay still, she cut off his shirt. Sweat rose in a sheen on his body. She unzipped his pants carefully, then began at one side to cut them, all the way down. Every inch of his lower body was beet red.

He'd also gone commando, which distressed her because it seemed very wrong to be looking at him. Yet he was so big that for a moment, she grew very still. Her desire for him, never far away, returned inappropriately and now her body felt flushed and hot.

She took a moment to return to the bathroom to fetch a towel. She had to cover him up, for her sake and because at some point he'd come back to himself. The last thing he'd want was to be fully exposed while tied down.

Laying the towel across his hips, she returned to the basin.

The next washcloth she dipped in the water she used on herself. What came away from her was dirt from the cave and more blood, probably from what had been on Marius's clothes. She groaned. She had to be filthy.

But she set all these thoughts aside and for the next half hour washed Marius repeatedly until his skin resumed a more normal hue. She scrubbed beneath him as well. The sheet was soaked, and if she could manage to change it she would.

A couple of times she heard him whisper, "Thank you." She answered quietly each time, "You're welcome." But she was never quite sure he actually understood her.

She found a clean sheet in a cupboard in the bathroom and set about replacing the damp one beneath him, which became a project all in itself.

She only stopped when a round of thrashing ensued, then she went back to work.

At least two hours later, he finally seemed to be resting, though his breathing seemed labored. Seeing that he was the calmest he'd been, she hunted through a chest of drawers on the wall adjacent to the bed, found one of his clean T-shirts, and went into the bathroom and turned on several showerheads.

Stripping out of her clothes, but keeping the chain wrapped around her wrist, she stepped into the spray. Never had a shower felt more glorious than in this moment. She got all the dirt off her body and out of her hair, then let the hot water beat on her now very sore shoulder and back. Siphoning Marius's power, she sent what healing she could into her muscles. Happily, it worked. Maybe she wouldn't have a bruise the size of Puget Sound on her back after all.

"Shayna?"

She heard Marius's voice and slapped in quick jerks at the handles to shut off the water. "Marius? Are you there?" She didn't know how else to ask if his mind had come back to him.

"Momentarily." He sounded hoarse.

"I'll be right there. I was just taking a shower, cleaning up."

She quickly dried off, slipped on his navy T-shirt, wrapped her dripping hair up in a towel, then returned to the bedroom.

His eyes were open, but he looked haggard and pale. "How are you feeling? You don't look so good."

"Shayna, I'm sorry to ask this of you after all that I've put you through, but I need blood. I'm not gonna make it otherwise. Can you donate?"

CHAPTER 5

Shayna stood all the way across the room, staring at an almost naked man, spread-eagled and begging for her help. She'd known him a few hours and here they were, the sorriest pair ever.

She could feel his weakness through the chain still wrapped around her wrist. Death wasn't far away.

His question didn't require an answer. Of course she'd donate. Maybe Marius had thrown her into a nightmare, but he was a good man and deserved to live.

She crossed to the nearest side of the bed, which put her on his right side. Crawling across the bed reminded her that she was wasn't even wearing panties.

She scooted close, dragged the towel off her head, and offered her wrist.

"You should probably lie down next to me. This may take some time."

For some reason, the proximity made her nervous, not because she was afraid of him, but because neither of them had much on. She lay down beside him, arranging herself as best she could. "Should I release the chains?" He seemed so changed, so much like himself.

"Not yet. I think the worst is over but I'm not sure. Just hold your wrist tight to my mouth."

She felt his fangs emerge and after he gave her a couple of instructions about angle and pressure, he struck. She gave a squeak at the sudden sharp pain, but was surprised when it dissipated so quickly.

Closer, he sent mind-to-mind.

She pressed her wrist down so that he could form a seal with his mouth.

Good. That's good.

And he began to suck.

Suddenly she was very tired as though until this moment, she hadn't been able to let down, to let herself feel where she was really at. She worked to get comfortable, not caring that he was naked or that she only wore one of his thin T-shirts.

But as she relaxed into him, the steady suckling at her wrist brought forward what she'd been trying to ignore from the first time she'd actually exchanged words with him in Seattle. Maybe it was the blood-chains, but her desire for him rose like a wave in heavy seas, pummeling her self-discipline and making her long for what she'd already seen between his legs.

She knew the pleasure of being with a man and she missed sex, the touch, the connection, the raw physical nature of it.

As he began to take from her, she felt his strength returning, and the blood-chains soon started to tell a different tale. His hips rolled more than once and she had to know. She lifted up just enough to see that he was fully aroused.

The sight of his cock pushing to make a tent out of the towel strengthened all the sensations she'd already been feeling. But she couldn't possibly act on her animal needs. It wouldn't be right.

Marius was bound to the bed and she'd be taking advantage of him.

She settled back down and though breathing hard, she forced herself to think of anything other than having sex with her captor.

Marius had never tasted an elixir so sweet or so pure as what flowed into his mouth and down his throat. Shayna tasted as he thought she would, of woman and delicate flowers combined.

He moaned because he couldn't not moan. *Your blood, Shayna, is like nothing I've had before. Thank you.*

I can tell that you're feeling better.

Much.

There were things he should explain, like how the experience of feeding at the vein had close sexual connections, but he couldn't. He was exhausted from this latest, and hopefully last serious bout of recovery. But he was fully erect and wanted sex in a way that shocked him, even bound as he was. If he could have pulled Shayna onto his groin then buried himself deep, nothing would have made him happier.

From the moment he'd first seen her close up in Seattle, he'd wanted her. Kissing her more than once had fired him up.

There was nothing appropriate about how he felt, but the fact that her response appeared to match his own didn't help matters at all. He could smell her desire, which made his lips and mouth suck harder and his hips arch. What he wouldn't give to have her hand on him, or her mouth. Yes, that sweet perfect mouth of hers and her full lips kissing the hard erect length of his cock.

"Marius?"

Yes. He waited, holding his breath. He could tell she was in a state, that she desired him in the same way he wanted her. But he couldn't ask for sex.

"Do you need me?"

He finally released her wrist and turned to look at her.

"What do you mean?" He ached in a way he couldn't even explain except that in this moment he felt built for Shayna and he wanted to give her what had always been meant just for her.

"Do you need sex?" she asked. "I mean, is that part of what you require right now?"

He wanted to say yes, because he was sure she'd be with him for that reason alone. But he shook his head. "It's not critical. I just want you. That's all."

Shayna slid her hand down his chest, fondling him gently, rubbing his pecs. He groaned. "Part of me knows this can't be right since I hardly know you. But—"

"I know. It isn't right. We hardly know each other and you've done so much already. Feeding me is all that I require." He strained against the leather straps, wanting to take her in his arms and pull her down to him, hold her close.

He'd never wanted anyone the way he wanted Shayna in this moment. But he restrained himself and tried to calm down. Still, her blood seemed to be working in his body in a way he'd never felt before.

"I want to do this with you, even though I can't believe I'm even saying it. I want to be with you."

"You have a need as well. I can feel it, Shayna, but I need you to know that this would have to be about you. It would be too selfish of me."

"I've never felt this way before." She shifted to look at him. Her lips were swollen.

"Maybe just kiss." Maybe if he could kiss her, he could settle down.

She nodded and leaned up to plant her lips on his. He shivered and moaned. Her tongue swept over his lips. He parted for her and the tip of her tongue touched his.

He cried out against her mouth. "Shayna."

She kissed him again and once more her tongue swept inside his mouth. He pulled on her tongue with his lips.

This time she gave a cry and kissed him hard, her hands rubbing up and down his arms.

Maybe it was being bound, and having no control, or maybe it was the blood-chains, or that a beautiful woman kissed him, but he swore he was harder than he'd ever been.

Shayna, I need you. He ground his hips into the mattress, arching and moving, trying to reach her.

His eyes were closed as her hand crept down his chest. She fondling his pecs again while her tongue swirled over his. *You're so muscled, Marius. Your body is god-like. I can't seem to help myself. Is it okay if I touch you like this?*

God, yes.

Her words worked him up and once again he thrust his cock upward, needing to be between her legs.

Slowly, her hand moved lower, her fingers stroking the bottom of his thick pecs, now the curve of his abs. And still her mouth worked him, reaching in, taking hold of his tongue.

Sucking.

He groaned heavily.

She rubbed her palm over the ripples of his abs. His cock wasn't far away now, just a few more inches. He wanted her hand on him, stroking him. He could come like this.

Take the towel off.

Good idea. She kept kissing him as she slid the towel away from his groin.

I need you, he whispered through her mind.

Her body writhed against his and she slung what he realized was her bare leg over his thigh. Oh, that's right, she'd taken a shower and she wore only his T-shirt. She pushed against him now in strong thrusts of her hips.

So close.

Her fingers swept lower. Then she touched him.

He groaned again. She kept kissing him as she drifted her fingers up and down his cock.

Marius, this is so wrong. I don't even know you, but I'm caught up in this. Is it all right if I keep going?

Yes, please, Shayna, do whatever you need to do. Use me. I'm desperate for you. Taking your blood has done this to me.

She drew back and looked down at him, her eyes dilated. She breathed hard through her mouth. "I want to mount you, but I need to know that it's okay. You've been through this terrible thing here, in this bed, and I don't want to hurt you or take advantage."

He stared at her, unable to believe the words she'd just spoken, that she expressed so much concern for him.

"I want to feel my cock buried inside you more than anything in the world. I'm here for you."

"I feel exactly the same way."

Shayna was burning hot with need to mount this vampire for about a dozen reasons she *didn't* understand. And truthfully, she was shocked by her behavior. Marius was someone she'd only known for a few hours.

Yet there it was again. The chain-bond helped her to feel as though she knew him inside and out, had always known him.

She took her time, wanting to savor what was about to happen. She kissed a slow line down his chest and swirled her tongue over his thick, weighty pecs and stiff nipples. The tight beads felt like heaven on her tongue.

Though bound by the leather straps and the chains, his body undulated with need.

She took her hand off his cock and instead stroked it down his muscled thigh. With the other hand, she played with the rise and dip of the muscles along his arm. She hadn't known a man could feel this way.

"Shayna, my God. Shayna." His voice was deep and hoarse, more signs that he was worked up.

As she sucked and tugged on his nipples, she glanced at his upright cock, the tip weeping. He was so ready and he couldn't keep his hips still.

He would need friction to come and she wanted that friction to be all her.

She also wanted her mouth on him but she knew he was too far gone. It wouldn't take much for him to explode.

Feeling more powerful than she ever had in her entire life, she rose up on her knees and slipped off her T-shirt. She wanted him looking.

His gaze fell to her peaked breasts. "You're beautiful."

She had full breasts and took each in hand, cupping them. He licked his lips and she knew what he wanted. "Do you want a taste, Marius? Do you want to feel my breast against your mouth, suckle my nipples, the way I suckled yours?" Had she just said these things? Who was she? Yet everything felt so natural and so good.

"Yes." His voice sounded like it had just fallen down a deep well.

She angled over him, holding her left breast in her hand, and positioned the nipple over his mouth. He lifted his head reaching for her, and when he latched on he groaned heavily.

Her back arched because it felt incredible to be suckled in this position, to have him pulling on her. "Marius, that feels so good."

Shayna, thank you for this.

She smiled, her eyes closed as pleasure pulled between her legs. *It's all my pleasure, Marius. Seriously. This is so amazing.*

But after about a minute, her body had reached that critical state of needing the same kind of friction that he needed.

She pulled her breast away from his mouth and felt him

reach for her and protest. But she swung a leg over his hip then lifted up. She caught his rigid cock in her hand, holding him in place.

He released a series of grunts and gasps, his neck and upper body arching as though trying to reach her. As she met his now frantic gaze, she slowly lowered herself, taking him inside. She moaned and a shiver went through her. He felt so damn good.

He shouted in response, his mouth open, his back arched. And once more, she could feel how much pleasure it gave him that she was surrounding him like this. The blood-chains on her wrist helped her to feel his pleasure, which in turn heated her up another degree.

As she lifted her hips, gliding along his cock, she groaned yet again. "Marius, I can feel what this is like for you. The chain at my wrist is amazing."

"I know. I can feel your pleasure as well."

His head rocked back and forth. The muscles of his arms bulged and he pushed his hips into her as much as he could. The chains that bound him tight to the bed didn't give him a lot of leeway, but enough that he could work her. As she rose up and down, pistoning over him, he matched her with an upward thrust.

She leaned over him, planting her hands just above his shoulders, and began to move. She loved doing this, more than she ever thought she would. She loved being over a man like this. And siphoning his power, she went faster.

"Shayna, I'm going to come."

"I want you to come."

"Let me do something for you."

She had no idea what he intended. "What? Yes. Anything."

"Let me do the work. I can move really fast and it's important to me that you have pleasure right now, a strong release."

Shayna stilled before she'd even formed the thought to stop moving over his cock, but not because he'd told her to. She'd never heard a man express an interest in her release before. The experience was so novel that all she could do was stare into his hazel eyes. Finally, she murmured, "I'd love that."

A slow smile spread over his lips. He was so beautiful.

His gaze fell to her breasts and once more his tongue made an appearance. She rose up just enough to support herself on one arm and slid her thumb into his mouth. He suckled greedily as he met her gaze.

Then, as promised, his hips and cock went to work.

It was a light flutter of movement first, hitting her in just the right spot. She cried out.

"Look at me." His voice was barely more than a hoarse whisper. "And keep looking. I want to watch you come, then I'm going to fill you with all I have to give."

She nodded. The flutter became a strong, deeper movement but the speed stayed the same, an unbelievably quick thrust inside her.

She moaned.

Then he went faster, something an ordinary man could never do. And all she had to do was hold herself in position.

Pleasure built. Her face and chest grew flushed. She felt certain that this would be unlike anything she'd ever experienced before.

And just when she thought it couldn't get better, he went deeper still, all the while sustaining the same extraordinary pace.

The orgasm hit her like a tornado of sensation, so that she writhed on him and cried out. Pleasure streaked through her well, pushing past her abdomen so that her whole body felt full of fire. She stared into his eyes. *Marius*.

You're beautiful like this.

Pleasure rolled for several seconds, but as she began to come down from the pinnacle, she realized he hadn't come. He slowed his thrusts.

He kept thrusting.

"You didn't come," she said, kissing his forehead, his cheeks, his lips.

When she drew back, his cock felt firm, but something had changed. She met his gaze because she could feel something waiting just beyond her consciousness. "Marius, what is it? What's happening?"

He shook his head and she sensed he wasn't sure. "I know that your blood did something to me and right now I'm feeling a new layer of power flow through my body."

She glanced at his shoulders and arms. "You're bigger."

She watched as he began to pull on the leather wrist strap. The muscles of his right arm grew corded and defined. "You're going to break through."

He didn't say anything, but a moment later the leather separated from the chain. Still easing his hips up and down so that he worked her with a slow thrust, he turned his head to his left wrist. The next moment the second leather strap broke free.

"Marius, should I be afraid?"

He met her gaze as he slowly rose up and surrounded her with his arms. Though his legs were still tied down, he kissed her and embraced her, the feel of his thick muscles like heaven against her breasts. *Marius, you feel wonderful.*

When he drew back, she felt his entire right leg flex. She had to watch, as he pulled with strong, consistent effort—and as though the leather had been made of tissue, it simply came apart.

And still he thrust inside her.

Chills went up and down Shayna's spine. She'd already come, but she could feel Marius's intentions. Her breathing grew labored and her nipples rose into stiff peaks.

He flexed his left leg and with a sudden guttural shout, he was free. At almost the same moment, he levitated then flipped her so that she landed on her back with a vampire buried inside her and moving in deep grinds of his hips into her sensitive well.

"Oh, God," she shouted. "Marius!"

He began to move into her now with every ounce of his power, slowly building his speed and pushing her toward ecstasy again. She gripped his shoulders, savoring his size.

This was more than she could have imagined would happen.

"Look at me, Shayna."

She met his gaze and the commanding intensity of his expression held her enthralled. She couldn't look anywhere else but into his hazel, gold-flecked eyes. She panted in deep grabs of air. "I'm so close."

"I can feel that you're ready and I'm going to speed up again."

A cry left her lips. She dug her fingernails into his shoulders, still panting. And as the orgasm began to release, she cried out over and over. The pleasure was like nothing she'd known, and still he held her gaze, thrusting into her.

His breathing grew harsh as well and she could feel his cock now, experience his tremendous pleasure, the result of the chain she held in her hand.

Ecstasy hit and he roared, the sound of his voice, very vampire, pulsing over her as he thrust.

Another wave of pleasure arrived unexpectedly so that her cries joined his. Lightning strikes of ecstasy whipped through her repeatedly, expanding up through her chest until she couldn't breathe. Stars flashed through her mind.

Just when she almost passed out, his movements finally began to slow and the orgasm passed like a beautiful ocean wave washing up on shore.

She was left feeling as though she'd just flown through the heavens, touched the moon, then floated back to earth.

She lay slack on the bed. "Marius."

Nothing else followed, just his name. There were no words to express what she felt, what he'd done for her. He was the first man she'd had sex with in a year, and because of her previous troubles with Michelson, she felt free in a way she hadn't in a long time.

Marius stared into Shayna's eyes and leaned down to kiss her. "Thank you."

She nodded. She looked incredible with a flush on her cheeks, her lips still swollen, and her eyes glittering. "I should say the same thing."

Still connected to her, he stroked her cheek with his thumb and kissed her again.

"I can't believe we just did this. I'm pretty much shocked by it all, and yet it felt so easy with you, so natural."

Marius felt the same way, though he was having trouble aligning all that he felt. Mostly, he felt a tremendous gratitude for what Shayna had done, that she'd gotten him through the worst of his recovery process, that she'd fed him, and finally that she'd had sex with him. Even now, he could tell that she felt a whisper of concern that she'd broken out of her usual standards and slept with him. He owed her his life.

"I understand," he said at last. "But just so you know, this isn't something I would normally do, either."

"Really?" She seemed so surprised.

He chuckled. "Really."

He still couldn't believe he'd just had sex with her. He'd kidnapped her out of Seattle, brought her here in great pain, forced her to be witness to things she should never have seen, and now she'd given him release.

Slowly, he eased out of her. He grabbed the T-shirt she'd worn, then planted it between her legs. He smiled, loving that he'd left so much of himself inside her. He also loved that she didn't seem embarrassed. "I'm going to take a shower," she said. She scooted to the side and he had a wonderful view as she walked across the room, then disappeared into the bathroom.

He sat up and shifted his legs over the side of the bed, the cool stone beneath his feet. He saw the plastic tub and memories surfaced of feeling something cool on his face and his body, something that had made the experience tolerable when for the early part he'd felt as though he'd walked through a fiery hell.

The lump of his cut-up battle leathers and his T-shirt told their own story. Shayna had done that for him.

He owed her so much.

He thought back to the moment when he realized that

her blood had empowered him and that he'd be able to break free of the bonds. Something had happened inside him as each strap broke, as though the release of each binding had freed a part of him long dormant, something lost on Daniel's punishment table.

He felt alive and aware, more sensitive to his surroundings, and acutely aware of Shayna.

He felt her in the shower, soaping up her hands and washing her arms, her abdomen, and deep between her legs. He wanted to go there again, repeatedly. He wanted to chain her up in his secret New Zealand cave and never let her go.

He planted a hand against his chest. He felt the secure beating of his heart, his pecs where she'd suckled him, and the seat of his soul that he knew was expanding.

What the hell had Shayna's blood done to him?

When he heard the water shut off, he decided that Shayna didn't need to see him naked right now. It was one thing to be bound on the bed and suffering through blood-madness recovery, even to have made love, but another thing to have his big, muscular body in her face.

He crossed to his nearby built-in closet and grabbed a robe. He found a second one of his that would work for her.

He took it to the bathroom and, keeping his gaze away from her, he hung it on the back of the door. "Thought you could use this."

"Thanks. That's really thoughtful and I love the paisley in your robe. Is that silk you're wearing?"

"Yes."

"It's a great look for you."

He would have left, but she grew very still and he sensed something from her, as if she was in shock. "What is it?" He turned toward her. She held the towel to her chest and it hung well past her knees. She was covered up—and then again, she wasn't.

"Marius." She had tears in her eyes. "This was what I saw, back in Seattle. The vision that I had, while standing on the sidewalk, of the future, of you and me. Do you remember? I said those exact words, *I love the paisley in your robe. Is that silk you're wearing?*"

Marius stared at her. "I remember now. I thought you'd fainted but instead you were having a vision. And this was it?" He held his index finger pointed toward the stone floor.

Her lips curved. "Yeah, this was it. I'm flabbergasted all over again." She started moving her towel over her breasts and down her abdomen. Now he should leave, but instead his gaze got hooked on watching her breasts as she continued drying off. He could feel her thinking hard again, trying to figure it all out.

She met his gaze a couple of times, which encouraged him to wake up. "You're okay with me standing here? Am I invading your privacy?"

At that, she smiled fully. "Marius, you just invaded my body, I think I can towel off in front of you."

She hung up her towel, spreading it out fully to dry, and all he could think to say was, "That's a good idea, hanging the towel up, I mean. This cave is near a water source and has issues with damp."

Inwardly, he rolled his eyes. He was such a romantic, talking about mildew issues. Next, he'd be tell her about bat removal and how best to deal with guano.

She crossed the room and for a moment, he stalled out again. What was it about a naked woman that took a man's breath away? He wasn't sure what she intended because she was coming straight for him. He blinked a couple of times, especially when she stood right next to him.

He was about to ask something equally lame, like whether or not the hot water had run out, when she reached past him and plucked the robe from the hook.

Right now, he felt like he was about twenty years old again.

"I don't suppose you have a brush I could use. I haven't got any of my things with me."

"Right."

He finally put his feet in motion and set her up with a brush. He showed her some other things she could make use of, like a toothbrush and toothpaste. He finally left the bathroom and sat down on the edge of the bed. "We should eat," he called out.

"I'm starved. Do we have food here?"

"No, but I can take care of that."

Rumy would help out in a heartbeat.

Once he'd connected telepathically with Rumy, he sent a mental image of the cave. Rumy promised he'd bring a meal and a few other provisions. Marius suggested some girl-type stuff for Shayna, including some clothes if possible.

By the time he hung up, he felt grateful all over again for having a friend like Rumy. He knew he wouldn't have survived otherwise and not just recently but probably a dozen times over the past several decades when a battle against the darker forces in his world had turned bloody and lethal. More than once, Rumy and his team at The Erotic Passage had patched him up.

When Rumy arrived, Marius didn't leave the bedroom doorway. He didn't want Rumy to see Shayna even in his robe, though the garment hung well past her knees. None of his rooms had proper doors and he felt protective of her. She didn't need another vampire looking at her until she was dressed.

"Thank you," Shayna said quietly.

Marius had his back to her while she slipped into the jeans and T-shirt Rumy had brought. There were other clothes as well, but the casual set would do in his home.

She'd already blow-dried her hair so that it hung in two straight lines over her shoulders. Her eyes and face had a healthy glow, a real sign she was siphoning his power. "Any aches?"

She shook her head as she straightened the bottom of the T-shirt. "How do I look? Presentable?"

One thing that was true of either human or vampire females: They worried about their looks.

He went to her and settled his hands on her shoulders. "You look amazing."

"Thank you." She put a hand to her stomach. "I've been smelling the food and I'm starved."

"Then let's eat."

As he led her into the living area, Rumy held up one of Marius's antique LPs. "How the hell did you find this Billie Holiday?"

"I have an agent, always looking. Paid a fortune for it."

"No doubt."

Marius turned toward Shayna. "I'd like you to meet Rumy, a good friend and owner of The Erotic Passage." He turned toward Rumy. "Meet Shayna Prentiss."

"It's nice to meet you, Rumy."

"And you. I hear you saved our boy's ass here."

She glanced at Marius. "And he saved mine." She nodded several times, but when she looked back at Rumy her gaze fell to the LP and she blinked.

Marius asked, "What is it? Something wrong?"

Shayna stared at the vinyl record that Rumy held in his hands. Marius had asked her something, but she was too caught up in staring first at the LP then at the cave's different living areas to process his words or to respond.

She moved slowly in the direction of the sitting area.

"Shayna," Marius said quietly, tracking next to her. "Are you having another vision?"

"She has visions?" Rumy sounded stunned.

She turned and shook her head at Marius. "Not a vision this time. I'm just . . . looking."

She'd had this experience before, when she'd arrived in Honduras at a remote village and knew she'd stepped back in time. It was one thing to read about a civilization, to study its current political difficulties, to get a sense of how the community organized itself. But to be in the middle of a undiscovered civilization like this one was a new playground altogether.

Until this moment, Shayna had been too busy staying alive, or helping Marius through his blood-starvation recovery, or even having sex with him, to completely assimilate that she was an outside observer in an entirely different world.

Her heart thrummed as the anthropologist in her came alive.

This part of the cave had a similar decor to the bedroom, the pieces made of fine-honed teak and leather. Some of the walls had been tiled with slabs of rich polished granite, others were left in a raw state, while a third evolution involved the chiseling of the original cavern stone into intricate patterns, clearly the work of craftsmen. In a couple of places, she saw the same pattern as in Chile and in his bedroom here. She began to wonder if she was looking not at a unique sculpting design, but rather a language, similar to ancient cuneiform.

Her heart thrummed a little harder.

She waved a hand at the wall. "Is this something your world encourages? The chiseling of designs in stone?"

Both Rumy and Marius responded. "Yes."

She could have spent a solid year just studying the sculpturing techniques and patterns of their culture alone. The one on the ceiling intrigued her because it ran at a perfect right angle to the wall that separated the kitchen from the living area. The space had been engineered on so many levels.

She even felt a cool breeze moving through, constantly freshening the air. She had so many questions and wished she had her iPad with her to start making notes. Her gaze moved around each space swiftly. She'd left her iPhone in her other jeans and wanted to be sure to take more pictures before she left.

Marius moved close to her, sliding an arm around her waist. "You're enjoying this, aren't you?"

"Well, yes, of course." She turned to look at him. He'd fed from her. The man was a vampire, a warrior in his culture, a man fighting for his entire civilization. And she had the profound honor to stand witness, in this moment in time, to what was transpiring in his world.

But she was also being rather absent from both men.

She glanced from Marius to Rumy. "Sorry, it's the scientist in me and a great deal of curiosity that I'm having trouble restraining right now. I guess you could say I'm just assimilating your world." She turned to Rumy. "I'm being rude. Forgive me."

"So Marius kept me informed and you've sure been put through the wringer. How you holding up?"

She lifted her hand that held the blood-chain. "I'm surviving mostly because I've been able to siphon Marius's power, which is an incredible and, at critical times, a healing experience." She glanced around. "There isn't a single light in evidence, but everything appears to be glowing."

"Yep," Rumy said. "Vampire power."

She shifted her gaze back to him and smiled. He was shorter than Marius by several inches. He clearly worked out and liked showing off his tight, muscular body in a snug black T-shirt and gray tailored slacks. His shoes had that handcrafted look. The tips of his fangs showed, though, which apparently had left calluses on his lips. He kept his curly hair cut close to his head, and not even his fangs could detract from his well-groomed appearance.

Rumy moved in her direction, extending his hand toward the dining and kitchen area. "I imagine by now that you're starved, especially after what you've been through. I've brought some of the best food around."

Shayna sat down at the dining table and watched the men unearth the carry-out food and arrange it on plates. Marius opened a bottle of wine, a Chianti to go with an antipasto salad, a savory pasta puttanesca, and loaf of bread.

And in that moment, with the men serving her a wonderful meal, her gaze fell to the blood-chain wrapped around her wrist and laced through her fingers. Her eyes suddenly filled with tears.

Only a few hours had passed, but she felt as though she'd lived a lifetime. She knew that Marius wanted her to stay, desperately, but some questions deep within her heart remained unanswered.

Glancing once more at the intricate stone carvings of the walls and ceiling, she shifted her gaze to Marius. "Will you show me the rest of your home after we've eaten?" Maybe something about his culture, hidden in the carvings, would give her the answer she sought.

Marius held two glasses in one hand and the bottle of wine in the other. "Of course." He moved toward the table, Rumy behind him. "Ready to eat?"

"Absolutely."

Rumy settled several plates on the table, some containing the food and two blue earthenware plates ready to be filled. Marius set the glasses at each place setting, then poured the wine slowly.

He rounded the table and took his seat adjacent to her.

Rumy patted his hands on his thighs. "Okay. You're all set." He waved a hand toward the living area. "Along with the clothes, my friend Eve sent along some toiletries. Just let me know if you need anything else, Shayna, and I'll plan another trip in."

"I will and thank you so much."

Rumy nodded to Marius then lifted his hand, his fingers twisted close to his ear, in the call-me motion.

"I will."

Rumy waved, shifted to altered flight, and left.

Despite the fact that she had a decision looming over her head, Shayna savored every bite of the excellent meal and each sip of wine.

When she finally finished eating, she knew the time had come to figure things out. But before she did anything else, she went to her jeans and pulled out her iPhone. She wanted to take some pictures of the familiar carvings.

CHAPTER 6

Shayna followed Marius to an arched stone opening past the kitchen. The hall sloped downward, but again her vision caught the same, familiar carvings that involved repeated straight lines. The more she saw the patterns repeating, the more she felt certain she was looking at something similar to cuneiform, a type of written language used by the cultures of ancient Mesopotamia. She wasn't an expert by any means since her field was cultural anthropology and not linguistics, but her curiosity was aroused anyway.

She might have been headed to Malaysia for her fieldwork, but seeing Marius's undiscovered world was like being in a candy store.

An expansive opening to the left revealed a room she would call a study, with a broad, uncluttered desk. In the center sat a laptop. He moved toward it and the chain around her wrist vibrated softly.

He ran a finger through a line of dust. "I haven't been here in over a year." His voice was quiet, reflective.

She recalled now that Daniel had imprisoned three of his sons for supposed acts of treason and that he'd tortured each of them.

How quickly her reason for being in his home came flying back at her. She knew she should choose helping him and saving the human women she'd seen being treated like animals. She wasn't even sure what held her back.

Except, of course, the obvious: that she risked her life and all her plans by remaining in this cave. She'd worked hard toward all that she'd planned for her life—to study, to become an expert in her chosen field of study, to teach. How could she throw all of that away for a culture completely unknown to her?

She hardly knew Marius.

She'd turned over control of her life to a man once before, and the results had been disastrous for her. The affair she'd had with Michelson had begun as a thrilling experience because he'd been like Marius, very passionate. But their relationship, even in the bedroom, had been about her sacrificing for what Michelson needed at any given moment.

Michelson had been her role model, living the life she wanted. He was dedicated to his work as an anthropologist and spent hours on his research every day. By the time she'd recognized his "passion" for the selfishness that it truly was, he'd shattered her self-esteem with his demands and constant criticisms.

She'd needed months, including several intense weeks of therapy, to get herself back on track and to reestablish her self-esteem. She'd also made an important promise to herself to be wiser in the future.

How wise would it be to jump in and join Marius? How was that choosing for herself?

Yet somehow she knew life was more complex than simply analyzing the pros and cons of the situation. She could feel how in tune she already was with Marius's world. For one thing, she'd just had sex with him, as shocking that still seemed to her rational mind.

An oil painting of a hawk soaring through a massive cavern above a river hung on the wall behind the desk. Tall filing cabinets in what looked like mahogany flanked a table bearing a decanter and cut-crystal tumblers.

"You like whiskey?"

He nodded. "A fine single-malt."

He moved in front of her, crossing to the right. Another smaller tunnel opened into a tall cavern that clearly served as a library, with more of the unique carvings. Hundreds of books, most of them bound in leather, lined several tall bookshelves, each sunk into the stone walls. Comfortable leather club chairs and a matching couch sat in the center, while off to one side a large table and tall, ladder-back chair invited the stacking of books and papers and lots of research.

She drew a deep breath. "I could live in this room." She'd spoken the words aloud without thinking.

She moved toward the grouping of furniture where a globe of the earth sat on a tall wood stand. She examined the names and realized she wasn't looking at human earth, but at the location of every cavern system on the planet. Most of the names were familiar earth-based names but usually followed up with the word *system*. She glanced at him. "I see a name in Egypt—the Pharaoh system. So this globe reflects your world."

He nodded.

She stopped the globe at New Zealand. Several systems were labeled, one of them the Hawk system.

"Does the hawk have meaning in your world?"

"It's a symbol sometimes of courage, sometimes of dominance and strength."

She met his gaze. He personified these qualities but she had the feeling that he didn't think of himself in that way.

He was close to scowling again and she could feel his impatience, even his disapproval.

Marius saw how tightly Shayna clutched the chain, still wrapped around her wrist and threaded through her fingers. He felt her tension and sensed her indecision.

He'd never been more frustrated in his life. Why couldn't she see how much she was needed here?

He'd already made the decision not to force her to stay, yet every cell in his body screamed that she was the one, the answer to the crisis howling through his world.

He feared saying too much or not enough.

If he knew her better, he'd know how to proceed, what to say to encourage her.

Instead he had to do what was for him the hardest thing in the world: keep his trap shut.

He led her from the library, which he could tell had caught her attention. Her heart rate had increased and what had she said? That she could live here?

For a few seconds he'd felt hopeful, but no decision had followed.

"Where is your fieldwork," he asked, at last.

"On a small, primitive island in Malaysia. I've been planning this trip for years."

The words spilled from his mouth. "All those women you saw in the Dark Cave system had plans as well."

She turned to him, her light-blue eyes wide and accusing. "That's not fair, Marius."

He remained silent for a moment. He knew she hadn't had an ideal life by any stretch of the imagination, but she'd never been enslaved or tortured.

Finally, he said, "You're right and I shouldn't have said it." Yet he was glad he had. If she was going to walk away from this, he wanted her to know that he believed she was doing the wrong thing.

He gestured to a small doorway at the far end of the space. She followed behind as he showed her several guest quarters, simple rooms with en suite bathrooms.

A billiard room surprised her. "You must have expected to have guests one day."

He shrugged. The small talk was setting his nerves on fire. "Maybe. Someday." How could he think about entertaining when his world was in crisis?

"You're angry."

"Of course I'm angry. I don't understand how, after all you've seen, you could hesitate." There, he'd said it straight out.

She grabbed his elbow, forcing him to stop. He turned to glare at her.

"Well, let me explain it this way. Imagine aliens abduct you and you end up in their society and they tell you you're the only one who can fix their world but you'll probably have to give up your life to do it. How quick would you be to jump in?"

"I don't think it's a fair analogy."

"That's because you're the alien in my world. I'm sorry, Marius, but this is really shortsighted on your part. Your world has had this problem for a long time, yet you haven't been able to do anything about it. And I'm not even sure I can really help in the way you think I can." She folded her arms across her chest. "You're asking too much."

His frustration pounded inside his head but only because he feared for his world and knew in his gut that she could help.

He also respected her position. But what would it require to convince her to stay, to work with him . . . to be with him.

Maybe that was the real issue. He hated the thought of Shayna leaving his life so soon. What he'd shared with her, even over a period of hours, he'd never shared with anyone. He might not understand the why of it, but she meant something to him.

And he wanted her to stay.

What Marius had said was both harsh and unnecessary and had ticked Shayna off. If she'd been less compassionate, she would have seized on his criticism and used it as an excuse to walk away.

But she held her tongue, knowing that the right decision would come in its time. Though she might be young by comparison with his long life, she knew enough to give herself the space she needed. If she was going to stay, to forge a chain-bond with Marius, her commitment had to be one hundred percent.

As he started down another hall, she heard a distant sound that at first she couldn't place but soon realized was a fairly strong waterfall.

He marched ahead of her, his shoulders tight. She felt his frustration like a stinging sensation on her skin.

She rubbed her thumb over the chain on the inside of her palm, feeling a need to apologize—but for what? For being human? For having needs beyond what the man in front of her wanted on her behalf? And that felt way too familiar. Her entire relationship with her adviser had been built on how much more important his projects, his interests, even his sexual satisfaction was more than anything she needed.

Maybe that was why she resisted. She wanted a say in what mattered in her life, her journey, her chosen path, no matter whether lives were at stake or not. On an essential level, she wanted to know that she mattered in the scheme of things.

The stone hallway opened up to a massive cavern, a waterfall, and a stream, part of which flowed through a natural adjacent pool. "You swim here, don't you?"

"I do."

Vampires swimming, another new, surprising reality. She stood staring at the water dumbstruck all over again.

To the right, an alcove had been dug out of the stone wall and fitted with a bar and a poolside lounging area. It was so strange to think of how this fit with her own world's images of vampires as pale, statue-like creatures surviving only on blood and living primarily to kill people.

Marius was the exact opposite, flesh-and-blood, caring, and hoping to save his world.

The repeated patterns in the stonework along the back wall of the alcove caught her eye. Had to be cuneiform. How much she'd like to stay in this world just to study these patterns and see if she was right that this was the written form of an ancient language.

He turned to her, frowning slightly. "What is it, Shayna? You seem all lit up."

She released a long sigh and moved toward the pattern, running her finger over it. She told him what she believed it was and asked him what he thought.

Marius shrugged. "I really don't know. It's familiar enough in our world. I guess I always assumed it was a carving design. A lot of the patterns have names. This one is called 'Waves of Lines.' Descriptive enough, but hardly an indication that it has meaning beyond the variations in each group of lines."

"You're right. The name only describes what it looks like." Many of the lines were slanted and grouped so that they occasionally gave an appearance of waves.

On the opposite cavern wall, across from the alcove, was yet another image of a hawk, this time on a massive scale. She was reminded again how well she could see in the dark.

She also saw the same stone carving, more prevalent than ever, rows and rows of Waves of Lines.

The chain wrapped around her wrist began humming against her skin, stronger than before. The more she stared at the wall opposite, especially the carvings, the stronger the vibration became.

"Shayna, what's going on? My chain is practically singing against my skin."

She met his gaze but shook her head. "I don't know. I just really feel drawn to the carvings beneath the hawk." She gestured across the river. "There, on the opposite side. Can you carry me over so that I can have a closer look?"

"Do you think it's another vision?"

"I don't know."

He drew close and opened up his right arm.

As if she'd been doing this for years, she stepped onto his right boot and slid her arm around his neck. He pulled her against his side and at the same moment levitated to carry her quickly across the swirling pool and the stream. He landed on a shallow ledge from which the craftsmen must have worked to carve the image.

When he set her on her feet, she slowly walked the length of the carvings about twenty feet. "I'm still amazed by the level of artisanship and I'm feeling the need to put my hands on it." She glanced at him. "But first, Marius, I need to know you'll support me no matter what happens here, no matter what I decide. Can you do that?"

He dropped his gaze for a moment and released a breath that carried an almost hissing sound. The chains told her he battled within himself, but finally he said, "Yes, I promise you, I will. I'm desperate, that's all. But we're a resilient species, and if you feel you have to return to Seattle, I'll figure things out. Again, I just have a tremendous sense of urgency, which is why I pushed you."

"I get it. I really do." She felt his sincerity and knew that despite his frustration and even his anger, he'd stand by her.

She turned toward the carvings once more, knowing that once she put her hands on it, something would happen, maybe even another vision. "I think I'll need you to hold me steady."

"I think so, too. The chains are practically burning my neck now."

"I know. Me, too." When he slid his arm around her waist and drew her close so that if she stumbled or passed out, he'd keep her from falling into the river, she held her hands out flat and placed them on the carvings.

Marius was right: This was another vision.

The air seemed to bow and her body with it, but Marius held her fast.

Shayna, what's going on? Do you see something?

It's so strong this time, more than before.

A vision?

Yes. She was sure it was, though she saw nothing yet.

Tell me?

As soon as it takes shape.

At first, she saw nothing, she only felt that what resided on the other side of the vision had breadth and weight.

Oh, Marius, whatever it is, it's massive. That was the only way she could think to describe what it felt like.

A fleeting image came to her of a room so large that she'd never seen anything like it before—only not a room. Definitely a cavern. But waves flowed over the vision so that she could only catch glimpses, like a dream made up of fleeting images. She thought she saw a man wearing a long cape that draped to the floor. Another man stood on something ten feet higher, speaking in a loud voice that also came and went but she couldn't make out the words.

The vision dissipated and, for a moment, she thought that was it. Then another came and took its place. The setting was very different, in a much smaller cavern. The dark waves through the vision again made it difficult for her to understand what she was seeing. But she saw enough to recognize that a man she'd never met before, a vampire, stood beside a stone wall, a sledgehammer in his hand. He began slamming the thick head against the stone and with just a few strikes, the wall began to crumble.

The waves still made it so difficult to see. Why were they there? Was she blocked from within or was this some kind of interference outside herself?

When he was done, dust rose, then settled quickly enough.

The unknown man spoke to her in a deep resonant voice. "These have been waiting for you, Shayna, for over four millennia."

He'd called her by name. He knew her.

More waves.

But she kept working on capturing images until she saw herself pass through an opening in the now crumbled wall.

She felt anxious seeing herself like that, and the waves hurt her mind. Finally, she saw herself sitting at a work-table, looking down at an ancient clay tablet. She was cleaning it very carefully with a soft brush.

And this was in the future.

Her future.

Dizziness and blackness overcame her.

The next thing she knew she stared up at Marius's face. Glancing around, she saw that she was back in his living room and he held her cradled on his lap. "What happened?"

"You passed out."

"I guess I did." She slowly sat up and shifted to sit beside him, wincing. "I have another headache." She touched the top of her head with the chained-up hand, feeling the rough texture on her scalp. She laughed suddenly. "I think this is ridiculous."

"What? That you fainted?"

"No." She held up her hand for him to see the chain. "This."

He looked confused, a frown between his brows. "The chains are ridiculous?"

"No, that's not what I meant."

She'd run out of excuses, that's what she meant. There wasn't a single part of this world that didn't have a god-damn call on her soul. "And you're absolutely sure this chain will help us form a tracking pair?"

He nodded, his lips compressed once more in a tight line. His eyes flared.

Slowly, she unlaced the chain from around her fingers, and slid it off her wrist.

Marius planted his elbows on his knees, made a fist with both hands, and pressed his joined fingers against his lips. She could feel he held back a wall of emotion. She also knew he expected her to just give the blood-chain back and ask to be taken home.

Instead, without giving it another thought, she slipped the chain over her head.

Marius drew in a quick breath and leaned back against the couch cushions. He closed his eyes, clearly overcome. "Shayna," he whispered.

She set a hand on his shoulder. "Look at me."

His eyes were wet when he opened them. He held his arm wide and she took full advantage, shifting to once more sit on his lap and throw her arms around his neck.

"I have to do this," she said, weeping suddenly after all the holding back. "Of course I have to do this."

She felt the bond of the blood-chain click into place, and Marius was right: She felt more connected to him than ever before.

Which meant she could sense that he was completely overcome as well.

He held her tightly and rocked her. "I don't know what to say. I thought you were going to leave."

"I know. Me, too."

"What was the vision about?"

She shook her head. "All these waves made it difficult to see, just a lot of disjointed images." She wanted to tell him about the clay tablets, but she held back. "Is it okay if I don't share everything? I mean, I'd tell you if I thought it was important, but I think this vision was meant for me, to help me make up my mind."

She felt him weigh his response, that he hesitated, but finally he let it go. "Yes, it's fine. I'm a little too wound up and too controlling. But this experience must also just be about you to have real meaning. I believe in the rights of the individual more than anything."

In a moment of clarity, she understood something important about the situation. "So that's why you've had so much guilt in taking me out of Seattle."

"I know now that I wouldn't have taken you at all, not without your consent, if Daniel's men hadn't show up."

"Well, it's probably better this way. I'm a hands-on kind of person. I learn better through touch and experience. I'm not sure if I could have made a decision to help without going through all of this."

"Doesn't make it right."

She could feel his guilt pounding him once more, stronger now because of the chains. She wondered all over again why he felt this way—and was it just him, or was it a condition of all vampires to be saddled with excessive remorse?

Of course the actions of Daniel, who lived entirely

without a conscience, told her that Marius's guilt-laden suffering was all about him and not peculiar to his race.

She also felt the profound depth of his gratitude, and that was enough.

After a long moment, she pulled away from him, using her shirt to wipe her face. "How about we get a good night's—or rather, day's—sleep, then find this fucking weapon before your lunatic father does."

Marius chuckled and nodded. "Sounds like a plan."

Marius awoke with an unexpected pressure on his chest. He was groggy but had never slept better in his life.

Absently and with his eyes closed, he reached up to his chest to remove the thing causing the pressure and found his hand suddenly caught in Shayna's hair.

"Nhn" came back at him. "Zat you?"

"Shayna?"

"Uh-huh. I feel like I could sleep for a year."

"Me, too. Never felt like this before. Almost drugged." Even his speech was slightly slurred.

Slowly he opened his eyes to stare up at the ceiling of his New Zealand cavern bedroom. This was good. He'd awakened in the same place he'd gone to sleep. He just didn't understand why he felt this way.

He tried to put it into words and finally stumbled across the reality that he felt peaceful, honest-to-God peaceful—which made no sense at all except that Shayna had agreed to stay and she'd put on his blood chain.

She'd told him that the vision was personal, meant only for her. He got that and didn't press her. After all, the only thing he really cared about was right here, still pressing on his chest, her arm slung across his abdomen and dangerously close to his wake-up erection.

He slid his arm around her shoulders.

He could get used to this, waking up slowly, Shayna in his arms.

She wore a thin dark-purple nightgown that went well with her almost white-blond hair.

The chain at his neck was very quiet, an indication she was still in a sleep state, so he let her be.

The trouble was, his arousal wasn't diminishing, not even a little, and that surprised him. Instead desire for her suddenly rolled through him like a wave lifting a boat.

"Anything wrong?"

"Hard to explain. I'm trying to understand."

She drew in a shuddering breath. "You smell wonderful, Marius, have I told you that?"

"You asked about it." Oh, God, now his gums vibrated and dammit, he couldn't keep his fangs from descending. None of this had been done consciously. His hips rocked.

Shayna finally lifted her head to look at him and her eyes went wide. "Your fangs? Do you need to feed?"

What he wanted was to push her onto her back, drive between her legs, then drink from her throat for about an hour. He felt almost maniacal with sudden need.

He gritted his teeth, then finally said, "I need the bathroom."

"I can feed you if you want."

"No." The word came out harsher than he'd intended. "I'm sorry, I'm not myself right now."

She rolled off him to flop back against the pillows. He'd worn pajamas, something he'd done strictly for Shayna's benefit. He got up and made a beeline for the bathroom.

But he'd only taken three long, quick steps when the

chains warned him that if he went farther he'd most likely land on his ass.

"Hold up," Shayna called out. "The chains are pulling."

He stopped up short and glanced at her over his shoulder. He was still making a tent out of his pajama bottoms. "Sorry. I forgot. It's that proximity thing I told you about just before we went to bed." The chains wouldn't let them be farther than ten feet apart at any given time, one of the reasons they'd shared a bed.

"Right." She slid from bed and given that her silk nightgown showed a lot of cleavage, he averted his gaze. He needed a shower. A cold one.

As soon as she drew close, he continued on. With Shayna waiting by the sink, he went into the small space that housed the toilet. He had a hard time taking care of business, knowing that Shayna was right there, until he heard the water running and what sounded like Shayna splashing water on her face.

Okay, that helped.

He shook his head. In all the concern and frustration about getting her to stay, he'd forgotten the logistics the chains would require.

When he finished, she still looked sleepy-eyed but beautiful. She'd combed her hair, straightening a careful part.

"Coffee?" he asked.

"Oh, my God, yes. I come from Seattle. We drink it by the gallon."

Taking her to the kitchen, he served up some scrambled eggs and toast from provisions Rumy had brought.

After three quick bites, she took a breath. "I don't usually have a meal right away, but I'm starved."

"I can fix you more."

She got a funny look on her face.

"What?"

"Nothing. I mean I appreciate it, but I think this will be enough."

He glanced at the frying pan. He didn't know what had caused her sudden distress, but he could feel that his offer had struck a note that caused her to feel anxious. He just didn't know why.

Shayna could feel Marius's confusion, but she couldn't enlighten him. The whole thing was too humiliating. How could she tell him that what had caught her off guard was his offer to fix her additional food.

He offered, just like that.

With Michelson, she'd been expected to cook and take care of him. After the affair had ended, she honestly couldn't recall one incident in which he'd put her first, or made any special effort on her behalf.

Instead she'd been left with a terrible feeling of worthlessness that had taken a lot of effort to overcome. One of her friends had called it right: Michelson was an asshole.

Only now, a year after their breakup, could she even think about what had happened without cringing. And the last thing she wanted to do was tell Marius how she'd let herself be treated or the horror she'd experienced the last time he'd tied her up.

It had been thrilling at first to be bound loosely with a rope and to have Michelson make love to her. But the last encounter had left her with nightmares. He'd never gotten rough, nothing like that, but he had a habit of leaving her in that position, insisting he'd be right back, but minutes had grown to an hour then two.

The last time she'd been with him, he'd abandoned her for hours. She still felt panicky when she dwelled on the experience for any length of time. She could still feel the bindings on her wrists and ankles.

"Okay, what the hell are you thinking about, Shayna? Because the chain at my throat is just about tearing into my skin."

She dropped her fork so that it clattered on her plate. "Oh, God, I'm so sorry. I was thinking about my ex maybe a little too hard. He wasn't a good man."

When Marius got a fierce look in his eye, she lifted both hands. "He never hurt me. He wasn't that kind of *bad*. Just really, really selfish, and I was so starstruck by his exalted 'professor' status that I let myself get sucked into a toxic relationship." She waved one hand at him. "So just stand down, mister. Now my neck is burning."

Marius planted his hands on his hips and looked anywhere but at her. She watched him take several deep breaths. "Okay. Fine." He met her gaze. "Want to talk about it?"

"No. I really don't. It's been a year since we broke up, but part of me is still a little raw." She attempted a smile. "Instead, I'm going to keep enjoying the eggs you made me."

He sat down adjacent to her and busied himself drinking his coffee and buttering his toast.

It was such a homey scene except for the fact that he was a big man and his navy T-shirt clung to his shoulders and pecs. She had a hard time not checking him out. Again.

As she slid a forkful of eggs into her mouth, she remembered what it had been like to make love with him after he'd suffered through his blood-madness recovery. Part of her still couldn't believe she'd done that and was truly shocked at her behavior. But another part wanted to do it all over again.

His gaze slid to hers and she looked away, her cheeks warming up. He leaned close, offering a half smile. "Neither of us will be able to hide much, I'm afraid."

"I'm getting that, loud and clear."

She took another bite of her eggs and met his gaze. She loved his eyes. That's what she decided. "Your eyes are extraordinary, gold flecks and hazel. Really unusual."

He sipped his coffee. "Thank you." He stared at her over the rim of his mug and his gaze held. "You're beautiful, Shayna. You know that, right?"

"I'm not sure how to respond to that, except to say thank you. Although I will confess that I hate how young I look. I'm twenty-four and I'm still carded, every single time. It's annoying."

"I suppose it would be." But he smiled.

The reality of what she'd just said, complaining about being carded, sank in and she shook her head. "That was really insensitive of me given what all these women go through."

He frowned slightly. "I didn't mean for you to feel bad about just talking, but what's going on in my world is never far from my thoughts."

His ever-present guilt heated up the chains. She touched them, surprised by their warmth. Everything was definitely improved and enhanced. She saw Marius, the dining area and kitchen, even her food as though in early evening light before the sun has gone down completely. Yet there wasn't a single light on in the cave.

She seemed to be siphoning Marius's power more than ever as well, a steady stream that helped her to feel strong and very much alive. Putting the chain on had done that for her and had also heightened her sense of what Marius felt from one moment to the next.

Right now, his thoughts had continued down the guilt-path and though she knew she was taking a risk, she felt compelled to address the issue. "Marius, I don't mean to pry, but may I ask you a personal question?"

His gaze snapped back to hers, and she felt some of his tension dissipate. "Given that you've agreed to stay and that you put the chain on, I want you to think of it as your right to ask any question that enters your anthropological head."

At that, she smiled. "You may want to take back that offer because if you haven't figured it out already, I'm already prone to digging."

He chuckled. "Yes, you are. But I'm also very serious. I owe you answers so long as you're with me."

Settling her fork on her plate, she leaned forward, holding his gaze. "And I, in turn, give you permission to refuse to answer any question that you find intrusive."

"I appreciate that, but I'm sure it'll be okay."

She took a deep breath. "I want to understand the guilt. I've felt it coming from you almost from the first and it's hard to take." She touched the chain at her neck. "What comes through is oppressive. You were thinking about something just a moment ago. Can you tell me what it's all about?"

At that, what had been a sense of goodwill between them dimmed as if a passing cloud had blocked out the sun. "When you've lived as long as I have, you've seen a lot of things, *done* a lot of things. But what I'd been thinking about had to do with the last women I couldn't save, the ones Daniel used to try to break me. I held their lives in my hands and couldn't do anything about it."

She knew he spoke the truth—that he really had been thinking about the women tortured and killed in front of him in the Dark Cave system. She could also sense there was more, but perhaps it was just as he'd said: He'd seen a lot of stuff in his life, more than she could possibly imagine. She didn't feel it was right to press him further on the subject. "Thanks for telling me. I know this isn't easy for you, either, this bond we share."

"I don't like talking about any of it. I don't see the point."

"Yeah, I'm getting that as well. But to change the subject, there is something I'm really curious about. I haven't seen much of your world yet, but based on Daniel's slavery enterprise, he must have accumulated an enormous amount of wealth. What does he spend it on? I take it it's not on university endowments."

Marius laughed outright. "I've never heard of him donating to anything."

"So apparently he doesn't believe basic PR is necessary in your world."

"You've got that exactly right. He's a sociopath and does what he wants when he wants. As for his wealth, I always supposed he plowed it back into the human clubs he owns, the places he's set up around the world from which he plucks beautiful women for his Dark Cave operation."

Shayna nodded but for reasons she couldn't explain, she found this a less-than-satisfactory answer. Her reading had taught her that men of power rarely limited themselves to one endeavor and from what Marius had said, Daniel had already positioned himself to take over the vampire world merely by gaining control of the last extinction weapon. Had he done more than this?

Marius rose, took his plate and mug to the sink, and began cleaning up. Shayna shook her head once more, her thoughts shifting again to how different he was from Michelson. She couldn't even call her former lover by his first name anymore. She remembered how excited she'd been the first time he'd asked her to call him Greg. That was the moment for her when she'd let herself fall the rest of the way in love with him. She believed, at least at the time, that he'd finally seen her not as a student, but as an adult.

Suddenly she realized Marius stood right next to her and he was upset. When she looked up at him, she gasped. "Your fangs are showing. Why?"

"What were you thinking about? Because it sure as hell wasn't me."

She rose to her feet, uncertain what to do. The chain at her neck vibrated with a new and very different layer of heat. She stared at the tips of his fangs and held her breath. He was furious, but it made no sense to her.

She touched the chains, which always seemed to help her zero in on what was going on. Then it dawned on her that Marius was jealous or something close to it. "I was thinking about my ex."

"Well, you need to stop."

"You can tell my thoughts were fixed on another man?"

"Yes. And that your feelings were tender this time, not like before."

"But why the rage?" She really didn't understand why

her thoughts about Michelson had created such a violent reaction.

He pressed a hand to his forehead and squeezed his eyes shut for a moment, but his fangs remained in a partially descended state.

When he opened his eyes, he held her gaze firmly. "This is a very vampire kind of reaction, Shayna, enhanced because of the chains. I didn't mean for this to happen. And I know it's because of the bond and because I've fed from you, but I need you to avoid thinking about any of your previous boyfriends, especially your sexual experiences with them. You can be mad all you want, but try not to dwell on the other stuff."

"You mean like fondness or sexual interest?"

"Exactly. Damn, that was like a lightning strike through my chest."

"I had a moment of remembering what it had been like with the professor early on, how naive I'd been, that I'd fallen hard for him, all starry-eyed and, yes, inexperienced. But I'll be more careful."

"Thank you. I'd appreciate it. And this isn't your fault."

She laughed. "I know. It's the proximity and how much we can sense from each other." Her gaze fell to his lips. His fangs still hadn't retracted, which, of course, made her curious. "May I touch them?"

"What?"

"Your fangs."

"Shit, they didn't retract, did they?"

"No. So what does that mean?"

"That I'm aroused."

Only then, as she let the chains speak to her, did she figure out all that was going on with him in this moment. More than that, he wanted something from her right now.

"Marius, you want to be back at my throat, don't you?"

His eyes darkened. "Yes, that's part of what I need."

Her own desire, so quickly ignited when she was this close to him, rose once more. She planted a hand on his chest. "I knew this would be part of the equation if I put on the chain—and if you feed from me right now, I want to do the other thing as well." Her cheeks warmed up. She'd never been so boldly in her life.

CHAPTER 7

Marius had no rational thought right now, just a powerful instinct full of need and desire. He knew the chains only enhanced what was already there, but sensing Shayna's emotions, full of desire for her ex, had shifted his gears.

She was bonded to him now and he needed her focused on him and not on other men. He curled his hips against her. He wanted sex as much as he wanted to drink from her vein. He licked a line up her throat.

"Marius, I feel drugged with need."

He knew exactly what she meant, but all he could do was make a kind of chuffing sound that came from deep in his throat. "I'm going to tap in. I need you, Shayna. I need what only you can give."

"Yes. Do it." Her body was in motion and her fingers clutched at his biceps, forcing them to flex and release then tighten once more.

He switched to telepathy. *I'm going to move you up against the wall.* He levitated as he spoke, lifting her with him.

Good idea. I'm glad I didn't put on my jeans.

Once he had her against the wall, he pushed his PJ bottoms down and she lifted the hem of her nightgown. He drew back just enough to look into her passion-drenched eyes, her lips parted.

He lifted her leg, holding it against his hip, then angling his body. Still holding her gaze, he pressed the tip of his cock between her legs.

She moaned and made small gasping sounds. "Marius. I need you so much. This is crazy."

"I know." He didn't even know how he got the words out.

Then he started to push.

Shayna cried out. "You have no idea how good that feels."

"Yes, I do." He kissed her, rimming her lips with his tongue. "The chains tell me so much. I can almost feel the pleasure you're experiencing."

He loved that she was so ready for him.

He glided into her, thrusting slowly with both his cock and his tongue, matching the movements. Her hands once more grasped at his body, plucking at muscles here and there.

I want you to feel pleasure with me, Shayna.

I am. I will. You're so damn built, Marius. You make me feel like I won the lottery.

At that, he drew back, smiling. "You're so beautiful and your eyes have darkened."

She nodded, lips parted.

Because of their bond and who he was, he already thought of her as *his woman,* another effect of the chains. But that meant that *his woman* should have more pleasure than she'd ever known before.

He cupped the back of her neck, holding her steady as he thrust inside her, curling his hips each time. "How does that feel?"

Her lips moved as though she tried to find words, but couldn't bring anything intelligible forward. He smiled. "Good answer."

He kissed her again and moved faster this time. *I want you to come at least once before I tap in. Blood has an exquisite taste when it's full of passion.*

That's . . . I don't know . . . wonderful . . . feels so good . . . so built.

Her disjointed thoughts pleased the hell out of him. Her body pulled on him low. He knew it wouldn't take much so he drew back once more. "I'm going to do this fast for you, like last night."

She gasped and nodded. *Please, please, please.*

He wanted to watch her come. As only a vampire could do, he moved lightning-fast. Her body arched, her chest swelled, then she cried out. He almost lost it because the sight of her caught in ecstasy, her face growing flushed, had his balls tightening, ready to release. What was it about this woman that got him going?

Having learned a thing or two in four hundred years, he forced himself to calm down. As her body began to relax, he slowed the pace, but kept driving into her steadily. She was breathing hard. "That was amazing."

His gaze fell to her swollen lips, which he plundered all over again, always moving into her, thrusting deep.

The orgasm had caused her arms to grow limp as she slung them over his shoulders. He loved giving her pleasure, having her satisfied. But he'd soon have her ready for more.

His own need rose as he left her lips and kissed a line down her neck.

"God, yes," she whispered.

He licked several swipes over her vein, forcing it to the surface. When he felt the pulse beating beneath his tongue, he gave her a quick warning. *Ready?*

Please, yes, now.

His fangs emerged fully and he struck in a swift bite then clamped his lips around the wound and began to drink. When the first savory drop hit his mouth, he groaned. He thought he'd imagined it before, but now he was sure that he'd never tasted anything like Shayna's blood—and he'd sampled tens of thousands over the years, human and vampire.

She moaned and writhed against him and he kept driving into her as well, the motions so linked that he had no problem sustaining both at the same time.

He slid an arm around her waist, pinning her tightly to him.

The more he drank, the more his muscles responded, filling with added power.

Her fingers now gripped his shoulders. *You feel so good, Marius. Bigger. Is that possible?*

Yes. Your blood is this miracle, building me up. My God, who are you, Shayna? It's never been like this.

This is a dream. Her voice in his head forced his hips to pump faster. She cried out. *So good. You'll make me come again.*

That's the plan, but I'm close, too. And I want to come while I'm feeding.

I want that, too. She cried out repeatedly, then, *Faster.* The word forced his hips into hyperspeed again.

The time had come.

His body erupted, an exquisite streak of pleasure flowing through his cock and repeating in pulses that had him writhing against her and groaning. With his lips still sealed to her throat, he kept sucking, holding her undulating body in place while her cries of ecstasy filled the cavern.

He continued to pump, and pleasure flowed until finally her cries drifted away and his cock had released the last drop. He was breathing hard, Shayna as well.

She lay draped over him, making small sounds of contentment like a laugh and a groan combined. He stayed with her in this position, his lips still holding her throat, no longer sucking, just enjoying the connection.

He kept her pressed against the wall for a long time, releasing her throat in stages, wishing he didn't have to. When the small wounds were sealed and had begun to heal, he let go completely.

She then settled her head against his neck and he petted her hair, stroking the length down her back. She had beautiful silky hair, very straight with a fine texture.

"Marius?"

His chest ached at the lovely sound of her voice. "Yes?"

"I'm glad I stayed."

"Me, too." More than he wanted to admit.

He still felt pumped all through his body and somewhere deep in the core of his being, a new kind of power rumbled, increasing little by little. He didn't know exactly what it was, but he loved the feel of it.

What mystified him, however, was why Shayna's blood had brought these two things: that he became physically stronger as never before when he drank from her, and that being with her like this allowed him to experience a new level of power.

She sighed deeply. "But you know I'll have to leave one day, when my job here is done."

His chest ached a little more. "I know, which makes me all the more grateful that you're here now."

She ran her fingers over his back. "I don't ever want to leave."

He knew exactly what she meant. "Maybe I'll just keep you pressed up against this wall for the next decade. How does that sound?"

She drew back to meet his gaze, laughing. "Perfect." She slid her fingers through his hair. "Do you know, I keep getting this weird feeling that any minute I'm going to wake up in my Seattle apartment and realize this was all a dream."

He searched her eyes, trying to picture himself in her shoes, trying to understand how weird and frightening so much of this must seem. "And I wish for your sake that was true."

She smiled and nuzzled against his neck once more.

"How about I take us back to the bedroom right now?"

She lifted back slightly, her hands on his shoulders. "You mean like this? Still connected?" Her lips curved.

He dropped a hand to her bottom and held her firmly. "Why not?"

She giggled. "Then take me straight to the shower."

"You got it."

As the water from so many showerheads beat on her body, Shayna thought she'd one day have to have a setup like this. She felt like she was being massaged as she slowly turned in a circle, lifting her arms now and then.

She washed her hair and only as she was rinsing off did she wonder how the cave even had hot running water.

She glanced up at the ceiling carvings and tried to picture the routing of pipes.

She had so many questions.

Marius waited for her near the sink. She hadn't felt the chain tug at her neck, but he was sticking close.

Once she was done, Marius took her place and she set about blow-drying her hair, brushing her teeth, just like a normal woman except that she was deep underground in New Zealand of all places.

With her hair dry, she opened up the makeup Rumy had brought for her, which included, of all things, several sets of false eyelashes, something she'd never wear. She laughed. She liked Rumy a lot, but the most she ever put on was a little lip gloss and mascara. Occasionally she'd add eye shadow for a night out.

When Marius emerged, he wrapped a towel around his waist, which of course left the breadth of his massive chest exposed. Just looking at him, her heart rate increased.

He caught her gaze in the mirror, brows raised.

Busted. Warmth climbed her cheeks. He seemed to understand, because he smiled.

"Sorry," she said, laughing at herself. "But you're so incredibly gorgeous. I can't help looking and appreciating."

He turned toward her, his lids lowering. "Don't say stuff like that to me unless you want me to haul you back to bed."

She was so tempted and remained staring at him for a long moment.

Aware, however, that she had a job to do, she took a long shuddering breath. "I think we should focus on the extinction weapon. I mean, if I have this tracking ability, then a little practice might help."

"You're right."

She gestured toward the doorway. "I should probably get dressed."

"Uh-huh." His gaze drifted over her shoulders and the line of cleavage that the towel had created.

She made the hard decision to look away from him, desire swirling through her abdomen once more as though she hadn't just made love with the man. She hurried past him, sure that if she kept staring into his eyes, she'd probably grab him.

She was still stunned by how quickly she'd entered into a sexual relationship with him. A new host of questions arrived within her mind. Did vampires have the power to seduce women? Had he employed those powers on her? Were vampires more likely to engage in a sexual relationship quickly or was he just like a human male and if the opportunity presented itself, he dove in?

Yes, so many questions, best not asked, at least not at this time and in this context. She should at least get dressed.

He followed her into the bedroom.

She turned her attention instead toward working this weird, latent ability of hers. How would a tracking ability work in the first place?

Just as she reached the bed, she decided to experiment. She stood very still, closed her eyes, and turned inward. She held the thought in her mind that she needed to find the extinction weapon.

And just like that, a vision hurtled toward her in a fast-flowing stream.

Marius, a vision? She reached for him and felt his arm surround her.

The relief she felt at his touch allowed her to keep going. The same annoying wavy lines, however, that had been there from the first prevented a good portion of the images from becoming distinct, just like before.

She even squinted trying to see better, but all she could detect was what seemed to be that same massive space, with rows of stone seats. People moved about, bent over as though doing menial chores like cleanup of some kind—or at least that's what it looked like. The waves made it impossible to see clearly.

When she heard Daniel's voice, she panned around and he came into view, though the dark, disruptive lines gave her only partial glimpses. But she could hear him really well. That's when she understood she was seeing this in real time, not in the future.

Two other men stood near Daniel, each as big as Marius.

"Quill, what do you have for me?" Daniel had a deep voice and he was speaking with one of Marius's brothers, one of two that had aligned with Daniel.

"Our best lead yet on the weapon." He handed Daniel a sheet of paper.

Daniel scanned the contents, one brow lifting slowly. "What do you think, Lev?"

The other brother spoke up, though the lines obscured his face. Still, she heard him well enough. "There's mention of the red hood on this one, which is why we believe the tip is solid. We've had at least twenty mentions of a weapon with a red hood and shiny black base. This has to be it."

Before she'd fallen asleep, Marius had shared more bits of information about his world. In this case, Daniel had set up a tip line about the weapon just as Rumy had.

"So it looks like you're going to Sweden. And Lev, I want you both to go."

Lev smiled, as if he didn't often get to go on missions like this one.

Through the difficult wavy lines she watched Daniel smile and clap first Quill's shoulder, then Lev's. These were the sons loyal to Daniel, dedicated to his ambitions. They were just a few years older than Marius and his brothers.

Shayna's heart thumped. If this was her tracking ability at work, she felt encouraged that both Marius and Rumy were right and that she truly could help in this situation.

But as she stared at Daniel, he turned in what felt like her direction, his brow pinched, but he didn't make eye contact so she knew he couldn't actually see her. When he spoke, however, a jolt of fear went through her. At that exact same moment, Marius tightened his arm around her, perhaps sensing her disquiet.

"Are you there, Shayna? Is that you spying on me?" Daniel smiled. "And do I detect lovemaking? Have you already seduced my son? Clever girl. But I'll be waiting for you."

The waves in front of the vision grew more severe so that she saw less and less, and now her head hurt again. Was Daniel creating this interference or was the problem hers?

The fact that he must have sensed her presence caused her to pull away from the vision completely. She kept pulling until she felt the connection actually break.

How did Daniel know what she'd been doing? How had he been able to detect she was there? And yet Marius had already told her he was one of the most powerful vampires on the planet.

"Shayna, I can feel your distress. What is it? What happened? What did you see?"

She drew out of Marius's arms to face him, holding his gaze. "Daniel. I just saw him in the vision, but he somehow knew I was there. I don't think he could see me, but he could tell I was there. He even called me by name." She didn't reveal that somehow Daniel had known they'd been making love. It was just too creepy.

"Shit," Marius murmured. "My father has tremendous power, more I think than anyone knows. Did he threaten you in any way?"

She shook her head. "Not really, but he said he was waiting for me. What did he mean by that?"

"Don't pay any attention to that. My father is a master at manipulation and inciting fear."

"But do you think he really knew I was there?"

"He seems to have some kind of sixth sense, maybe even his own ability to see the future, I'm not sure. So was that it? Was the vision just about Daniel?"

"No, in fact I think it's good news." She then related everything she'd seen and heard, first about the large space then about the final extinction weapon, and that Quill and Lev were there, ready to serve.

"They were the first of Daniel's spawn and he broke them. This is good to know. My brothers are both powerful in their own right, so I'll know what I'm up against."

Marius dipped his chin, eyes squinted slightly. Shayna watched his gaze shift back and forth in quick flashes. She could almost see him formulate a strategy. When he was finished, his gaze snapped back to hers. "We need to start accessing the more mobile part of your tracking abilities, the part that can detect location. So what I want you to do is to focus on the weapon as it was described in the vision and on the location in Sweden. Can you do that?"

"I'll try and we'll see what happens." She drew a deep breath and settled her shoulders, trying to relax while she did as Marius suggested.

She took a series of deep breaths, letting them out slowly. Images began to drift in her direction, of a snowy landscape and low light, of the geography of the Nordic lands. She felt as though she were already in motion and began flying at a fantastic speed toward a vast snowy outcrop. Then suddenly she flew through the snow in altered flight, landing in a vast cavern space half filled with what looked like a flow of water that had frozen solid.

Leaning up against the cavern wall, well away from the glacier-like ice, was a red piece of metal about four feet square. She glanced around. No one else was there.

But the image, so clear in her mind, started filling up

with the dark, wavy lines once more, then finally winked out.

She drew back and stared at Marius. "I was there. I saw the red portion of the weapon."

He nodded, smiling. "That's it. Now let me gather my weapons."

She'd almost forgotten. He'd probably be battling again, something she'd pressed way back into her recent memories. "Right."

He moved across the room quickly. She was so caught up in the recent vision that she didn't follow him. The chain vibrated softly, gave a slight tug, then the pressure ended as Marius reached his dresser.

She stared at him, fully aware that twenty feet separated them now, well beyond the original proximity distance.

Slowly, while his back was to her, she moved away from him, returning to the bathroom. She kept waiting for another tug on the chains, but none followed.

"Marius?" she called out.

"What? Where did you go?" He sounded so normal, but she heard the doors to his dresser opening and closing, so he wasn't really paying attention.

"I'm in the bathroom. Notice anything strange about that?"

Everything grew very quiet, until she heard him moving back in her direction.

When he arrived in the doorway, he held his chain up. "What the fuck?"

She shrugged. "Something happened. I got this funny feeling, sort of like a vibration while you were moving away from me, then a small snap. You might have been too fixed on gathering your weapons to have been aware of it."

He shook his head, clearly perplexed. "I don't know what this means." He started backing up, clearly wanting to test the issue for himself. She moved to the doorway to watch how far he could go.

He kept moving well beyond the earlier ten-foot boundary, then stepped through to the hallway beyond. *I'm going to levitate from one end of the cave to the other.*

Sounds like a plan. This issue needed to be tested now.

She could sense he was in motion and moving faster. *I'm down by the waterfall and still no tug.*

This is incredible. I still feel bonded to you. I can sense that you're stunned.

I am that.

He returned suddenly in altered flight to stand in front of her. He put his hands on her arms. "I knew that your blood had done something to me, but dammit, I think it's given me a bit of Ancestral power, the kind Daniel has."

"Really?" This was good news. "That's fantastic."

"I know. Okay, let's get dressed. We need to find out what else I've got going on, and we need to get to Sweden."

She followed him into the bedroom and stood back as he drew a pair of what he called battle leathers from the dresser.

She stood back, watching him lose the towel and plant a foot into the pants. Marius went commando, which warmed up her cheeks all over again at the sight of his ass, as well as his movements that had his muscles rippling all over again. He was like an amazing wild animal.

As he zipped, he glanced at her over his shoulder. "Are you watching me?"

She sighed. "More than I should."

"Well, I'm glad. I like you looking at me and I like even better how that makes you feel." He shrugged into a snug black T-shirt then crossed to a cabinet in the far corner. He began sliding battle chains into thin slits in the leather pants. Larger rings dangled from the top, undoubtedly for ease of removal.

"This change between us is about you, Shayna. Your blood has pumped me up."

"I guess it has." She moved closer and felt down both arms. "You are bigger. I mean, I thought so at the time, but you are." She then reached down to touch one of the rings. "Are these the chains you battled with last night?"

"No, this is a new set. Those need to be cleaned up and polished. I'll get to them eventually, but right now you're my priority—and getting that damn weapon."

The part of her that had boundless curiosity, that had caused her to choose anthropology in the first place, launched into hyperdrive. The questions flowed rapid-fire. Why did he carry so many weapons? What was the advantage of the long chain over the short? How many daggers? Why did he carry different sizes? Did the battle situations dictate which weapon to use, and how did he make the decision?

He smiled and finally answered the last question. She'd hardly given him time to do more than that. "I make my decision by instinct mostly at this point." Seeing her interest, he took a couple of minutes and showed her each weapon, even demonstrating how the long chains spun and describing how with the exact right flick of the wrist the chain could incapacitate the enemy. The short chain was used for strangulation and, with enough force, decapitation. The daggers didn't require explanation.

She'd watched him fight, and the other vampires as well. She could still hear the whirring of the chains, the grunts of the men, and sometimes the crack of a head against stone.

"You don't use guns?"

"No, but I think that time is coming, another reason we need to take care of Daniel's threat in our world. You asked earlier what he spent his money on. If it's been the acquiring of handguns and assault rifles, we'll have a war on our hands like nothing my world has seen before. Now come with me. Let's see if Rumy provided the right clothes for a trip into the cold northern lands."

She sensed that he'd shifted into what she could only think of as "warrior mode." He vibrated with a new level of energy, and she could feel that his heart rate had increased.

She followed him across the room to the inset closet in which she'd stowed the clothes Rumy had brought her. He pulled out a fur-lined jacket. "You'll need this. I know that you're streaming my power, but you'll feel the cold. If what you've described is accurate, we're heading to what is called an ice cave. It will be like a freezer in there."

"That would be my guess as well."

He reached down and pulled out a pair of fur-lined boots. "Better put these on." He looked her up and down, then handed her a pair of jeans and a long-sleeved T-shirt. "You should be okay with just these as opposed to long underwear, which I doubt Rumy provided anyway."

"Any socks?"

He pushed a few things around and hunted through the shelves. "Well, just these." He handed her a pair of thin black ankle socks.

She took them. "These will do."

He stepped back and gestured to one of the middle shelves. "You'll want to pick something out yourself."

Ah, bras and thongs, mostly lace and sexy as anything. Marius turned away and stared up at the ceiling while she lost her towel. And in what she'd come to learn was Rumy's style, when she put her way-too-snug bra on, then the shirt, the low cut in front revealed another long line of cleavage. Marius had shared a few details about Rumy as well, and one of them was the fact that he believed if a woman wasn't dressed up in something sexy, she didn't have a grain of sense. Clearly, owning a sex-club complex as Rumy did had given him a skewed view of the world.

Fortunately, the jacket would cover things up.

She pulled on the boots, which fit really well. Despite the bra choices, she'd have to thank Rumy later for his attention to detail. Shrugging into the jacket, Marius turned back to her, then held out his arm for her.

He now wore a tight-fitting vest as well, also loaded with weapons, and as she hopped onto his booted right foot and slid her arm around his neck, she could feel the daggers beneath.

He put his hand to her face. "Ready for this?"

"Absolutely. But how do you know where to go?"

"I'll head northwest in the direction of Europe. As we get closer to Sweden, you can guide me in. Not sure how it'll work, but I'm confident we can figure this out."

"Sounds good. Now what do we do about the fast-flight issue I have?"

He smiled. "I've been thinking about that and I have a feeling it's not going to be a problem. If our proximity issue is gone, you should be okay."

She smiled. "Then let's go." But her heart hammered hard. When she'd seen the vision, the cave had been empty. However, that didn't mean that something could change by the time they got there.

As he switched to altered flight and took off, she closed her eyes, not wanting to see the stone wall rush at her. He soon had them high in the sky, flying faster and faster, but she didn't feel a thing, not a single twinge of pain. *Marius, this is amazing.*

No pain?

Not even a little. Incredible.

While he flew, she watched the moving landscape below, the breadth of ocean, then the shape of the Indian subcontinent. Soon the Middle East and Eastern Europe. Maybe twelve minutes had passed, but not much more, before they were descending. As she looked down she saw a good portion of Europe stretched out below. He'd taken her high into the air, high enough to get a bird's-eye view of this part of the planet.

Soon enough he started to slow, then finally hovered in the air. *We're close now. Try forming a picture in your head of the pathway into the cavern system. I'll admit, I've never been here before. I don't think it's inhabited.*

Okay. I'll see what I can do. She brought the vision forward, and as before, it arrived with the dark wavy lines. She felt a sudden disappointment that Marius's increase in power hadn't translated into her images improving. She began to think the problem lay with her.

She directed the destination point toward him as though speaking telepathically, then asked, *Are you receiving this?*

I am, though it's difficult with all the waves.

I know, I'd hoped they would have disappeared by now, especially because you have more power. I've even wondered if Daniel has been interfering, but I'm beginning to suspect that the problem is mine. The question is, do you think you can make your way to the weapon with what I'm giving you?

He set them in motion again, though much slower this time, as though hunting. *I'm not sure. See if you can bring up the vision again and really focus.*

Shayna closed her eyes and worked on bringing the images forward. She'd seen it much more clearly earlier. Michelson's critique of her came back, roaring through her mind: *You lack focus, Shayna, you always have. Even your papers have this singular disappointing absence of purpose and commitment.*

The vision grew even more muddled as her ex's criticisms rolled through mind.

She knew he'd messed with her head, that all the negative things he'd told her during their six-month relationship weren't true. But at a time like this, her confidence took a plunge.

However, she refused to let Michelson dominate the moment. Dipping her chin, she brought the vision up once more. She took several deep breaths and let her mind relax. Her ex was wrong and right now she meant to prove it.

This time when the location filled her mind, she immediately sent it in Marius's direction. Though still riddled with the strange wavy lines, the image was much clearer. She could make out all the elements now, including the size of the cavern, the massive flow of ice at the northern end, and the red square metal piece that she knew belonged to the extinction weapon.

But suddenly the image revealed a new element: Daniel and his security team. *Did you get all this? I'm seeing Daniel and his men.*

I see them.

So do we head back to New Zealand?

She heard him laugh. *Hell, no.*

Shayna's heart flipped over a couple of times. *You mean we're going in, even though Daniel and his men are already there?*

Damn straight. Hey, this is what I do and there's something more, what you've given me. I know that I can take them, and I wouldn't have before you fed me. But if you're worried, I can leave you outside the cavern or even topside. Your choice.

Shayna really appreciated his attitude. In fact, given what she'd been used to, she was stunned. She actually had a choice. She was almost light-headed with the power he'd placed in her hands, to choose for herself, for her safety, for whatever the hell she wanted to do right now.

As she considered her options, she focused on the cavern and instinctively felt that she needed to be there, that she'd have a part to play.

Leaning away from him slightly, she met his gaze firmly. *I'm in. I trust you, and I'm in.*

He held her gaze for a long moment, and she saw admiration shining in his eyes. *You have more courage than any woman I've ever known.* He planted a full kiss on her lips and she swore that for the rest of her life, she'd let what he'd just said to her rule her life.

Let's go.

He nodded. *And as soon as we land, I want you to disappear like you did before.*

I will. And you're absolutely sure you can manage this many warrior-types?

I can do this. Trust me.

"Trust me." On principle, she hated those exact words. How many times had she heard them roll off Michelson's tongue, always with that condescending tone as if she were an idiot. "Trusting him" had usually meant that she'd had to give something up like a personal boundary, a belief, or her precious time.

But she worked hard to set her prejudice aside because in this case, Marius had spoken the words. And on a fundamental level, as well as in this situation, she did trust him.

One more deep breath. *Let's do this thing.*

He flew once more, and because passing through anything solid still freaked her out, she closed her eyes. She could tell by the way the air felt full of feathers that they were passing through solid rock.

The flight lasted longer than she'd expected, but she'd once heard that cavern systems could go on for hundreds of miles.

When at last he began to slow, she could feel that they were within just a few yards of their destination.

One more wall of rock, then we'll be inside. Marius's muscles had begun to twitch.

Shayna's heart rate skyrocketed. *And I can feel that a portion of the weapon is just behind this wall.*

Ready?

Yes.

He passed through the stone and touched down just inside, which placed them against the wall opposite the massive flow of ice.

Quill and Lev stood by the red hood of the extinction weapon off to her left and Daniel levitated just above the ice, his men in an arc in front of him, weapons in hand.

The bluish-white ice created a perfect backdrop for the would-be dictator, dressed all in black. Daniel had a flare for the dramatic.

He didn't look at Marius, however. Instead, he'd trained his gaze fully on her.

She felt him beating at the edges of her mind, trying to establish contact. The power that he focused in her direction made her tremble, but the last thing she wanted was Daniel in her head, communicating telepathically. Streaming more of Marius's power, she blocked him mentally, looking away as he continued his assault.

Disappear, Shayna. His voice was a steel command inside her head.

She didn't hesitate but took another hit of Marius's power, opened up the pathway that let her do this impossible thing, then made herself invisible.

Most of Daniel's security team had their hands on daggers or short chains. But at least two of them spun the long chains, and she thought that whirring sound would live in her mind forever.

Marius stood slightly hunched, knees bent, ready for action. He radiated so much energy and power right now that she swore he gave off a slight glow. Yep, something had changed within him.

Daniel levitated slowly, moving forward, away from

the ice. He smiled, something that seemed more sinister to Shayna than if he'd scowled.

He no longer tried to make contact with Shayna. Instead, all his attention was now on Marius.

She didn't understand why Daniel didn't tell his men to attack or why he flew until he stood on the floor in front of his men now, as though he had no fear of what Marius might do.

But she felt Marius's level of determination. Even this was stronger than before.

Still, he faced over twenty men and she couldn't imagine how he was going to defeat them all.

CHAPTER 8

From the time he'd fed from Shayna, Marius felt power swirling through him as never before, heightening his perception, awakening latent power. His gaze flashed from one powerful guard to the next in quick milliseconds.

"My son, my patience won't last forever and I can feel your power awakening. You're beginning to realize who you are in our world and I want you with me, to rule beside me. Join me now, and once we have the extinction weapon in hand, I'll let you destroy it."

He knew Daniel intended to lull him with talk, but Marius was having none of it. Not tonight. He had a woman to protect, someone he was coming quickly to value. It was clear to him she had a unique place in his world.

He also fully intended to get out alive and to take this portion of the extinction weapon with him.

He didn't bother to answer Daniel. Instead, he saw the moment for the unique opportunity it was.

He moved his hands like lightning and before Daniel had blinked he had a dagger in his chest and had slumped to his knees, staring at the finely crafted piece of steel as though thunderstruck.

And at the same time, four of his men had daggers in their throats, all thrown by Marius.

Another blink and two more were down.

He moved faster than he'd ever moved before. Several of the guards were now grouped around Daniel to protect him, others were dead, the rest in shock. Quill and Lev shouted things he couldn't hear.

Using the short chain while levitating, along with altered flight to disappear and reappear, he decapitated man after man before any of them knew what was happening.

With his lightning reflexes and enhanced vision, he saw two men moving in what would be Shayna's direction, maybe on Daniel's command.

He flew in a quick, straight shot, intercepting them both, a long chain whirring in one hand. Before a dagger left the hand of his left opponent, Marius flicked his wrist and the long chain flew swiftly and wrapped around his neck.

The other opponent let a long chain fly as well. But with perceptions Marius had never had before, he stepped sideways, caught the chain mid-spin, and with another flick sent it back to its owner, catching him around the neck. He'd never done that before and he didn't know anyone who could.

Daggers now flew in his direction. *Shayna, are you all right?*

I'm in the air high above the battle. I'm safe.

Marius caught and returned each dagger, striking home each time, so that a moment later the battlefield was silent. Those not dead stared at him, including Quill and Lev.

He hovered in the air, his gaze sweeping over the field, making sure that no one feigned injury and attacked him.

He needed to know if he'd killed Daniel, but he didn't dare draw close—not when Quill and Lev could attack. By then, he was hovering high in the air, plotting how to get to Daniel and finish him off. Being this close to offing Daniel was more than he'd hoped for.

The next moment, however, Daniel and the remains of his team vanished, along with the Quill, Lev, and the extinction weapon. He felt the effect of his father's power. Only Daniel could have done that.

But he left bodies on the ground.

Marius dropped to the floor of the cave, his boots landing with a thud. He felt almost light-headed that he'd come so close to ending his father's life. Moving to the spot where Daniel had bled, Marius stood over this small victory.

Shayna, come join me.

He watched her become visible then float down to him, her eyes wide. "How did I levitate like that? I couldn't before. Is it the same power that you just exhibited? Marius, you moved so fast. At times you simply vanished."

"Was that what it seemed like? That I disappeared?"

Shayna touched down on the cavern floor, her nose pink from the cold. "That's exactly what it was like, as though you fought the battle from an invisible place."

He glanced up at the ceiling. "And you levitated."

"I did. I saw that the weapons were flying really fast and I was afraid I'd get caught in the crossfire. I thought the thought and the next thing I knew I'd bumped into the ceiling a little too hard." She rubbed the top of her head and winced. "I have a small knot right now, but even so the power I'm siphoning from you is taking care of it."

He hardly felt like himself. "It is incredible. Mostly, I don't understand the source."

"Marius, not to be insensitive, but I'm having a hard time with all this. Can we leave now?" She splayed her fingers, gesturing to the corpses.

He wished he could leave, but he and his brothers had rules about returning any place of battle to its former condition, at least as much as possible. "I have to take care of this mess first. This is one of the ways we keep our world hidden from yours."

"Sure. Okay." Something caught her eye, and as he followed her gaze he saw that she'd just recognized the carvings that she'd been asking about the night before.

"Why don't you check it out, while I oversee cleanup?"

She nodded and picked her way over to the wall near their initial entry point.

He dipped into the deep side pocket of his battle leathers and withdrew his iPhone.

Rumy's voice came barreling on the line. "Marius, how's it going? Are you still in New Zealand? Anything I can do for you?"

He glanced around and explained about the recent encounter.

"Holy shit! You almost had him, didn't you?"

"Almost, but not quite. He'll be more careful next time."

"No doubt. So what do you need me to do?"

"Order cleanup." Marius turned in a circle. "Fifteen dead."

"Got it. I've got your GPS. Stay put and I'll have a team up there in a few minutes." The cleanup crews were some of the fastest fliers around. They specialized in removing any sign of their civilization, especially in an unimproved cavern system like this one.

While waiting for the crews to show up, Marius turned in a circle, always staying on the alert. At the same time, he gathered up his weapons. The crew would clean them for him, one of the many shit-jobs they did and for which he would always be grateful.

Shayna had her phone up at the carving-height level, taking more pics. He felt her usual curiosity, but also her concern. Levitating, he joined her.

"So what have we got here?" He wondered if he should mention that when she returned to Seattle, he'd probably have to strip her phone of all these pics. He decided that was a conversation for a different night.

She placed her hand on the carvings. "I'm convinced more than ever that it's important I understand these symbols."

"Maybe we can address the issue with Rumy."

She turned to smile at him. "He would definitely be one of the places to start. If I were studying your culture, I'd probably seek him out as my prime source of information."

"And you'd be wise. He knows everyone in our underworld."

She frowned slightly. "So I have to ask, did you kill Daniel?"

Marius shook his head. "Not a chance. That dagger

could have sliced his heart in two, but his self-healing ability would have knit it back together before three beats had passed."

"Well, that at least explains why you're not doing cartwheels."

"Cartwheels, huh?"

"Celebrating."

He chuckled softly. "No, it's not time to celebrate yet." He looked her over. "Are you sure you didn't get hurt?

"Not even a little."

"May I check?"

She glanced down at her body, frowning. "Of course, but really, I stayed out of the fray."

Despite her assurances, he felt her arms and legs, slid a hand down her back, and opened her coat to examine her torso. If his gaze got hung up for a moment on her cleavage, he took a deep breath, then cleared his throat. "You seem to be fine."

"I told you, so why did you check?" Though the words sounded accusing, her tone was still more intrigued than offended, very typical of this woman. She wanted details about everything.

He met her gaze. "Sometimes adrenaline, in a battle situation, prevents the pain from hitting the nerve centers in the brain until later. Then, of course, you're in for a world of hurt the moment the feel-good fades."

She pushed her hair away from her face. "I'm okay, really. But I'm still trying hard not to look at all these dead men." She shuddered.

"Then keep taking your photos." He glanced behind him. "The cleanup crew should be here anytime now."

"I know." She turned back to face the wall, then stepped sideways a couple of feet and took more pictures.

At the same time, the crews arrived.

Marius nodded at the lead man, who inclined his head in return, then quietly started issuing orders. More men arrived, along with a handful of women, dropping down from altered flight, stretchers in hand. A couple of them carried emergency medical kits, but none was needed.

Bodies were quickly loaded onto the stretchers and covered up with heavy, rubber sheets. As soon as the straps were secured, each team of two took off.

"Wow," Shayna murmured. "That's incredibly efficient."

"It's a good system."

The leader spoke quietly into the com at his shoulder and a minute later a new, larger team of at least a dozen men arrived. Most had tanks strapped to their backs, of varying sizes.

"Ghostbusters," Shayna murmured.

He smiled. He knew the film well. "Not exactly. Just a little stain removal, then steam cleaning."

She drew close to him and watched the process as the final part of the cleanup took place. "Again, wow. So parts of your world function really well."

"I'd have to agree with that analysis."

Once the leader made a circuit of the space and pointed out a few missed spots, he dismissed the crew, each slipping into altered flight and disappearing. When only he remained, he picked up Marius's weapons and approached drew close. "How are you, warrior?" He handed Marius his weapons, now pristine and dry.

"I'm good, Joe, thanks for asking." Marius loaded his vest and battle leathers once more.

"We were all sickened when the Council of Ancestrals gave in to Daniel and he imprisoned you and your brothers. We appreciate what all of you have done for us. Just wanted you to know."

Marius settled his hand on Joe's shoulder. "And I appreciate what you do." He then took a moment and introduced Joe to Shayna.

"Pleased to meet you, Shayna." He smiled. "And you should know that you have a good man here. One of the best."

"I know."

Marius glanced at her, feeling the chain at his neck vibrate with the warmth of her emotion. She really meant it.

"Blessings to you both," Joe said, lifting a hand in farewell. He turned and launched, gliding upward into altered flight, then through the stone with the ease of at least two centuries of practice.

Shayna's gaze drifted over the now pristine battlefield. She shook her head, and he felt her disbelief.

He chuckled and slid his arm around her shoulders. "Let's get out of here and see if we can't access your vision-tracking ability again. If I recall, Quill and Lev had a long list of possibilities to go through to figure out where the rest of the weapon is. They've got one-third of it now, with that red roof section. But all we have to do is to keep them from getting the remainder." He held out his arm, and she climbed aboard.

He immediately shifted to altered flight but made his way slowly in a northerly direction just in case Daniel had some of his men waiting for him in the south.

"I was sure glad I had the jacket and boots on. That cave was cold."

"Yep, the ice creates a real freezer effect."

Shayna had closed her eyes when Marius launched, unwilling to watch him head straight for a solid wall. She wondered how long it would take before she wouldn't flinch. For now, eyes closed.

She sensed when he'd moved high into the air. She had no problem opening her eyes at that point. But approaching anything solid made her tremble.

He moved swiftly, faster than ever, and yet she had no pain now. She wondered what it meant or why Marius's power had increased so suddenly.

With her arm wrapped around his neck, she thought about what the leader of the cleanup crew had said to him, thanking him for his service to their world. He was clearly well respected.

She slipped into telepathy. *Marius, you're revered in your world, aren't you? Rumy definitely had that vibe going on and now Joe.*

I wouldn't use the word revered, *exactly.* She could feel how uneasy the compliment made him. *Although I'm sure it would define how Adrien and Lucian are viewed. They're both older and they've done so much more than I ever could to help our world.*

As Shayna took in this statement, the oppressive guilt returned just like that. He'd spoken about feeling guilty about the women that Daniel had used to try to force him into joining his team, yet somehow she knew that another, difficult issue lay beyond his distress. *It's hard for me to believe that your contribution hasn't been as significant as your brothers'.*

Well, you'd be wrong. You just haven't been here long enough to know the truth.

This time, not only guilt rode him hard but also a

profound sense of shame, as though he'd done the unforgivable.

So what did you do, Marius? Because I'm feeling your guilt again, a heavy weight that you carry with you all the time.

As they flew south, he grew very quiet. She couldn't imagine how many tens or even hundreds of miles they'd already flown—his speed was amazing.

Finally, he said, *The chains don't lie, so I know I can't pretend that what you say isn't true. I live with a constant remorse about things I've done, terrible things, but I have no intention of revealing the details. I'll only say this: What I did cost my brothers years of suffering and I shouldn't have lived. It's as simple as that.*

What could she say to this admission? Though she found it hard to believe that Marius would have done anything to have hurt his brothers. *Well, I just wish you didn't have to live with so much guilt.*

He adjusted his arm around her waist, getting more comfortable. Shayna held on tight. It was a long way down.

Marius's voice once more flowed through her mind. *If I could undo what happened, I would, but I can't. So how about we shift our focus. While we're in flight, I'd like you to try tapping into your tracking ability again. We have something a lot more important to deal with than my past crimes.*

Fair enough.

Shayna took a moment to make the shift from Marius's shame and remorse to her latest struggle, grappling with a strange power that still didn't function properly for her. She closed her eyes once more and focused her thoughts on the extinction weapon, but as before the waves appeared, blocking a good portion of the images that wanted to come to her.

She wished she had more confidence generally because maybe then the waves wouldn't even be there, obscuring half of what otherwise she might see. She could even hear Michelson laughing at her. *A half-ass job as usual, Shayna.* He always thought it was funny to point out her shortcomings.

She forced the unhappy thought away. So now here she was, needing to be fully present in a life-threatening situation and finding it hard. Besides, what did she know about these abilities that Marius's power allowed her to express? They were like clothes she'd borrowed, but that really didn't fit.

Still, she pressed on. This much she could do: She knew how to battle through even when she didn't know what she was doing.

Despite the ever-present waves, images emerged slowly of Daniel asleep on a couch, bare-chested, his hand on top of the knife wound, his complexion pale. She sensed nothing would happen for a while since the man causing so much trouble was temporarily incapacitated.

She shared what she saw with Marius. *All I see is Daniel, on his back, eyes closed, recovering.*

He's still lying down?

Yep.

Huh. I must have gotten deep into a vital organ.

Shayna said, *I'm guessing by how high the wound was that you pierced his left lung. But I'll never forget how surprised he looked when your dagger struck home.*

You and me both.

So why do you think you've had a sudden increase in power and ability?

I'm really not sure, but I keep coming back to the one constant: My power increased each time I fed from your vein, especially this last time. Nothing else in my life is different. Just you.

Well, I have a different view altogether.

While in flight, with clouds whipping by like soft feathers against her face, he drew back just enough to make eye contact. *And what would that be?* He seemed genuinely bemused.

Call it an instinct, but I think it's possible you might have more latent ability than either of your brothers, possibly even more than Daniel.

Marius, once more on autopilot, held her gaze. He even laughed. *Sorry, but that's just not possible.*

Think about it. Daniel has all but begged you to come on board, and when we arrived in that cave, I think he could have killed you, but he didn't. No, he's holding back and I think it's because he knows your potential. He really does want you to rule beside him. He might even need you to make everything work.

Marius shifted his gaze back to the path ahead. *Well, you couldn't be more wrong. And if you'd ever seen Adrien or Lucian, you'd get the whole picture.*

You really look up to your brothers, don't you?

I do. I think, well, they're my heroes. There's no one like them, and I wouldn't be alive today if they hadn't gotten me out of Daniel's compound all those centuries ago. I owe them everything. No, I honestly think this latest power increase is about you.

Shayna didn't respond. She disagreed with him on an essential level, but she doubted he'd ever believe her. She already knew that whatever bad thing he'd done in the past was keeping him from seeing himself clearly. Maybe feeding from her had triggered a new power, but the rest was all Marius.

And she was feeling too much for him. Dammit, there was just so much to like about the vampire. She knew he had issues, but she loved that he was so loyal to his brothers, that he treated those around him so respectfully, and that he would sacrifice himself without a second thought for the world he loved.

And just like that, a new vision opened up, again with annoying wavy lines. Daniel once more, but his eyes were open now and even though it had been just a couple of minutes, he looked better. The bastard was healing fast, just as Marius had said he would.

Quill was there again, with Lev standing in the shadows of his brother's stronger personality. Quill's complexion had turned ruddy. "You should have killed Marius when you had the chance, Father. Why didn't you? You could've taken them both out and, as a result, he almost killed you. When will you figure it out that Marius is your real enemy, not the hope for the future you believe him to be."

Daniel shifted slightly on his couch to face Quill. "I find your incessant jealousy unbecoming."

"You owe me, Father, not that traitor."

"But he will fulfill a need of mine that you can't. He's the one that . . ." He said something more, but the presence of the lines occasionally marred the audible portion as well. When Shayna could hear him again, he was saying, "Have you chosen the next location? Let me look at the list of places again."

As usual, the vision faded in and out so that she could only catch glimpses. Something was in the background, that same sense of a vast space, perhaps a cavern as large as a skyscraper, but she just couldn't tell. Maybe it was night somewhere and Daniel was on a chaise longue outside.

She couldn't hear the men speak, but she saw them and watched their lips move. By this time, the waves were making her nauseous.

When the image sharpened once more, Daniel handed the list back to Quill. "Fine, then check out the Costa Rica cave and if for whatever reason Marius should show up, don't kill him—and that's an order. You're to try to bring him back here. Use whatever means you can. We need him. If he ever discovers . . ." But the remainder of his words faded with the lines.

The vision dissipated, in part because she really couldn't take the waves a second longer.

She shared the information with Marius.

Where in Costa Rica? Did either say?

Nope.

All right, Shayna, see what you can do. Try focusing on the weapon this time and on Costa Rica.

As Marius veered southwest, she felt his whole body wind up again in anticipation of finding something significant in Costa Rica. He sped up at the same time.

There's just one thing, Marius.

What's that?

She brought up her issue with the wavy lines, concerned that she was missing out on vital information.

Marius squeezed her waist. *Try not to worry about that right now. Just do your best. Let's find out what's in Costa Rica. And if we discover that the imperfect visions are a problem, we'll address that next. How does that sound?*

It sounds good. I'm just really worried about what I'm missing.

I'm getting that, Shayna. And I appreciate you going the distance with me right now.

She turned her attention to the new location and took a deep breath, trying to quiet her mind. Of course it didn't help that she felt Marius's excitement, his warrior readiness to engage in battle again. She knew he would be happy to take on Quill and Lev, who were clearly Daniel's minions in this final hunt for the last extinction weapon.

Still, she settled her mind and focused instead on the weapon, the one element in this situation that could bring complete victory for Daniel. She centered her thoughts on the square red component that Quill and Lev had removed from the Swedish cave.

She sensed that the recovered portion had already been taken to the Dark Cave system, something she relayed to Marius.

She continued to hold the image of the red roof in her mind, then let her tracking ability fill the rest in. She could see a different component this time, one with a smooth black surface, maybe enameled, but the same square shape and size.

When the image faded in and out once more because of the waves, she turned her focus to Quill, because she felt certain he was the key in this situation.

Once she did that, his serious, hostile face came into view and sure enough, he'd just arrived in Costa Rica. She could feel it with every cell of her body. The location locked into place.

I've got it.

That's fantastic. Let me have it.

She siphoned an additional burst of Marius's power, which gave her a flush all over her body, then sent the image to him through the same telepathic means.

These waves are hellish. I don't know how you stand them.

Shayna admitted to feeling the need to hurl a couple of times.

But you're not flight-sick?

Flying with you has become a dream.

Good. Okay, I'm locked on target and we'll be there in no time.

With a destination in hand, Shayna asked, *So what do you know about the caverns in Costa Rica?*

It's not a large system, but it holds over three hundred families.

What do you mean, families? Are you referring to procreation?

He laughed out loud. *Anyone else would have said children.*

She sighed, well aware of her foibles. *Yes. Children. Right. Do many vampires have children?*

At some point in our long lives, we hope to have children. But conception is rare and sometimes takes centuries. We have slow movers.

You're referring to sperm motility.

Again, he laughed.

Was that funny?

You're funny, you just don't know it. But yes, we have lazy swimmers, for which your earth population should be immensely grateful.

I see your point. You would have taken over our world by now.

I have no doubt of it. We have a population of only a few million, but look how close Daniel is to taking over both our worlds.

Shayna sighed. *Speaking of Daniel, I'm a little uneasy about Quill. Daniel told him not to harm you, but I know Quill wants you dead. Apparently you pose some kind of threat to his own position in Daniel's hoped-for empire.*

I don't see how. I'll never serve Daniel.

I know that, but it seems to me Daniel still holds out hope that he can find a way to turn you.

He won't, Marius said.

I have no doubt of that. Just be careful, that's all I'm saying. Daniel may have ordered him not to harm you, but I got the sense Quill has other ideas.

Marius squeezed her waist yet again. *Warning duly received. Now look out on the horizon. Land.*

I see it. The Yucatán Peninsula came into view, forming a recognizable horn that separated the Gulf waters from the Caribbean.

Now it was Shayna's turn for her own adrenaline to hit her veins and her heart started racing. While they were in flight, they were safe, but close to Quill, who knew what might happen. And the weapon was there. She could feel it now, as well as Marius's powerful intent to do everything he could to get hold of it.

Marius set his trajectory for Costa Rica and a minute later started a sharp descent.

As he penetrated the jungle landscape, Shayna had to close her eyes once more. The trees then the cavern system created the feathery feeling again, then nothing as Marius reached their destination point within this latest cave.

Shayna was taken aback by the unimproved state of the cavern, which was riddled with the usual dripstones.

Marius hovered in altered flight, five feet above the ground. Shayna sensed he'd take off in a heartbeat if he had to.

But only Quill, Lev, and what looked like the black base to the weapon awaited them. A small, faded blue canvas bag sat against the wall not far from the weapon.

Yet the lack of a security force alarmed Shayna, though she didn't know why. Something about the whole situation felt wrong. Why would Quill and Lev come here without a team of well-trained fighters to protect them, especially after having seen what Marius was capable of?

As Marius slowly lowered to the ground, his voice shot through her head. *I won't turn away from this battle, Shayna, so I want you to step off my boot then disappear like you did before.*

She didn't need to be told twice. As soon as he released her, and her own fur-lined boots hit the cavern floor, she pulled back into her safe, invisible place. Like before, as she siphoned Marius's power, she levitated toward the ceiling of the cave, though slower this time. She didn't need to deal with another goose egg on top of her head.

Marius stared at Quill, his oldest half brother. Lev, as the weaker of the two, Marius ignored.

All five brothers had had different mothers, each of them killed by Daniel when her son reached the age of four. The pain of losing his mother still lived in Marius and always would. He remembered her, and her love, the primary reasons he would never succumb to Daniel's persuasions. Marius's mother had taught him well during those early years, talking to him often, teaching him, and advising him.

When the torture had started, the primary reason he'd

survived without completely losing either his mind or his soul was because of the strength his mother had built into his character. Why Quill and Lev had chosen to align with Daniel, Marius would never know.

But Quill's choices had made him a murderer, rapist, and slaver, which meant that Marius would not feel any kind of remorse if he ended Quill's life right now. And Lev was cut from the same cloth.

Shayna's voice pierced his mind. *Marius, I'm uneasy about this setup. Something doesn't feel right to me.*

I know, I'm feeling it, too. But if Quill wants a battle, I'm ready.

She said nothing more, made no protest on behalf of her own safety, though he could feel her anxiety. At least he knew she was out of harm's way for now.

Off to the side, Lev stood with his arms crossed and a smug expression on his face as he guarded what looked like the base part of the weapon.

The Costa Rican system was known for built-up and, therefore, potentially lethal stalagmites and stalactites.

But he'd battled in all sorts of environments over the centuries and would be happy to take Quill on in this rugged setting.

"Well, brother," Quill said, pulling a dagger from the placket on his right thigh. "I've waited for this moment a long time. Don't forget, though, that I'm an Ancestral, which you are not, and I really don't plan to break a sweat despite how fast you moved in Sweden."

As with Daniel in the earlier encounter, Marius didn't wait to exchange a few useless words. With a dagger in hand, he launched.

For a split second Quill looked surprised; then he smiled. Marius struck home as he passed by Quill, then flew quickly through the maze of dripstones. When he turned, ready to battle Quill again, he saw his half brother staring down at the wound on his arm that Marius had inflicted. Like Daniel, he looked thunderstruck.

Quill then levitated, lifting his head and meeting Marius's gaze straight on.

Marius flew around a stalactite; Quill moved behind one.

Marius watched him, his vision growing acute. Quill charged at lightning speed.

Marius started moving faster, darting past the sharp downward growths, throwing himself out of reach of Quill's dagger. But Quill's Ancestral ability made him equally fast.

Marius's mind reached for a strategy and as Quill shot past him with his dagger stretched in his direction, Marius dipped, rolled, then struck with blinding speed.

His dagger connected for the second time and Quill shouted his pain, followed by another long cry of pure rage.

Quill faced Marius once more, flying in and out of the stalagmites, his nostrils flaring as he turned his dagger over and over in his hands. He now bled from his stomach and his arm, but neither wound was serious enough to stop the battle.

"So why have you gained so much speed, brother? I can feel that you're not an Ancestral. Is it Shayna? Daniel says she's special and he wants her. And you know Dad, he always gets what he wants." Quill moved slowly, watching, calculating. He matched Marius in size and muscle mass.

Marius understood Quill's ploy. While he chatted, he was also self-healing, giving himself time.

Quill suddenly shifted to altered flight and disappeared from Marius's view. Shayna's voice shot through his mind. *Quill is behind you, strike now!*

He didn't question Shayna, but moved in a lightning whirl and caught skin, muscle, and bone.

Quill dropped out of altered flight and rolled off the fat end of a stalagmite, falling into a pool of water. His ribs were exposed, his body writhing.

Lev's behind you now.

Marius once more turned and swept his arm in an arc, but Lev leaped back and his blade struck only air. Lev lifted both his hands, the universal form of surrender. "Give me Quill and you can take the weapon."

Marius thought it a perfect trade and nodded.

But the smile on Lev's face told a different story.

Quill vanished first. Lev swept in a quick flight to the black base of the weapon, took hold of it easily in one hand, then shifted to altered flight. He disappeared instantly as well.

What the fuck?

Marius glanced at the remaining faded bag. He knew exactly what it was and that Quill had definitely disobeyed his father.

Oh, shit.

Shayna, appear now. This is a trap. We have a split second to survive this.

The moment she showed herself, he shifted to altered flight, and like a rocket aimed for her, grabbed her, and flew them both straight through the rock, the jungle, and up into the air. He held Shayna close, pulling her arms and legs in tight to his body, shielding her as best he could because, at the same time, the bag that was a bomb exploded behind them.

A blast like this was one of the few things that could cause a problem in altered flight.

The force of the blast propelled them farther. He took shrapnel in his lower legs and buttocks. He rose higher and higher, wrapping a disguise around himself and Shayna, then headed east in the direction of Italy.

There was only one problem: He couldn't feel his legs.

Shayna, are you okay?

Yes, but something's not right with you. You're flying funny.

Just hang on. I've been hit. Let me contact Rumy.

Marius switched telepathic frequencies, focusing on Rumy.

But when Rumy opened to him, Marius couldn't get his SOS out because Rumy said, *Marius, we're in deep shit here.*

Great, because I think I took something in the spine, I'm losing altitude, and I need help, Rumy. I'm in altered flight heading east across the Caribbean. But what's going on there?

Daniel's got his men posted outside The Erotic Passage. He's waiting for you.

Marius's head swam, but he forced himself to concentrate and to keep flying. His speed faltered and by his best calculation he was at least fifteen minutes out. The blast had hurt him badly.

Rumy, you've got to intercept me. I'm too far from my home in Chile and I can't make it to Lake Como. I'll try to get us into one of the islands.

Can you head to Cuba?

Cuba, right. Excellent caves. He shifted course.

I'm on my way now. I'll bring help. Rumy disconnected.

Marius felt Shayna's hand on his face. *Hang tough, Marius. I know you're hurt. Would my blood help?*

Shit, yes. He grabbed her arm and without thinking or giving her a warning, he bit hard and began to drink.

He felt her whole body jerk in his arms; he'd just caused her a boatload of pain. *I'm sorry.*

It's okay. I'm fine now. Drink.

He realized that he'd lost a lot of blood and as he drank he feared he was losing even more because he couldn't heal what he couldn't either see or sense.

Shayna, I've got something lodged in my spine that's preventing me from feeling my legs. I need you to remove it. I've got hold of your arm, but do you trust me enough to release my neck in order to pull away from me and see what's going on back there?

He felt the depth of her fear at letting go of him, and once again his guilt rose like a wave. He hated that he was asking so much of her, but it couldn't be helped. *You can do this.*

I'm so damn scared, but I'll try.

It'll be okay, just let go of my neck in easy stages. Can you do that? Then you can feel how much I have hold of you. And your blood is helping, it really is.

He felt her begin to relax her arm and to let it glide over his shoulders, but their momentum caused that same arm to fly back and she slipped off his booted foot.

As promised, he had hold of her, but his weakness caused him to tumble midair. He closed his eyes and worked at righting himself. He could hear her screaming, but he never lost the grip on her arm. Slowly and carefully, he pulled her toward him as he made the adjustments. When he was in a vertical line to the earth, he opened his eyes and reset his course to Cuba.

He held her close. She was crying in her fright and panting hard as she tightened her hold on him.

He sensed that he needed more of her blood, a lot more, which told him one of his wounds was mortal in nature. If he didn't get feeling back in his lower limbs, he wouldn't be able to heal it.

First things first. *Shayna, can you hear me? I've got to get feeling back in my legs. I'm bleeding badly now.*

Yes, just give me a sec to calm down. She trembled in his arms.

But after a long, difficult minute, she slowly released his neck and once more began moving her left arm around his back, inching across.

I think whatever it is, it's lower down your spine.

He felt her hand, then nothing.

I've got it. It's a dagger. Lev must have done this on his way out. Marius, can you heal from a spinal injury?

Yes, but there's something else I have to know. I've been losing too much blood. The explosion might have done something even worse to me. I need to know if my legs are still there?

Marius!

Please look. I've got to know what I'm working with here.

Shayna crawled up his body to look over his shoulder, and kept crawling until she was bent over him. *Rock us back and forth. If your legs are there, I should be able to see them from the momentum.*

Marius slowed down and, while still moving toward Cuba, he started the rocking motion.

I'm not seeing anything yet, rock more. That's it. Two

more rocks, then she called out. "Marius, I can see them."
She switched back to telepathy. *Your legs are intact, but
blood is trailing into the air.*

*Okay, next I need you to get the knife out of me. I can
only stop the bleeding if I can feel the source.*

*But you'll be in an enormous amount of pain. The ex-
plosion pitted your legs. Your boots are half gone.*

Marius took three deep breaths. *I'll be okay. Just pull
out the blade.*

He felt her calm herself and finally said, *Okay, I've
got the handle. Ready?*

Do it.

She told him what she was doing, step by step, until
the blade was free.

He felt the result in increments as he sent his self-
healing well into his spinal cord and second by second
sealed up the wound. But the moment he restored the
nerves, it was like a fire pouring into his lower extremities. He shouted a string of profanity, long and loud.

Shayna clung to him then pressed her wrist up to his
face once more.

Again, he hurt her with a second desperate strike of
his fangs, once more sucking hard. But each swallow
eased him and powered him. Quill was right: Shayna was
special.

Despite her blood, however, he now shook all over
from the hit his body had taken and he kept losing altitude. At least the healing had started.

The next moment, however, he saw two vampires in
flight, both big men—and they didn't belong to Rumy.
Shayna, we're in trouble. Incoming.

She shifted, an arm around his neck. Without thinking,

she threw the blade she had in her hand, the one she'd taken out of his back, with surprising expertise. Immediately one of the men had a dagger in his neck and fell from the sky clutching at the blade.

The other reached Marius at almost the same time, but then suddenly he stopped midair, looking around. At first, Marius didn't know what had happened until he realized that Shayna had made them both invisible.

He breathed a sigh of relief and kept flying. *Can you hold us in this invisible state?*

For a little while. That was close.

You saved us. But Shayna, have you ever thrown a dagger before?

No, but I've watched you and I think the chains did something. I just sort of knew how to throw. How strange is that?

You're amazing was the only thing he could think to say. His mind had started winking out, but he took her arm once more and continued to drink from her while he worked at healing his body and at trying to support their altitude.

More than once Daniel's men showed up, apparently following their trajectory, so he chose to drop them another forty feet. After that, he saw no more of the enemy.

He contacted Rumy again just as Cuba came into view. *I'll be putting us down inside the system, one of the undeveloped back ends. But Shayna has us invisible and I want to keep it that way.* He told Rumy about his injuries.

I'm bringing in a healer. We're five minutes away from your position.

Okay. Heading into the cavern now. And my mind is going.

I understand.

He flew slowly, while still taking Shayna's blood. She'd grown very quiet, and the chain at his neck lay silent.

He'd put her through a lot.

He stopped drinking as he penetrated an uninhabited cavern. "Shayna, you can make us visible now."

"K." She was hardly audible, but when she released her power, he could feel the difference between the two states.

Rumy, where are you?

Almost there. I've got a bead on you.

Good, because I'm seeing spots. He lay down on a patch of hard rock that was relatively flat and dry. He was in so much pain, he couldn't think, but he held Shayna in his arms. She'd grown limp and something about that bothered him, but he couldn't put enough thoughts together to know why.

A few seconds later Rumy stared down at him, but he wasn't smiling. Instead he peeled Shayna away from him and spoke over his shoulder. "Shit, he drank too much. She'll need a transfusion right away."

Marius saw a couple of med techs, but he couldn't make sense of what Rumy had said. He tried to say something, but Rumy put a hand on his shoulder. "Just lie quiet. We'll take care of both of you. I'm taking you to my villa. You'll be safe there."

No one had ever seen Rumy's villa, so that had to be impossible, which meant Marius was hallucinating.

The healer put her hand on Marius's forehead and a

wonderful sensation of peace flowed through him. He felt more hands lift him up. The next thing he knew he was on his back, on a stretcher, and moving in altered flight.

A wall of blackness descended, then nothing.

CHAPTER 9

Shayna had no idea where she was when she woke up. She lay in a bed, wearing a light-blue cotton gown she'd never seen before. But whose bed? And she had an IV attached to her arm that ran red. A transfusion?

She stared up at a beautiful ceiling made up of purple crystals. The room had three regular, Seattle-type walls, and only one of carved rock. This had to be a house built inside a large cavern, yet it still had a partially human feel.

She released a deep breath because the squared-up walls reminded her of her Seattle apartment. It felt so human that for the first time in the past two days, she almost felt at home.

The linens had a fresh smell as though they'd hung out on a line and dried in the air and the sunshine. So where was she? Heaven maybe.

Her last thought had been that she'd needed to warn Marius to stop taking her blood. While he'd been drinking from her in flight, she'd started feeling light-headed and dizzy. But he'd been half out of his mind with pain and his own blood loss. If he fell from the sky, they'd both be dead.

She also recalled having a serious doubt that he'd be able to make it to Cuba, then landing in a cave. He'd asked her to make them visible, but that was the last thing she could recall before she passed out.

Now she was here, but she had no idea where "here" was.

She lifted her arm, and the tubing that carried replacement blood into her body. So was this a medical facility? And whose blood was this? A vampire's?

The dizziness returned accompanied by a boatload of fatigue. Marius wasn't nearby—that much she could sense. She quickly reached for her blood-chain and breathed a huge sigh of relief when she found it intact. The bond held.

She tried to go back to sleep but couldn't. She was too worried about Marius. Was he okay? Had he survived his injury?

She reached out for him. *Marius?*

Shayna. Good. You're okay. I'm here. They're working on my legs.

How long have we been here?

A few hours.

And exactly where are we?

Rumy's villa in the Como system, very private and

*more secure than any other place on earth. Daniel can't
get to us here.*

Thank God.

I'm going to send someone to you.

Okay.

She honestly couldn't manage more than that. A few
minutes later, a woman showed up with a tray of food.
She wore a woven gown of some kind and her dark-brown
hair was drawn back in a twist. "Are you hungry?" She
smiled when she asked.

Shayna put a hand to her stomach. "Starved." She
didn't wait to be told but scooted up in bed, propping
pillows behind her.

"I am always hungry after I've donated to a vampire."
She settled the tray over Shayna's lap.

"You're human?" Shayna was shocked.

"I'm a refugee out of the slave trade here in the vampire world. I'm originally from San Francisco, and yes,
very human." She glanced down at the tray. "But have
some of this soup. It's homemade with organic vegeta-
bles and you will feel a hundred percent better once you've
eaten. I promise you."

Shayna had so many questions, but that wasn't exactly
new. She lifted the spoon and dipped into what proved
to be a thickened broth with beans and bits of ham, car-
rots, and celery. Her stomach growled, telling her to get
on with it, the faster the better.

The first spoonful was like heaven, and she felt as
though she hadn't eaten for weeks instead of just a few
hours. She had to work to calm the panic she felt.

When she'd settled down, she glanced up at the woman.
"What's your name?"

"Yvonne and you're Shayna. I've been told that you're

in a grad program in anthropology and that you might have a few questions for me."

Shayna's brows rose as she took another spoonful of soup. Apparently, Yvonne had been warned. She smiled as she responded, "Only about a hundred."

When Yvonne chuckled and said "Fire away," Shayna knew she'd found a friend.

Marius hurt, especially in his lower extremities. Hours later and despite his own healing efforts and a team of specialists, he was still in pain.

Rumy had finally brought in a surgeon since the bomb that had exploded had planted shrapnel everywhere. Fortunately his trajectory and the way he'd held Shayna cradled in his arms had spared his upper torso as well as her body from injury.

But even his ass hurt.

Rumy stood nearby in an expensive black silk shirt, arms crossed over his chest. He grinned at Marius.

"What are you smiling about?"

"You're alive, dammit, and you shouldn't be."

"Fuck off. I'm in pain."

Rumy made a sad face. "Oh, poor powerful Marius."

He didn't exactly want sympathy, but Rumy was pissing him off.

The surgeon snapped on his gloves. "Roll onto your stomach and let's get this shit out of you."

At that, his lips curved. Though it hurt like hell, he did as he was told.

He spent the next hour trying not to wince, especially since a few bits were big and had gone in deep.

*   *   *

The human, Yvonne, had talked steadily with Shayna for hours. She'd long since finished her soup, but she'd heard enough to confirm yet again that she'd done the right thing in staying with Marius.

Yvonne had escaped from the Dark Cave system after eighteen months of sex slavery. Shortly afterward, Rumy had taken her in. She'd lived in the villa, deep in the Como cavern system, for over thirty years. But she didn't look like she'd aged, which begged yet another question that Shayna needed to ask, unless the answer surfaced by itself. The woman appeared to be so peaceful.

"It took years to recover from what I went through in Daniel's system, but now I have my children, three of them, and a vampire husband I'd never leave. He's one of Rumy's security detail here in the villa."

Ah, that explained it. Yvonne was bonded to a vampire, and apparently that kind of proximity had an anti-aging effect on humans. Very interesting.

According to Yvonne, over two hundred people lived near the villa in what had grown to be a small village. The community had a central store and a park, and a school for all the kids—of which there were fifty now, of various ages. And all because Rumy had taken former slaves into the villa for rehabilitation. Many refugees had passed through, but a large number had fallen in love with different members of Rumy's security outfit and made homes here.

Shayna thought the whole thing so fascinating that she wished she could spend a solid year doing fieldwork in the village. How much she would learn!

Yvonne had been near death when she'd arrived. "I was one of the few lucky ones. I would have been dead in a couple more days. I couldn't keep anything down and our handlers loved to torture us repeatedly at that point, when we were of no use servicing the clientele. We'd then be used in betting pools to see how long we'd last. Bets would be placed up to the minute and various tortures were performed as part of the process. I'd just entered that horrible phase when one of the vampire guards snuck me out. I don't know how he did it, but now I'm here, and we're married."

"So was he working undercover for Rumy, then, that the guard-now-your-husband actually took the risk to get you out?"

"Exactly. Rumy had him there to keep tabs on Daniel and his operation. But that was the last run he made. Rumy pulled him out for good after that, feeling it would be too much of a risk for him to return." Her eyes twinkled as she smiled. "But I think the truth goes deeper. Rumy knew the guard loved me, so for his sake and mine, he brought the guard here to serve on the villa security team. Rumy is a gem if you haven't figured it out by now."

"He's amazing. And funny."

Yvonne chuckled. "He is that. And short. And he has that adorable lisp because of his fangs."

"Why are his fangs like that?"

Yvonne rolled her eyes, then lowered her voice. "Don't tell anyone, but he used vampire Viagra when it first came out. Overused, I should say. And he didn't pay heed to the label warnings. Now he can't retract his fangs."

Shayna started to laugh and for a long time couldn't stop. Yvonne laughed with her.

When Shayna finally settled down, she marveled at Yvonne's fortitude and that she could speak of what had happened to her so easily. But no doubt that ease had come with time.

She touched her blood-chain, aware that Marius was still in a lot of pain. "Can you go find out what's going on with Marius? I don't understand why he's not healed up yet and I know that if I ask, he won't give me details."

"Men," Yvonne responded, but smiling at the same time. "I'll be happy to find out what's going on."

Because Shayna had finished her soup, Yvonne took the tray away, promising to return as soon as she had word about Marius.

Shayna sipped a glass of water and kept sipping. Yvonne had encouraged her to drink a lot right now. Vampires released a serum when they tapped into a vein that replenished the blood supply quickly, but liquids really speeded up the process.

So she sipped, wondering if she'd need to donate again given all that Marius had been through.

Now that she'd eaten, had her transfusion, and was hydrating, her usual energy and accompanying restlessness returned. She wanted to be up and doing, to see Marius for herself, and to have a look at the vampire–human hybrid village.

Her heart pounded at the thought that she would be able to observe the combining of two cultures, brought together, as so many were, through an act of violence. She knew from her studies that war and the accompanying rape of women frequently produced offspring who then impacted how both cultures moved forward.

She really wanted a chance to speak to more women, like Yvonne, who had fallen in love with and married vampires. If her own heart beat a little stronger because of these thoughts, she tried to ignore what simmered in the back of her mind. Even so, the thought formed itself for the first time, shaking her to her trembling knees: Could she have a life with Marius?

She had to be out of her mind to even be thinking such a thought, yet there it was, staring her in the face. She had to admit at least this much to herself: that beyond feeling an enormous attraction to the man, she also respected and valued him.

She smiled at the ridiculous thought of making vampire babies with him. Yet Marius's mother had been human, and even Yvonne had three children.

She leaned back against her pillows and closed her eyes. These thoughts were too hard and too impossible to even consider. She forced herself to recall all her excellent plans, her love of anthropology, and her desire to teach others what she knew about a subject she loved.

Having ordered her thoughts, she turned her attention to the one thing that could get her back home to Seattle more swiftly, before her affections became firmly attached: She had to get the remaining part of the extinction weapon. As far as she could tell, Quill and Lev had just secured the top and the base to the final weapon.

Yet she felt uneasy. The wavy lines that dogged her visions had left out important aspects about both Sweden and Costa Rica. She was sure of it. In fact, she'd begun to suspect that both trips had been a ruse, or at least a lure. Daniel knew Shayna was with Marius and that she had tracking abilities. He would have known she'd be on the trail of the weapon.

When she thought back to what Daniel had wanted Quill to do in Costa Rica, to try yet again to persuade Marius to join their world-domination efforts, somehow she knew that Daniel already had the weapon. In fact, she was sure of it. Yet she also knew that the wavy lines had marred her ability to get the whole picture, and before she offered up any more vision-type information to Marius, she needed to get rid of those lines. She strongly suspected that she would have known about the bomb if she'd had full access to the last vision.

When Yvonne returned and reported that Marius had just finished having the last of the shrapnel removed, and that he'd had the work done without anesthesia, Shayna groaned. "I can't even let a dentist touch my mouth without several shots of Novocain."

Yvonne smiled. "These vampires are tough, especially the fighting men."

Shayna considered laying her problem before Yvonne, but the woman was human and showed no real signs of the kinds of strange power that Shayna could access.

She needed to talk to a vampire. Maybe Yvonne would know someone who could help.

Once Yvonne knew what she needed, she nodded wisely. "I know exactly who you should talk to. Let me have a chat with Rumy and see if we can bring her in. She's different, though, and she'll have a bizarre take on things, but she's also incredibly perceptive in a surprising way."

Yvonne was ready to take off, but Shayna called her back. "Listen, I'm going stir-crazy in this bed. I feel fine and I'd love to get up and get dressed, but I don't have any clothes."

"Oh, of course." She crossed to an armoire, a lovely antique, and opened the doors. She gestured to the clothes hanging inside and stacked on shelves. "Rumy stocked it so you're all set. Consider these yours."

Shayna held up her arm still hooked to the IV. "What about this?"

"Let me talk to Rumy. He probably knows what the orders are."

She was only gone a couple of minutes before she returned wearing a smile. She quickly removed the IV. "You're all set and I think Marius is out of surgery as well." She glanced at her watch. "We'll have our main meal in about an hour and we'd love for you both to join us. We eat together as a community once a week so it will be a madhouse potluck, with fifty lively kids running around."

Shayna smiled and something inside her relaxed. "That sounds wonderfully normal."

Yvonne offered her another smile then left, closing the door securely behind her.

Shayna breathed a big sigh of relief. She really needed to be moving. It was one thing when she felt so faint, but now that she was recovered, she had a job to do—and ultimately a life to get back to.

If she and Marcus could find the damn weapon, she'd have plenty of time to finalize her plans for getting to her fieldwork in Malaysia.

As she hunted through all the blouses and tops, all cut way too low, of course, she finally decided she'd have to wear a tank top backward and a second shirt like normal. The rest was typical Rumy fare: black lace thongs, sexy lace bras that would force her breasts up and out, and snug jeans. She ignored the stilettos lined up like aggressive troops going into battle, relieved to find a pair of flats. She'd be comfortable and could hopefully keep the take-me-now factor on low rumble.

She stripped off the cotton nightgown and stepped into a lace thong. The bra was a little snug and her breasts, always on the full side, poured from the cups, as usual.

The closet had a full-length mirror so she couldn't help but look.

She was almost sexy.

She ran a hand down the narrow curve of her waist. Michelson had said her proportions were all wrong, her waist too small, her hips too big, her legs too long.

Shayna, are you all right?

Marius's voice in her head startled her. *I'm fine. I'm getting dressed.*

It's just that you felt angry all of a sudden. I sensed all this renewed energy then a shift that felt like you wanted to hit something. You're sure you're okay?

Something is bothering me, she responded, still looking at herself in the mirror, *but it has nothing to do with you or this situation, just an asshole I'm pissed at right now.*

But not me?

Of course not.

Good. I was worried. Rumy told me you'd needed a transfusion. I'm so sorry.

You couldn't help it, Marius. You were losing blood and trying to keep us both in the air. But you got us safely to Cuba, and Rumy took us the rest of the way. We're on the mend and I'm so glad you're out of the woods. What's the prognosis?

I have healers with me now. I should be good to go in a few minutes, then I'll come to you.

I'll see you then. She felt Marius shut down and thought it was a good thing, at least for now, because she had something important to think through and it had to do with her ex.

She continued to look at herself in the mirror, turning so that she could see her firm ass. She ran three miles a day come rain or shine and had for years. She was fit and, dammit, she looked it.

She looked good.

In fact, she looked hot. Her breasts spilled out of the underwire bra. She shook her head, hearing Michelson's complaints about her basic anatomy. "That lying sonofabitch," she said aloud. "I'd put his head in a meat grinder if I could. Asshole."

"So who are we talkin' about and please dish, because I like your style, my beautiful blond one."

Shayna whirled toward the doorway, startled by the sudden arrival of a woman who had to be over six feet tall.

"Who are you?" The woman was also blond, but with really long hair caught up in a ponytail that still hit her mid-buttocks. She was beautiful, with ice-blue eyes that had an upper slant at the sides—cat's eyes, they'd be called. She wore a ton of makeup, snug leopard-print pants, black, leather flats, and a black silk bustier that left little to the imagination.

The woman was stacked.

"I'm Eve. Didn't Rumy or Yvonne tell you I was coming? Yvonne called and said you need a consultation." Her gaze fell to Shayna's cleavage. "Well, don't you have pretty breasts. I could use you in one of my shows, if you're game." She had a wide mouth and eyes that sparkled.

"One of your shows?" Shayna slid into her jeans and quickly donned the tank top.

"I own and operate a club in The Erotic Passage, all consensual and aboveboard. No slaves, nothing that hurts anybody. You'd be a hit."

Of all the things Shayna had experienced so far, none

had come close to astonishing her as much as meeting the owner of a sex club who dressed the part and didn't mind recruiting humans.

Shayna's lips twisted into a smile. "I like sex well enough, but I'm really not interested in performing on stage."

Eve chuckled. "But we could do the whole anthropologist-meets-vampire thing. My clients would go crazy. Do you wear glasses?"

"A bit cliché, don't you think? And the answer is no I don't, and again, no, not interested."

The funny thing was, Shayna wasn't offended at all by the offer, though her senses told her Eve was only half serious anyway. No wonder Yvonne had spoken of her as not being in the mainstream. So what was it—could Eve help, or did this world lack counselors generally?

"I'm seeing a few questions pass through your eyes. I've been told you like to dissect all kinds of issues."

Shayna shook her head, collecting herself. "Yep, I'm known for my inquisitiveness, but please come in. Yvonne is something special, and she really believed you could help me."

"I hope I can, but if not, then we'll figure out what to do next."

Shayna liked her. She was the kind of woman that lived life full-out, nothing held back, and she doubted she ever apologized for anything. Eve also seemed to have an undercurrent of common sense and kindness about her.

Shayna started to close the armoire door then caught sight of her reflection again. Glancing down, she realized in putting on the tank top she'd forgotten about her original plan to wear it backward. "This will not do."

"What? Marius will love it."

"That's not the problem. All the other men will as well, and that won't fly."

Suddenly Marius appeared in the doorway, scowling as he looked her up and down. "No, it sure as hell won't."

"Ah. The man has arrived." Eve turned toward him. "Rumy said you were in bad shape. How you doin', warrior man?"

"I've been better." He glanced a second time at Shayna, still frowning.

Eve laughed. "Well you look fantastic, like you always do."

Marius turned toward Eve, a different kind of frown forming a trough between his brows. "So what exactly are you doing here?"

Eve explained, which gave Shayna a chance to just look at Marius. He may have been at death's door not long ago, but right now he looked amazing. He must have just showered, because his hair was damp, and Rumy had provided him some clothes. He looked sexy as hell, wearing blue jeans that fit his muscular legs beautifully and a long-sleeved navy T-shirt, open at the neck so that his blood-chain showed.

A small tremor went through her at the sight of the single-chain, and what it meant, how connected they were.

She touched hers and her heart rate sped up.

When he glanced her direction, she could see the question in his eyes, but she just smiled and shook her head. In the back of her mind she knew she needed to flip the T-shirt, yet somehow she wanted him looking at her just like this, with her breasts spilling out.

They'd been through so much recently that she'd forgotten for a moment what this part of her relationship with him was like, the powerful sexual drive toward him that took so little to ignite.

Marius kept glancing in her direction, probably aware of her thoughts because of the chains, though he continued to speak in a quiet voice to Eve. Shayna probably could have followed their conversation, but she was too caught up in looking at Marius to listen or to even want to.

Eve finally turned in her direction. "I'll catch up with you later, during the potluck they've got going on in a few minutes. After dinner, you and I can talk about what's going on. Right now, our favorite man here needs some alone time with you—at least that's what I'm getting." She put both hands on his shoulders and kissed his cheeks, each in turn. Shayna could see just how much Eve respected Marius, something Shayna had witnessed repeatedly now, from every quarter.

She wondered if he had any idea how much he was loved in his world. Somehow she doubted it, and she knew his guilt prevented him from seeing himself clearly.

Shayna waved as Eve slipped past the door, closing it behind her.

Marius didn't move though. "Hey," he said. Once more his gaze drifted over her chest, and she felt his desire spike.

"I should change this shirt," she offered.

"In a minute. But besides the fact that the shirt you're wearing is hot as hell, I just want to look at you, to see that you're safe. That means more to me than anything."

Her heart swelled and for a moment she honestly couldn't breathe. She'd expected him to say a number of things, even to pick up his earlier thread about not wanting her to wear the shirt. What she hadn't thought he'd express was how much he'd been worried about her.

Her feet started moving in his direction and when he headed toward her and opened his arms, she gave a little yelp and ran to him. As she landed hard against his chest and slung her arms around his neck, he caught her up in a full embrace.

"Hot as hell." He'd said that to her. Michelson had expressed nothing but criticisms. Marius was a new world for her in every possible way.

A very pure affection rippled through her, for this man she hardly knew, and she hugged him hard. He responded in kind, holding her fast for a good long minute.

"This feels way too good, Shayna. And I meant what I said, you look fantastic in that shirt."

She couldn't resist. She drew back and let him look at the low-cut top and her breasts pouring over the edge. "Rumy has a very specific idea about the kinds of clothes I should wear around you."

"He's pretty hopeless that way."

He caught her hips and connected low while he looked down at her cleavage. "But I think I *love* this shirt."

She opened her eyes wide. "But you came in and announced I couldn't wear it."

He chuckled, his voice low and husky. "And you know damn well why. As I recall, you shared my opinion."

She smiled. "Yeah, I did. I do. And I have no intention of wearing this in public. But why would Rumy think this was okay to wear in a family setting, around kids?"

"Actually, this is tame by his standards."

She looked down at her breasts. "Well, I'm definitely not used to being on display like this, but Eve said something about using me in her show."

Marius groaned and shook his head. "She owns and operates The Ruby Cave, a very successful BDSM club in The Erotic Passage. I don't recommend that you take her up on her offer." His eyes glimmered with amusement.

She chuckled. "I already turned her down." She thought for a moment, then, while still keeping her hands on his shoulders, she said, "As I recall, you've never been here before, right, to Rumy's villa?"

"That's right. Rumy has kept this place very private. It's probably the most secure location in our world. And he has one helluva security force here as well."

"Well, did you know that Rumy has brought a number of sex slaves here?"

"No, we hadn't gotten that far. I was having way too many pieces of shrapnel removed from my body."

She told him about Yvonne, her marriage and children, and about the local village.

He shook his head in disbelief. "All I was told was that we were having some kind of potluck or something. I thought it was a strange choice of words for what, at the time, I thought would be a meal served to his security team."

"That would sound strange, as in fighting men organizing a potluck."

Marius laughed.

As she stared into his gold-flecked eyes, and drifted her fingers over the tough muscles of his shoulders, she asked, "So, not to change the subject, or anything, but have you seen any of Eve's shows?"

Marius didn't answer right away, but a speculative light entered his eye. She could tell he was weighing his responses and finally opted for, "A few."

"Being careful, I see. Gauging your words."

Marius chuckled. "Trying to."

Shayna couldn't help but laugh. "This is such a different world. I'm used to having my nose in a book and here you are, a vampire warrior in your world, and we're here in Rumy's secret villa with Yvonne and all the other former slaves who live here, and talking about Eve's sex show."

"So how many former slaves are we talking about?"

"Yvonne said they had at least two hundred people living here, fifty of them children."

"Fifty children? Wow. How is that possible?"

She shrugged. "You have to remember that the women are human and probably have brought our quick-procreation genetics to the table." She thought for a moment. "Why did Rumy bring us here? I mean, if he's kept it secret for so long, why now?"

At that, his tension returned, a heavy vibration through the chain at her neck. "When I contacted him after we left Costa Rica, he said that Daniel had The Erotic Passage crawling with his men—otherwise, Rumy would have given us an apartment to use. He just didn't think we'd be safe anywhere else. We're targeted now, both of us."

"What do you mean targeted?"

At that, his expression grew grim. "Daniel has called out a warrant for our arrests. Apparently, I've committed treason and you're a CIA spy sent to expose our world."

At that, Shayna burst out laughing. "Really?" She wrinkled up her nose. "Who's going to believe that? I mean, me? A spy?"

"The truth doesn't matter, only that he's offering a reward for the capture of either of us of two million dollars apiece."

"Wow. Two million. I guess he's serious, but I have to

say I think this smacks of desperation." She smoothed her hands over his shoulders. "He definitely wants us out of the way."

"I think you're right." He then searched her eyes. "Are you sure you're okay?"

"I'm fine. I'm not hurt. I was tired after the flight and I needed to rebuild my blood supply, but they gave me a transfusion and some soup. I'm also siphoning your power again so I feel great."

"That's not what I meant. When I spoke with you earlier, telepathically, you seemed angry about something."

"Oh. That. Yeah, well, I was thinking about my ex and realizing he was a bad man. Until I met you, Marius, I didn't have a decent frame of reference. I've lived on my own a long time and I barely knew my father. The boys I've dated have all been so immature, which was why Michelson fooled me. He seemed all grown up, caring, smart.

"But when I really look back at the way he talked to me and the way his words made me feel, I'm disgusted that I was ever with him or that I ever believed a word of his left-handed compliments or his outright slurs, all meant to be helpful criticisms. Especially when he demeaned my body."

Marius's brows rose. "He found fault with your body? That's not possible."

"All the time. He thought my breasts were too big and my hips too wide. He thought my knees were bony."

"He wasn't just an asshole, the man was blind." He narrowed his gaze. "Or he had a small cock. That could explain a lot."

She bit her lip and felt guilty saying it, but she said it anyway. "Well, there was that."

Marius smiled and finally Shayna released a long-held sigh, something she'd been holding back for months now. "I thought the world of him as a teacher and I wish now I'd had enough wisdom to not get involved with him. He did inspire me to take up anthropology as a profession and I'll always owe him that because I'm built for this kind of work. But he hurt how I viewed myself."

"That's unforgivable."

She shrugged. "What Daniel does is unforgivable. What Michelson did was controlling and self-serving. I'd like to see his ego flogged, but I want Daniel dead and I never thought I'd say that about another person in my entire life."

CHAPTER 10

Marius drifted his gaze over Shayna's face slowly, memorizing each feature so that he could remember her when she left his world and returned to her life in Seattle. His chest ached in a way he'd never experienced, which was one more reason he needed to get this job done, keep the final extinction weapon from falling into Daniel's hands, and get Shayna home.

He was already attached to her. He couldn't deny what he felt anymore, how one out of every two thoughts turned to her, how the whole time the surgeon had worked on him he'd thought of little else but getting back to her.

And he sure as hell couldn't blame the chains. The tradition in his world made it clear that blood-chains could only reflect what already existed, which was why couples who argued a lot, but tried the chains out to see if they would improve the relationship, only ended up arguing more.

He sensed he and Shayna were highly compatible and could probably develop a strong relationship. But on an essential level, they both knew she would have to leave.

The thought, however, made his chest hurt even more.

When he slid his hand behind her neck, she caught his arm. "Marius, what are you thinking about? You feel so sad suddenly, but I have no idea why."

He shook his head. "It's simple. I was just wishing everything was different, in every possible way, that I was human or you weren't, that you didn't have a life to go back to, that I had a different life here. That's all."

Her emotions shifted to match his. "I was thinking just a few minutes ago how much I care about you even though I barely know you. We seem to connect on a level that has surprised me and makes no real sense. The disparity in our cultures is so great that you might as well have been living on the moon. Yet I feel likc I know you, really know you."

He drew back enough to meet her gaze. "Me, too." He leaned into her and slanted a kiss over her lips.

She responded as he expected her to, with a soft moan, a sound he'd come to love. He explored her lips and her mouth, memorizing the feel of her in this way as well. He didn't want to forget anything about her.

She slipped her arms around his neck and leaned into him so that he felt her well-supported breasts pressed against his chest. He held her close and curled his hips into hers, wanting her to feel his arousal.

She responded by writhing against him and uttering another moan.

He deepened the kiss, stroking in and out of her mouth as he pushed his hips into her. He wanted to take her to bed and do it right. He wanted her under him, looking into her eyes as he brought her repeatedly. He wanted to lock his hands with hers, to be completely joined, then he would take her blood.

The thought of it set his heart racing. He gripped her bottom and began working her, pushing against her mound.

Marius, I'm so close and all you're doing is kissing me and holding me.

He drew back, breathing hard. "I wish I could finish this right now, but there'll be a call to dinner any second."

"I know." She searched his eyes. "I want to go to bed with you. I want that so much. I mean, I know we've had sex, but I really want to be with you. Does that make sense?"

"I've thought the same thing, so, yeah, it makes sense. Maybe after dinner?"

She nodded, but he saw the concern in her eyes.

He thought he understood. "You're thinking about the weapon."

"Yeah. It's really been bothering me and at some point soon, I want to talk it over with you. I've had some thoughts about what I think is going on."

A knock sounded on the door right behind Marius. He felt Shayna jump. "Yes?" He wasn't willing to invite anyone in, not until he'd calmed the hell down, and definitely not until she'd changed her shirt.

"Rumy sent me to tell you that we're gathering for the communal meal." He didn't recognize the woman's voice.

"Thank you. We'll be there in a couple of minutes."

"I'll let Rumy know."

He released Shayna and she stepped away from him. "I need to finish getting dressed and brushing out my hair."

As she walked over to the armoire, she took off her shirt then turned it around. He wondered why she felt she needed to wear two shirts, until she put on the second one and saw that it was low-cut as well. He shook his head. Rumy really was hopeless.

A few minutes later, he led her out of the villa and onto what proved to be a front lawn that led to an underground river. Linen-covered tables and chairs, as well as a laden buffet table, sat to the left, as well as the village Shayna had told him about. There had to be dozens of houses about a quarter mile off as well as a park with trees and a large playground.

The front lawn of Rumy's villa stretched all the way to the river's bank. For quite a distance, Rumy had built up the river walk with a low wall to keep the young children safe.

The river itself was fairly broad and had been further improved with a beach area and a shallow pond for swimming.

The cavern itself was massive, larger than any he'd ever seen except one in the Himalayas a couple of centuries ago. Rumy's cavern was easily five hundred feet in height at its tallest point and well over two miles long, maybe even more. But it was the sound of children in the distance, all headed toward the villa, that got to him. So many in one place was nothing short of a miracle in his world, though he was pretty sure that Shayna had it right, that human females had brought their enhanced baby-making abilities into the mix.

"This is like a dream," Shayna said. She slid her hand in his and squeezed, adding another layer of ache to his heart. She looked wonderful, her blond hair parted in the middle, brushed to a shine, and reaching to mid-back. He ignored how young she looked and how young she actually was compared with his four hundred years.

He watched more villagers arrive, adding to the already groaning buffet table, setting down the dishes they'd prepared. He'd lived a warrior's life for such a long time that the sight of traditional home-cooked meals, from all parts of the globe given the range of ethnicities represented, made him long for a different kind of life.

Mostly he ate food on the run at human fast-food restaurants anywhere around the globe, or at any of several excellent restaurants in The Erotic Passage. But he couldn't remember the last time he'd sat down to a family meal.

"I know I had soup just a bit ago, but I'm still really hungry. Can you believe the aromas coming from that table?"

"No, I can't."

The next few minutes were spent greeting Rumy again as well as Eve. Rumy also introduced them to his security team, made up of no less than thirty men, most of whom had married former slaves.

Shayna saw Yvonne, the woman who had served as her nurse, and joined her to meet her family. Eve followed and both Marius and Rumy enjoyed watching Yvonne's husband avoid looking at Eve's ample and well-exposed chest.

Rumy elbowed him. "She's a good person. Shayna, I mean. I take it she saved your ass again by donating."

"Yes, she did." He told Rumy about what had happened in Costa Rica and on the flight to Cuba, which had Rumy whistling. He then eyed Rumy. "You have one helluvan operation here. Was this always your plan? To rescue slaves?"

"Not hardly. It just sort of happened. Yvonne was the first. She belonged to Daniel, a favorite of his, and you can imagine the hell she went through. He made a fortune off her and of course used her himself. One of my men who worked undercover at the Dark Cave system got her out of there, which meant I couldn't send him back. I knew your father would have hunted her to the ends of the earth to bring her under his control, so I took her in. After that, well, I couldn't help them all but if I heard of women who'd escaped, I'd search for them and bring them here. As rare as it was to get out of the Dark Cave system alive, I thought they deserved a shot."

"You've done a good thing."

"Least I could do."

Rumy glanced at the blood-chain at Marius's neck and frowned. "And you're sure you're still connected to Shayna?"

"We are. I know it's seems strange, but we don't have the usual proximity issue, and I can carry her in altered flight without a problem—but no, I can't tell you why. However, I can tell you what she's experiencing moment-to-moment, as clear as a bell, so I know the bond holds."

"Well, this is a real mystery." Rumy rubbed his lower lip, just between his fangs. "But that might explain why, when I told Gabriel what was going on and suggested he have the set of double-chains ready for you, he said it wouldn't be necessary."

Marius was grateful in this situation that Gabriel hadn't pushed the issue, but he wondered what it was Gabriel knew that he didn't.

Rumy's phone rang and he stepped away, only to cover the phone and turn back to Marius. "Something at The Erotic Passage." He grimaced. "One of the club owners. No big deal but I'd better take it."

Marius nodded. He turned his attention back to the potluck. The children had already started going down the buffet table, and mothers hovered nearby to help them fill their plates.

Eve left Yvonne and Shayna, and returned to stand next to him. "Isn't this a surprise? Rumy's commune?"

Marius smiled at her. "Astonishing. And he just told me about Yvonne."

Eve's gaze traveled her direction. "Yeah, she gives me perspective. I've lived an exceptional life. I've always done as I pleased and I've never had to deal with anything like what these women have been through. Daniel needs to be put down."

"Yes. He does. No question."

He waved an arm to encompass the full stretch of river. "Do you know what's funny about this? I always thought Rumy kept a harem of women here to satisfy his every whim. I imagined orgies at his villa. Never kids, families, or potlucks, for God's sake."

"I know. It's extraordinary, but then I've had all these years to get used to it. Of course, that meant I had to pretend I'd never been here, and I really had to keep my trap shut about how great he is. But I've helped as best I could with the transition for these women."

"So you've been coming here for years."

"I have."

He felt Shayna reach for him telepathically. He caught her gaze from across the lawn. *What is it?* he asked.

Would you mind if I sat with Yvonne and her family? Now that you and I don't have a proximity issue, I'd love to get to spend some time with her kids and her husband. I have so many questions.

He couldn't help but smile. He recognized the particular thrill Shayna was experiencing when she knew she had a rare opportunity to explore an aspect of his culture, something she might not get to do again. He wouldn't have denied her for the world.

He nodded. *You do whatever you want.*

She held his gaze for a moment, then nodded. *Thanks.* And with that, without even another glance at him, she turned back to Yvonne. He could tell she'd asked yet another question, this time of the vampire husband.

Marius shifted toward Eve. "She's dining with Yvonne and her family."

"I'm not surprised. You know, I like your woman. I like her a lot."

His woman again.

"Don't start with me, Eve. She can't stay and everything I do from this point forward is to keep Shayna alive so she can go back to the life she has planned for herself."

"Fine." She lifted both hands in surrender. "But you're an idiot to even think of letting her go."

He resisted rolling his eyes. "A few minutes ago, when you were with Yvonne and Shayna, what did she ask you?"

Eve grinned. "Sure you want to know?"

Marius suspected Shayna would have asked about The Erotic Passage, and he was curious. "Absolutely."

Eve leaned close. "She asked me how long my period lasts and when I ovulate and if that helps sales at The Ruby Cave."

If he'd just taken a sip of something to drink, he would have spewed it everywhere. "What?"

"You said you wanted to know. Actually, the moment Yvonne's husband turned away to discipline one of the kids she asked at least five similar questions, all in a row."

Marius laughed and Eve joined him.

Eve eyed him. "You know, you haven't done that in years, not that I can recall—laugh, I mean. She's done that for you."

His amusement gave way to a warmer feeling as his gaze once more drifted in Shayna's direction. "She's unusual, even for a human. She's an academic and she wants to teach."

"She can teach here, in our world."

"I know, but why would I ever deprive her of a normal human life? That would be impossibly selfish."

"But you deserve to be happy, Marius, more than anyone I know. Why shouldn't she be part of your life?"

He didn't respond. He and Eve had argued this subject to death in past years, what she believed he deserved and why he knew she was completely wrong.

She elbowed him. "So how is it with her?"

With his gaze fixed on Shayna as he watched her lift one of Yvonne's children and balance the girl on her hip, he said, "She's great. Very easy to be with. And she has a helluva lot of courage."

Eve made a disgusted sound. "I meant the sex. Jesus, you are an idiot."

He sighed. "We haven't really done it yet."

"Yes, you have. I know you have. I can smell it on you."

"No, I mean we have, but we haven't. Hard to explain and I really shouldn't be discussing this with you anyway."

"You need to throw that woman on her back and give it to her good, that's all."

This time, Marius did roll his eyes. "Let me try to say this in a way you'll understand. The chain-bond ramped things up, but we haven't really been close yet. And maybe it's better that way."

She mocked him in a singsong way. "Because she's going home." She made another disgusted sound with her lips. "You're being really obtuse, Marius. Besides the fact that she smells like a woman falling hard for a big, beautiful bone, she's already enamored of our world. I'll bet you that after a trip to your secret New Zealand home and a swim in that pool you've bragged about more than once, she sticks."

"You're on. And in return, I want you to take a week's vacay from The Ruby Cave."

Eve's eyes went wide. She'd never left The Erotic Passage longer than two days, not in all the decades her club had been open.

Marius pointed an accusing finger at her. "See, you're addicted to your work so much that even the thought of taking a week off leaves you gasping for air."

Eve lifted her chin, but brought the end of her ponytail around and flipped it a few times. "Fine. You're on. But this is one bet I'll win." She let her ponytail drop. "And now, to change the subject. Do you know what she needs help with? Why she wanted someone to talk to besides you, I mean?"

"I don't know except that her visions are really bugging her. I know she wants to do better at it, but I have no idea how to help her."

"Well, after dinner I'll have a talk with her. Maybe I can gain some insight."

After the communal meal, Shayna walked with Marius and Eve back to the villa. The structure was made of cream-colored, unpolished marble, a really beautiful look, but different from the ones down by the river. The village homes had the look of the surrounding stone, but the villa was all Rumy, a reflection of his love of all things Italian.

Rumy had returned to The Erotic Passage with the hope that he could eventually report back on Daniel's movements.

The villa structure included a large inviting foyer and a curved staircase leading to a second story. The front of the villa faced the river.

As Shayna walked up the steps, she turned back and saw that on the other side of the river, Rumy had planted a whole bunch of trees. "How does everything grow so well underground, without sunlight?" The commune had an enormous vegetable garden as well that served the entire community.

"A special system of grow-lights," Eve responded. "I've seen them and they're amazing. The whole community is asleep during the hours the lights are on, otherwise it would be intolerable for vampires."

Shayna waved a hand. "But this level of light is acceptable to you?" She glanced at Eve.

"Sure. We can adjust to most artificial light really well, but the ones used for growing plants are industrial-strength and mimic sunlight, which we can't handle except during altered flight."

"Absolutely fascinating."

She turned toward Marius and Eve and saw that they were watching her, both smiling in an indulgent way. "I've been asking too many questions again, haven't I?"

"Not at all."

"No, I've been insufferable. Admit it."

Marius slid his arm around her waist. "You're being yourself."

She held his gaze. "Tedious, would you say?"

He shook his head.

She winced. "Aggravating?"

"You do realize you're asking questions about how annoying the asking-of-your-questions has become?"

She groaned. "I'm ridiculous, but I really am fascinated."

Eve murmured. "I'm going to win that bet. I just know it."

"What bet?"

Marius glared at Eve, who in turn laughed. The vampires had something private going on between them and though her usual curiosity had her dying to know why, Shayna held back the probing questions that sprang to her lips.

Eve cocked her head and caught Shayna's gaze. "Ready to talk?"

"I am."

"Do you want Marius with us, or not?"

Shayna glanced at him and weighed the situation. "Actually, I think he should be with us. I mean, my problem, whatever its source, affects him as well since this is about my visions, or rather, my impaired visions. Although, I have to say I'm not sure you can help with that."

"If not, I'm sure I'll be able to send you to someone who can."

She led them into the villa, to the sitting room off to the right. A large picture window had a view of the grove across the river. "Well, let's all sit down, you tell me what's going on, then I can best answer you one way or the other."

When Shayna sat down on the couch across from the window, she glanced up at Marius and patted the seat beside her. When he sat down, he took her hand and gave it a squeeze. He really was the sweetest guy, especially for someone who looked as fierce as he did.

"You can tell Eve anything. She's good people."

Shayna smiled. "I know."

Eve sat opposite, in a club chair off to the left that angled toward the couch.

Shayna decided to just launch in and offered up a sampling of the visions, her thoughts surrounding those moments, and how the wavy lines had blocked what she could see from moment to moment. "The thing is, I don't think it's about power, since I'm streaming Marius's all the time and the flow is amazing." She put a hand to her chest. "I mean, really amazing. So I honestly think this has to be about me, that I'm doing something wrong."

Eve held Shayna's gaze. "You mentioned that during one of these visions, you'd started thinking about your professor, the man you had an affair with. What was your relationship with him like, and was it a recent breakup?"

"Not real recent. A year ago." She then found herself unburdening her soul with all sorts of details about Michelson, his demeaning way of offering criticism, his complaints about her body, her work ethic, that she didn't have a tidy desk.

"And what was the sex like?"

Shayna turned toward Marius and met his gaze. She felt really uncomfortable discussing this in front of him. He'd grown tense as well, and she felt a certain amount of hostility emanating from him.

He took a deep breath. "Do you want me to leave?"

Shayna was about to express her gratitude that he understood when Eve immediately intervened. "On no account should Marius leave right now. I think I understand what's going on with you, Shayna. But Marius needs to hear this. All of it. I suspect something happened in the bedroom with Michelson, didn't it, something bad? And if I'm right, trust me, it will affect every area of your life, including these visions."

Shayna had never told anyone the details of her last sexual encounter with Michelson, the straw that ended her relationship with him.

She must have grown really quiet and her distress no doubt thoroughly communicated itself through the chains, because Marius leaned forward to meet her gaze. "Did he hurt you?"

"No, not exactly. No. It was more like neglect, but it was profound. I've just never really talked about it before. Once I ended the relationship, I was done. I mean, I had some counseling, but I didn't talk about this one part."

Eve spoke in a quiet voice. "Take your time and start with whatever comes into your head."

Shayna found her eyes filling with tears. "It was that old saying, *All of a piece*. Michelson was—is—a completely self-absorbed man. I know that now. He might even have sociopath tendencies." She stopped as though her vocal cords had just shriveled and wouldn't let her go any farther.

"You can do this," Eve said, more firmly this time. "And I think you'll find it very healing and probably the release you need to get these visions unblocked. Okay?"

Shayna licked her lips, her mouth suddenly dry. "I fell hard for Michelson. He was a man I admired a lot for his work in the field of anthropology. I knew going in that I was a starstruck student, an absolute cliché, but he was handsome and inspiring and unattached. I wouldn't have dated him if he'd been married, or anything like that.

"The sex was glorious at first, but I honestly think it's because I was so deluded, so infatuated with him. I couldn't get enough of him. So in those early days, I didn't notice how critical he was of me, I think because it began so gradually; how I looked, what I wore, my makeup, my hair, comments about how I studied, that he thought I was messy and disorganized. He'd make suggestions on improving everything but never seemed to be satisfied when I made the changes. I kept waiting for some kind of affirmation that he finally approved of me.

"Then, about three months into the relationship, he brought out a few of his neckties. The first time he bound me to the four posts of his bed was really intoxicating. I mean it turned me on and though he might be critical of me, the sex was great, or so I thought. The first few times were really exciting."

Eve nodded. "It can be a profound experience. Bondage is as much about trust as it is about the thrill. So when did it go wrong?"

Shayna ignored the increasing tension in Marius and took a deep breath. "The first time things started going bad, he left me spread-eagled on the bed, tied up at both wrists and ankles, saying he'd had an inspiration for an article he was writing, but he wanted to write it down immediately and that he'd be right back. I was stupidly exhilarated that I could be a muse for such an important man. And he came back ten minutes later.

"Part of me thought it a little odd, but again I believed in him and he'd already trained me to think much less of myself than I deserved and to keep him on a pedestal. He'd get angry at even the slightest interruption in whatever project he was working on. I'd learned early on not to disturb the waters when he was engaged with his work."

"It got worse each time, didn't it?" Eve asked. "The length of time he'd be gone, that sort of thing?"

"Yes. I tried talking to him about it, but he invoked how important I was as his muse, which of course led to a lot of guilt and fear on my part."

She could feel that Marius's level of tension had now jumped several notches, but she had to see this through.

Eve spoke to Marius. "Dial it down, warrior. Please." To Shayna, she dipped her chin. "Go ahead. Tell me about the last time."

Just thinking about it brought tears flowing down Shayna's cheeks, something she hadn't intended or thought would happen. "I had no pleasure that time, and hadn't had for the last few sessions as far as that goes. I faked it the whole time because of course he'd get mad if I didn't appear to be enjoying sex with him. But I was barely aroused. The truth was, I was afraid of being left tied up again. And by then, he had only one goal, to have his release, which he would insist gave him some kind of inspiration for his work that he had to attend to while I was lying tied up in his bed.

"But this time, when he left me, he was gone for hours. But he didn't go to his desk and work. Not this time. No, he got in his car and left because I heard the car on the gravel drive pull away. I screamed my rage not once but several times as the hours passed. Later, I fell asleep, having worn myself out.

"When he came back, he told me how thrilling it was to know that I was waiting for him. I remember forcing a smile and telling him how glad I was that he'd had a good time because by then I was scared to death."

"You thought he'd hurt you?" Eve asked.

"Yes and no. Truthfully, I was afraid that if I gave vent to the rage and humiliation I felt in that moment, I'd kill him. I'd go into the kitchen, wait till he was asleep, and take a knife to him. I'm not proud of having had those thoughts or feelings, but it was one more reason I knew this would be the last time I was with him.

"I ached from head to foot from having been in the same position for so long. I had bruises on my wrists and ankles from trying to get out of the knots, because he sure knew how to tie them."

"No one heard you screaming?"

"He has a big piece of property outside the city limits. So the answer is no."

"Shayna," Eve said very quietly. "Let me make this clear to you. He isn't just without a conscience, he's a psychopath and I'm sure if you compared notes with some of his previous girlfriends you'd find he'd been practicing this routine for a long time. My guess is each time he lures another young woman in, he pushes the limits to see how far he can go. He'll keep escalating as well until he's done something a lot worse than leaving a woman tied up on his bed while he goes out with some friends."

Shayna finally leaned back against the couch cushions. "I've had those thoughts as well, but dismissed them. I've even thought about going to the police."

Only then, after she'd said it all, did she become fully aware of the state of Marius's emotions.

He rose up from the couch and shouted in a kind of guttural animal way that made her stiffen her arms, pinning them to her sides, preparing for what, she didn't know. But the vampire was in a rage.

Eve rose up as well and went to Marius. She got in his face. "Knock it off. You're not helping. You're scaring her. Look at Shayna, Marius. Look at her."

He shifted his gaze to Shayna and in quick stages, he got his temper under control. "I'm sorry, but I want to kill him for doing that to you. I want to kill him. Do you understand?" His hands were balled into fists.

Shayna jumped up and ran to him. He opened his arms as he'd done before and she fell into them. The floodgates opened and she wept on his chest and he just held her, petting her back. She actually hadn't known until that moment how much Michelson had traumatized her, how much fear she'd had of what he might do to her, what he could have done, how much of a victim she'd become. "I didn't understand. I didn't. I thought I was fine. I just thought I needed to realize he was bad for me. I didn't understand. Who would ever do that to another human being?"

The rage Marius felt went bone-deep. His whole body felt on fire with suppressed anger, feelings from his childhood and now for Shayna's past. He knew exactly what it felt like to be tied down and abandoned. Daniel had once left him shackled, bruised, and cut up on the table for two days, one of the times he'd almost died.

The feeling of impotence left him enraged beyond words. The only difference was that Michelson had somehow drawn the line at not inflicting physical pain beyond the hurt the bindings would cause. He never hit her; therefore, he could justify what he'd done to her.

He met Eve's gaze and saw the speculative look in her eye. She had her arms folded over her chest as though she, too, had to hold herself together by sheer force of will. She'd bought a lot of slaves in the past for the purpose of healing and freeing them.

"I'm so sick of this shit," Eve said, shaking her head back and forth. "I love what I do, but everyone involved participates by choice and no one is hurt or left to suffer like that. I hate what this man did to you." She unfolded her arms throwing them in the air at the same time.

"Me, too," Marius said quietly.

Shayna still wept. "Me, three." She hiccuped, then drew back to look up at him. "I didn't expect to start crying like this."

He wiped her cheeks with his fingers. "And I'm sorry I lost it. I wasn't even the one injured, but I hate that he put you through that. If he walked into this room, I'd pound him into a pulp."

She drew a deep breath. "Right after me. You know, it was one long seduction at first; then he slowly turned into a control freak and wore down my self-esteem just a little bit every day until I actually let myself be treated that way. The first time he abandoned me for the sake of his 'inspiration,' setting his needs well above my own, I should have kicked him in the nuts." She pulled out of his arms and lifted her top shirt to wipe her face.

He could sense she was working hard at calming herself as she turned in Eve's direction. "So what do I do next? I mean, do you think just admitting how blind I was to what I'd actually experienced will help me with the visions?"

Eve paced, a frown between her brows, her ponytail swinging. "I'm trying to figure that out but I do have an idea. Sometimes it helps to relive traumatic events by way of proxy, but change the outcome." She stopped in her tracks and held Marius's gaze. "Shayna should see my next show. With a couple of tweaks it will be perfect, since the submissive is a woman."

Marius shook his head. "Eve. No." He didn't want Shayna exposed to a full-on show like the kind Eve ran in her Ruby Cave club.

But Shayna placed her hand on his arm. "Actually, I think Eve has it right. My gut tells me that I would benefit from it because I'm guessing the woman either breaks free or the man releases her the moment she's ready to be free."

Eve nodded. "He releases her."

"Yes, that's it." She nodded and met Marius's gaze.

Marius could hardly bear the thought of Shayna, with her relatively innocent background, having to watch one of Eve's performances. He thought maybe she didn't understand. "Shayna, these shows are explicit and I do mean explicit. X-rated. Lots of nudity. Nothing is left to the imagination."

"I can feel how concerned you are. But don't you see, this is a big part of your world. The extensive sex-club complex that you, Rumy, and Eve have each described to me as well as Daniel's sex-trafficking operations are two sides of a cultural coin. Not to say that new laws and policing actions aren't needed to protect the unwilling and the innocent. But at some point down this path we're on, it might help me to find a key to taking Daniel down. Don't you see? This is all of a piece. It all works together somehow."

"I want to protect you."

"But that's not your job, Marius, at least not in this circumstance. I definitely value your physical protection in a battle situation, but this is my field—understanding your culture and coming to terms with what my ex did to me. In this case, I don't need you to run interference for me."

He was completely taken aback by her determination. "I'm just feeling so damn guilty because I dumped you into this situation."

She smiled and rubbed his shoulder. "You're right. You do have a responsibility in that. But later, I was the one who agreed to stay, and from that point these are absolutely my choices. So you can stop with the guilt now. Got it?"

Something inside him eased and he nodded. "Got it."

She turned to Eve. "When's the show?"

"In about half an hour and given that Daniel is hunting the pair of you, I'll need to make some special security arrangements. Still, it'll be a risk." She looked them over. "You'll want to change as well. My clientele is fairly high-end and if things go south, you'll want to blend in. In fact, I'm going to take off right now and arrange things but I'll call when everything's set up. Okay?"

Marius nodded, Shayna as well. Eve smiled as she shifted to altered flight and disappeared through the wall of the house.

Marius took hold of Shayna's shoulders and squeezed gently. "And you're sure you want to do this?"

Her gaze flitted around in that processing way of hers. "Absolutely."

"Okay, then, let's get changed."

He put on a pair of tailored slacks, a fresh black T-shirt, and a short, black leather jacket that concealed at least four daggers and two battle chains. Afterward, he paced the foyer, waiting for Shayna.

He was nervous as hell, for more than one reason. He'd admitted to having seen several of Eve's shows, but what he hadn't confessed was how much they'd turned him on. And it wasn't just the sexual component. Maybe because he'd been chained up as a child, some sick part of him also got off on the idea of bondage. He'd been damn aroused when Shayna had mounted him while he'd been in restraints and recovering from blood-madness.

Truth? He'd loved it.

And he'd loved it even more when he'd broken free.

Twenty minutes later, Eve called, letting him know that Rumy's security expert had built up a disguising shield behind which they'd be invisible while they watched the show. Only an Ancestral of Daniel's power would be able to see through that kind of disguise, so Marius had to trust that his father wasn't actually the one hunting for him at The Erotic Passage. Eve also encouraged him to stay for the entire performance of the first couple, which would last about twenty minutes total.

"Let Shayna see the end. That will be the important part for her."

"Okay."

When he hung up, he was jittery and Shayna still hadn't emerged from the bedroom.

When he heard heels clicking on the tile floor, he stopped and turned toward the doorway to the bathroom.

She appeared and he swore his heart stopped.

"Holy shit" left his lips. "You look fantastic." Her long, straight hair was pulled back on one side with a small silver clip.

"Marius, I'm sorry it took so long, but the dresses were all absurd. I chose this one because it had the most fabric."

But he wasn't complaining and he knew one thing for sure: He'd be throwing a whole lot of wood tonight. He moved toward her like he was floating, then he realized he'd actually levitated, a perfect metaphor for exactly how he felt, like everything would rise tonight.

She wore a simple black silk dress, cut low to reveal all that cleavage of hers. And the dress was short with a sheer red insert cut halfway to her hip bone. The inset would give the dress just enough give if he wanted to lift up the fabric and cop a feel.

When he reached her, he did the only male thing he could think of. He pulled her up against him and ground his erection against her abdomen.

She gasped. "Oh, Marius, how are we going to get through the next half hour?"

"I don't know. I could take you to bed right now."

"I'd go with you."

He debated. Despite the work Eve had gone to on their behalf, all he wanted to do was pick Shayna up and throw her on the bed.

And she would have let him. If he hadn't believed her words, her light floral scent, so full of sex, rose all around him perfuming the air. He'd never been so into a woman before.

But plans had been put in place and he needed to set aside his current hunger for what Shayna needed.

He opened his arm wide and Shayna carefully perched on his fine Italian leather shoes with just the balls of her feet. The stilettos she wore could do some serious damage.

As soon as she was situated with her arm around his neck, he made his phone call, one-handed, letting Rumy know they'd arrive in about fifteen seconds given that the villa was part of the same Como system as his extensive club complex. Rumy let him know that he had a number of his security team, in plainclothes, scattered throughout the club in case Daniel and his crew showed up.

When he hung up, Rumy made telepathic contact and guided Marius into the club, to the exact position behind the enhanced disguising shield, one more layer of security.

Once Shayna was standing beside him, he contacted Eve, letting her know they'd arrived.

A moment later the lights dimmed.

Marius hoped to hell that Eve was right about the show and about Shayna. He'd hate for anything to go wrong right now.

CHAPTER 11

Shayna slid her arm around Marius's waist and drew up tight against him. She'd never been to a place like this before. She'd never even watched porn on her computer.

Now here she was in an upscale sex club, holding on to a vampire she had the serious hots for, and ready to watch strangers have sex.

And not just the performers on stage, by the looks of it, since more than one couple nearby was doing some serious fondling. *Sex club* was right.

The room itself was beautiful. The walls reflected the name of the club in crushed red crystals, floor-to-ceiling, setting the entire space in a red glow.

About half the audience sat at tables enjoying drinks;

the rest stood around the perimeter of the room. Most were, as Eve had suggested, well dressed, so that if she and Marius lost the shielding disguise for whatever reason, they'd fit right in. The thing was, she was already aroused and found herself stroking Marius's arm. She was tall anyway, but in the heels she was just a couple of inches shorter than him, which meant she could kiss him easily if she wanted to, and she did.

She almost suggested it, but the music swelled, a pulse of blues that had her whimpering.

"Anything wrong?" His deep voice had a husky resonance.

"Oh . . . nothing."

He chuckled softly, switching to telepathy. *If it's any consolation, I'm in pain and the show hasn't even started.*

Marius, how about a kiss?

He turned into her with a quick grab of lips that became a strong, promising drive of his tongue that had her panting all over again. God, she loved being with this man.

Eve sauntered onto the stage. "Hello, my lovelies. We've planned something special for you tonight. First up, a schoolgirl learns an important lesson."

She put her fingers to her lips, then blew a kiss. She cracked a long black whip at the same time. Her leopard-print outfit had disappeared and she was dressed all in red leather that featured serious cutouts, including both breasts.

Shayna looked at her nipples carefully. She was pretty sure that Eve had used makeup and glitter on them.

She wondered how Marius was handling all this exposed flesh. Glancing up at him, he was staring at the ceiling.

Her turn to laugh.

Two well-endowed men in very snug briefs wheeled a slanted four-poster bed onto the dark stage, a black fitted sheet on the mattress. They both had beautiful, muscular bodies, part of the show.

The female performer entered the stage wearing a fantasy costume: a short white blouse tied just beneath her large breasts and a minuscule red-and-black-plaid skirt that revealed everything, including a dark landing patch.

She wore pigtails and enormous black-rimmed glasses.

Shayna knew without having to be told that this was for her benefit. In any other circumstances, she would have been too raw to have watched the performance. But tonight it felt right, exactly what she needed.

Also, she trusted Eve. The woman had amazing instincts.

The student sat down on the side of the bed, bounced a couple of times on the mattress, and made an O with her lips while turning to smile at the audience.

A smattering of laughter followed.

Two women entered the stage in only black lace thongs and an arc of visible red glitter above each exposed nipple. "The professor wants us to prepare you for your lesson."

"Do whatever you need to do."

They began undressing her and touching her at the same time. Using neckties, they bound her to all four posts, kissing all over her body until the schoolgirl writhed and whimpered.

Once the bound girl was all alone, the scene was all too familiar to Shayna. Except suddenly she knew what she wanted Marius to do to her. And she felt sure Eve would approve.

The thought made her knees weak.

You okay? You're trembling.

Marius?

Yes.

Shayna took a breath, then said, *I want you to do that to me when we return to the villa. Would you be willing?*

He caught her arm in his hand, then suddenly she was in his arms and he was kissing her hard, his tongue pummeling her mouth again. *I want to, but could you handle it? Could you trust me?*

Of course I could trust you, without hesitation. And maybe that's why. I want to know the thrill of it, to have you command me, then take me.

He groaned heavily.

Eve cracked her whip, drawing Shayna's attention back to the stage. Marius released her, but continued to hold her arm in a firm grasp. She felt how aroused he was, just like her.

The professor entered the stage barefoot, wearing what looked like a graduation gown.

"Hello, Professor. I'm ready for my lesson."

Maybe the dialogue left something to be desired, but Eve made up for it as she approached the man from behind and slowly removed his gown, sliding it off broad muscular shoulders and arms to reveal a fully erect cock.

I don't want you looking at him.

Marius's sudden voice in her head made her jump. She shifted slightly, turning toward him. His eyes glimmered in the dark. *Then give me something to look at, Marius. We're behind a shield and no one can see us. Can you do that for me?*

Is that what you want?

You know it is. There it was again, the boldness that seemed so out of character for her.

She felt Marius actually tremble as he turned to face her and unbuttoned his slacks, then unzipped. He was fully erect as well.

She peeled back the pants just enough to expose him. She drew close to him once more, leaning into him, and as the couple got busy on stage she used her hand and felt him up, from the base of his thick hard stalk, slowly sweeping upward to fondle his crown.

She blessed her stilettos again, because he settled his lips on hers and kissed her while she played with him. Desire flowed through her abdomen, down between her legs. She moved against him in slow undulations, her free hand wrapped around as much of his back as she could reach.

He found her breast and dipped inside her bra, stroking and thumbing the tip.

Oh, Marius, this is driving me crazy. I want your beautiful cock inside me.

He kissed her harder, now pummeling her mouth with his tongue, letting her feel exactly what he intended to do to her.

But after about a minute he left her breast, caught her exploring hand with his, and made her stop. He was breathing hard. He pulled her up against him and held her. *We'd better just watch the show.*

She shifted her attention to the stage and watched as the professor kissed his student all over, using his tongue in parts, suckling her breasts until finally she begged for him to use his rod and teach her the final lesson.

She watched him enter her and her own body clenched with need.

Soon. Marius's voice both soothed and excited her.

She couldn't wait.

She almost asked Marius to take her back to the villa right then, but Eve had told them to watch the finish.

The professor was rolling into her, the woman's legs and wrists struggling against the bindings. One by one, he began releasing the neckties, and with each release the woman wrapped an arm around the man, then a leg, then she was free, holding him and crying out as he thrust into her.

She screamed her ecstasy and with a few dedicated swift thrusts, the woman entered paradise.

Moans and cries filled the small room as other couples climaxed along with them. Applause followed.

How do you feel? Marius asked.

Like I know what this would do for me. I want this with you so bad. Can we go back to the villa?

That's the plan.

He held out his arm and she stepped on his foot, carefully of course.

He kissed her cheek. "Hold me down low for the trip. I want to feel your hand on me again."

She slid her fingers down what was still really hard. She whimpered as she touched him, savoring the feel of the silky skin covering the hard stalk.

She kissed his neck as he flew, speeding through rock and other caves. She kept her eyes closed and focused on what she wanted more than anything in the world right now.

The next thing she knew she was back at the villa, but not in the canopy room, in a different space altogether. "Eve also set this up for us. She wanted it to be a surprise."

There was a waterfall in this room near a bed that had four short posts. Hanging from each were several long black cords made of silk, waiting for them. Candles were lit all around the room, and red rose petals dotted black silk sheets.

"Marius, this is perfect."

Marius didn't say anything to Shayna; he just undressed while watching her do the same. He felt her excitement and her nerves, the two blending to arouse him even more.

The bed was oversized, even for him, which would allow for movement. Eve had done this, providing him the right tool to take Shayna the distance.

He understood Eve's thinking as well, because the experience with Shayna, when he'd broken out of the restraints, had done something for him, set something inside him free.

He wanted Shayna to feel the same way.

She stood naked and trembling, her nipples peaked in the cool, moist air, her light-blue eyes glittered. His gaze raked her and what was already hard, stiffened a little more.

With his clothes off, he went to her, sliding both hands beneath her long beautiful hair to cup her neck. He kissed her, a full wet kiss, his tongue piercing her mouth, her hands gripping his arms and digging into his muscles.

Marius.

Her voice in his head made him groan. He drew back and looked into her eyes. "I want this for you. I want you to know what it's like to be bound, pleasured, then set free."

She nodded. "I want to be bound by you, Marius."

He felt the level of her arousal, almost off the charts,

and he loved it. Leading her to the side of the bed, he commanded her, "Stretch out on your back."

She didn't hesitate, which was one of the things he loved about Shayna: Once committed, she jumped in.

She looked so beautiful lying before him. He chose not to tie her up right away. Instead he moved to position himself over her, his knees between her legs. He settled his lips on her neck and sucked. *When I have you bound, I'm going to drink from you.*

She whimpered. *I would love that.*

He drew back, looking down at her. "You like when I feed from you."

"It's been the most exhilarating experience I've ever known, especially when you make love to me at the same time, when we're connected low."

She was a generous woman, something she probably didn't realize.

"Let's get you tied up then."

She drew a shuddering breath and nodded.

He moved around to the other side of the bed, but didn't immediately use the cords. Instead he placed kisses over her forehead, sliding his hands down her chest to fondle her breasts.

Marius, you always surprise me.

He kept kissing her, wanting her to know with each touch and caress, each press of his lips to any part of her body, that he valued her. *I want you to have the pleasure you were denied. I want you to know how much you've come to mean to me in just a couple of nights together.*

Her chest rose and fell. She stroked both his arms and hands as he kneaded her breasts and pinched her nipples gently.

He sensed that she'd fallen into a languid state, one full of surrender and willingness.

The time had come.

He moved slowly, savoring what the blood-chain bond told him: that Shayna floated on the desire she felt, her body humming.

He bound her wrists first, taking his time, giving her slack with each so that she had some freedom of movement. She would be able to touch his shoulders and arms, but she wouldn't be able to embrace him. She could also bring her legs close to his and make contact, but she wouldn't be free to wrap herself around him.

Once she was fully bound, he moved back to look down at her. His gaze slid over her breasts, her navel, and between her legs. He saw how she glistened—a sight that brought his hand to his cock. He stroked himself and savored what he saw.

"Marius, you have no idea how much what you're doing, and how you're looking at me, turns me on." Her hips dipped into the mattress, rocking gently.

He released his cock and began at her ankles. He kissed each of her legs, going back and forth, moving slowly upward.

"I want to touch you, but I can't."

He looked up at her while nibbling on the inside of her thigh. *And I love that I have all this power over you right now, that I can do anything to you and there's nothing you can do about it.*

He felt a shiver race through her, goose bumps riding her flesh. She found his words thrilling. He stroked the outsides of her thighs with his hands while he kissed his way closer and closer to the small line of blond hair that made his mouth water.

The scent of her sex became an intoxicating fragrance. He'd loved the way she smelled from the first, like something floral and lush that had to be tasted. Now he was going to eat until he was full.

He slid his hands and arms under her buttocks and began to feast.

Shayna trembled, head-to-foot, from the feel of his mouth on her low. His lips surrounded her fully as he suckled. The next moment his tongue flicked over her, afterward moving in a long sweep over her clitoris.

She writhed and cried out and he kept feasting, kept repeating his suckling, flicking, and sweeping movements.

Her hips rocked and she wanted her hands surrounding his neck, his arms, his back. But she could only barely touch his shoulders.

He had her bound.

He had control of her.

And she loved it.

Chills raced through her as he dipped lower still and his tongue penetrated her. She felt him inside her now as he drove quickly in and out.

"Marius," she cried out. Images of the show at The Ruby Cave slipped through her mind, intensifying what Marius was doing to her. She'd needed this desperately, and now Marius was taking care of her.

He moved faster and because her cries had grown steady, he went vampire-fast, using his phenomenal speed. And just like that she flew over the edge, ecstasy grabbing her up for a flight that took her into the heavens.

He kept driving his tongue into her, so that the orgasm rolled on and on, pleasure flowing, streaking, filling up her abdomen and swelling her chest. Her cries echoed to the cavern ceiling and back.

When the moment passed and her body began to settle, he kissed his way up her abdomen, nipping and sucking repeatedly wherever he landed.

She wanted her hands on him so bad, but with each impulse to touch him came the tug of the cords and the reminder that he was in control. What was it about being restrained that made her clench?

When he reached her breasts, he slowed his progress and focused his attention on tending to her, using one hand to prop himself up. He used his free hand to cup her breast as he swirled his tongue over the nipple and covered her with his mouth. He sucked her greedily, which had her hips arching and dipping so that she was once more becoming aroused.

"Marius, that feels so good. You have no idea."

I can feel your pleasure, Shayna, one of the wonderful perks of the blood-chain bond. And what I'm sensing from you moment to moment, how my tongue, my lips, my teeth feel to you, has me hard as a rock.

"Let me touch you, Marius. I want to feel your cock in my hand while you do that. Let me give you pleasure at the same time."

He looked up at her and slowly shifted his hips until her hand could fondle what she craved more than anything. She loved the feel of his cock and took her time exploring him with her fingers. She ran her hand the length, then returned to the crown, to pluck at him, teasing the sensitive ridge so that he groaned as he sucked her breasts.

But she needed more. "Marius, I need you inside me. Now."

He left her breast and returned to plant his knees between her legs. "Is that what you want, Shayna, my cock driving deep?"

The slack in the cords allowed her hands to stroke his shoulders. "Yes. I want you drinking from me and driving into me. That's what I want."

"I love doing this."

She nodded and as he placed his cock at her opening, she cried out. "You feel so good." He pierced her with what was so essentially male. And he'd pierce her again with his fangs.

She wanted it all.

Marius could hardly believe how much he could feel Shayna's pleasure and, at the same time, feel his own. The dual sensation had him grunting as he pushed into her, then pulled back, pushing farther each time, making his way deep inside her body.

Making love to a woman had never been like this before. He'd marched into new territory without realizing that's what he'd done. But she was a new land to explore and he was loving it.

He planted his hands on either side of her shoulders and curled his hips. He was seated deep by now and he wanted her to feel the length of him as he moved in and out. With each thrust, he drew back just to the point he could slip out of her, then drove back in.

Each time her body writhed beneath his, her head would roll on the black sheets and a new cry would leave her mouth. He could feel the exquisite sensations his cock brought her, making him harder still. If he hadn't had so much experience, he'd have lost it by now. But he wasn't four hundred years old for nothing.

He sustained the slow pace, watching her passion build.

Finally, she focused her gaze on him and between gasps said, "Drink from me, Marius. Please, take all that you need. I want to do that for you while you're giving me so much pleasure, while I'm bound like this."

He leaned down and kissed her, adding a line of kisses to her throat.

She moaned as he licked above her vein. His vampire nature called to her body and the vein rose, her heart rate increasing, getting ready to deliver what he needed to survive.

Saliva flooded his mouth and his fangs emerged, two sharp points, ready to penetrate Shayna in a new way.

He grazed her throat with the duller sides of his fangs. *I'm going to bite you now.*

In response to his words, her hips jerked, sending a streak of pleasure along his cock.

He arched his neck, then struck to the exact right depth.

Her blood hit his mouth and he moaned as he retracted his fangs and began to suck. How could he explain what her blood was like, as though it had been specifically created just for him. The flavor was ethereal and bold, the texture like silk.

But it was what happened to him when the elixir hit his stomach and began streaming into his bloodstream that stirred his soul. Energy started to vibrate through his veins, and his muscles expanded. He could feel his essential vampire power thrum to life. He knew that was why proximity wasn't an issue with them anymore and why she could now travel with altered flight at great speeds and not become sick.

Her blood had somehow permanently altered his power level. For that, he owed Shayna more than she could ever possibly understand: She may have made it possible for him to battle and defeat Daniel.

As he drove into her and sucked her vein, his need for release strengthened.

He felt Shayna straining at each of the cords, yet thrilling to them at the same time.

The heels of her feet rubbed the backs of his knees in anxious jolts, the only way she could reach him with her lower limbs. Her hands plucked at his shoulders, digging her nails in.

Shayna?

I'm here. Marius, this is beyond anything I've ever known. I wish I could tell you what it's like to have you moving inside me and drinking from me at the same time. I feel like I could fly. I swear it.

I can sense your pleasure. And he really could. *Can you tell what I'm feeling?*

She was quiet for a moment, then: *That you're ready to explode, but more than that. I think your body really loves my blood, really responds to it, as though I'm not just feeding your muscles but the depths of your vampire being as well.*

Yes, that's exactly right.

She squeezed his shoulders. *You feel damn amazing, bigger when we make love.*

How close are you? He needed to know. He had to make this mutual, this last run at flying into the stars.

If you just do your vampire thing, I'll come, but I have to warn you, I might scream this time.

She was breathing hard and he loved it.

He wanted to look at her, but also knew she'd love experiencing her orgasm while he drank from her.

He began to thrust faster and she cried out, sinking her nails into his back.

Shayna, stay with me, right with me.

I will. God, you feel so incredible and I can feel what you're experiencing now, how your cock feels gliding in and out of me. Oh, Marius.

He sped up once more, this time having to work to keep his lips around her neck. The restraints helped.

She writhed beneath him now. *I want to be free to hold you, Marius.*

He knew something in that moment: Shayna could siphon his power and do this herself. It was something she needed to do. *Just break the cords.*

By myself?

You can do it. I know you can. He was so hard right now, he ached, but he held back his release. He wanted her to come when she broke free.

I can't.

Yes, you can. Siphon more of my power. You can do it.

He felt her shift internally as she began to draw more of his power into her, then tug with all her might on each cord at the same time. The first pop sent her right arm slapping against his back. She cried out at the same time.

He kept drinking and working her with his hips.

Guttural sounds came out of her. He felt another tremendous wave of his power flow through her and with just a flick of her left wrist, she broke the second cord.

You're doing it.

I am! And I feel like I could fly. Her hips moved against his.

Finally, he released her neck so that he could look into

her eyes. He stared at her, curling his hips, working her deep.

She gasped as she used her now free hands to move over his pecs, his shoulders, his arms.

"You're breaking free, Shayna. Now tear apart the cords that hold your legs captive."

She tapped into his power once more and pulled on both ankles at once, staring into his eyes. The connection he felt to her in that moment was profound. And just like that, the remaining two cords broke and she surrounded him with her legs.

Tears flowed from her eyes down the sides of her face and into her hair. "I think my life just changed forever."

He nodded. "I know that feeling."

"My God."

He smiled and kissed her. She surrounded his neck with her arms and kissed him back. "Marius, can you bite me a second time? I want to finish this while I'm feeding you."

"Absolutely." She slowly rolled her head the opposite direction so that he had a new vein to pierce.

As before, he licked her throat, encouraging the vein. Her hands began a serious exploration of his neck, and back, and now his shoulders. Her touch fired him all over again.

His heart ached, he wanted this so much, even though he'd already taken from her.

But this time, she was free. She'd siphoned his power and liberated herself from restraints that she couldn't before.

When he punctured her throat this time, she cried out and he felt her grip him low.

She was really close.

He began to drink and once more drove into her. She was so wet, so aroused by all that had happened between them. She hooked her legs behind his thighs so that her well seized his cock, claiming possession.

He sped up once more, thrusting heavily at the same time and sucking hard at her neck.

Small cries came from her mouth as he drove them both toward ecstasy. His own body felt on fire now, heat pouring out of him, his cock a missile ready to launch.

And he was giving his woman what she needed. Nothing felt better or more profound. And he wanted her full of his seed, bearing the mark of his scent to warn off other vampires.

The distant thought occurred to him that only vampires of Ancestral power could do that, could create a mark that other vampires could detect. But he knew that was what he was doing as he powered down her blood and thrust faster and faster.

He felt her grow very still as he drove into her and he could feel that with just his movements, he was taking her the distance.

Her voice began a cry that turned into a shout, then a scream.

He could feel her pleasure as his cock began to pulse, his seed shooting through him and creating a lightning bolt of sensation that had him leaving her neck and shouting with her.

He felt her grip his cock repeatedly. In response, he delivered a second load that had him crying out once more.

Pleasure on pleasure.

She writhed and screamed as another orgasm caught her up and carried her to the pinnacle again.

And just when everything should have grown quiet, he felt a third wave launch, for both of them.

He drove faster as he came, as she came, as together they reached the top of another mountain of shared ecstasy. She held him pinned in her arms, crying out, shouting and holding him fast.

It seemed like an eternity before his body began to settle and her grip on him lessened.

Slowly her legs released him, then her arms. She lay on her back, her hands touching his shoulders lightly, her eyes closed. She breathed hard in deep gasps, her mouth open.

When at last he lay slack on top of her and his own breathing had evened out, he smiled.

He didn't want to leave her body. Ever.

She stroked his hair and the back of his neck, using both her hands. She kissed his forehead repeatedly. He felt her gratitude, a perfect reflection of his own.

Shayna knew now that on every possible level, she'd never really had sex before. She'd had a few thrills, yes, but never sex.

She felt so connected to Marius, truly one with him, that she never wanted to leave.

He was her man.

He always would be.

That thought, so out of left field, hit home, striking deep and burning a hole through her heart.

Marius was her man.

She rubbed his back, savoring the dips and falls of his muscular shoulders. She hugged him repeatedly.

He lay very quiet on top of her, his weight a layer of pleasure all on its own. He was still buried inside her and in a half state of arousal that felt really good, beyond good. Amazing.

The cords were still attached to her wrists. She lifted one to look at it. She wouldn't have been surprised if she'd snapped the wood off. Instead, the cord had shredded near the knot around the post.

That moment, of breaking free, had released something tremendous inside her, a rush of euphoria equally as profound as the series of orgasms she'd just experienced.

She truly felt liberated from the emotional pain and trauma she'd endured at Michelson's hands.

She could move forward now, and it crossed her mind that she needed to have a long conversation with the Seattle Police Department. She wanted the trauma that she'd experienced at Michelson's hands on record just in case any other women came forward. She might even have to charge him for what he did. Better to stop him now than to have his criminal mind decide to step up his game and actually murder the next woman he got involved with.

Marius stirred and lifted himself up to look at her. He kissed her. "Thinking about things?"

"Yes." She told him she now intended to visit the Seattle PD and to report what had happened to her. "I just think it ought to be out there."

"I think that's wise." He shifted, easing out of her. "I'll get you something."

"Thank you."

He left the bed, heading for the bathroom, and a minute later brought a washcloth back to tuck between her legs. He kissed her on the lips then returned to the bathroom.

As she lay in bed, the vision of all those village

children going down both sides of the potluck table suddenly whipped through her head.

What if Marius got her pregnant?

But she was so full of feel-good hormones that she released a deep sigh and wallowed in the delicious feeling of bringing a child of his into the world.

She knew the sensation would pass, but for just a moment, as she heard the distant shower wind up, she let herself enjoy the fantasy. If she stayed with Marius, she'd get to have sex with him a lot, and probably make babies, and live out her life with him. She'd meet his brothers, Adrien and Lucian, both of whom had already bonded with human women. Her children would have aunts and uncles.

She turned on her side and stared at the waterfall. The rock behind glittered and a soft light below created a kaleidoscope of images.

She laughed at herself for thinking about vampires and making babies.

Fortunately the hormones began to fade and reality began to return in quick whips of time.

She had a life to get back to in Seattle, a doctorate to complete, students to teach, a dissertation to write, and fieldwork in Malaysia. She was on a good strong path, one fit for her. Her time with Marius was just a dream, something to be valued and treasured always, but not *her* life.

She wasn't a vampire and she needed to keep reminding herself of that truth. She also had the last part of the extinction weapon to locate. And maybe this time, her visions would be pure.

She lifted her arm and slowly began unknotting the cords at her wrists, then her ankles. The shower shut off and she slipped from bed, gathering up her dress at the same time.

She felt Marius's tension now and knew that his thoughts had turned in a similar direction to her own.

She met him in the doorway. He had a towel wrapped around his hips, water beaded between his heavy pecs and dripping from his hair.

He said only one word. "Daniel."

"I know. I'm thinking the same thing."

He shook his head. "I just don't want you to think this wasn't . . . extraordinary, because it was."

She put a hand on his cheek. "You don't have to explain. I think we're both in the same place. We have a job to do and I have a life to return to."

"And even if we get the weapon, we've only staved off Daniel's ambitions. The use of the weapon would have secured his domination of this world as well as his intention to take over yours. But the absence of the weapon wouldn't have ended his driving madness. One way or the other, I will still have a boatload of work to do."

She nodded. "I'm with you, Marius, one hundred percent. I know we have something special between us, but it makes no sense to even think about having a future together. And right now, I need my shower."

She moved past him, set her clothes on top of a nearby hamper, and walked into yet another massive shower. The thought went through her mind that maybe it had been built for orgies, but then someone like Marius, as big as he was, would take up at least half the space.

She smiled as she flipped on three of the seven showerheads. Once the water was flowing, she thought *what the hell* and turned on the rest.

Shayna couldn't know it, but Marius hadn't budged an inch from where she'd left him in the bathroom doorway. First, he'd watched her move in the direction of the shower, enjoying her narrow waist and full hips, the sensual movement of her bottom. Afterward, he'd remained leaning against the door frame, sensing her enjoyment of the shower and all that water beating on her body from every direction.

He was in deep shit with this woman.

He understood that now.

Maybe if he hadn't made love to her just now, all bound up by the silk cords, he wouldn't be feeling this way. But he'd never known this kind of intimacy with a woman before and his soul longed for more. His heart actually ached at the thought she would leave and never return, that she could be content on any level with her life as an anthropologist apart from him.

Her voice pierced his mind suddenly. *Hey, what's going on? You feel really sad right now.*

Just ignore it. He paused before adding quietly, *Please. No problem.*

The last thing he wanted to do was to talk about any of this. He just wanted to get on with things and see if they couldn't locate and seize the extinction weapon. Then he could take her back to Seattle and leave her there. He could return to his job as an anti-Daniel activist without having to worry about her safety or how he could keep from falling in love with her more than he already had.

He finally left the doorway, disgusted that he'd let his emotions get away from him. He let Shayna know that he was heading back to her bedroom to get dressed and that when she was done with her shower, he'd come back to get her.

Sounds good. She sounded cheerful enough, but he sensed her own disquiet, an inner conflict over their recent lovemaking against the reality of their situation.

Once he'd donned battle leathers with the intention of having Shayna access her tracking ability again, he used his phone and contacted Rumy.

"Not a good time," Rumy said. The tension in his voice had Marius reaching for one of his daggers. Something was going on.

"Is that my son?" Daniel's voice penetrated the airwaves. Looked like dear old Dad had recovered from his second stab wound. "If you don't get your ass over here to talk to me, I'm taking your pal, Rumy, back to the Dark Cave system and stringing him up like I did you."

Marius grew very still. This was no time to react to anything Daniel had to say, including his threats. Besides, he and Rumy had talked strategy for years, working through several scenarios that might involve Daniel's intrusion into The Erotic Passage.

Daniel was definitely in the middle of making his play.

He took a deep breath. He would hate more than anything to have Rumy's torture or death on his hands, but Rumy hadn't been around this long, rubbing shoulders daily with the entire vampire underworld, without having a few plans in place.

Rumy finally said, "Don't sweat it, Marius. I'm about to serve my guest some tea and cookies."

Shit, Rumy was going to blow up part of The Erotic Passage.

Marius hung up and slipped his phone back into his deepest side pocket. He packed his battle leathers full of chains and daggers. Thinking Shayna would probably want a little more time with the shower, he headed back to the waterfall room.

Shayna took her time drying off, her thoughts having returned to making love with Marius.

She felt changed, born anew, and the terrible oppressiveness she'd carried with her because of Michelson had disappeared. She hadn't realized the extent to which his purposeful tearing away at her self-esteem over the course of their relationship had left her burdened.

Now the burden had vanished like a heavy stack of firewood set ablaze and reduced to the weight of ashes.

She would always feel grateful that her bizarre journey into this unknown world had released her from something she hadn't even known existed.

When she started blowing her hair dry, making use of the high setting, she became aware of how sensitive even her hearing had become. She tried to imagine what this was like for vampires, living with a heightened auditory capacity. She knew that the extinction weapon used an extreme decibel level to kill vampires. If the sound of the blow dryer bothered her, what would a high-pitched sound do to a full-blooded vampire? She could only imagine the pain.

With her hair sufficiently dry, she returned to her dress and pulled her iPhone from the small side pocket. Still wrapped up in her towel, she scrolled through the various pictures she'd taken of the stonework, enlarging the parts that looked like an ancient language, and just let her eyes wander over the lines and shapes. She felt certain she was looking at the key to understanding something important about the vampire world, possibly even about Daniel.

The anthropologist in her wanted to spend the rest of her life exploring the intricacies of a culture lived at night and in the depths of secret, hidden caverns. She'd want to delve into the earliest traditions, charting the evolution of the society through the ages. If she had more time, a study of this kind could even offer an understanding of Daniel and possibly even the best means of corralling the beast.

She set her phone on the counter and made use of a tool she often employed when studying a culture. She took a deep breath and got very relaxed. She let all she knew about the culture surround her, imagining the spiritual and social aspects of what she'd seen now float around her head. She let her memories of the physical night-to-night activities move through her. She envisioned the sensuality of Marius's world and of the vampire life generally, perhaps a result of cavern-based living.

She added in the sex-slavery component that had become a partially accepted element in a disproportionately large segment of the vampire-world population. She saw the driving scientific elements that she recognized all around her, serious feats of engineering that allowed for hot water, and fresh-flowing air, even for electricity and grow-lights and extensive underground gardens, and for the development of a weapon with genocidal application.

To all of this, she added the reverence she felt whenever Marius spoke of the children of his world and the rarity of procreation. The sheer absence of young minds in need of guidance would alter how an entire culture spent its hours, established its essential morals, developed its basic theory of education.

A former vision returned, the one she'd felt had been meant just for her. And she could see everything so clearly, just as she'd hoped she would. She took a moment to revel in the change, that nothing inhibited her visions now.

She saw herself once more in the room stacked full of clay tablets, rising all the way to the carefully carved ceiling, and hidden deep within a cave. She could feel the location, that the cave was somewhere in Egypt, which actually made a lot of sense. A large portion of ancient civilization came from that region of the world. Vampires, it would seem, had always borrowed from their surrounding human communities. Why wouldn't they have developed their own brand of cuneiform?

But what wouldn't she give to enter that room, a thought that caused her heart to beat hard in her chest.

While she saw this vision, a sense of urgency began to work in her veins, troubling her thoughts. She felt the pressure of another vision and because she was already in a receptive state, she let it come.

What unfolded before her eyes, however, brought tears flowing down her cheeks.

She saw death.

CHAPTER 12

By the time Marius returned to the waterfall room and found Shayna caught in the grips of another vision, a faint vibration shook the villa. He knew Rumy had blown up the front part of his offices.

If he hadn't believed that things were quickly coming to a head, he believed it now.

He stood in front of Shayna and settled his hands gently on her shoulders to support her, but he felt such pain coming from her that he prepared for the worst.

After a moment, she opened her eyes.

"Marius, I just had a horrible vision about something that happened a couple of hours ago." She looked around.

"But what shook the cavern? An earthquake? We have them sometimes in Seattle."

"No, not an earthquake." He explained about his phone call to Rumy, about the strategies they'd discussed if Daniel became more aggressive and what he believed had just happened.

Shayna put a hand to her forehead. He could feel her distress, so he shifted to slide an arm around her shoulders. "Tell me about the vision. What did you see?"

"It was awful. Daniel already has the weapon in his possession. I wanted to discuss this with you earlier, that I had a feeling both the trip to Sweden and the one to Costa Rica were just lures, to try to get to you—or to us, maybe, I'm not sure."

Marius felt as though he'd just been hit in the gut, hard. Daniel had the weapon and what came from Shayna felt like she'd witnessed the holocaust. "What did you see?"

"Quill fired up the extinction weapon."

Because she was trembling, he set her in motion, guiding her back to the bed. "Why don't you sit down and tell me every detail."

He already hurt deep into his soul, knowing what he was about to hear.

She sat down and planted her hands on her legs for support. "I want to stream this for you, Marius. I think you should see it for yourself."

He didn't want to do this. He didn't want to watch a massacre. But what he wanted didn't matter. "Okay." He sat down on the bed beside her and took her hand.

She closed her eyes. *Ready?* Her telepathic voice, full of her distress, made him flinch.

Yes. Go ahead.

As the first image showed up, he realized that her issue with the visions was gone, something in other circumstances he would celebrate. But not now.

The vision played like a movie. He was looking at the cave where Daniel had killed all those women in front of him.

This time, a large metal cage had been assembled in the center of the room and inside were females, all vampires. Sex slavery wasn't human-specific. A lot of clients preferred vampires because they were much stronger physically, could take greater abuse, and could self-heal quickly.

The women looked confused but otherwise sat close together, some holding one another for support. Each bore bruises and cuts.

He felt nauseous and wanted to look away, but he had to stand witness to this horror.

Shayna panned back, part of her gift, and the weapon came into view with its red hood, silver main housing, and shiny black base.

He could see a simple metal flip switch. A human woman, shackled and very thin, with bruises all over her arms, waited close to the weapon. She glanced over her shoulder to look back and to her right, her eyes wide with terror.

Shayna panned back farther and there was Quill, a maniacal smile on his lips, madness in his eyes. He had his arms crossed over his chest.

The next moment Quill shifted to altered flight then nodded to the human.

She flipped the switch and the weapon hummed to life, making a sound that vibrated at first in the lower registers. The female vampires began to rise to their feet. He sensed their mass anxiety.

The vibrations grew increasingly higher-pitched and as his own eardrums began to ache, the women started to scream, holding their hands to their ears.

It all happened so fast, the women tearing around wildly, ramming into one another, screaming, followed by blood pouring from their eyes, noses, and ears.

They began to drop suddenly, one by one in quick succession, and he knew they died, just like that. Quill appeared to be safe while in altered flight. He nodded a second time to the woman, who flipped the switch once more and the vibration stopped.

As the vision ended, Marius opened his eyes. He realized he'd let go of Shayna's hand to press his palms against his ears. The vision hadn't carried the full measure of the vibrations, but his ears hurt and the pain extended through his skull.

"Are you okay?"

He felt Shayna's hand on his back and nodded. "I'm fine, but they're all dead."

"They are and it was horrible for them and so fast," she said. "I didn't think it would be so quick."

He sent healing power to his ears and to his mind so that after a minute, he no longer hurt, just his chest because of the mass murder.

He gave himself another minute to absorb and to recover, then turned to Shayna. "Can you tell me if the weapon is still in that location?"

He watched her close her eyes again. She shook her head, but she suddenly gripped his hand. "Marius, I've found it, but you have to see this. I don't understand why it's in this place. This makes no sense."

"Go ahead and stream it."

The images arrived like a new onslaught. The weapon sat on a land bridge within a large cavern. Below were a couple hundred human slaves, all staring up, milling around, nervous. Something was going on.

He opened his eyes and met her gaze. "This isn't a vision, is it?"

She shook her head. "It's just the location, here and now."

"The Dark Cave system?"

She nodded. "Yes, but it feels like a trap."

"I couldn't agree more."

This time her shoulders rose and fell with a quick intake of breath. "We have to go get it."

"Yes, we do."

"But how? Because I'm convinced we'll be attacked."

"Let's get you dressed, then we'll make a plan."

"I need to get my dress." She stood up and headed back into the bathroom.

He followed after her and watched her start tidying up the space, something she didn't need to do. He didn't understand at first until he saw that her fingers trembled as she wrapped up the hair dryer and put it away on a wood shelf beneath the sink.

She was in shock.

When she started wiping down the sink, he went to her. He turned her to face him and surrounded her with his arms. "It'll be okay."

She hugged him hard. "I'm scared," she mumbled against his shoulder. "I don't want to be, but I am. It was awful to watch them die."

"I know and you have every right to be freaking out right now."

"I want to be stronger than this."

He rubbed her back up and down. "You're doing just fine. I'm so proud of you."

After a moment, she calmed down and gathered up her clothes. "I'm ready."

He flew her to her original room. She went immediately to the closet and he picked up his phone again and placed a call to his brother. When he heard Adrien's voice, guilt poured over him once more, that old remorse that lived in him like a wound that would never heal. "Marius. We've been hoping we'd hear from you, but didn't want to call." A phone ringing at the wrong time could alert the enemy.

"I wanted to let you and Lucian know what's going on. And I want you to share with Gabriel what I'm about to tell you." He quickly outlined all that had happened, beginning with his call to Rumy and the later explosion. "I knew his mind, Adrien. He'd always said if Daniel started moving in on The Erotic Passage, he'd destroy the whole system before he let that bastard take over anything."

Adrien was silent for a moment. "Sounds like Daniel's serious this time. He's making his move."

"We think so, too. Shayna and I are going after the weapon. She's seen the location. I know you're in hiding, but if things go wrong, you may need to go after the weapon yourself. I know your woman, Lily, has the same tracking ability as Shayna. I need you both to be our backup in case things go south."

"We will. Just keep us informed."

"And there's something else; Daniel had Quill kill off a number of vampire sex slaves by firing up the weapon. It happened so quick; they died so damn fast." He then relayed the vision that Shayna had streamed for him, answering any questions that came to Adrien's mind.

Adrien huffed a heavy sigh. "Daniel has to be stopped."

"I'm getting the feeling that something big is on the horizon."

The tension level in Adrien's voice rose a notch. "What do you mean?"

He shifted to look at Shayna, watching her slide into a pair of jeans, then zip up. She already wore a long-sleeved T-shirt, cut low, which she mitigated by putting on a dark blue tank top backward like before. She sat down on the edge of the bed to put on socks and a pair of running shoes.

"Just a feeling. Be sure to let Gabriel know. And be ready. I might need your help in the next few hours."

"I'll tell both Lucian and Gabriel. And don't worry. We'll contact Rumy and see what's going on. We've got your back."

Marius hung up and slid his phone into the deep pocket of his battle leathers. He turned to Shayna and told her what was going on.

"I heard most of it," she said, standing up and straightening the outer T-shirt at the hem.

He crossed to her and once more took her shoulders in hand, meeting her gaze straight on. "Shayna, I can go by myself on this one. You'd be safe here with Rumy and the other refugees."

She shook her head and had never looked more serious. "No, you'll need me. That much I know. I can feel it."

She patted his vest and down the sides of his pants. "Good. You're fully armed."

He couldn't help it; his lips twisted into a smile. Shayna

was checking to make sure *he* was ready for war. "Of course I'm armed."

"I guess that was a silly thing for me to do, but I'm nervous."

"Me, too."

She rolled her eyes. "You are not."

"I hide it really well, but only an idiot goes into battle unafraid."

"Okay."

"Okay, then."

He opened his arm and she hopped onto his foot, slinging her arm around his neck. She held his gaze for a moment, then kissed him full on the lips. "Let's go get that weapon, warrior."

Shayna had never been so frightened before, though she didn't really understand why this situation was worse than any of the others. Except that Quill could fire up the weapon and Marius could die, which would mean she would be trapped in Daniel's lair. There was that.

As he flew her east, in the direction of the Dark Cave system, she thought back on all that had happened beginning with first meeting Marius in Seattle, seeing him from the corner of her eye in flight and wondering if someone had slipped her a roofie at the club she'd been at.

Now she was here, flying once more, experiencing no pain, just an almost paralyzing fear because of what might await them or the thousand things that could go wrong.

The flight took way too long, yet wasn't long enough at the same time. When he made his descent and they began to pass through rock, the sound of her heartbeat pounded in her ears.

He broke through the main cavern and there it was, the last of the extinction weapons, sitting on an eight-foot-wide land bridge above a large pit at least eighty feet across. She couldn't imagine what Daniel was thinking by putting it there except that it looked like a piece of bait. So if this was a trap, how did they get the weapon and not fall prey?

The ceiling of the cave rose another couple hundred feet. In the pit, all the human women, shackled, emaciated, and bruised, huddled at the edges, forming a large circle well away from anything that could fall from the bridge.

Her gaze became fixed on the weapon. A large hook in the center of the red top was probably used for transport. Maybe the original concept involved cranes for placement.

Shayna, Daniel is already here.

Where? I don't see him.

He's beyond the land bridge hovering about thirty feet away, with a very large force.

If we shift out of altered flight, can you sink a dagger between his eyes? Once the words left her mind, she realized just how deep she was into this world. She couldn't imagine Shayna-the-college-student ever talking so easily about killing someone.

Marius, I've been holding back siphoning your power, believing that you needed it to fight, but I think I should change that strategy. I need to see Daniel for myself. I need to see everything that's going on. Can I take more?

He turned toward her slightly. *Don't hold back. Take as much power of mine as you need. We're in this together and you're a big part of the equation. And you definitely need to see what we're dealing with here.*

She held his gaze for a moment, and some of her trembling stopped. He was counting on her, on all her weird abilities in his world, and she wanted to be ready for whatever Daniel threw at them both. *We're improvising, then.*

Not sure we have a choice, but given Daniel's level of power, it's probably best anyway. If he had an inkling of any plan we might have, he could anticipate my maneuvers and block them.

She nodded and shifted her gaze back to the weapon. Focusing on the blood-chain at her neck, she centered her thoughts on siphoning what she needed.

As the power began to flow, her ability to see through Daniel's disguise sharpened. The layers started to melt away until he and at least fifty of his men came into view. Her heart seized. They were all dressed in black and big like Marius, all hovering in the air, daggers and chains in battle-ready positions. Rough them up a bit and they'd look like a biker gang.

Daniel, smiling as always, hovered in the middle, Quill and Lev on each side.

She trembled all over again. Too much adrenaline. Once more she worked to calm herself. How were they supposed to defeat an overwhelming force like that?

Shayna, I can see a way out, but we'll have to play this just right, so let me ask you something. Could you levitate if I let go of you?

She searched her abilities and her body. *Yes, but only in brief spurts.*

Altered flight?

Yes. The same. Very limited.

Good. That's all we'll need for this. For now, I'm going

to keep holding on to you, hoping that Daniel and his boys missed that you've got these skills.

She began to see the direction of his thoughts. *The only way out of this is to set off the weapon and I'll have to do it, human that I am.*

That's what I'm thinking. I may have gained speed, but not enough to battle fifty soldiers, Daniel, and his sons all at once. But the timing has to be right.

Shayna gathered her courage. *And first, we have to lure them out of altered flight.*

Shit, you're trembling. There's still time to go back, Shayna.

At that, she laughed. *Not on your life. I didn't come all this way to run-and-hide now, but I appreciate the thought. As for the way I'm shaking, just ignore it. Call it battle nerves or something.*

You're doing fine. You're one helluva woman, and I'm proud to know you.

Marius smiled at her. In the middle of all this nonsense, he smiled. Her heart swelled, liking this man so much.

And he was proud of her.

Reverting her attention to the weapon, she said, *There's a switch in front. Do you see it?*

Yes. Marius's arm tightened around her waist.

It's off to the left, so be sure to position me on that side.

I'm going to move in now, Marius said.

Go for it.

He shifted from altered flight to levitation and flew steadily toward the land bridge. Daniel held his arm up, a gesture that appeared to keep his force in check.

"I'm here to take the weapon, Daniel. I can't let you keep it since I've already seen what it can do." He landed on the thick stone bridge, still holding Shayna tight against him.

Daniel moved slowly in his direction, shifting out of altered flight. Quill and Lev, and the rest of his force, remained behind. His penetrating gaze moved from Marius to Shayna. When he held her gaze, she felt him reaching for her mind, wanting to talk to her telepathically, but she blocked him. A chill went down her spine. If evil could take a form, it would look just like Daniel Briggs.

"Hello, Shayna. I see you've been enjoying my son. He's magnificent, isn't he? Marius was my best creation, he just doesn't know it yet."

Shayna wasn't sure where her boldness came from, but she said, "Are you sure this was your doing? I mean, I just don't see the resemblance at all." She glanced at Marius and back to Daniel. "I never saw his mother, of course, but I'm thinking he must take after her. I understand she was an exceptional woman."

Daniel's eyes narrowed. Shayna expected steam to start coming out his ears. Instead he shifted his gaze back to Marius. "You should discipline your woman, teach her not to poke the bear."

Marius didn't hesitate. "Shayna has a mind of her own and can say whatever she likes. It's not my place to censure her on any level. Besides, I think what she's said is true. I do take after my mother."

"More's the pity, son. She tried to make a weakling out of you, always coddling you and hugging you. But I made you a man."

Shayna felt Marius stiffen, his muscles flexing and

unflexing. *Hey, relax. That ego maniac is so full of shit.*

Marius glanced at her quickly, then laughed. *You're right.*

"Isn't this charming, but I should remind you that telepathy in company is very rude."

Again, Shayna spoke boldly, meeting Daniel's gaze again. "You think this is rude? Want to know what I think falls into the category of a social faux pas? How about killing off your female vampire slaves to test your extinction weapon? Yeah, I think that's rude."

Daniel stared at her. "So how did you know about that? Ah, of course, you had one of your visions. But I'm losing patience."

"And you're pissing me off."

Daniel physically moved to place himself in a direct line with Marius, purposefully ignoring Shayna. He was now only ten feet away. "How about we have a little contest and the winner takes the weapon?"

"What do you have in mind?" Marius's voice sounded dark to Shayna, full of intention.

"You split and each of your forms, primary and secondary, takes on ten of my men. You win, I let you cart off the weapon. You lose, well, you lose everything: You'll join me in my new government, I'll get the weapon, and Shayna, of course, will be sent to work in one of my clubs here. She'd do very well. And one more thing. While you're battling, Shayna stands beside me." He smiled, that horrible oily smile of his. "I'll keep her safe if weapons start to fly."

Shayna wasn't sure how she expected Marius to respond, especially since his muscles were twitching and he ground his jaw. She also had no idea what Daniel meant about primary and secondary forms. She hadn't come across that concept before. A dozen questions rose in her mind like a sudden burst of air bubbles rising to the surface, but she suppressed them.

"What do you say, son?"

"Agreed," Marius said. "But I want Quill and Lev to remain at the far cavern wall."

Daniel nodded, and his obedient sons immediately flew and hovered against the far stone wall.

Marius! What are you doing?

We need Daniel's troops out of altered flight, and this appears to be as good a way to get the job done as any. I want you near the switch and ready for my order.

There really wasn't time for him to explain further, she got that. So she responded, *I'm all in.*

Good.

He released her and Daniel flew straight for her, grabbing her by the arm and dragging her off to the side. He pinched her beneath her arm so that she cried out.

"What the fuck?" Marius shouted. "What did you just do to her?"

Daniel apologized. "I must have caught her delicate human skin between my fingers when I took her arm. Just an accident." He addressed Shayna. "Are you all right, my dear?"

She met his gaze, grimacing. "Don't you 'my dear' me, you sick fuck."

His nostrils flared. "You know I could destroy you with a thought."

"Well, that's what you're good at: destruction. I'd like to see you actually build anything of merit."

This time she watched Daniel grind his teeth. She knew he wanted to hit her or maybe even throw her off the land bridge, but he worked to control himself. After flaring his nostrils again, he nodded to Marius. "Now let's see what you can do."

"First, choose the men I'm to fight so that I can get a good look at them."

Daniel lifted his arm once and the entire force moved from altered flight to levitation. After that, he made a few gestures and twenty warriors separated from the main force, ten grouping off to one side, ten to the other.

Shayna felt Marius's sudden burst of excitement. He'd just accomplished the first part of their makeshift plan. But she wasn't prepared at all for what he did next.

She felt a profound vibration flow through her blood-chain, then watched as Marius suddenly became two of himself.

She stared in utter astonishment, unable to believe what she was seeing. And the division of his physical self was completely equal because each wore the same clothes and had the same number of weapons.

She could tell that the Marius at the right was his primary self, though she didn't know how exactly. He just felt stronger in some way, more present perhaps. But how was he doing something that seemed so impossible? Did he control the secondary Marius? Were they one consciousness but two bodies? Yes, lots of questions.

"We're a much superior race," Daniel said. "You should get used to that fact right away. Your days are numbered, Shayna. Human earth's as well. It's only a matter of time."

She wanted to say something cutting again, but truthfully seeing two of Marius forced her to admit that Daniel, in this case, was absolutely right.

"My God," she murmured.

"Precisely so," Daniel responded. He sounded so self-satisfied that she wanted to kick him.

Marius glanced at her. *Just be ready, because I don't know when I'll want you to hit the switch.*

I'm ready.

She grew very calm and focused all her attention on him, forcing herself to take deep breaths.

Both right and left Mariuses pulled out a long chain in one hand and a dagger in the next. Each dropped to a fighting stance, the long chains whirring.

What happened next gave her vision a workout. Marius moved so fast that at times he seemed to disappear. And twenty adversaries moved rapidly trying to keep up with him, often colliding so that the battle appeared to be nothing but chaos.

She wondered what it was like for Marius.

Marius had never been so in sync during a split-self battle. His consciousness had control over both selves, yet each operated independently. He moved as fast as he had in Sweden, whipping through the air.

The two long chains had already dropped two vampires down to the floor below, a good sixty feet. But it was his dagger and whip-like movements that cut throat after throat. His secondary self proceeded in the same way.

More bodies fell, one after the other.

He never stopped moving and watched especially for those moments when one of Daniel's men would collide with another. Twice he cut two throats at almost the exact same time, taking full advantage of their momentary confusion.

When one of Daniel's men sliced Marius's arm, and

sent his blade falling to the floor below, Marius drew two more blades out at the same time, flew backward ten feet, synced up with his secondary self. Each began throwing daggers at lightning speed. He caught throat after throat, a precision he hadn't had before.

He was ramped up high, ready to take on the rest of Daniel's men, when Shayna's voice pierced his mind. *Marius, we've got to do this now. Daniel's grip has slackened, something he doesn't realize. I'm going to throw myself off the land bridge while hitting that button.*

Give my about fifteen seconds. I need to reform first.

Got it.

Marius had no daggers left and drew out a short chain, as did his secondary self. Six vampires remained and while they waited for him to act, he reformed in a quick snap so that now he faced all six by himself. Even the process of bringing both selves together had speeded up.

He hung in the air, breathing hard, the remaining six of Daniel's force doing the same. The rest of the vampires had started moving in closer, very slowly and probably on Daniel's orders. He sincerely doubted his father would hold to the terms of wager.

He waited, shifting his gaze from one warrior to the next.

Ready? he asked Shayna.

Three . . . two . . . one . . .

Marius flew back toward the weapon and just as Shayna whipped out of Daniel's grasp, he watched as she flew sideways, hit the switch, then dove downward into the pit below, catching her levitation at fifteen feet. *Marius, I can't hold my levitation.*

I'm coming.

The vibrations started up and his head immediately

filled with incredible pain, something he might not have ignored, except that Shayna would die if he didn't reach her.

By the time he turned in her direction, she was in free fall. Though the piercing sound waves made it almost impossible to focus, he forced himself to shift to altered flight, then shot after her, barely catching her in his arms. He stayed in altered flight because the weapon wouldn't hurt him there. But what he saw with Shayna in his arms were the remaining vampires screaming and one by one falling to the stone floor below. The humans were still pressed up against the sides of the pit.

Even Daniel writhed, which stunned him. His father appeared to be incapable of switching to altered flight. Quill and Lev hovered over him but there was nothing they could do.

Daniel was caught in the grip of the sound waves.

For a long moment, Marius stared up at the land bridge, wondering if his father would die then and there.

"Marius, fly me back up to the weapon. This is our chance, right now. When I hit the switch, Quill and Lev will be tending to Daniel and we'll be able to take the weapon away."

He immediately rose to hover right next to the weapon.

Quill, still in altered flight, turned to glare at him. He couldn't hurt Marius, not while in altered flight. "You're killing him, you bastard."

"I'm not sure I can feel bad about that."

"Where's your fucking loyalty? He's your father."

"He's a psychopath butcher who gets off on it, nothing more."

Lev turned toward Marius as well and each, enraged,

suddenly split while in altered flight, so that he was looking at four opponents instead two.

"Your woman dies first." Quill's lips drew back and
his fangs descended.

Marius knew that he couldn't defeat both Quill and
Lev if they chose to attack. Each was at Ancestral status, and if Daniel died right now they'd take vengeance
on him and on Shayna.

He had a decision to make: Save Shayna and take the
weapon, or let Daniel die. And how much he wanted his
father dead. Daniel lay struggling to heal himself as the
vibrations and decibel level from the weapon took its toll.
He bled from ears and from his nose.

As though reading his mind, Shayna said, *Just let him
die, Marius. He's the real problem.*

He stared at Shayna. *But we'll both die in the process,
and Quill and Lev will have the weapon.*

This isn't simple.

He felt her debate within her mind, feeling, as he did,
that it would be hard to pass up an opportunity to take
Daniel out.

In the end, she released a heavy sigh. *They'd use the
weapon right away, wouldn't they?*

Yes, they would.

All right, Marius, do what you think is best.

He nodded. *I'm getting you out of here.* To Quill he
said, "Leave us in peace and Shayna will shut off the
weapon, just long enough for you to take him out of here."
He lowered them both to the side of the weapon with the
switch. She held out her hand. "She can move from altered flight to levitation all by herself so don't think for
a moment that I'll leave this state."

Blood started flowing from Daniel's eyes.

Quill glanced down at him. "Agreed."

The brothers reformed, then drew close to Daniel, ready to haul him away as soon as Shayna shut off the machine. Marius gave her the go-ahead.

He felt her shift to levitation and flip the switch. As soon as the weapon wound down, she slipped back into altered flight.

At almost the same moment Quill and Lev moved out of altered flight, grabbed Daniel, moved back in, and took off. They were gone in a flash.

Just for good measure, Marius had Shayna flip the switch once more. He was glad he did, because a new set of vampires flew back into the cavern, probably on Quill's orders. But each headed straight back out when the vibrations hit the air.

Marius let the weapon run for a full minute, then with Shayna in one arm and his hand gripping the hook on the top of the weapon with the other, he signaled for her to shut it down.

As soon as she flipped the switch, he hauled both Shayna and the weapon into altered flight and headed west, back to Egypt.

As Marius approached the Pharaoh Cavern system, he sensed that Gabriel, who owned the system, had added a new layer of security disguises. Despite his increased level of power, Marius could barely feel the presence of the caves below even though at least five thousand vampires lived there.

The weapon was heavy and he needed to set the damn thing on the ground, but he wasn't about to do that outside a well-protected cave. Daniel would no doubt have sent his men in pursuit; they could easily be following by only a minute or so.

Still in altered flight, he levitated above the system and pushed hard to reach Gabriel telepathically. *Can you hear me, Gabriel?*

Marius! Where are you?

Above the Pharaoh system. I've got the last extinction weapon with me, and Shayna.

A split second later an inbound path opened up and he slipped through. He could feel the disguise close up behind him equally fast. Gabriel, his surrogate father and the primary reason Marius had even one brain cell intact, was an Ancestral of tremendous power.

Marius penetrated a partially cleared-out cavern of immense size and a few remaining stalactites. As he set the weapon down, he saw the charred, melted remains of several pieces of machinery, no doubt the detritus of several similar weapons.

He released Shayna and she stepped off his foot, glancing around. "Are these what I think they are?"

"Yep."

The next moment Gabriel arrived with a security team of a couple dozen men. The latter spread out around the perimeter, daggers and chains drawn.

Gabriel grabbed his shoulders and hauled him into a quick, hard embrace. "How the hell are you, son?"

Gabriel represented everything good in this world as well as the hoped-for future of the race.

"I'm better now that we got the weapon. But listen, we left behind about two hundred women in the Dark Cave system. Is there any chance you have a security team that could try to get them out?" He then outlined how the battle had gone and that, in addition to the women, they'd find fifty dead vampires.

He glanced at Shayna for a penetrating moment, then back to Marius. "I'll take care of this right now." He drew his phone from the depths of the long, woven robe he wore and made a call. He spoke quietly and when he was done he nodded to Marius. "They're on the way."

"How? Don't you need the location?"

Gabriel glanced at Shayna. "I picked it up from your woman, sort of an afterimage of the entire journey. I'll keep you informed."

Marius stared at him for a long moment. Gabriel had always kept his cards close to the vest and he suspected that the man he called his surrogate father had a number of quiet ways he'd been working to undermine Daniel. That he had the power to simply order one of his teams, over the phone, back to the Dark Dave system, and to be so confident of success, gave Marius a hope he hadn't had in a long time.

He nodded to Gabriel, then gestured to the weapon. "I'm hoping this is it, the last of the experiments from the 1950s.

"But let me introduce you to the woman who made this possible. Gabriel, this is Shayna Prentiss from Seattle. Shayna, this is Gabriel, one of the leaders of our world, though currently lying low."

Shayna extended her hand and Gabriel took it in both of his. "Welcome to the Pharaoh system. From the depths of my soul, thank you for your willingness to help us. My people will sing songs about your sacrifice for years to come."

"That's very kind, but it hardly feels like a sacrifice. More like a mission."

Gabriel smiled. "Yes, it was that. Whatever brought you here and gave you the courage to face so much horror, I'm grateful. And this last one, gaining control of the weapon, has saved our people an enormous amount of suffering."

"I saw it in operation, in a vision. It was horrible."

Marius saw the shadow cross over Shayna's face and knew she was thinking about the female vampires in the cage who had perished. He quickly slid an arm around her waist.

Gabriel grew very solemn, his lips pressed into a grim line. "Visions of any kind can be a difficult burden to bear. I hope in time that what you saw will be eased from your memories."

"I hope so, too." Her gaze shifted to the weapon. "But at least we got it."

Both Gabriel and Marius turned their attention to the weapon as well.

Marius let go of Shayna and moved to slide a hand down the angled red roof. "We need to deactivate this thing right now, but you should clear the room. The lower casing has been retrofitted with a battery pack so that it can be fired up anywhere. One flip of the switch"—he rounded the machine and pointed it out—"will send out killing sound waves that would take us all down within seconds. Although the waves can't penetrate altered flight."

Gabriel called out, "Disperse to altered flight."

The response of his team was almost instantaneous. The men levitated as one and shifted to altered flight, each hovering in place. Impressive.

Gabriel, however, remained standing stoically nearby but Marius refused to do anything until his good friend was safe. He remained staring at him resolutely, until Gabriel's lips quirked and he joined his security force.

Marius carefully tilted the weapon on its side to expose the lower casing. Flipping a compartment with a simple mechanical slide plate exposed a battery pack. He reached in and within a few seconds, he'd disabled the machine, removing eight packs all linked together.

He was about to set it upright again, when Shayna caught his arm. "Join Gabriel and his men and let me test it out. We don't want an accident because we've been tricked."

He held her gaze, frowning slightly. "What made you say that?"

She narrowed her gaze. "Because Daniel is devious and this would be right up his alley."

At that, he smiled. "You're absolutely right. We'll err on the side of caution."

"So good ahead, shift."

"Yes, ma'am."

Shayna grinned, which made her look like she was about sixteen. But he obeyed and shifted to altered flight. When she flipped the switch, the damn thing went off, the vibrations of the weapon shaking the ground and trembling through the air. She hit the switch immediately, shutting it down.

"That bastard," she shouted.

Marius dropped out of altered flight. He asked for a sledgehammer, intending to pulverize the weapon then and there, but Gabriel, on solid ground once more, intervened. "I've got a better idea. Let me get my detonation squad in here. They'll be fully protected and

I think our best course will be to blow this damn thing up."

Marius thought it was the best idea he'd heard yet. "Let's do it."

But he couldn't leave. In fact, everyone stayed while the team was brought in and the explosives rigged.

Shifting to altered flight with Shayna held tight in his arms, he took her away, moving past a wall of stone to hover in a nearby unimproved cavern as he mentally did the ten-second countdown.

The explosion rattled through the immediate cavern surroundings. After a couple of minutes, the squad gave the all-clear and everyone moved back in.

Marius thought he'd always remember the burnt, chemical stench of the space as one of the best smells in his life since the last remaining weapon lay scattered in smoking ruins.

"Are we sure this is the last one?" Shayna asked.

Gabriel turned toward her. "Why don't you do a search? From what I understand, now that you've had so much contact with this weapon, you'd be able to find even the smallest part of one."

"I will." Then she did something that surprised Marius. She moved close and took his hand. *Will you support me right now? I mean, with your power? I'm afraid I'm still shaking.*

God, yes. Whatever you need.

For some reason, his words caused her lips to part as she stared at him, searching his face.

What? For a moment, he thought he might have offended her somehow, but he wasn't getting that through the chain-bond they shared.

You have no idea who you are, that's why I'm amazed

right now. You're one of the most supportive men I've ever known.

He was taken aback. *Okay. Thank you, I guess. But why wouldn't I be when you've helped us all so much? My God, it seems like such a small thing.*

At that, she smiled. *Maybe.*

He moved in close, sliding an arm around her waist. *Ready when you are.*

She closed her eyes and he felt her begin her locating search. He also sensed the clarity of that search, that her skills had improved tremendously. Between the visions that were no longer marred with dark waves and what he sensed right now, he knew that Eve's experiment had proved exactly the right therapy for Shayna. Her abilities felt solid in a way they hadn't before.

Of course, she was siphoning his power, a steady stream that flowed out of him, something he loved. But Shayna had changed.

She took a long time as she extended her locator ability, and the minutes piled up.

Everything okay?

I'm trying to be thorough. I'm going continent by continent. The Western Hemisphere is clear.

He shared that with the group and a cheer went up.

He felt Shayna falter for a few seconds because of the noise, but she quickly put herself back on track.

A few minutes later Shayna sagged against him as she opened her eyes. "I didn't find anything and trust me, I cruised the entire globe. There's nothing there."

Gabriel smiled. "While you were doing your search, I had another locator do her search—Adrien's woman, Lily. She didn't find anything, either. I think we're good to go."

The cheer that went up this time shook the air.

A wave of something Marius didn't recognize at first flowed through his body and he kept cheering. The biggest, most dangerous obstacle his world had ever faced no longer existed.

He immediately called Rumy, who communicated the news to his security team. More cheering resonated through his phone.

Gabriel finally quieted everyone down and added another bit of information. "The team I just sent out, a hundred of my best men, got the slaves out, the ones living in squalor beneath the land bridge. No sign of Daniel, either. The women are safe."

"Thank God," Shayna murmured as another cheer went up.

When everyone had once again grown quiet, Gabriel dispersed his team but gave permission at the same time to spread the news far and wide. The latest threat to the peace and safety of their world had just ended.

Turning to Marius, Gabriel clapped a hand on his shoulder. "Well done. Now I have something I want to give Shayna with your permission, but it's something of a surprise. Will you allow it?"

"Of course." It went without saying that Marius trusted Gabriel with his life.

CHAPTER 13

The process of using Marius's power and her own innate locating ability to search the earth for any trace of a remaining extinction weapon had left Shayna feeling strung out. But she couldn't imagine what kind of surprise Gabriel had in store for her, although a hot bubble bath sounded really nice about now.

Shayna knew Gabriel was a really important person in Marius's life. He was an exiled leader of their world and a father figure for Marius and his brothers. He was handsome with strong cheekbones, piercing gray eyes, and short, spiked black hair. Beyond that, he radiated a kind of warmth that instantly made her trust him.

"Follow me," the Ancestral said.

She hopped on board Marius's booted foot, a much easier task to accomplish given her running shoes, and settled against him. How comfortable the process had become since the first painful flight out of Seattle. She felt as though years had passed instead of just a couple of days, that she'd lived a lifetime with the man holding her tight and helping her feel secure.

The trip was short given that both men could fly at lightning speed, but the trajectory took them deep into the North African earth through cavern after cavern. A lot of the cave systems were layered one on top of the other, often amounting to hundreds of nonlinear miles—an unfathomable number.

Marius landed them in what proved to be a large, comfortable guest suite, with a broad, thin waterfall extending the entire length of the dining area. Soft lights at the base set the blue-flecked wall behind the water glittering.

All the furniture appeared to be made of mahogany with freestanding walls separating the rooms. Glancing up, she understood why. The tall curved ceilings were kept in their natural light-blue crystals, a physical structure very familiar to her. "Oh, my God, this is a geode, or at least part of one." She'd never been more surprised.

Gabriel smiled. "Essentially, yes, one of the larger ones in our world. When this one was discovered and excavated, portions were shipped elsewhere to other dwellings to be shaped into new architectural features. But this is the original. I kept it for myself and had it made into a haven of sorts."

"So you sometimes come here? This is part of your home?"

His smile broadened. "Not exactly. I have felt for a long time that someone would be coming into our world who

could put this space to use, if just temporarily. Once I
heard about you, Shayna, I decided that if the situation
permitted, I wanted you to stay here."

"Really?" His decision had shocked her, although suddenly Gabriel seemed very familiar to her, but she couldn't
quite place him. "Why?"

"I'll get to that in a minute." He then went on to show
them the various rooms, which included a large library
with hundreds of books, several worktables covered in
sheets of leather, magnifying glasses on stands, and
brushes that Shayna knew were archaeological tools.

Awareness started to dawn.

There was even a sledgehammer leaning against a
wall. She laughed and went to it, touching the handle. Was
it possible?

Her heart rate soared as she turned back to Gabriel and
recognized him and the space from one of her first visions, the one she'd known had been meant just for her.

What's wrong? Marius quickly moved in and once
more slid his arm around her waist.

Nothing, she responded quickly. *I'm fine.* She'd forgotten that she hadn't shared this particular vision with Marius.

Her gaze skimmed the wall next to the sledgehammer.
The fact that she'd already seen what lay behind the wall
set her to trembling all over again.

Shayna, this isn't nothing.

Turning toward him, she confessed that she'd seen this
in a vision and her eyes filled with tears.

You're overcome.

*I am. But just wait until you see what lies beyond that
wall.*

Gabriel didn't say anything. He just stepped up to the wall, moving with the same lithe, muscular grace that Marius did. Gabriel picked up the sledgehammer and smiled. He let the handle slide through his fingers to the end. "You might want to step away for this."

Shayna felt Marius's confusion as they both moved back about ten feet, but her own mounting anticipation almost had her floating.

Gabriel drew the hammer back then struck the wall. Just like that the thin layer of stone crumbled, revealing an arched doorway.

She was already in motion and stepped over the rubble to move inside. Everything was as it had been in the vision.

Marius's voice sounded from behind her. "What the hell is this? Are these clay tablets?"

Gabriel's gaze drifted slowly up the tall stack. "Our history."

"You mean our written history?"

"Cuneiform," Shayna said. "Like all those pics I've taken."

Gabriel removed the nearest tablet from one of the shorter stacks and held it out for Shayna to inspect. She shook her head slowly from side to side. "This is absolutely amazing."

She understood now that most modern vampires believed the symbols to be an ancient carving design, since so many of the stone patterns had names and origins.

Marius drew close. "So this is what you were talking about."

"Yes, it is, like ancient Sumer."

"Then this is our language."

"The written word." Shayna didn't dare touch the tablet. Something this old, probably several millennia, needed to be handled with care.

"Where shall I put this?" Gabriel asked.

Shayna's throat had grown very tight as she met Gabriel's warm gaze. "On the table, please. I presume you have gloves I can use."

He nodded, moving back into the room with all the tables and equipment. "I should have used them as well, but I was too impatient." He carried the large, heavy tablet back into the workroom.

Shayna forgot about everything else, including Marius. She knew the men hovered and responded quickly to everything she requested, including additional lighting and a different chair, one that swiveled and rolled. She had them set two of the tables at right angles. She requested a computer and within a few minutes had a complete working setup because Gabriel said he would do anything she wanted and she took him at his administrative word. The man knew how to run an organization, just like Rumy.

Marius brought her a glass of iced tea. She caught his hand and looked into his eyes. She blinked rapidly. "This is beyond anything I'd ever expected or hoped to experience in the entire course of my life."

"Good. I'm glad."

He kissed her hand and, for a moment, she almost lost sight of her goal, which apparently involved finding the key to the old language as quickly as possible.

But Marius released her hand quickly and she resumed staring at the tablet now lying beneath the large magnifying glass.

She found that the same phrase repeated itself in the

carvings in the various caves, which would make sense. Maybe it was a blessing, or perhaps a warning—she couldn't be sure.

Hours passed.

After she had stretched her aching back for the tenth time, Marius rubbed her shoulders. "Dinner just arrived."

She met his gaze over her shoulder. "I just realized I'm famished." And that's when she felt his need hitting her in a series of strong waves. The man was blood-starved.

She'd been so caught up in studying this incredible sealed-up find that she'd blocked all sensations flowing from him. But what she found beyond his hunger was something so close to affection, maybe even love, that she almost stumbled when she left her chair.

The earlier question took a new shape in her mind. Could she have a life with Marius, a real life full of love and belonging, in this hidden world?

Marius took Shayna's hand and had started to lead her to the dining area when she caught sight of the doorway to the tablet room and stopped in her tracks.

"The debris is all gone. When did that happen?"

He squeezed her hand. "I think that was going on about the time you were exclaiming over the quality of the tablets and the clarity of each imprint."

He could see she was about to expound on the same theme, so he reminded her that dinner was waiting.

"Right, yes, right. I really am starved."

Marius seated her and poured her a glass of red wine.

"This is a feast and I don't think I've seen this dish before."

"It's wonderful," Marius said. "It's a bulgur salad made

of cracked wheat, tomatoes, onions, parsley, and an olive oil vinaigrette."

She put a large spoonful on her plate and took a bite. "That's heavenly."

He sipped his wine and watched her for a few moments. He needed to feed from her vein badly because of the recent battle, but he wanted this time to be about Shayna.

And he wouldn't have disturbed her, not even if he was close to death. He knew what the tablets had meant for her, the joy that such a tremendous discovery had been, something that Gabriel had kept secret for well over five hundred years, probably longer. He'd given her one of the finest experiences of her life by allowing her the privilege of a first look at the ancient treasure and history of the vampire world.

He understood that she was looking at the footings of his entire civilization.

And so did Gabriel.

But Gabriel's motives weren't entirely pure.

While Shayna had been busy exploring the tablets, Gabriel had told Marius that though the extinction weapon was no longer a threat, he knew Daniel had to be removed from power. He was hoping that something Shayna might learn, or perhaps had already learned, about their world would provide them with a clue as to how to unseat the most powerful vampire of the past two millennia.

Marius sampled the fare as well, savoring charred chicken kebabs cooked with onions and peppers, the salad, and a very fine hummus served with chunks of bread torn from a soft round loaf.

"Marius?"

He glanced up at her. "Yes?" He cut one of the chicken pieces in half, speared it with his fork, then added a slice of red pepper.

She had her elbow on the table and waved her fork in the air back and forth several times. "How did you do the split-self thing, the one with a primary self and a secondary one? Of all the things I've seen in your world, that single act astonished me the most. How can you battle as two people?"

He could do more than just battle, but he decided that was more than Shayna should have to deal with right now. He shrugged. "Actually, I'm not sure of the physiology of it and it's not something all vampires can do."

"But you can. And your brothers?"

"Yes."

"Is there a working theory as to how the process functions?"

He sipped his wine. "Well, some think it might be a sort of super speed—being in one place but moving fast enough to appear as though you're in two different locations."

"Is that what it feels like to you?"

He shook his head. "I don't know. Not exactly. I think it's just a function of our world, like altered flight. It just is. We walk, we levitate, we fly, we have visions, we create strange intricate disguises, and some of us can split into two beings for short periods of time."

She settled back in her chair appearing to absorb his answer. "You are a unique race."

At that, he smiled. "Thank you. Now it's my turn. So what do you think of the tablets? Is this a code you can break?"

"Historical linguistics isn't my field of expertise," she

said, dragging a piece of bread through the hummus. "I've only had a couple of classes, though I am completely fascinated by the subject. Is there anyone in your world who knows the ancient language, who speaks it, and perhaps created a working alphabet?"

"You could start by surfing our Internet."

She took a sip of wine and leaned back in her chair, her gaze sliding over the waterfall. "If I could just get that alphabet, I could work at a translation. Then I think I might have something for you."

"I'll see what I can find out as well."

She met and held his gaze. "Thanks. Marius, I'm sorry I haven't been paying attention to you and I do know that you need to, you know, hit my vein."

The thrill that her choice of words created rocked his entire body. He had to take a really deep breath to keep from launching straight at her throat.

She leaned close and took his hand. "I wish I could have captured the look on your face right now."

The scent of her sex suddenly permeated the air. Her response to him had been present almost from the beginning, something that had kept him on fire for her.

He squeezed her fingers, losing all appetite for the food on his plate. His desire to haul her into the bedroom intensified.

This time Shayna took a deep breath, another sip of wine, then turned her attention to her plate. After a bite of hummus and bread, she didn't look at him when she said, "Eat."

Marius picked up his fork and followed her lead. He took one forkful of the bulgur salad, then another. For what they'd both been through, she was right. They both should replenish their reserves.

"Do you really think I'll be able to help by looking over these ancient tablets?"

"Gabriel seems to think it's worth a shot, and I would count on his opinion for that. He's been an Ancestral as well as part of the policy-making sector of our world for a long time. Daniel has tried to off him several times, but he seems to stay one step ahead of the bastard.

"He helped develop the courts, which Daniel recently undermined and took over. No one in our world has had enough raw power to match Daniel. And over the years, a lot of our most influential leaders have had to go underground in order to survive. Many, of course, were assassinated through the years."

She dabbed at the hummus. "So in your opinion, Daniel has been working for a good long while to consolidate his power, including trying to take possession of a working extinction weapon."

Marius nodded. "A year ago, when he arrested Adrien, Lucian, and myself, he launched this particular nightmare. Before that, we'd worked hard to keep his ambitions in check. We patrolled the world nightly and battled his forces when they tried to strong-arm our leaders or engage in kidnapping and torture. As soon as he took over the Council of Ancestrals, and afterward our five main courts, he arrested us and sent us to the Himalayan prison. At least half the Council went into hiding at the same time."

She fell silent and continued to eat steadily, but her eyes flitted about in that searching way of hers as though seeking answers to questions she hadn't yet posed.

"I hope I can help," she stated at last.

"You've already done so much. But please, don't feel obligated to stay. You've done what we set out to do, to capture the weapon. This"—and he waved in the direction of the workroom—"well, I'm sure there are experts in our world who can take over."

At that, she turned toward him, laughing. "Obligated?" She gestured with an arm flung in the same direction as his. "I've been given the opportunity of a lifetime, my deepest heart's desire. No, Marius, I don't feel obligated. More like, I'm wondering how I'll ever leave."

The words struck Marius to the core of his being and that same thrill returned, riding his nerves like an electric storm. Desire hit next all over again, so that this time he was on his feet and didn't hold back.

He sensed her own responsive need for him and clattered her fork on her plate. She rose at the same time, stretching her arms out to him so that he'd caught her up in a tight embrace before he realized it.

The feeling, the desire, was damn mutual. "I want to take you to bed and make love to you. How does that sound?"

"You'd better," she murmured, then kissed him hard. When she parted her lips he drove his tongue inside so that he felt her body weaken against his.

He caught her up in his arms and carried her to the bedroom. But as he turned toward the bed, he laughed. "I wondered why Gabriel had gone in here just before he left. The man's a romantic." The covers were pulled back and three long-stemmed white roses lay on the dark-blue silk sheets.

Shayna leaned her head against the crook of his neck. "He thinks we're lovers."

Marius turned her just enough to look into her eyes. "Aren't we?"

She shivered. "Oh, yes, we are at least that."

And right now, he wanted what he'd never thought to have in his entire life: He wanted Shayna to be *his woman.*

Shayna lay facedown on the bed, one of the thornless roses clutched in her hand, the intoxicating rich scent adding yet another layer of pleasure.

Her clothes were gone and just before Marius had told her to stretch out on her stomach, she'd caught a glimpse of his naked body. All that sheer masculine brawn had made her more than willing to do whatever he wanted her to do.

That, and she trusted him.

She felt his hands first on the backs of her thighs, his thumbs kneading the swell of each of her buns. He pressed his fingers into the outside of her thighs, massaging gently.

She released a sigh. The man could touch her anywhere and she'd grow limp and yielding, just wanting more.

Her fingers played over the white velvety petals as he swept his hands lower and pushed her legs apart. She felt the mattress move so she knew he'd climbed between.

It was exciting to know he was behind her—but she couldn't see all of him, just glimpses now and then when she craned her neck. He'd lit a single candle, a very bright spot given how well she could see, but it had the advantage of casting light and shadow over his muscles.

He planted his hands on either side of her shoulders and she felt his stiff cock as he slowly slid it up her crack all the way to her waist, letting her feel him.

All that maleness made her hips rock, pushing into the mattress.

He covered her hands with his and locked their fingers

together. She gripped him hard in return. She needed this experience with him more than anything, to be this close to him after all they'd been through, to be physically joined with him. The blood-chain was one extraordinary experience, but nothing could ever replace the sheer physicality of sex.

He kissed the back of her neck repeatedly, and she arched enough so that his tongue could reach the vein.

I want to take you from behind and drink from you like this. Would that please you?

She moaned softly. *Yes, it sounds wonderful. Ah, Marius.*

Yes?

No question, really. I just like saying your name. She said it aloud this time. "Marius."

While still laying kisses over her neck, he dipped low to push his cock between her legs. He released her right hand and slid his arm under her stomach, pulling her up onto her knees. He swept her long hair off her right shoulder well away from her throat, then used his hand to find her entrance.

She cried out at the mere feel of his cock starting to push inside. "I love how that feels."

"You're so wet for me." He drew back, gripped her hips, and with firm thrusts made his way inside. He took his time and with a steady rhythm, in and out, began building her pleasure.

"I love doing this to you, Shayna."

She was already breathing hard because it felt so good. She supported herself on her arms, something she found easy to do because his power constantly fueled her. As he pushed in she started pushing back, which caused him to groan. "Damn, that feels good."

She moved faster and he did the same. At this rate, it wouldn't take long. "Marius, drink from me."

He leaned over her. "We need to slow this down."

"You're right. You get me so excited."

"Same here."

Once more, he kissed her shoulder, her neck, her back, but kept his hips moving, though at a much slower pace. She closed her eyes and savored. She loved the way he smelled, that summer grass scent of his. She turned her head a little more and his lips sought out her mouth. She shifted, turning farther to meet him.

When he kissed her, she moaned all over again. His tongue pierced her deep, swirling inside. His cock matched the movement, and she groaned heavily because he hit her just right.

Oh, Marius, that feels way too good.

So, of course, he did it again.

And again.

He held her tight at the waist so he never lost his rhythm and kept her in place on the bed. She had the thought again that before Marius, she'd never really known what sex was, on any level.

The blood-chain helped, because she could feel his pleasure, another sensation that kept her tightening around him deep inside because she knew how good it felt to him.

He kissed down her chin and once more began to lick all up her neck, finding the exact spot where the vein would rise.

She loved that sensation and it made her clench deep within all over again.

Drink from me, Marius.

Do you want to feel my fangs? Do you want me to nip your vein and take from you?

She moaned and writhed against him. *Yes. Please, yes. Now.* She whimpered. She couldn't help it. It all felt so good, so incredible.

When he drew back, she knew he was lowering his fangs. Her whole body stilled. The strike was quick, then his lips formed a seal and he began to suck.

This time he groaned heavily, his cock pushing inside her. *You can't know what you taste like, Shayna. But it's amazing and your blood fires me up.*

His cock grew harder, bigger, and he pushed more heavily now. Each thrust made her cry out repeatedly.

He went faster and faster, the suckling sounds another added sensation.

I'm going to come. She wasn't sure how she got the words out.

I want you to come, Shayna. I can hold back but I want to feel your orgasm and I want to taste those sweet flavors as I drink from you.

The orgasm began to pulse, driving along her clitoris then up inside her body as he whipped in and out. The sensations kept flowing, so that she could hardly breathe. She knew she was moaning or shouting or something because it felt so good.

A powerful wave of pleasure flooded her abdomen, her stomach, her chest. She shouted repeatedly, her hips flexing into each thrust until the wave softened on the shore.

He slowed his hips at the same time, the sucking at her neck as well, easing her down.

She worked to catch her breath as he continued to drink.

That was beautiful, Shayna. I felt your pleasure, what it's like for you to have my cock buried deep.

And I felt how close you were. I want you to come, Marius. Are you ready?

God, yes.

He thrust heavily now, but he wanted something more, something he had a hard time putting a word to, something that made no sense. He finally let go of his hold on her vein and kissed her shoulder, her throat, and the back of her neck once more. He loved taking her in this position, covering her.

He remained kissing near the top of her spine, then licking in that place as well. He angled his head but kept his fangs in check. With Shayna, his fangs were always one breath away from emerging, something else that remained a mystery for him. Why did she bring such strong instincts pounding through his body?

And here was another one: that while still thrusting his cock into her, he felt a need to bite her, though just with his teeth and not breaking skin.

Shayna, will you let me do something to you? Will you permit me to bite you here, at the base of your neck, where I'm licking? I won't use my fangs, I promise.

Her whole body writhed in response. She hardly needed to speak the words; he'd had his answer. But what followed sent another thrill streaking down his body and straight through his cock. "Marius, do whatever you want to do. I feel a drive in you that needs to be satisfied. Bite me hard, if that's what you want to do."

He kept licking the base of her neck. "Bend your head forward. Yes, just like that."

He angled slightly, then took as much of her in his mouth as he could, grabbing hold of her nape with his teeth and clamping on.

Shayna cried out. *You have no idea how good that feels. Oh, God, Marius, I'm going to come again.*

He had complete control of her, the way animals in the wild could control other animals. He held her firmly and speeded up his thrusts at the same time. He could feel the excitement coursing through her and loved hearing her guttural cries as he plunged in and out.

She gripped his cock now with her internal muscles, in the same way he had command of her neck. His balls tightened. *Shayna, I'm close. I'm going to go faster.*

Do it.

He moved with a speed only his kind could attain. Her pleasure began to rush through her as his release came. A geyser of fire exploded through him, streaking through his cock. But he held on to her neck, biting down just a little harder.

He heard her cries of ecstasy and he grunted deep from his gut. The intense sensation caused his vision to falter. He'd never experienced anything like this.

The orgasm eased down, but he wasn't done. He knew his power had increased, but apparently what came with it was more than one release.

He was breathing hard, still working her low but slowly.

She panted and pushed her hips against him.

I'll be coming a second time, Shayna. You ready?

Yes. My whole body is thrumming with a kind of vibration and all because you're holding my neck. I wish I could tell you what it feels like.

But he could tell; the chain at his neck told him everything. *I can feel it, Shayna, and it feels the same way to me, another point of connection.*

He started moving faster and her body released another wave of moisture that had him pumping hard.

When she came this time, she screamed and the intensity of her pleasure forced him to release her neck and rise up. He held her hips in place and thrust. She arched her neck, still crying out repeatedly.

As before, his balls tightened and he let go.

Pleasure rushed through his body once more, intense and fiery as he gave her his essence. His arms felt bulked up, his thighs, his back. He roared, lifted his head, feeling her pleasure roll and his own drive to the pinnacle finally peak. He groaned heavily. He'd never had such a profound orgasm.

He felt Shayna's ecstasy crest. She breathed hard as the last of her cries left her throat. As her arms gave way and she stretched out flat, he moved with her, firm enough to remain connected to her. He lay on top, his body rising and falling with his own harsh breaths.

He felt so fucking good.

She stretched out her hands and he covered them, once more linking fingers. The three roses lay askew.

Marius felt so much in this moment that he couldn't separate the strands of his emotions. Gratitude, mostly, rose to the surface. He was so thankful she'd stayed in his world long enough to help him find the final extinction weapon. And what an extraordinary thing that something about her had increased his power almost as though he was an Ancestral. The fact that he had no proximity issue with her at all had him baffled and amazed.

But he was also grateful for this: how much just being with her had deepened his life in ways hard to explain. He hated the saying, but he honestly felt more complete as a man, even as a vampire, because she was in his life.

He felt her emotions as well, mostly that she was caught up in the feel-good of sex. Her breathing had evened out and her fingers worked his, stroking him gently, a very affectionate movement.

"Marius, the way you caught my neck in your mouth was incredible. I want you to know that. I don't know what it did, but I had these sensations rippling through my body, straight between my legs because of it. I definitely want to do that again."

He shifted slightly, angling once more, and bit her in the same place, giving her neck a soft shake.

She giggled and his cock jerked. She moaned. "I want to stay like this forever. Just like this. I love the feel of you still connected to me."

He released her neck and reclined his head off to the side of hers once more, half on her arm, half on the pillow. He could get used to this—a thought that sent a shard of anxiety moving through him.

"What is it?" she asked.

He decided to be honest with her. "I keep having a powerful desire to beg you to stay with me, but I know it can't work for so many reasons, most of which you already know."

"And some come from me." She released a heavy sigh. "I want to face you to have this conversation. Can we do that?"

He nodded, then disengaged, pulling from her slowly. He hadn't wanted to, but she was right: The moment required some talk.

As he shifted off her, he would have left the bed to

fetch her a washcloth, she but she caught his arm. "Don't go yet." She tugged him back to her so that this time, he lay on top of her face to face.

She caressed his face and leaned up to kiss him. He responded, kissing her back.

She rested her head on the pillow. "I wish we could keep doing this, Marius, stay together forever. Part of me feels so strange about being here now, as though I can't imagine ever leaving. Yet I've only been here a couple of days. I fault the intensity of what we've been through for that, as though we've lived together for a hundred years."

"I feel the same way." But the situation felt deeper than that, something he couldn't explain. "I keep thinking about how drawn you are to the tablets and our ancient language, to all that we are as a society."

"But don't you see? That's because I'm an anthropologist."

"Are you sure it isn't more than that?"

She held his gaze, searching his eyes. "I honestly don't know." She looked away from him, but this time her eyes didn't flit around. Instead, it was as though she was searching deep within herself. Finally, she said, "Can we visit the refugees tomorrow night? The ones that Gabriel had his men rescue?"

At that, he laughed and shook his head.

"What?" She seemed genuinely surprised.

"Well, for one thing, we were talking about the unique aspects of our relationship including how drawn we are to each other, and suddenly you want to visit with the refugees."

She smiled sheepishly. "Oh, I can see how you would

think that. But here's where my mind went. I know that for me everything shifted when you originally took me through the Dark Cave system. The plight of all those women supported my decision to stay. The longer I'm with you, the more I want to stay, so I think I need more data to help me understand my relationship with you and how I might fit into your world here. Does that make any sense at all?"

Marius hated just how much his heart soared with even a hint that Shayna might stay. Yet at the exact same moment, the other powerful reality of his life flowed through him in a painful agonizing wave. He shifted, rolling onto his back to lie next to her.

She leaned up on her elbow to look at him. "Marius, what is it? I don't understand. I was talking about seeing the refugees and the next moment that horrible guilt is on you again. I wish like anything that you'd tell me the whole story. I feel that you've held on to something for a long time, and you need to let it go. What happened that you feel as though your life must only be about making war, about battling Daniel and his kind? Won't you tell me?"

He stared into her eyes. He wanted to tell her the truth, but he knew it would change things forever, even ruin what he had with her right in this moment. If she knew the truth, she'd walk out the door and never look back. He settled his arm over his forehead, partially shading his eyes. Yet he had to tell her something; he owed her that much.

"I won't go into the specifics, but I will tell you this." He felt how quiet she'd fallen, almost reverent. "I betrayed my brothers in the worst way possible."

When? How?

Her questions hit his mind like swiftly thrown daggers. He moved his arm to his side and stared at her. "Shayna, I just told you I didn't want to talk about this in detail."

She clamped a hand over her mouth. "I'm sorry. The questions slipped so fast through my head that I must have shifted into telepathy without thinking. Pretend I didn't ask. And you know how I am with the questions."

He nodded and settled into the pillows. "I think that's all I can tell you, but that's the guilt you keep feeling and it's the main reason I've fought as hard as I have. I've been trying to make up for this for the past four hundred years."

"Do your brothers know?"

"Of course they know. They were punished for what I told Daniel."

"So this happened when you were a child?"

He nodded, but nothing else would come. "Let it go, Shayna. Just know that I'll never be free of the remorse I feel."

"It's impacted your life, hasn't it? I mean, that's why you're not married, why you haven't found someone to share your life with."

"I'm sure it's one of the reasons."

He glanced at her and the odd thought went through his head that maybe another reason was that he'd been waiting for her all this time. Even Gabriel must have felt it, how special she was. Why else would he have opened up the secret vault of tablets just for her, a human?

But the weight of his guilt had settled in hard and he rolled from bed.

Wish I could help. Her voice, full of sympathy, made him cringe.

He didn't turn to look at her as he headed to the bathroom, but let his thoughts fly. *Wish you could as well.*

The next moment, he heard running feet and before he reached the shower, she caught him from behind, wrapping both her arms around his chest, holding him fast.

His throat tightened painfully.

He overlaid her arms with his own, holding her fast just as she was holding him. For a moment he couldn't breathe. All the air had rushed from his lungs, and his eyes burned. He wished like anything that this woman would stay, this lovely, eccentric question-riddled human, with her long white-blond hair and light-blue eyes, with her tenderness of heart, her love of other cultures, and her beautiful willing body.

God, yes, he wanted her to stay.

An hour later Shayna sat on a park bench deep inside the Catskill system in the state of New York. The cavern was one of the more massive ones she'd seen and had been cloaked in an intricate layer of disguises that not even Marius could detect, let alone see through—Gabriel's handiwork, no doubt.

The Catskill refugee center housed five thousand former female slaves and even a few men, mostly human but with a smattering of vampire slaves as well. She and Marius had learned that Gabriel and Rumy together had built and paid for about a dozen of these centers throughout their world, all hidden, and they'd filled each to capacity. Apparently they'd had several black-ops forces working in secret over a long period of time, stealing slaves out of a number of sex-slave organizations around the globe.

She sat facing a large park, where a number of women wandered about and talked in groups. A massive complex, built into the adjacent cave wall, formed the dormitories and gathering rooms, as well as several classrooms that served the refugees.

A couple dozen of the latest refugees that Gabriel had recovered from the Dark Cave system sat with her. The women had told her all about the rescue mission, that a hundred male vampires had suddenly just shown up and that the extraction had taken less than two minutes.

She kept shaking her head in between all the comments. Something wasn't adding up, which was why she kept pelting the group with her questions. She just couldn't seem to get to the center of something very important, something critical to the vampire world.

She asked the group at large. "So if I've understood correctly, what you're saying, especially those of you who had been enslaved for over a year, that neither Daniel nor his two sons Quill and Lev was even in residence for most of that time?" She had always supposed that Daniel would have spent most of his time in the Dark Cave system, engaging in the orgies he sponsored and sold.

A murmured ascent went around the group. An Indian woman spoke up. "You could always tell when they were gone. The vampires left in charge became more relaxed, and there were fewer assaults. Some of the guards even protected us from customers who became too rough. Daniel would have been furious at such leniency and more than once he beheaded vampires for treating us kindly."

Everything about that statement spoke to Daniel's character, but something else as well. Was it possible that the Ancestrals, which all three men of these men were, enthralled those vampires around them? Although sheer intimidation could make vampires and humans alike behave in ways they might otherwise not. This was a cross-cultural condition: Faced with the prospect of torture and/or death, most will succumb to the required behavior.

Of course she left her supposition open to further study, observation, and analysis. She resisted drawing absolute conclusions, life being an absurdly dynamic process, always changing. Even her presence here in the vampire world had given new meaning to the concept of change being the only constant.

But the larger question remained. "So where did Daniel and his sons go? What were they doing when they were gone? Were there rumors?"

A fair-haired Russian slave, more emaciated than most of the slaves, responded. "More than once I heard he was building something in one of the largest caverns in this world, but I do not know where it would be or what it was."

Others confirmed the rumor.

She mentally reviewed all that she knew about the horrors of the Dark Cave system, leading her to pose a question for which she expected no particular answer. "Were any humans ever given special treatment, so they didn't have to work as sex slaves?"

To her surprise, the response was an overwhelming affirmative accompanied by a shocking bit of information: Most of the women were put through a series of tests, and the brightest were actually administered standard IQ tests. As she continued asking her questions, she became increasingly alarmed since the consensus seemed to be that at least five and maybe as much as ten percent of the arrivals of the past year were sent elsewhere, presumably not to work in the clubs.

"And the rumors about where they went?"

The Russian responded once more. "To the same system, the one with the enormous cavern."

CHAPTER 14

"So what happened when you set off the explosion?" Marius sat at a distance from Shayna. Rumy sat beside him on one of dozens of benches scattered throughout the park.

Rumy shook his head. "I'd hoped Daniel would buy it, but no such luck. I think he read the light in my eye before I shifted to altered flight and the room blew."

"What did he want?"

"He wanted you. I don't know what bug crawled up his ass, but he seems determined to get you and not necessarily to kill you. I didn't see this with either Adrien or Lucian. I think he wanted to get all three of you to join forces with him, but he honestly didn't give a rat's ass if Lucian died out there on the lake. No, he seems to want you for something."

"Well, he can go fuck himself."

Rumy chuckled. "Tell me how you really feel." He smoothed down his tight curls. He kept his hair cropped and oiled. "The thing is, Marius, there was something different about his security detail."

"How so?"

"They wore something new that looked like real uniforms. It just seemed odd."

"In what way?"

He shifted toward Marius. "For one thing, there was a line of weird-looking marks above a silver emblem. The emblem was a hawk. I'd never seen anything like it before. Have you? When confronting Daniel? It had, I don't know, a professional look, a branded look."

Marius shook his head. "No, I can't recall ever seeing anything like that. I know he kept his men in black, but hell, that's what we all wear to remain invisible when we fly through any city at night. Black is standard and sensible. But, no, I've never seen a hawk emblem before."

"What do you think it means?"

Marius crossed his arms over his chest. "Haven't got a clue." His gaze was fixed on Shayna. He purposefully kept her in sight and right now he felt a new emotion from her: She'd changed from anthropologically curious to pretty anxious. Something the women had said was distressing her.

"So what the hell happened in the Dark Cave system? I heard some of the refugees say they thought Shayna was committing suicide when she threw herself off some kind of catwalk."

Marius told him about her ploy and how well it had worked.

Rumy's eyes went wide. "And this woman isn't trained military?"

Marius had to laugh. "No, not even a little."

"She sure has guts."

Marius nodded. "That she has."

Rumy elbowed Marius. "You're into her."

"Shut your trap."

Rumy laughed. "I could hardly blame you. She's gorgeous. Quirky, but beautiful. And those breasts, a vampire could—"

He got no farther, because Marius moved like lightning and now had hold of Rumy's throat. "Don't ever go there again."

Rumy's eyes widened and he nodded slowly. He coughed and sputtered when Marius released him. "Sorry. My mistake. Won't happen again. But you're not into her, right?"

"Cute."

"Just sayin'."

Marius resumed his seat, settling his gaze back on Shayna. He felt uneasy for reasons he couldn't explain and rubbed the back of his neck. Something was bugging him. Maybe it was Shayna's distress or what Rumy had told him about the new uniforms that Daniel's men were wearing.

Or maybe that Rumy had it exactly right: He was so into Shayna.

An hour later Shayna sat next to Marius in a quiet part of the Catskill system, in a private room within the complex.

She sipped iced tea and kept rubbing her forehead. Rumy sat opposite her, leaning forward with his elbows on his knees and his hands clasped together.

She'd been trying to express her concern over Daniel's activities, but felt her data was too vague to make a strong enough impression on the men. "All I'm saying is that I think Daniel's been up to something for the past year. I think that's why he's been absent so much from the Dark Cave system."

Marius sat next to her, but shook his head. "The women can't know that for sure, that he was rarely there. It seems completely out of character for him. The man loves to spend a good portion of his time hurting his slaves."

"I'm not saying he didn't do that. All I'm telling you is that the women knew when he was in residence and when he wasn't. The guards' behavior alone would tend to confirm their side of things."

Rumy glanced at Marius. "She has a point."

Marius met Rumy's gaze for a long moment, then shifted to stare at Shayna. "So you think Daniel's in this unknown cavern of massive proportions, but doing what?"

Shayna shifted, angling her body toward him. She even put her hand on his arm. "What if he's building infrastructure." She then related what the women had told her about the IQ tests. "Maybe he's been using the most intelligent slaves to help him do basic accounting, manage projects, order building supplics, that kind of thing. That way he could definitely keep his whole operation on the down-low."

Marius stared at her. "He administered tests to the women? Why is this the first I've heard of anything like this?"

Shayna shrugged. "Maybe nobody thought to ask the refugees."

Marius laced his hands behind his head and released an exasperated huff of a sigh. She could feel that his head had started hurting and that a kind of oppression had taken him over. She tried to imagine yet again what his life had been like, what it was to be a vampire in this culture, all the ramifications, and to have fought against Daniel for four centuries.

Everything was still so new to her that even with her trained mind, she couldn't quite fit the pieces together. Of course she'd only been exposed to the most violent aspects of this world for an extremely short period of time. How could she possibly understand either Marius or his world sufficiently to make a real assessment of what she'd learned tonight?

Rumy leaned back in his seat, folding his arms over his chest. His tongue made an appearance, touching the inside edges of his ever-present fangs. "You know, I hate to say this, but I've always wondered about Daniel. What a waste of talent to build a massive sex-slavery operation when he could have put his abilities to use on behalf of our world. Hell, he could have founded his own university."

Shayna couldn't help herself and started to giggle, which turned quickly into full-out laughter the more she thought about what Rumy had said.

"What's so funny?"

She slapped at the air a couple of times. "I don't know. Daniel as the founder of a university? What would the classes entail? Basics of Abduction One-oh-One, How to Create Propaganda for the Complete Sex-Slavery Operation, an Introduction to BDSM, Including Tools of the

Trade? Of course those sound more like community college trade classes than university-level. Maybe more like, Ethnography and the Use of Torture as a Form of Sexual Expression." Maybe her fatigue from having been battling in Marius's world almost nonstop had begun showing or perhaps her youth, because neither of the vampires cracked a smile.

"Shayna, are you all right?" The sound of the slight lisp that Rumy used in her name—and all because of a vampire version of Viagra—set her off again.

She laughed herself out after a few minutes during which time Marius brought her a cup of what turned out to be fairly weak coffee. He sat down beside her again, occasionally patting her knee.

She sipped the warm brew and suddenly missed Seattle and an espresso that had real weight. She sniffed the air. She could smell the water from either a nearby underground river or a waterfall, both of which were in abundance in this world. Seattle was a very damp environment as well because of the city's thirty-eight inches of rain each year and the proximity of Puget Sound.

After a few minutes, she regained her composure. She apologized to the men, shoving her hair away from her face with her free hand.

Marius rose to his feet and started to pace. She knew that his level of anxiety had grown. He paused at one point and told her about the new uniforms on Daniel's security detail with the hawk emblem. "Rumy said that there were strange markings above the silver hawk's head."

Shayna stared at him. "A hawk? Didn't you once tell me that besides courage, in your world it's also a symbol of domination?"

He nodded.

Shayna took out her phone and crossed to Rumy. "Did they look like this?"

He angled his head a couple different ways to get the best view of the photos. "I think so, something like that."

She looked up at him, then at Marius. "Do you think Rumy could share that with me the way I share images with you—telepathically, I mean?"

Marius got a funny look on his face, something she couldn't at first define, until his emotions hit her like a hurricane-force wind. He clearly didn't want her communicating so intimately with Rumy, or any other man.

The way his possessiveness made her feel in that moment weakened her knees. She knew it was a vampire thing, but it was also very male and sudden images flew through her mind of making love with Marius just a couple of hours ago and of Marius lying on top of her, his front to her back, and still connected.

He sniffed the air and suddenly she was in his arms. He held her tight and rubbed his hand up and down her back, something he often did. *You smell wonderful.*

And the way you think about me, Marius, this possessive thing took me right back to bed. The suddenness of the memories has my head reeling. And Rumy's grinning like an idiot.

Marius released his tight hold on her but didn't completely let go. He glanced at Rumy. "Sorry, just having a moment."

"Yeah. I can see that. But you're still not into her, right?"

Marius glared at him, then said, "Can't let you share with Shayna."

Rumy's grin broadened. "Didn't think you could. Besides, I'm sure Shayna really didn't understand what she was asking."

"I'm getting the picture now. It's a vampire thing having to do with the blood-chains."

"Exactly," both men said at once.

Shayna addressed Rumy. "Well, can you put the images into Marius's head? Then he can share them with me."

For a moment, Rumy looked dumbstruck. "Are you saying this is normal stuff between the pair of you, this kind of sharing?"

Marius responded succinctly. "Shayna gets visions."

"I know that, but then she can put them inside your head?"

Marius nodded.

"You know that's fucking Ancestral power, right? I mean, the average vampire can't do that, but an Ancestral can. Marius, have you taken the leap?"

"Not that I know of."

Rumy wagged a finger between them. "But you don't have the proximity issue, either."

Shayna shook her head. "And flight's a piece of cake now as well."

"Huh." Rumy frowned heavily, then added with a clap of his hands, "Well, okay. Marius, let me give it a shot."

Shayna watched him close his eyes. A few seconds later Marius said, "Got it."

Turning toward her, Marius smiled. "The image is really clear. Ready?"

"Sure." And there it was, a picture, clearer than a photo, of Daniel in Rumy's office, the room that was now destroyed, and smiling in that horrible way of his. He wore a snug shirt with the silver hawk emblem and above it the symbols, six altogether with the first symbol repeated two times.

She blinked and stared at Marius. "I'll bet the first word is the ancient version of either 'the' or 'one,' and I'm feeling a need to get back to the Pharaoh system. I have some studying to do. But my guess is that Daniel has a plan and that he's been working on it a long time. And if he's made use of your ancient language, then my guess is that I'll be able to find an English translation somewhere, if I keep hunting through your Internet. And Marius, I'm going with my gut here, but I think he's been building something big and that despite our destruction of the extinction weapon, he won't be needing a weapon to bring his ambitions to life."

"Fuck." Marius drew close. "Then we'd better get you back to Egypt."

While Shayna dove back into her work, Marius paced the adjacent library. With each pass, he caught sight of her. She was on the computer, one that had access to his world's private Internet. She tapped away, her shoulders tense as she worked, her mind completely focused.

The tablets that she'd been examining were arrayed in precise order on the table at a right angle to her computer, but her own papers and notes lay scattered in front of her. He got her: She needed some chaos so that her mind could remain fluid.

Unfortunately, the more he walked, the more distressed he became. The revelations from the refugee camp had set his mind down a new path, and Shayna had posed the right question: What if Daniel was up to something that didn't involve either his sex-slavery operation or the extinction weapon?

"Marius, come here."

The tension in Shayna's voice put him in motion and he joined her at her work desk.

She glanced up at him. "I found this obscure site after going through about three hundred search pages. One of your French scholars has translated some of the ancient language and I was right about the first word. According to his partial working dictionary and subsequent English translation, the repeated word stands for 'one' as in 'only' or 'exclusively.' Maybe Daniel knew this or has had his own people on the translation himself, but his choices can't be either accidental or decorative." She put her finger on the screen. "This is what I have."

As Marius read Shayna's translation, his heart thudded in his chest. "'One Earth, One Race, One Ruler.'" He felt as though every concern he'd ever had about his world coalesced in this moment. "You're sure? You're absolutely sure?"

She nodded, a deep frown between her brows. "He's talking about both our civilizations, isn't he? The human race and your world."

"Yes."

"Marius, there's something else. There was more than one symbol for 'ruler.' This one, the one that Rumy saw on Daniel's uniform, means 'one who has conquered' as opposed to an inherited position and I sincerely doubt there was anything like 'casting votes' back in the day. And the use of new uniforms with an emblem and a stated purpose emblazoned on the fabric indicates a high level of organization. But can Daniel really hope to achieve total domination without the extinction weapon? I thought once we'd destroyed it, he'd lost his opportunity."

Marius settled his palms on the soft leather surface.

The trouble was, he knew she was right. One hundred percent. His father had never lacked for ambition. "It appears
that Daniel thinks he can."

"What are we going to do?"

He glanced at her, surprised by her use of "we." He
searched her eyes, aware just how much he appreciated
her presence in his world, her willingness to help, to spend
hours as she had just now searching for answers.

She'd helped him get the extinction weapon and now
she'd interpreted the meaning of the symbols on Daniel's
shirt that had translated into a serious warning about his
current plans.

"Thank you," he said.

She glanced at the monitor. "For this? You're welcome,
I guess. I mean, this really was my pleasure."

"I know."

And just like that, he knew it was time for her to go
home, to go back to Seattle. She didn't need to be part of
what would be happening next in his world. And she definitely deserved better than being caught in a war that had
nothing to do with her. She'd called it right early on: The
problems in his world belonged to the vampire civilization, no one else.

She rose to her feet almost at the same time. "Marius,
no, I don't want to go."

He almost laughed. "Did you just read my mind?"

She smiled but looked so sad at the same time that
his heart felt crushed. "No, of course not. I felt what
you're feeling and it came as a profound sense of finality.
But I don't feel ready to leave." Her gaze flitted around.
She blinked several times, and he watched tears fill her
eyes.

"It's time."

She met his gaze once more and took several deep breaths. He felt her pulling inward and he didn't like the sensation because she was gathering her emotions and shutting them down. "I've been here long enough, interfering in a way I never would have in a culture I'd come to study. Of course it's time for me to go. I can see that. I know you're right."

She drew another deep breath, then suddenly a wave of grief hit Marius, emanating first from Shayna, then swelling within him at almost the exact same moment. "Oh, God, Shayna." He opened his arms and she fell against his chest.

His throat tightened all over again as though he had a noose around it. Tears burned his eyes. His shirt grew damp and the soft sobs that came out of her tore at his heart, making him wish so many things at once, but mostly that she would stay with him forever.

He held her for a long time, rubbing his hand up and down her back until the worst was over and even his own sadness had dimmed. Emotions always felt eternal, but they weren't, and this would pass like everything else. The only constant in his life was the sudden guilt that surged within him yet again as he remembered the sins of his past, the real reason he'd always be alone.

I wish I understood your suffering. Her voice was the softest murmur through his mind.

He'd miss this as well, the intimate sharing of telepathy, something he'd been able to do with her from the beginning, as easy as shifting into altered flight, like feeling feathers through his mind.

And I wish I could explain it.

I hope one day you'll be free of this, because it's like a living thing inside you.

She'd said it exactly right. A python inhabited his soul, tightening at times until he could hardly breathe.

But he'd done the unforgivable and the only thing he could ever hope was that if he continued waging war against his father, maybe then his continual sacrifice could make up for his betrayal of his brothers.

She drew back and he stared down into reddened eyes and cheeks, but she looked as beautiful as ever. "You think that what you've done crossed a line that can never be taken back."

"You don't know who I really am."

She shook her head. "You're wrong. I know exactly who you are. You're one of the kindest, best men I've ever known." She put her hand on his face and reached up to kiss him.

He drank the kiss in, knowing it might be their last. *Thank you for everything, Shayna.*

After a moment, she pulled away from him. He saw that her eyes had filled with tears once more, but it couldn't be helped. She turned back to her worktable and began gathering up her notes.

He was a little surprised that she didn't make more of a push to stay. "You're okay with this, then?"

She glanced at him over her shoulder. "Of course. I never really belonged here. I'm an intruder and I should leave."

"You're not an intruder. How can you say that?"

"Maybe I used the wrong word, but I'm human and this is your world. I'm trained by profession to be very respectful of the customs of other cultures. In some ways, my involvement here has gone against my training, but that doesn't matter now."

At that, he chuckled. "You weren't invited here as an anthropologist, Shayna. I abducted you."

"You sort of abducted me. Mostly, you saved my life." She glanced around. "This was amazing, though, a gift I'll always treasure for so many reasons."

He glanced into the adjoining room, at the tall stacks of tablets, waiting to be studied and translated. "I can see how you'll miss this."

"Oh, Marius, you're such an idiot." And before he understood, she'd thrown herself against him once more and slid her arms around his back, holding him tight.

He was an idiot and the thought came to him that he'd never have to watch her leave his world if he just stood here for the next hundred years holding her in his arms.

Shayna leaned her head on Marius's shoulder and sighed heavily. His hand moved up and down her back, soothing her as he'd done many times before. She didn't want to leave, even though she knew it was the right thing to do. In the two days they'd been together, she'd grown attached to him.

Maybe the bond of the blood-chains had forced them to grow close, but in this case proximity had bred a very deep affection. If she didn't know better, she'd actually say she was in love with him.

Love.

Oh, God.

She was.

She hugged him harder still.

Love was what she felt right now. She would define it as nothing less.

She loved Marius and probably always would.

What she couldn't know was whether or not what she felt, if given the chance, could stand the test of time. Did she love him enough to leave Seattle, to set aside the life she'd planned for herself, the one that seemed as far away from her as the moon right now?

Part of her wanted the chance to discover if this could be something more than just a sense of kinship as a result of having shared hardships with him.

Always analyzing, that was her. Even now, she couldn't just let Marius go, she had to extrapolate and wonder, asking herself a dozen what-if questions.

She released another sigh and forced her brain to shut down. Instead, she just savored the feel of his muscular body, the one that had held her, loved her, caressed her, and given her unimaginable pleasure

She would definitely miss the sex. All future relationships would pale in comparison.

I loved having sex with you.

He nuzzled her neck. *Same here.*

Drawing back, he leaned close and kissed her forehead. "I'd offer to do it again, but I don't think that would be wise."

"No, it wouldn't." She had to leave.

Finally, she pulled away from him and continued gathering up her papers. "I suppose you should take me home pretty soon. Now that we've made the decision, I don't think I want to hang around, although I do have a concern. Is there a chance Daniel will come after me, in Seattle, I mean?"

"He might, but I'll make sure that you have a security detail on you for as long as needed."

Holding her notes in her hand, she held his gaze. "And what do you plan to do about Daniel?"

"I intend to take him down."

She put her hand on his arm suddenly. "Marius, you should tell your brothers how you wronged them."

He appeared shocked. "I can't do that." He shoved a hand through his hair, and she felt his remorse flow through him yet again.

"Tell them. It might help. It might even surprise you. I think you've carried this damn thing long enough."

"You don't understand. My brothers are all I have. They'd never forgive me."

"Well, I would."

He laughed harshly. "Only because you don't know the truth."

She grew very still. "You're right. I don't know, but isn't four hundred years of service a proper length of time for atonement? Because I'd bet my life that you never betrayed them in all that time."

"No, I never did."

"So as I recall, you were a child when this thing happened."

"My age doesn't change what I did."

"Well, there's no point arguing, and once again I'm intruding way too much. But would you mind if I had a little time just to be here, before we left? It's a way of saying good-bye, because I'm pretty sure I'll never be back."

He nodded. "Whatever you want to do."

She could hear his phone ringing as he suddenly slid his hand into his pocket. He glanced at the screen. "It's Gabriel. I'll need to take this."

He moved quickly away from her into the adjacent room.

Shayna watched him for a moment, then sat back down in her chair in front of the computer screen. She almost went right back to work as she clicked the mouse and the Frenchman's dictionary popped back up on the monitor. She was a worker bee by long and enjoyable habit, so it took her some doing to close the search engine for good.

Knowing she'd fall into a funk, she rose from the chair and pulled on her gloves. She decided to use her last moments examining the tablets as her way of saying farewell.

She brought a new tablet from the stack, placing it beneath the magnifying glass, getting lost in the imagery within her mind, trying to picture the vampire so long ago who had made these indentations in the soft clay.

She often made up scenarios in her head. Would the scribe have kept a beverage in a cup nearby? Did he smoke hemp rope beneath a canvas with some of fellow scribes during his breaks? Did he have an exercise program to keep fit while spending most of his life hunched over slabs of clay?

"What do you see?" Marius settled a hand on her shoulder.

"Just looking at the level of detail, the precision of the length of each indentation." She glanced at him. "Everything okay?"

"Actually, yes. My brothers are coming here, to Gabriel's conference room, to discuss the possibility that Daniel is up to something. We'll be talking new strategies as well."

"Good. That's good." She wanted to ask a few questions, but held back. Her job here was done. Still, she smiled. "I don't suppose you could let me stay here while you have your meeting."

She felt the tension drain suddenly from Marius. "I'd like that. I really would."

She turned and put her hand on his shoulder, caressing him. He responded by taking a step toward her and sliding his arm around her waist. She moved closer still, pressing up against him.

A soft moan escaped his lips as he tilted his head and kissed her.

Shayna slung her arms around his neck. She hadn't meant for this to happen, but her need for him rose like a tsunami. Desire flowed through her until she writhed against what had become firm really fast.

But this wouldn't do at all. She was leaving.

She drew back. "Marius, what is it with us?"

"I don't know." He chuckled and leaned his forehead against hers. "But I have a meeting I need to get to and now I'll have to calm down before I can show my face."

She smiled, loving this between them, wishing like hell it didn't have to end.

She said nothing more, but waited with him. She took care not to fondle his arms, one of her favorite things to do. She didn't even speak, but let her breathing settle down.

After a couple of minutes, he released her completely. "I'll probably be gone for at least two hours. But when I return, I should probably fly you home."

She nodded. He stepped away and shifted to altered flight. A moment later, he was gone.

Shayna stood staring at the empty space, grateful to have this respite before facing her empty apartment and her miles-away life.

But just as she turned back to the magnifying glass and the ancient tablet beneath, a man's voice forced her to grow very still. "I think my son has fallen in love with you, which means that my current plan has worked out perfectly."

She turned, and Daniel was just there, stroking his goatee and standing ten feet away. He'd broken through Gabriel's layered cavern disguise that even Marius hadn't been able to penetrate, and now he smiled at her in the middle of the room full of ancient tablets.

She squared her shoulders. "I'm guessing you're not here to share a cup of coffee, maybe have a little chat. I have so many questions—"

"None of which I intend to answer."

Instinctively, she picked up one of the tablets and threw it at him, but they were large and heavy. He laughed as it dropped to the floor several feet in front of him and broke into pieces.

Before she even blinked or saw him move, she was trapped in Daniel's arms, flying through rock then into the air above North Africa.

How did you find me? I can't believe you actually got through Gabriel's disguise.

She felt him laugh again. *Remember that sharp little pain in your arm, the one you might have thought was a pinch? Let us just say that I embrace technology in all its forms.*

A tracking device?

Shayna, you certainly don't lack for intelligence. And he laughed again.

CHAPTER 15

Marius sat down at an ebony conference table thinking he'd never been so glad to see all these men gathered in one place. He couldn't remember the last time he'd been with both of his brothers, as well as Gabriel and Rumy, at the same time.

He sat across from Adrien and Lucian, while Rumy sat on his right. Each of his brothers bore a resemblance to Daniel, just as he did, their parentage impossible to refute.

Adrien had thick dark hair to his shoulders and muddy teal eyes with brown flecks, while Lucian had gray eyes and kept his black hair cut short. Both were handsome men, six-five to six-six, and muscular like thoroughbreds.

He loved them and loved being with them, though he always felt separate because of what he'd done. In the past, he'd used a lot of humor to mask what he really felt.

Gabriel sat at the head of the table and had provided coffee. Marius sipped from a heavy red mug, his thoughts disjointed. He didn't want Shayna to leave. He needed to find a way to end Daniel's reign. He also wondered if Shayna was right. Maybe he should finally confess his sins to his brothers.

But would they ever forgive him?

"So what's your plan? With Shayna, I mean," Gabriel asked.

"I'll be taking her home, of course. We've already discussed it. She has her life well planned." He went on to speak about her fieldwork in Malaysia, her intention of earning her doctorate, her love of anthropology. The words flowed and he couldn't seem to stop them. He then launched into all the ways she'd helped him and saved his ass over the past two very short days.

He ended with, "Shit, I'm going to miss her so much."

No one said a word, maybe because they were stunned by his admission. But both Lucian and Adrien were fully bound to human women whom they now lived with.

He glanced at each in turn and saw eyes full of compassion. But all that did was fill him with his usual remorse.

Clearing his throat, he shifted the subject to the critical matter at hand. "So, I take it we're all here for the same reason."

"Yep," Adrien said. "To go after Daniel and bring him down for good."

Marius related Shayna's most recent discovery, of a

hawk emblem on Daniel's shirt and those of his security team, as well as the symbols above the hawk's head.

Once he was done, everyone at the table fell silent as the tension in the room rose a notch.

"Is there anything else?" Gabriel asked, a tight frown between his brows. He scrubbed the side of his head, just below the spikes.

Rumy jumped in. "Marius, remember what Shayna learned at the refugee center. Tell them what she said about the IQ tests."

"IQ tests? What the fuck?" Adrien had never looked more surprised.

Marius shared what Shayna had learned from the most recent group of refugees out of the Dark Cave system. He especially emphasized the amount of time the women believed that Daniel and his other sons spent away from their massive sex-slave operation.

A new heavy silence fell on the room as all eyes turned to Gabriel. Marius's surrogate father had always been the unacknowledged leader of the vampire world, at least the portion who wanted better things for their world, like civil law and the ability to enforce that law through a decent court system.

But Gabriel turned to Marius. "You're the one he's after, the one he's wanted more than any of his sons."

Marius wasn't sure he'd heard right, even though Shayna had once said something similar. "That makes no sense to me, none at all."

"Then tell me this, where's Shayna right now?"

"You know where she is. I left her in the guest room with the tablets."

Gabriel angled his head and narrowed his eyes. "And how far away is that in terms of yards or even miles?"

Most vampires could tell distance by an innate homing ability. "The guest room is two point three miles from here."

"And is that a single blood-chain around your neck or a double?"

He felt agitated by the question, especially since the answer was so obvious. "You know it's a single." He touched the links anyway.

"I rest my case."

Marius held his gaze. At the edges of his mind, he knew where Gabriel was headed, but Marius couldn't bring himself to say it. "What's your point?"

Gabriel's gaze lowered to the single-chain around Marius's neck. "That you're wearing a single blood-chain and you haven't risen to Ancestral status, but your woman is two point three miles distant. How is that possible?"

"Shit," Adrien murmured.

"Holy fuck." Lucian leaned forward. "Even after I rose to Ancestral status, Claire and I couldn't be more than sixty yards apart." He gestured with a swing of his hand toward Gabriel. "I needed a lot of practice to broaden that distance to encompass a couple of miles."

"Same here."

Lucian pushed his hand through his short black hair. "How much fucking power do you have?"

Both of Marius's brothers wore the double blood-chains that had helped each to achieve Ancestral status.

Marius rose to his feet and addressed Gabriel. "There has to be some mistake or some bizarre explanation. I mean, both Adrien and Lucian outperform me in every possible way."

Gabriel lowered his chin, his eyes holding Marius's gaze fast. "Because you've kept it that way. For reasons

I've never understood, you've held back. You always have."

Marius recalled Shayna saying something similar, if not about holding back, then about insisting he might be special, might have something more to offer—and that Daniel was after him.

Gabriel continued. "You told me about what happened at the Dark Cave system. But the bottom line is that Daniel had intended to kill Lucian, and he would have but Claire helped him escape. He's never made a serious attempt on your life that I know of. And he could have taken you out any number of times over the past two days. Admit it."

Marius left the table but he began to pace. He rubbed his forehead. He felt dizzy and sick at heart. Maybe he had held back, but he knew why.

Was Shayna right? Did he need to confess the truth even though he felt ill just thinking about it? Was it possible he had the kind of power Gabriel believed he had, that he might be special?

Lucian rose as well. "Marius, if what Gabriel is saying is true about you and your abilities, you have to try to embrace who you are. We need you because it sounds like you'd be able to battle Daniel and defeat him."

Marius felt panicky. "Maybe there's something off with the blood-chains. That has to be it."

Gabriel was on his feet and Adrien as well. They began moving in his direction and a terrible nausea came over him. His mind flew back to being on Daniel's table, his skin and muscles split open to the spine. Daniel had forced him more than once, through the terrible pain he inflicted, to betray the plans that his brothers had made to get the three of them out of Daniel's compound.

As the men converged, he had to speak the words. His family needed to know what kind of man he really was. When they stood in an arc in front of him, he said, "I betrayed you more than once. Adrien. Lucian. I betrayed you. " He felt like his heart was on fire, like it would incinerate and burn up his entire body because the words had left his throat.

"What do you mean?" Adrien asked. "When?"

"Yeah, what kind of betrayal are you talking about? When exactly did you do this?"

He rubbed the back of his neck. He could feel the top of the scar, the one that Daniel had created through repeated incisions down the length of his spine. "Three times we were going to escape and each time I told Daniel about it. I couldn't help it. I betrayed you. I was in so much pain and I told Daniel all about the plans. There, you see how special I am?" He shouted his rage at having betrayed his brothers, who had protected him countless times by taking Daniel's punishment in his stead.

"Three times?" Adrien asked.

Marius knew with every cell in his body that today he'd be separated forever from the family he loved, from his brothers and Gabriel. They'd have every reason to cast him out for good.

And he'd deserve that. "I've tried with every ounce of my strength all these centuries to make up for what I did, hoping somehow that I'd be able to atone for my betrayals. But I know now that nothing can make up for it. Daniel would make me listen to your screams in the hallway. He'd chain me there so I'd have to hear what my betrayals cost each of you."

"So you did this three times?" Lucian stared at him, repeating the same thing Adrien had asked.

Marius straightened his shoulders. "Yes. Three." He felt empty inside, but the confession also relieved him of the burden he'd carried. Even though he'd have to go forward by himself, at least the truth was out. The python that had lived within his body all this time dissolved and could hurt him no more.

But a strange thing happened. Both Lucian and Adrien began to smile, something Marius didn't understand at all. Smiles turned to ridiculous grins and after that his brothers started to laugh. They laughed so hard that tears began to run down their cheeks.

"I don't understand." He turned to Gabriel, who in turn shrugged.

Finally, Lucian grabbed Marius by the back of his neck, pulling him to touch foreheads. "Marius, I wish you'd said something before now. We all caved. Three times each." He then drew upright and held Marius's gaze firmly. "Daniel made each of us give up the truth about our escape plans. Do you think I was stronger than you or Adrien? Think about how sharp that blade was. You weren't alone. It just had never occurred to me that you believed our earlier plans failed because he'd gotten the truth out of you. In reality, he'd figured things out on his own. And remember, we were kids back then. The servants could have alerted him to our bungling efforts. The final escape just involved being cleverer than before and a little luck. That's all."

Adrien drew close and planted a hand on Marius's shoulder. "We both thought you knew, Marius, I swear it, or Lucian and I would have said something before now. Damn, I hate that you've carried this all these years. I'm so fucking sorry."

Marius was in shock as he drew back slightly and

shifted his gaze back and forth repeatedly between Adrien and Lucian. "So I'm forgiven?" It seemed impossible.

Lucian shrugged. "There's nothing to forgive. Not a damn thing. We were all caught in the grips of that psychopathic monster we had for a father."

Marius remained standing where he was for a long time, processing what he'd just learned. Daniel had played them one against the other, yet somehow Marius had been too young to figure that out. He tried to recall if the subject had ever come up before. Even if it had, Marius suspected he'd been deaf to the discussion because of his intense guilt over the betrayals.

"Be well, Marius." Lucian sought his gaze.

Marius stared at him and felt the last of his guilt leave him. This, too, had been Daniel's fault: that he'd carried something all this time that wasn't his to bear.

After a long moment, he planted a hand on each shoulder. "I was sure that once you knew the truth about what I'd done, I'd never see either of you again. I lived with that fear all my life, of losing you both."

A joining of arms around shoulders followed, all three brothers together, full of shared love and grace and the bond because each had suffered at the hands of their father in the same way.

When Marius drew back, he met Gabriel's gaze. His surrogate father smiled and nodded. "I know what courage that took. Well done. But I'd like to suggest something."

"Sure." Right now Marius would have agreed to anything. He was happier than he'd ever been and the release of all that guilt made his chest feel like it was stuffed full of cotton. He'd never felt so free.

"Given everything that you've said about Shayna, and

these latest revelations that seemed to come from her own perceptions, why don't you keep her with you a little longer? I think we need to know what Daniel's up to, and it seems to me she can help with that."

Shayna.

Though he couldn't explain why, he knew that his coming to terms with what had haunted him for centuries would have an impact on how he viewed her. More than anything, he wanted to share what had just happened and that her encouragement to confess the truth had given him that extra push to bare his soul.

He turned physically, angling in the direction of the guest room some two miles away through the intricate Pharaoh system. He could feel the trajectory of their shared guest room the way he could feel himself breathe.

He glanced at his brothers, then at Marius and Rumy. He even smiled. "I'll be right back."

He didn't wait for an acknowledgment, just shifted to altered flight and sped in the direction of the room with all the tablets. Somewhere in the middle of flying, however, he realized he couldn't *feel* her at all. He wondered if she'd taken off her blood-chain.

As he touched down, he touched the matching chain at his neck, but got nothing in response.

And the tablet room was empty.

Anxiety flowed through him and quickly turned to panic. "Shayna!" he shouted, turning in a slow circle, reaching for her repeatedly.

But she wasn't in the guest suite.

A tablet lay broken on the floor several feet away from the table, the only sign that something must have happened in this room once he left. Shayna would never have broken a tablet unless something extraordinary had happened.

He opened up his telepathy but still couldn't find her, couldn't reach her, something he'd never experienced with Shayna once she'd put the chain on.

He returned swiftly to Gabriel's conference room. The men were laughing, until he arrived. Both Adrien and Lucian dropped into fighting stances then relaxed, but each expression grew instantly concerned. "What's wrong?" Adrien called out.

"Shayna's gone. I don't what happened." He described the emptiness of the rooms and the broken tablet.

Gabriel spoke Marius's thoughts. "Daniel has her."

Once the words were spoken into the air, Marius held his arms wide and hands upraised.

How long had the monster had his woman? Had he hurt her already? Would he have had reason not to?

Rage, both ancient and new, flooded his veins with fire. He let that fire grow, heating up his limbs, his torso, the very center of his soul.

Daniel had been the creator of all things evil in his life, starting with the murder of Marius's mother when he was only four, then all that torture both he and his brothers had endured, then the ensuing slavery of both humans and vampires throughout their world, more maiming and murder.

And now he had Shayna.

Marius moved in a slow circle, hands wide and outstretched. He reached for something he didn't understand, except that it had a name: *power*.

He lifted his chin and started drawing in what had been gifted to him through his father's genetics and the latent ability that his mother must have possessed and which Daniel had sensed four centuries ago.

He took deep breaths, reaching into his gut, opening his soul wide. Power surged through him, filling every cell of his body. His shirt grew tight around the flexing muscles of his shoulders and arms. His thighs expanded, pressing against the leather and the weapons he carried.

And finally, a roar came out of him, filling the cavern, a roar that would echo throughout the world birthed to the vampires and given to them by the ancient ones, those who had gone before and built this world.

Ancestral power and something more, something greater, filled his bones, his blood, his muscles. Strength came to him, as nothing he'd known before.

He opened his eyes and saw the room as though it moved in circles spinning around him, though he was the one that moved.

When he finally stopped, he saw the stunned expression on each of their faces. But he didn't have time to process what it might mean. Instead, he moved to stand in front of Gabriel, noting that he now looked down at him from increased height, as though he'd gained an inch or two. He searched Gabriel's eyes, then his mind, whipping through quickly, something he'd never been able to do before.

"Gabriel, you've built an army, haven't you."

He heard both Lucian and Adrien exclaim from behind him. "What?"

Gabriel nodded. "Rumy as well. We both thought it prudent and began the project ten years ago. Just when we would have started taking our intentions public, Daniel took over the Council of Ancestrals, gaining control of the courts, then imprisoning the three of you. We waited. We would have come for you, but—"

"You couldn't do that. I understand. You weren't ready to face Daniel and he would have probably killed us and broken your army. You did right to wait. Now is the time."

"It sure as hell is and you're the one to defeat your father. Through the years, I had glimpses of what you could become, but I didn't see this, and I certainly didn't see what hindered the process. I also know that what you've become was what Daniel wanted to harness. You were the real weapon he's been after all this time."

Marius closed his eyes, and because he was now more than even an Ancestral, he felt the breadth of his ability to communicate. He also understood how Daniel had found Shayna and captured her with no one the wiser. At first, he'd thought his father had been that powerful. But now he recalled that Daniel had done something to Shayna on the land bridge when he'd held her arm in his hand. She'd cried out at the time, but Marius had thought she'd been frightened by his touch. Now he knew his father had planted a tracking device beneath her skin.

Marius searched for Shayna and found her hidden behind a thick layer of multiple disguises. He couldn't see her but he felt her. Slipping into her mind, he spoke softly. *Shayna, it's me. Hold steady. Try not to show any emotion right now because we're engaging telepathically. Just tell me first if you're okay.*

He felt her calm her mind. *I'm fine. But this is a trap. Don't come. Do you hear me, Marius? Don't come. He intends to bind you and somehow use you in his takeover plans, though I have no idea how any of that would work.*

Marius grew very quiet, because as she had from the

first, Shayna stunned him. Daniel had abducted her, but instead of Shayna begging him to save her, she offered a warning: "Don't come. It's a trap." Who else would have been thinking not of herself, but of him?

God, he loved her.

And there it was, the complete revelation of the true state of his heart, nothing hidden or held back because of misplaced guilt.

He loved her.

You're not to worry about me, Shayna. All I want you to do is to send me an image of where you are, of your current location. I can't see through your eyes right now, because Daniel has this place heavily disguised. But if you'll place an image within your mind, of the widest panorama possible, I will find you.

No, please don't, Marius. All he can do is kill me.

Shayna, I'm coming whether you help me or not. It would be a helluva lot faster and easier if you would do as I ask, but it's up to you.

I don't want you to get hurt.

His heart swelled at the words. *Can you trust me right now, Shayna? Because I'm telling you that's not going to happen.*

Of course I trust you. I have almost from the first, even when I was flying through the air out of Seattle. He felt her mind settle into its usual determination. *Here goes.*

A jumble of images rushed at him, but eventually one came forward with perfect clarity and Marius couldn't believe what he was looking at.

Stay calm. I'm coming.

He felt Daniel's telepathic approach and shut down the communication so that his father couldn't read it.

Opening his eyes, he stared first at his brothers and

Rumy, then Gabriel. "You won't believe this, but Daniel has built a massive arena large enough to hold fifty thousand troops, in an extremely well-disguised system. And every seat is filled with men shouting triumphant war cries. Looks like they're preparing to go to war." He glanced from Daniel to Rumy and back again. "Either of you got an army that large?"

Rumy grinned, his fangs pressing into his lower lips. "Hell, yeah, and they've been itching to go after Daniel and his men for a long time now."

Adrien asked, "So where are we going?"

"To the Himalayas."

Where it all began.

Shayna stood very still on the central black stone platform of the arena. Daniel had made it clear that if she moved, he'd hurt her using his blade, and he'd enjoy watching her blood flow. She had no choice but to stay put.

She tried really hard to hold it together, but her fingers trembled and nausea boiled in her stomach.

Earlier, he'd taken her from the tablet room in the Pharaoh system after she'd instinctively, but without effect, thrown one of the ancient clay tablets at him. He'd brought her straight here, into one of the dressing rooms, then turned her over to several of his slaves.

They'd dressed her in a light-green floor-length gown, split up both sides to the waist. She'd fought them, of course, but they'd finally given her a shot of some kind of fast-working paralytic. She'd never been so frightened in her life: She wasn't able to move even a muscle. She couldn't even blink.

Minutes later, with several vampires working on her, she was given another shot and the feeling in her arms and legs slowly returned. But oh, her head hurt. And she couldn't siphon Marius's power, so right now she'd reverted to a fairly fragile human state.

A glance in the mirror told her she'd been dressed up for either a stage performance or to be put to work in one of the Dark Cave system's upscale clubs. The front of the dress was cut halfway to her navel, and her breasts were squeezed together with the most uncomfortable bustier ever created.

Her blond hair now sat high on her head and dressed with pheasant feathers and she had teal glitter on her cheekbones that fanned upward to her temples. Thick false eyelashes weighted her lids.

She even wore five-inch stilettos, a nightmare all on its own.

Marius was also on his way, which made her sick with worry. How could he battle and defeat either Daniel or the tens of thousands of his seasoned soldiers now cheering their leader maniacally?

Daniel stood in what appeared to be a throwback to ancient Rome, with a shiny black breastplate over his chest and a black velvet robe trimmed with silver hanging from his shoulders all the way to the floor. But he'd kept the leather pants and glossy boots.

She had to admit, he looked the part of a man intending to rule two worlds. He kept turning in a circle and every time he raised his arms, the soldiers' cries rose and swelled to a deafening roar.

His sons Quill and Lev stood off to his right side in similar attire, except in burgundy, and of course the capes were much shorter. All three men wore snug leather pants and black boots laced up the front.

But beyond the central depression of the stage, the

arena rose like a massive football stadium. She couldn't even see the height of this cavern or the length.

Most frightening of all, however, was the simple fact that Daniel had gathered what looked like a full-blown army into the black stone seats of the arena. Tens of thousands of vampires, all in uniforms that bore the hawk emblem and the ancient symbols for "One Earth, One Race, One Ruler." They shouted so loud that even Shayna's less sensitive ears ached.

Off to the side on a raised platform, a vampire sweating rivers and waving his fists and arms kept urging Daniel's army to cheer. She'd listened to a few lines, but it seemed like typical propaganda with phrases like *The good of the few must be sacrificed for the good of the many,* which usually meant that individual freedoms would be eradicated at the whim of the dictator until Daniel had full control of everything and everyone. From what she'd learned, the entire vampire culture embraced the rights of the individual above everything else.

More mentions of Daniel's benevolence and plans to improve the lot of every vampire in their world made her stomach turn. She had only to think about what existed in the Dark Cave system to know what Daniel's world would actually look like on a global scale. He excelled at so many things, and "spin" would naturally be one of them.

The most telling aspect of the arena, however, was the circle of sunlight on the central stage that shifted slightly as the earth moved on its axis. She hadn't actually seen what happened when a vampire got burned, but she'd felt Marius's profound aversion to sunlight. And a sunlight-based killing zone in the arena was the perfect psychological threat to keep Daniel's followers in line.

She'd soon realized that the visions she'd had early

on, though marred at the time by the dark wavy lines, were of this space. As she looked around the arena, she saw one of the reasons for Daniel's success. He paid attention to detail, from the use of symbols as a powerful promotional tool, to the careful engineering of the whole arena structure, the torch lighting that added a strong, wild tension, the branding colors of black and silver and a smattering of maroon reflecting power and strength. Daniel had clearly spent money, time, and considerable effort in creating an infrastructure for his ambitions, all built, of course, on the rape, torture, and murder of human and vampire slaves.

She wanted to reach out to Marius, to warn him about the pool of killing sunlight and the reach of his father's plans. But she knew that despite Daniel's outward focus on keeping his soldiers cheering and stamping their feet, he watched her closely.

Suddenly she knew that Marius had arrived, even though she couldn't see him at first, because his power flared through her entire body. She was siphoning once more and it was all she could do to keep from crying out.

She took it in, breathing deep and feeling such a profound sense of relief that she swayed on her feet.

Still, she kept her telepathy shut down. Neither did Marius try to reach her.

But he was there. She could feel him in every cell of her body.

She looked around, trying to find him. But he could have been anywhere given the number of bodies in the arena.

Marius hovered behind a layer of disguise not far from Shayna, and invisible even to Daniel, something he would never have believed possible. He held himself in altered flight, fully aware of the changes in his physical body and in his level of power.

He sensed that Shayna knew he was there, but he didn't dare try to contact her. And he had to spend a helluva lot of energy not reacting to how she looked or that fifty thousand men leered at her. All part of Daniel's ploy, no doubt, to distract him when he arrived.

He streamed the images of what he saw, the arena and Daniel's army, the deadly patch of sunlight and Shayna, all straight into Gabriel's head. He could even hear, despite the enormous distance between northern India and Egypt, what Gabriel said aloud to Adrien, Lucian, and Rumy.

Gabriel had finally revealed that he and Rumy had been building a secret force for a long time, in various locations around the world. The Ancestrals in hiding had all agreed that one day Daniel and his forces, however big they might prove to be, would only be defeated by military action.

But these efforts had been the biggest secret of the vampire world, kept hidden even from Marius and his brothers. Because Daniel kept his sons as perpetual targets, Gabriel and Rumy had made the decision early on to keep this knowledge from them. Marius had concurred with the wisdom of this part of the plan. Daniel had many forms of torture and knew how to get information if he really wanted it.

Right now Gabriel streamed images back to Marius of each of five forces, from different parts of the globe, tens of thousands of vampire warriors, already in the air and headed toward northern India. Marius saw them like a movie inside his head. Because he knew when each would arrive at the Himalayan system, he could calculate the exact moment when Gabriel's invasion of the arena would take place.

He couldn't reveal himself until the precise moment when the invasion started, otherwise Daniel might be able to intervene with his enormous power and end the battle before it began. He could create layered disguises over his army, however, or even with a single order cause them all to disperse.

So Marius waited.

He had a full minute remaining before the first of Gabriel's forces penetrated the arena. Marius had already created a path through the layered disguises that Daniel had put in place, more evidence that Marius's level of power had gone into hyperdrive.

As he scoped the entire arena, he knew he had to make Quill and Lev a priority. If not, they'd do everything in their power to protect Daniel; Marius wouldn't stand a chance.

The best and simplest solution possible came to the forefront of his mind. Prior to his confession to his brothers, he probably wouldn't have thought to reach out to them; his guilt would have held him captive.

But now he didn't hesitate. Adrien and Lucian hovered just outside the system, waiting for Marius's orders. He reached for them both at the same time, and forged a telepathic conversation among all three of them. His powers truly had entered a new, incredible phase.

Adrien, I need you to take out Quill. Lucian, immobilize Lev. If either of them or Daniel has even a split second to act, we'll lose our chance to end their reign once and for all.

Adrien said, *We're with you, Marius. Just waiting for your orders.*

Marius felt Lucian's telepathic stream kick in. *Just tell us what, when, and where.*

I'm going to stream the stage area for you both. Marius closed his eyes and did the impossible: He sent two sets of images flowing in different directions at the same time. *Have you got the locations locked in?*

Two affirmatives.

Lucian added, *Clear as a fucking bell! Damn, Marius, you've got some serious chops.*

The words, coming from his brother, pleased the hell out of Marius. *In fifteen seconds, the first of Gabriel's force breaks through. On my mark.* Marius started counting down, finally reaching, *Three . . . two . . . one . . . Go!*

At the same time that the first massive force pierced the cavern above the arena, Marius watched Lucian and Adrien bust through.

Marius turned all his attention to the man who had caused endless pain, death, and destruction through the vampire and human worlds for centuries. He whipped in Daniel's direction, leaving altered flight and dropping his disguise barely a split second before he plowed into his unsuspecting father.

Off to his right, Adrien and Lucian did the same with Quill and Lev. Several rounds of battle cries flooded the air above the stage as Gabriel and Rumy's men engaged Daniel's army.

Game on.

Marius's momentum took him and Daniel to the arena floor, ten feet away from the patch of sunlight. He landed on top of Daniel and delivered three quick blows to his face.

Daniel used the force of his power and threw Marius into the air, adding a blow to the chest at the same time.

The air rushed from Marius's lungs and he hung in the air working to recover.

Daniel didn't immediately attack. Instead he stood in the center of the arena floor looking all around him, his lips parted, his eyes wild. He reached for the robe at his shoulders and unclasped it, letting it fall to the floor, the breastplate with it.

To Marius's right, Adrien and Quill battled high in the air. On the ground, Lucian had his long chain spinning as Lev circled him with one of his own. But his brothers were both Ancestrals, like Quill and Lev, meeting the half brothers with equal power.

Recovered, Marius dropped to the floor twelve feet away and waited for his father to face him.

Daniel moved slowly in the direction of the pool of sunlight. Marius got the point and didn't care. One of them would end up frying, as good a plan as any for ending Daniel's miserable life. Marius had waited a long time for a chance to battle his father and because he'd embraced all that he was, power flowed through him as never before. He was something new and something *more*.

Like his father.

Against the cacophony of the battle raging through the upper reaches of the cavern, and as more of Gabriel's troops arrived and tens of thousands of men battled in the air, Daniel's voice entered Marius's mind. *I see you've embraced your power at last. Do you see what you are, know what you are now? What I created you to be? I foresaw this transformation.*

Marius began moving closer, slowly, watching the smallest flick of Daniel's fingers, the slightest shift of his feet or twitch of his eye.

Marius responded, *You're a liar, Daniel. You didn't foresee anything, or you would have been prepared for this attack. I think you hoped that I might reach, possibly even exceed, your power, but you didn't foresee it.*

And you've your mother's weakness. She had so much compassion but not enough sense. Try to break free of that right now. It's not too late to join me. Together— here he swept an arm to encompass the arena—*we can rule everything.*

Marius felt Daniel's power begin to pulse all around the arena.

Suddenly the battles that raged around him and Daniel slowed, then halted, fists and chains in mid-strike, bodies prone and dying, others gone.

Marius saw what would happen next because he couldn't move. Daniel launched at him and caught him around the neck, flipping behind him so that he had one hand pressed on the side of Marius's head.

Marius knew that in this moment, he was dead.

Daniel would snap his neck. He had more power than anyone knew and Marius's power, so recently arrived, was untried, unproven, undeveloped. He had raw power, but Daniel had been building his for centuries, well beyond Marius's age, taught by even viler creatures than he himself had proved to be.

This was a pattern in Marius's family, sons killing their evil fathers. In this case, it would be the other way around.

His gaze strayed to Shayna and he realized she wasn't immobile like all the others. Her gaze was fixed to his. He didn't attempt to touch her mind, to communicate; Daniel would know.

She began to levitate. Marius shifted his gaze straight ahead and focused on Daniel. "What do you want?"

"You know what I want: you and your abilities. I've always known you could do what I do. One day, with practice, you can do more."

Daniel released him, sweeping a hand over the still-life battle. "I want you to take charge of my army, to serve as my right hand. I would let you do whatever you wanted—and not just in a military sense. If you wanted control of the courts, I would grant you that. You could write the laws I know you value. We'll need laws in this new world of mine."

"But you'd have the veto vote."

"Of course." Daniel smiled. "But I don't know what you think your woman can do. I can feel her now, just inches away from me."

But Marius knew. *Back up, Shayna, now!*

The moment Daniel shifted his attention to Shayna, intending to hurt or possibly kill her, Marius flew at him and whipped his blade over his throat. He cut deep just as Daniel swept backward attempting to strike Shayna down. But she'd already shifted to altered flight.

She reappeared and grabbed Daniel by the arm. Marius stayed where he was because right now, she siphoned most of his power as she dragged him toward the pool of sunlight.

Blood poured from Daniel's throat. He clutched at his neck, spending his energies on self-healing instead of getting rid of Shayna. Marius moved in their direction, knowing that Daniel was self-healing faster than ever before. The wound was already half sealed.

Marius withdrew another dagger and let it fly. This time he'd aimed for the heart and knew he'd succeeded when Daniel arched, his mouth opening wide.

He made a halfhearted attempt to throw Shayna aside,

but he was too late. She dragged him into the pool of sunlight and Daniel screamed.

Hold him down. Keep him in place.

Shayna's eyes were wild as she planted a foot on Daniel's wounded chest. Even so, Daniel started to rise in the air, levitating with the power he had left.

Marius, I can't hold him!

Marius fell as he released the rest of his power to Shayna. She stood with one foot on Daniel's chest and pinned him to the stone floor. The sunlight kept burning through Daniel's clothes and started eating away at his flesh.

Shayna's hair came undone and flew in a wild mass around her shoulders. Only a human could have put Daniel in the light and let the sun do its work. She looked like something from her human mythology, her hair moving as though on fire, all around her head, her stiletto on Daniel's chest, holding him in place, her arms spread wide.

Stay with him until he's gone.

Shayna didn't look at Marius, but kept staring down at Daniel's dissolving face. *I won't let him up until there's nothing left. Ashes to ashes.*

Marius, weak from having turned over his power, sat on the stone floor several yards away.

The air battle had resumed the moment he'd cut Daniel's throat.

Quill lay gasping for his last breath, Adrien's chain around his throat. Lucian had beheaded Lev and flew toward Marius, a dagger in hand. He stood over him, waiting, moving in a protective circle. "I can feel that you've sent her all your power."

"She's keeping Daniel in place and the light is doing its work." Marius couldn't take his gaze off her, in part because it helped to keep the power flowing. And right now, Shayna was doing the most important job in this entire cavern.

Daniel's body twitched now and then but otherwise he'd stopped moving. And still Shayna kept her foot in place.

"Lucian, I need to stay focused on Shayna. Tell me how Gabriel and Rumy's troops are doing?"

"They're steadily tearing away at Daniel's army. The northern section is completely subdued and a portion of the eastern part of the arena. Another of Gabriel's regiments just came in. And another. This will be over soon."

CHAPTER 16

Shayna didn't take her eyes off Daniel, even though the sight and smell nauseated her, and she kept her foot hard on his torso.

But though she watched Daniel disintegrate, her inner gaze looked well beyond the emerging skeleton to the women who would soon be set free from the Dark Cave system and one day hopefully returned to their lives.

Marius's power was like a wind inside her, blowing constantly and filling every part of her with strength. Daniel had tried several times to rise up, but her foot, and the power she streamed, was more than enough to keep him in place.

At last she felt Daniel's life force completely fade, like smoke disappearing into the air.

Still, she held her position, holding him down even when his bones appeared. What did it take to truly destroy evil? If she lifted her foot, would Daniel rise suddenly, despite the fact that his bones were beginning to crumble? Could he even bring his ashes back to life?

Since she didn't know, she wasn't taking any chances.

And still she waited.

She waited until she began to feel Marius's power shift direction. And even then, she waited until she felt his arms surround her. "You can remove your foot now."

Nothing remained beneath her stiletto except a thin layer of ashes. "Are you sure? Once I'd taken in your power, I could feel what he was. He would have succeeded if not for you and your brothers."

"And you."

She glanced up at him, turning slightly. He levitated her into the air, moving away from the sunlight. "Wait, you were standing in the sunlight for a couple of minutes just now, when you were holding me?"

"I felt I was safe because of our bond. Apparently, your humanness protected me, which isn't the usual case."

She searched his eyes for a long moment. "Is it over, Marius? Really over?"

"What do you hear?"

She realized the arena had grown completely silent. She turned, casting her gaze in a circle as Marius turned her so she could witness the aftermath of the battle.

Gabriel and Rumy were in the center of the arena stage, standing beside Adrien and Lucian. Shayna saw that there were an awful lot of dead warriors everywhere, but new forces entered the building, many of them with white medic vests. The cleanup had already started and the dead were being carted away on stretchers, thousands of them.

She moved with Marius to stand with his brothers and Gabriel and Rumy, the latter of whom took one look at her chest then surprised her by removing his black shirt and handing it to her. He then got on his phone and requested a new shirt for himself.

"Thanks," she murmured, putting it on and quickly buttoning it up to hide her exposed cleavage. She also worked to smooth down her hair, knowing that something about the experience had caused it to fly around. Glancing at her feet, she reached down and unbuckled the uncomfortable stilettos then kicked them off.

Marius brought her close again, and she shifted to slide her arm around his neck. All the men were now watching the patch of sunlight.

Together they'd accomplished the impossible and she'd been a big part of it, something that pleased her human soul more than she thought she'd ever be able to communicate to Marius.

I get it. His voice was a quiet, soothing sound within her mind. *Remember, I can still feel what you're feeling and I understand completely.*

She kissed his cheek. *And you're feeling the same way. I am. I feel . . .*

Honored?

Marius squeezed her waist. *Exactly. Honored to have been able to finally rid our world of this monster.*

Shayna waited in the arena with Marius. Cleanup continued with precision so that corpses left in a steady stream and the cavern slowly emptied out. The familiar steam-cleaning happened at the same time, purifying the bloodstains from the stone.

She wasn't sure why, but she wanted to stay until the very end, a sentiment Marius shared with her.

Occasionally, she'd glance down at the pool of light and watch as even the ashes continued to be eaten up by the light.

When the arena was empty at last, she glanced down once more and spoke aloud. "Marius, look." She gestured to the sunlight. Only a few specks remained.

"Unbelievable."

Both Adrien and Lucian added the same sentiment.

"He's gone now."

Somehow, even the air felt cleaner.

When the last of the cleanup crews were taking care of the few remaining corpses, and the regiments had returned to their respective continents, Gabriel and Rumy drew close, both hovering in the air with ease.

Marius held Shayna close. Even though she could siphon his increased power and levitate alongside him, he didn't want to let her go.

He smiled as he met Gabriel's gaze. "What happens next? Because I have a feeling this is only the beginning. Am I right in thinking you probably already have a government ready to fall into place?"

Gabriel nodded. "And a new set of laws. We're adding a representative Senate as well. Corruption will always be part of our world, as it is on human earth, but we need a law-making body to at least hem in the unsavory elements. We must either dismantle the Ancestral Council or set different regulations in place on who can serve and how they get there—maybe by Senate appointment. And yes, I know, bribery will take a lot of people far. But if we're careful, we'll see some progress that will protect not just our own civilization"—here he shifted his gaze to Shayna and nodded—"but the human world as well."

"So I'm curious," Shayna began. "How do you plan to create the Senate? Will there be a voting process or do you already have a group of 'elders' "—she used air quotes—"who will be choosing the first candidates? And is this based on geography and cavern systems, or something else?"

When all the men started chuckling, she drew away from Marius enough to ask him with raised brows, "Are my questions inappropriate?"

He laughed. "As usual, you just have so many of them." He gestured to the arena. "And the timing might be a little off."

Shayna lifted a brow. "Oh, I see what you mean. Me and my damn curiosity. And would you look at the size of this cavern. And Marius, you won't believe what's below. There were dozens, maybe hundreds of rooms, like an enormous office building."

Gabriel said, "Yes, there are hundreds of rooms below, possibly thousands. I've had my men checking. There's a massive dormitory where the slaves who run Daniel's organization live. This was the heart of his operation, right here, and you were absolutely right, Shayna, about the women being separated out of the Dark Cave system based on IQ tests. The smartest landed here. And yes, I can see that you have a few more questions you'd like to ask about Daniel's operation, but I have a question for you, if you'll allow it."

Shayna loved questions. "Of course."

He glanced at Marius and his expression softened. *Do I have your permission?*

Marius knew what Gabriel meant to ask, and for some reason he was okay with it. He'd have to open the dialogue with Shayna soon enough, but he thought it might be a good thing for her to understand that he wasn't the only one who valued her.

He nodded and Gabriel shifted his gaze back to Shayna. "Here goes. Do you think we might be able to persuade you to stay in our world?"

Marius felt Shayna grow very still in his arms, a pensiveness that brought his own heart to thudding heavily. She turned to Marius. "I think that's something Marius and I need to discuss, probably at some length. Do I want to stay? Part of me does, absolutely. But should I stay? That is another question entirely."

Rumy smiled. "You'd be so welcome in our world. I want you to know that. We've kept our world separate from yours because of Daniel and because we need to find a way to govern ourselves better before we tackle a serious connection with the human world. But we've always had humans who've come to live here, to be with us, to embrace our cavern-based society. So please don't feel like you'd be the only one. You're not. Besides the women you met at my villa"—he jerked his thumb in Lucian and Adrien's direction—"just look at these two."

Adrien nodded. "And I hope you'll have a chance to speak with Lily before you make a final decision."

"Claire as well," Lucian added. "They've both heard a lot about you and want to meet you."

"I'd like that," Shayna said. She then smiled. "I might

even have a few questions for them. Imagine." Because she laughed, the men joined her.

With the arena now cleared out except for the cleaning crews, neither Marius nor Shayna could resist taking a quick tour of the extensive network of administrative rooms below. Marius kept them in altered flight the whole time so that they could pass through walls with ease.

When he reached the extensive dining hall, thousands of women were there celebrating the demise of Daniel's operation. Rumy had already taken charge and had flown in dozens of cases of champagne for the event. Paper cups might not have been as elegant as glass flutes, but it didn't matter. Daniel was dead.

Rumy promised to meet up with Marius and his brothers, as well as their women, for a shared meal. They needed their own celebration for what had begun as a terrible ordeal four hundred years ago and was now at an end.

After having seen the full scope of Daniel's Himalayan infrastructure, Shayna held tight to Marius as he flew her back to the Pharaoh system. She felt changed in a way she really didn't understand, except that Marius's power had taken her over. She'd even shifted into altered flight for a few seconds all on her own.

As he touched down in their guest suite and she caught the scent of the ancient tablets, she didn't know what she should be feeling. Mostly she felt dull, as though all the terrible things that had just happened along with the visual impact of the battle in the arena had laid a veil over her mind and heart.

"I'm feeling so strange, Marius." She stepped off his booted foot, enjoying the cool feel of the tile beneath her now bare feet. She was safe with Marius. No one could get to her here anymore. Only Daniel had been able to, but he was dead now as well as his powerful sons.

She felt beneath her arm then turned her back to Marius. "Can you get this out of me?"

"With pleasure."

Marius had to us a sharp knife and it hurt like hell, but Shayna was relieved when the device was out of her. Of course, she healed up in a few seconds because of Marius's power, but she finally felt as though the last of the connections to Daniel had been broken.

She could breathe. "I guess I just can't believe it's over. All of it. Finished."

Without thinking, she moved into the room with her computer and a few of the clay tablets spread out on the adjacent worktable. Marius followed, though he remained in the doorway, leaning his shoulder against the stone surface. She knew he was watching her and waiting, but she couldn't exactly figure out which thought to have first.

She crossed to the tablet broken on the floor and picked up the pieces, cradling them in her arms. She turned to Marius to make her confession. "Absolutely without thinking, when Daniel showed up I threw this at him. But they're really heavy. It missed him by two feet and landed in front of him."

She placed the remnants on the table. "I can have this repaired."

Marius moved toward her and put his hands on her shoulders. "No one is going to care that you broke this tablet. No one. And I'll see that it gets repaired. You don't have to worry about that."

Her throat seized all on its own. Gabriel had asked the

only really important question and she didn't know how to answer it.

She turned toward him and settled her hands on his arms, just below the shoulders. "I want to stay, but—"

"You're having doubts, a lot of them. I can feel it."

"Marius, I want to say something and I need you to really hear me and believe. Apart from whether I decide to stay with you or not, I'm in love with you. I swear I fell hard even when I thought you were a hallucination. I don't honestly know how that's possible because I've never been a big believer in love at first sight. Not really.

"And over the past several days, since we've been together, you've proven yourself repeatedly. I trust you with all my heart—more than any other man I've ever known." She drew in a deep breath, then swallowed hard. "But the work I do isn't just a profession, it's a calling, maybe in the same way you were called to battle on behalf of your world. I just can't feel good about walking away from the commitments I've made. Does that make sense?"

Marius had grown very still and for the first time since she'd held the blood-chain in her hand, she couldn't read him, she couldn't sense what he was feeling.

Her heart pounded in her chest as she waited for him to respond.

Finally Marius offered her a smile and even had a glimmer in his eyes. "Actually, I have a suggestion."

"You do?"

He nodded. "Well, since I've already made the decision that I will do whatever it takes to have you in my life, what if I got a sweet apartment in the Cascade system, not far from Seattle? It's a bit pricey, but I can afford it. And I'm sure, if I worked hard, I could find the same setup, or build one, in Malaysia. How long do you plan on doing your fieldwork?"

"A year. At least. Maybe more if I feel the need." Her throat once more seized. "You'd really do this for me?"

He took her in his arms. "In a goddamn, righteous, fucking heartbeat. I'm in love with you, Shayna, all that you are, not just how you might fit into my life. I know how important getting your doctorate is to you, your education, and your hope one day to teach."

"But in my world, not yours. I realize that I could have a place here." She gestured at the stack of tablets. "Just working with these could be a lifetime's effort. But my calling is to the human world. We have so much that needs to be done in our civilization worldwide and I've come to believe that not much will get accomplished without people like me who work hard to really understand each culture. With that understanding, real progress can be made. Without it, it's like trying to dig a trench using soup spoons." She took a deep breath. "Can you live with that?"

He smiled and smoothed her hair away from her face. "Shayna, you helped my world get rid of its biggest threat in the last millennium. I'm telling you that if you told me that the only way we could be together is if I stood on my head the rest of my life, I'd do it. I'd be crazy not to."

She blinked a couple of times. "You really are serious."

"Damn straight I am. But I should warn you that if you leave, I'll come knocking on your apartment door. I'd bring flowers, thousands of them, bottles of wine, chocolate by the ton, anything you desired to try to win you over." He lowered his voice. "I'd bring you books, too, lots of books, on anthropology, history, science. I'd even steal some of these tablets and put them on your door-step just to get you to open the door for me. I'll do what-ever it takes."

Tears burned her eyes. She grabbed his vest at the shoulders and tugged a couple of times, then slid her arms around his neck and held him tight. He did that thing he often did, rubbing his hand up and down her back, com-forting her.

"Shayna, I'm teasing you about coming after you. Say the word, and I'll take you home and you'll never see me again. But I want you to know how grateful I am for who you are. This time with you has been incredibly healing for me, something I didn't expect when Rumy sent me to Seattle because you had the highest score on the com-puter game he designed. You brought so much into my life that had nothing to do with either Daniel or the ex-tinction weapon. For that, you will always have my un-dying loyalty. If you ever need anything, you have but to ask and I'll come running."

Marius held himself in check, utilizing the tight control he'd learned from living as long as he had. He felt so much right now that he had to work extremely hard to keep his emotions from swamping Shayna. He didn't want to say too much or too little. Sometimes the war was won hold-ing tight to the middle ground and letting the moment breathe.

Finally she drew back and said, "I trust you, Marius. If you truly believe you can do what you've said, that we could have a cave apartment somewhere near Seattle, that I can pursue my studies or anything else I feel is impor-tant, then I'm all yours."

Marius didn't realize he'd levitated with Shayna in his arms until he hit his head on the cavern ceiling. "Ow."

Shayna laughed. "I did the same thing. Remember? That happened in Sweden."

He searched her eyes, his heart so full he couldn't speak.

Instead, he kissed her. Hard. And as soon as she parted her lips, he slid his tongue inside, thrusting and making all kinds of promises.

When he drew back, her beautiful sexy scent filled the air, a perfect match to his own need to take her to bed and make love with her.

As he slowly levitated back down to the floor, he realized Shayna's emotions were as euphoric as his own, as though a fog lived in her mind. She kept stroking his neck, his shoulders, his pecs, and pushing her fingers beneath his vest at an awkward angle. She was as anxious as he was to get down to business.

He picked her up, cradling her in his arms. He may have bumped into a couple of doorjambs as he made his way to the bedroom and the blue silk sheets once more.

Because he'd bulked up, he struggled a bit to get his leathers off and ended up on his ass.

Shayna laughed so hard and at first he thought it was because of his stupidity. Instead he finally realized she'd gotten her hair stuck in the zipper of her dress. "I need help!"

He got his boots off and his leathers then went to her aid, working her long white-blond hair out of the zipper.

By the time he helped her get her dress off, he was undressed and she wore a sexy bustier and a thong. He had his mouth on the mound of her breasts, lifting them out of the bustier at the same time, before he knew what he was doing. She'd already started panting when he latched onto one of her nipples and began suckling.

"Oh, God, Marius!"

His hands got busy, having a mind of their own, teasing her between her legs, stroking her bottom, lifting her knees, or squeezing her breasts while his lips kept working her.

"I need this bustier off. It's pinching me."

He flipped her over and untied the strings. She moaned with relief and he could see why. Her back was crisscrossed from the indentations the lace-up had created. He rubbed her back and slowly worked her out of her thong. But he kept her on her knees.

"Shayna, I have something I want to do with you, but only if you're comfortable with it. Do you remember what I did in the Dark Cave system, how I split into two separate entities and both of us fought?"

She turned to look at him over her shoulder. "Of course. And I still have so many questions."

He laughed. "I'm sure you do. But here's my question: I can make love to you like that as well. I can split into two parts, a primary and a secondary, and we can both have our way with you. What do you think? Interested?" He leaned close and kissed a line down her back.

She froze.

"What is it?"

"Two Mariuses. I think I'd faint if I wasn't already lying down. I swear it." She drew in a hissing breath through her lips. "Oh, two of you. My God." The sudden rock of her hips and the groan that left her mouth told him all that he needed to know.

"I take it that's a yes."

"Oh, yes, that's a yes."

With the added power he'd gained, it only took the smallest thought to split.

With his secondary self above, and lifting her into the air, his primary self slid beneath her.

Her eyes were wild, her nipples peaked. "I didn't know you could do this. You're touching me from behind and yet here you are beneath me. I think I might faint."

He nodded and smiled, levitating just enough to reach her lips and kiss her.

Drawing back, he said, "See if you can levitate and hold your position in the air. You'll be able to reach more of me with your hands that way and Shayna, I want you touching me. I love the way you touch my body, fondling every part of me."

She nodded, and he felt her rise into the air just a few inches, then slide her hands over her shoulders. "Make a sandwich of me in the air. Can you?"

"Hell, yeah." His secondary self stretched out over her, then he levitated so that he made solid contact under her.

"I'm going to die and go to heaven right now. There's so much of you. Oh, my God, two cocks." Her body writhed so that she rubbed him in front and behind at the same time.

"Damn that feels good, Shayna." He kissed her again, and the secondary Marius began working his mouth from the base of her neck down her body.

She whimpered and cried out. He suckled her buttocks from behind while in front he nipped at her throat, warming up her vein. He was in a state, locked onto her body and craving her blood.

His secondary self shifted so that he could catch Shayna behind the knee with one hand and draw her leg against his hip. At the same time, holding himself with levitation, he used his hand to guide his cock to her opening.

Her hands were driving him crazy. She plucked at the muscles of his arms and pecs. Her fingers played with his nipples, then his ass.

At one point she surprised him by turning her head so that his secondary self caught her mouth and kissed her. He watched the sensual movement of his secondary tongue pushing in and out of her mouth as he began to drive inside her low.

Keep kissing my other self. I love watching.

This is so unbelievable. Her voice sounded breathless inside his head.

She panted against his secondary mouth. He took the opportunity to begin licking a line up her throat since her neck was so beautifully exposed.

Hold this angle, Shayna. Just keep kissing my secondary mouth.

Okay, but this feels amazing. Two of you. I can't think. Oh, my God.

When her vein rose to meet his tongue, he once more spoke telepathically. *I'm going to bite you in this position. Would you like that?*

Yes. Do it. Marius, this is incredible. I'm so close. But first let me feel your cock in my hand.

His secondary self shifted sideways to give her access. She groaned as she stroked him. *Bite me.*

His neck arched and he struck, piercing her vein. When her blood hit, his whole body arched, which set her to writhing all over again. Feeling her hand stroking him while he drove into her, as well as the taste of her blood, almost made him lose control.

He loved surrounding her like this, giving her pleasure. Nothing seemed more important right now than that Shayna have her needs met, especially since once again she fed him with blood that nourished his soul as much as his body.

Shayna felt ecstasy begin to flow, a hot wave through her body as she held one cock in her hand and had another hitting her in just the right place so that she spasmed repeatedly.

She groaned, then cried out as the pleasure kept flowing. Her heart felt light and free as she held on to Marius, as he drank from her and as she met his most basic needs.

When he drew back and stared into her eyes, the pleasure heightened. He moved faster, vampire-fast, while his secondary self latched onto the back of her neck.

"Oh, God, Marius. You'll make me come again."

"I love you, Shayna, and I want you to come."

She could feel his release building. "I love you, too, and I want you to come just like this while you're looking at me. I want to see everything."

He nodded and went even faster, which ignited a second orgasm deep in her body. She gripped his buttocks and a slight vibration went through him, telling her that he was rejoining.

He flipped her in the air, shouting, but still holding her gaze. She landed against the bed and another orgasm began to pulse, pleasure on pleasure until she was crying out repeatedly.

His hazel eyes, flecked with gold, almost glowed as

he released into her, giving her all that he had. He continued to pump until her body grew lax, then he settled his hips and rested against her.

Still connected low, she slid her hands through his hair, leaning up to kiss him.

He kissed her back.

She sighed heavily, once more gazing into his eyes, unable to believe this tremendous bounty that had come into her life.

He stroked her cheeks with his fingers, a soft curve on his lips.

She smiled. "You look content."

"I am and very much at peace, something I've never known before. I owe that to you, Shayna."

She nodded. "Same here. I hadn't known how bad things had been for me until I got here, until I was with you and experienced your kindness and your selflessness. I feel that I owe you everything."

He kissed her again, gently.

Several hours later, in Gabriel's living room, Shayna stood by yet another beautiful waterfall, leaning against Marius. He had his arms around her, holding her close.

His brothers and their women, Lily and Claire, all helped set the table. Lily's son, Josh, played video games. Gabriel talked to his head of security and afterward crossed to join them.

Gabriel's smile was warm. "I'm so glad you're going to be part of our family, and I heartily approve of Marius's plan to keep supporting your work. You'll love the Cascade system. Beautiful waterfalls and a hotel with a wonderful swimming pool. Good people over there."

Shayna pressed Marius's arms. "And there are good people here."

Marius nuzzled her neck and Gabriel laughed.

Rumy arrived waving two bottles of Dom Pérignon in the air. "We have a lot of celebrating to do tonight. Eve said she'd be joining us in a few minutes, right after her last show. How does that sound?" A cheer went up.

"I'll get some glasses," Gabriel said. He crossed to take one of the bottles from Rumy.

Shayna owed Eve so much, the woman who embraced her sexual bondage side while facilitating healing through a lay counseling practice. She turned to meet Marius's gaze. "Do you think she would mind if I asked her a few questions?"

Marius grinned and his heart heated up. Claire, who now sat beside Josh, called to her. "I know you ended up here because you won a computer game online, but how are you at video games?"

"I love them. I use them to relax when I'm grappling with a difficult theory."

"Then join us."

Marius felt her hesitate. "Go ahead. I need to talk with my brothers anyway."

She reached up and kissed him, then planted herself next to Claire, who immediately handed her a controller. "Halo. I love this franchise. So how long have you played this game, Josh?"

Marius smiled, thinking that with Shayna's intensity, Josh may have met his match.

He stayed put, enjoying Gabriel's waterfall, a ten-foot sheet lit by three soft blue lights from below. The mass of blue crystals behind the waterfall set the entire room in a glow.

Adrien and Lucian drew close, each in turn clapping him on the shoulder.

"We're glad you and Shayna are making a go of it," Adrien said. "But it is amazing, isn't it, these women that essentially Daniel chose for each of us?"

"A huge fucking irony. I don't think this was what he planned at all."

All three men chuckled. The last thing Daniel would have ever embraced was the warm family group his three youngest sons had created out of the nightmare Daniel had delivered.

Daniel was gone now, as well as the sons aligned with him. Their world would have a chance to breathe now and to grow. Marius was under no illusions: They were just getting started in terms of managing the illegal activities that some of his kind were prone to.

Lucian spoke quietly. "Rumy thinks we'll have at least fifty cavern systems to uncover, each holding human slaves intended for Daniel's clubs."

Yep, he and his brothers had a lot of work to do yet, but they were no longer without power. Both Lucian and Adrien, wearing the Ancestral mark of the double-chains, had the corresponding power. Marius had something similar though it was agreed he might be the next evolution in his world. He wondered if just maybe his human mother was the cause—and wouldn't that be another wonderful irony? But then Daniel had chosen her as well.

Now that Daniel was dead, Marius could let a lot of things go. His past for one, and his fear of his emerging powers for another.

He would regroup with his brothers in a few days, when he'd had a chance to be alone with Shayna and to set up his new apartment in the Cascade system. For now, he'd never been so content, so at peace, so hopeful for the future.

A call to dinner brought him back to Shayna. They gathered as the family they were, especially when Eve arrived just in time, vampires with one shared purpose: to see their world become a safe, well-governed place in which all could thrive.

Gabriel said the blessing. "In times of chaos, even in the midst of destruction, we are ever grateful for that which feeds our bodies, whether served from the sacrificial vein or from fare on the table. May the fire of the eternal spirit ignite your life force tonight and evermore."

When Gabriel offered a short bow, everyone followed suit, then sat down to break bread together.

Marius held Shayna's hand throughout the meal, not wanting to lose touch even for a second. With Shayna on his right, he had to work to eat left-handed, but he didn't care. He'd found an extraordinary blessing and at least for now he honored that blessing by holding his woman's hand and occasionally bringing her fingers to his lips.

She hardly noticed, however, because she'd asked Gabriel a question and the man not only answered her but encouraged her to ply him with as many questions as pleased her soul.

There were a lot of questions that night.

And laughter.

And love.

And above all a sense of hope that had not existed in his world for a long, long time.

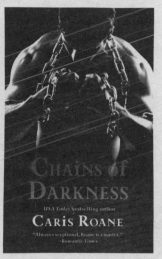